…ord…
fantasy writer working today, and *The Devil's Apprentice* is, true to form, a box of delights. It is entirely unmissable.'
Lavie Tidhar, World Fantasy Award-winning author

'She writes in a quiet but uncommonly witty style that can soar into elegance or mute dread.'
Publishers Weekly on *The Witch Queen*

WITHDRAWN

D1246039

Other books by Jan Siegel

Prospero's Children

The Dragon-Charmer

Witch's Honour

Here's the house without a door
Here's the room without a floor
Here's the cat that chased the rat
Here's the rat that bit the cat
Here's the dog that didn't bark
Here's the flame without a spark
Here's a candle to light the proud
Here's a spindle to spin your shroud
Here's a farewell where'er you roam
Here's a death knell to ring you home
Here's a church and there's the steeple
Open the doors and here are the people.

Nursery Rhyme

PROLOGUE
Ghost

Beyond the Doors
London, seventeenth century

THEY CALLED HIM Ghost, because of his colouring, and because he could come and go without a sound. After he had been in the city for a little while he almost forgot he had any other name.

It was a big city – the biggest city in the world – he knew that because they told him so, though it didn't seem especially big to him. The buildings were huddled into clusters or piled on top of each other, rickety structures of wood and pitch and tumbledown brick, with roofs that gaped between criss-crossed beams, and holes for windows, and doors that sagged from their hinges. Twisty stairs climbed up the walls, and broken ladders climbed down, and the streets and alleyways ran through the cracks in between. People and rats and cockroaches and pigeons all lived there like one big family, squabbling over every inch of space, every morsel they ate. When there was nothing else, they ate each other.

When Ghost first arrived the thing he noticed most was the smells. He had grown up in a world of chemical smells – chemicals that smelt like flowers, and chemicals that smelt like fruit, and chemicals that smelt like chemicals – but here the smells were all human. Human sweat, human dirt, human waste. To begin with, he thought it would make him sick to breathe it in all the time, but he got used to it very quickly, and after a while he didn't notice it any more.

The boys lived in a kind of loft with a chimney running through it and a creek underneath, a narrow tongue of water that joined the main river several streets away. In flood, it spilled into the cellars; in drought, it shrank and stagnated. Everyone threw their rubbish into it, presumably out of optimism since it had no current worth speaking of and the rubbish simply stayed there, until the rats ate it or it had grown a crust. At the front of the building, or what passed for the front, was a tavern called the Grim Reaper, which added stale beer and vomit to the cocktail of odours. By night it was a gloomy place, with one lamp and few candles, where people could meet other people without revealing any giveaway details, like names or faces or the contents of their tankards. By day it was even gloomier, with no candles to enhance the murk, and the dancers from the theatre would come there, Big Belinda's girls, drinking to forget their troubles, and laughing even when they had little to laugh at, and making lewd jokes about the men who crowded the stalls to ogle them. The theatres had reopened when the king returned, and now there were women on the stage, though respectable ladies looked down on them, saying they were no better than they should be. But the ladies would say that, since the dancers were pretty, at least to begin with.

Mr Sheen knew them all. He knew the girls and Big Belinda and the faceless, nameless people of the night. He looked after the boys, or so he told them, disposing of the day's takings and seeing the rent was paid and they got fed and clipping their ears when they spoke out of turn. He was thin and sallow and sinister, with old embroidery peeling from his coat like last month's scabs and a wig that was too big for him, a monster of a wig that, according to One-Ear, housed mice and spiders and even a nest of small birds. He had a raven which sat on his shoulder picking insects out of the wig and squirting white excrement down the back of the coat; if the boys didn't work hard and behave he said it would have their eyes. They were all afraid of the raven but

Weasel, who was the youngest (or seemed to be), was even more afraid of the wig, and would wake from nightmares screaming: 'The wig! The wig!' and claiming it was chasing him. Of course, Snot was younger still, perhaps three or four years old, but he was too young to count, and Mr Sheen only allowed him to stay because his brother, Filcher, stole enough for two.

Ghost was different from the others, right from the start. He could read and write and do sums. He knew how old he was – thirteen – while they could only guess. He stood a head taller than the tallest and although he was skinny he was strong, with arms like knotted wires. His skin was dead white and his hair was so fair it was almost white – even his eyelashes were white – but his eyes were dark and narrow, slots of agate in the pallor of his face. 'It's a shame he isn't pretty,' Big Belinda said. 'He might have been an angel, all pale and perfect – only the God of Whores made him into a freak. Haha!' Ghost knew he wasn't pretty. His face was thin and pointy, his nose sharp, his ears pixy-tipped after a bully in the Home had called him a Vulcan and nicked them with a pair of scissors when he was eight. He had dealt with the bully a year later, feeding him rabbit-droppings covered in chocolate which he said were real sweets, and after that they'd left him alone. It had taken a long time, collecting the rabbit-droppings, and persuading the cook to teach him how to prepare them, and the children said he was cunning, and revengeful, and patient as the grave (in childhood, a year is an age), and he believed them.

In the city, such qualities were the stuff of survival.

The week he arrived he tried to wash, if he could find any clean water, but then he realised his fairness marked him out, and it was better to hide behind a layer or two of grime like the other boys. He had learned long ago how to fade into a crowd or slip into a shadow, and the city was full of crowds and shadows. On the first day, the boys had found him and claimed him as their own. In the Home, he had had enemies and allies but no friends;

here, he had a family. He had Sly, Weasel, the twins, Ratface and Pockface, One-Ear, Maggot, Cherub, Filcher and Snot. There was another boy called Little Jimmy who hurt his foot and couldn't run fast, so a fat shopkeeper caught him and beat him till he couldn't walk, then the twins carried him back to the loft and Mr Sheen knocked him down. Two days later, he died. Bad things had happened in the Home, but no one had ever died, not even the bully who ate the rabbit-droppings. Ghost watched, and listened, and said nothing.

'You're a smart one,' Mr Sheen told him. 'I can make something o' you. You could be a highwayman like Daring Dick, with the gold chinking in your pocket, and the rich folk shrinking from the muzzle o' your barker, and you can go up the stairway to heaven like a hero.' And he cackled a croaking cackle, all brown teeth and bad breath, and the raven cawed an echo.

Ghost stole an apple a day to keep his teeth clean, just thinking of Mr Sheen.

He knew the stairway to heaven meant the gibbet, and Mr Sheen's praise was more than half malice, but he said only: 'I can't ride.'

The next market day, when they brought back their pickings, Ghost said: 'That lot's worth eight shillings at least.' He'd already learned the currency of the city. He was a quick learner, especially when it came to money. 'We worked hard for it. Harder 'n you. We want some.'

'Greed,' said Mr Sheen. 'Avarice and greed. Two o' the deadly sins, or so they say in church. I beat sin out o' my boys.'

He lashed out at Ghost, the way he had at Little Jimmy, but Ghost was faster and stronger. He blocked the blow and aimed a low punch with one knuckle crooked for maximum hurt, straight in the solar plexus. Mr Sheen didn't know he had a solar plexus, his education hadn't tended that way, but the punch knocked the breath out of him if not the stink, and he fell back with his wig all awry, and the raven flapped onto a beam, croaking a protest. The boys spread out in a circle to watch, terrified by Ghost's boldness and what might come of it. Then Mr Sheen pulled the dagger out of his boot, a mean little dagger with a rusty blade, and lunged for Ghost, slow and clumsy from having his breath punched out. But Ghost found the knife he'd brought with him, all new and gleamy, and it snapped out of nowhere into his hand, quicker than an adder's tongue, and Mr Sheen seemed to lunge himself straight onto it. His eyes opened wide in surprise, and he drew back swearing hoarsely, and there was a redness spreading on his clothes, bright as the paint Big Belinda's girls used on their lips.

'Help me,' he said, but no one moved to help him. 'Help me, you little buggers – you offspring o' rats and roaches – you lice in the pubes o' the city... As a father I've been to you, so I have, and now you turns on me. Help me... I'm dying.'

'Go and die somewhere else,' Ghost said, tossing him a rag to pad the wound.

Mr Sheen clutched it to his side and gasped: 'Peck out his glims!' to the raven, but the bird only squawked, hopping back onto his shoulder and eying the blood like next night's dinner. Then he stumbled out, cursing.

The injury wasn't serious but he took himself to a backstreet quack who stitched him with a grubby needle and cupped out the fever, and he was dead in a week.

In the loft, the boys looked at Ghost.

'What do we do now?' they said. 'He took care of us.'

'We take care of ourselves,' Ghost said. 'We don't need him.'

So Ghost became their leader.

CHAPTER ONE
Habeas Corpus

London, twenty-first century

NOTHING EXCITING EVER happens in a lawyer's office. Even criminal lawyers reserve their excitement for visiting their clients in gaol and moments of courtroom drama; in the office everything is staid, respectable, and essentially dull. If they are successful there will be an expensive desk, leather-bound lawbooks, discreet examples of modern technology like telephones and computers. If they are lower down the scale, the furniture will be second-hand shabby or mass-produced modern, with beige filing cabinets. Beige will feature somewhere, whatever their status. Beigeness and dullness are important hallmarks of legal premises, designed to assure the client that their chosen representative is someone who can use words like 'heretofore' and 'howsoever', when necessary in everyday conversation.

These particular offices were exceptionally beige and dull, even by the standards of the profession. The desk was elderly without being precisely antique, the telephones dated from a previous century (the switchboard operator wasn't sure which), the files were dog-eared, the lawbooks mouse-nibbled. This was an office where excitement had never intruded, crime had never been mentioned, divorce was another country. Its incumbent dealt exclusively with Wills, and Trusts, and property, which is about as unexciting as the law can get. His name was Jasveer Patel, newest member of Whitbread Tudor Hayle – a very old firm, which had long run out of both Whitbreads and Tudors and was down to its last Hayle. Jas Patel represented Progress, though he did his best to do it in an extremely dull (and beige) way. He was clever, earnest and bespectacled, his jacket blending with its background like camouflage colouring, his manner carefully cultivated to add a decade to his twenty-five years. However just now, despite his best efforts, he was gazing at his visitor in shock, and in consequence looked much younger. One of the things that had always contributed to the safe dullness of his job was that his clients were predominantly dead. He wasn't used to seeing them in his office.

Particularly when they had been dead for some time.

'I simply can't go on like this,' Andrew Pyewackett was saying impatiently. 'Flesh and blood won't stand it. Let's face it, they aren't meant to. Look at me, I'm already falling to bits – every time I remove my socks several toes fall off. I need to get out of this body and move on. Arrangements will have to be made.'

He wore a Savile Row suit some fifty years old – 'I never put on an ounce after I was a hundred!' – a jaunty little bow tie, and a very tall top hat pulled well down over his cranium. In the street, he had wrapped a silk scarf round much of his face and covered his eyes with tinted glasses, which was just as well, since although the lids had largely shrivelled away the eyeballs remained, round and staring and a-glow with unnatural life. He still wore his false teeth, which were aggressively new and shiny, though they fitted only loosely to his shrunken gums and were liable to become detached while he talked and clatter away by themselves. He had taken off his gloves and tapped with bony fingers on the desktop, shedding flakes of brownish skin like dandruff.

Jas Patel said: 'Er...'

'Don't you *er* me, young man,' said his visitor. 'I'm not having any of your *ers* and *ums*. I've had nothing but excuses from this firm since I died. It wasn't like that in Graham Tudor's day, I can tell you. What's happened to young Bunny Hayle? Don't tell me *he's* running things now. Not much good at the business – always chasing the girls. That's why we called him Bunny. At it like a rabbit, he was – up the skirt of any flapper he could find.'

'He's ninety-three,' Jas said, desperately trying to summon up some legal nous.

'Ninety-three? Huh! A spring chicken. I made it to a hundred and forty: porridge and treacle for breakfast and a glass of port every night. Died in December '99. Really annoyed me, that did. I wanted to see in the new millennium. If you ask *me*, it was the quality of the port. Ran out of Graham's Single-Quinta six months earlier, had to get some new-fangled stuff. Laid down in '78 – just wasn't mature. That's what did for me, I'm sure of it. I'd have made it to the big 2000 if it wasn't for that.'

'Well,' Jas swallowed, 'you're – you're still here, aren't you? In a way...'

'I'm dead,' Mr Pyewackett pointed out unnecessarily. 'Trust me, it just isn't the same. What's more, I want to get on with it. Can't hang around indefinitely with my bits dropping off. Fetch Bunny Hayle. He's been dodging my phone calls but he can't dodge me. Ninety-three indeed! Nothing but excuses.'

'Mr Hayle's retired,' Jas said. 'He only comes in occasionally to... to consult. I've been given some of his cases. The matter of your Will–'

'It's you, is it? What are you doing about it, hey? Seven years and you still haven't found my successor! I can't wait any longer. If you don't find him within the month the estate will have to go into the hands of the executors. I'm not one to shelve my responsibilities but I've looked after the place for over a century, man and corpse, and it's time for someone else to take on the job.'

'I understand the legatee is... is a Mr Bartlemy Goodman, of no fixed abode...'

'You understand, do you? Glad to hear it. Understanding is a good start.'

'Is he... is he a relative?'

'Of course not!' The dead man rolled his eyes until they spun in their sockets. 'Ran out of relatives ages ago. Never married, no brats. Maud – m' sister – had two boys, both killed in the Great War. One at Passchendaele, one on the Somme. Bad show. Broke her heart. M' cousins went to the colonies – imbeciles, if you ask me. We sent our crooks to Australia and our religious crackpots to America. Who'd want to join 'em? No one left now – no one I can trust. Has to be Goodman. I'm told he's just the chap.'

'But s-surely,' Jas stammered, 'you *know* him?'

'Never met him in my life,' Mr Pyewackett said blithely. 'Or since. Doesn't matter. He's the man. Got a reputation... in certain circles.'

'A reputation–?'

'For looking after things. That's what we need. The house has to be looked after. Can't have just anyone strolling in, wanting to buy the place, or sell it, or – God help them – trying to *live* in it. Could be a disaster.'

'It seems to be a valuable property,' Jas demurred. 'Is it... is it in a *very* poor state of repair?'

'No idea. Haven't been inside for years. Don't want people going inside, do we? Never you mind about *value*. Has to have a custodian to keep people out, for their own sake. Otherwise... it makes my blood run cold just thinking of the consequences.'

'*Does* it?' Jas asked, unable to refrain. He was beginning to get into the spirit of things.

'Don't be impertinent with *me*, young man. What's your name? Petal? Know what we would have thought of a name like that when I was a boy. Still, times change. Thank God I'm done changing with 'em. See here, young Petal, we've got to get this sorted out *now*. Till Goodman turns up, the place needs a caretaker. No offence – you seem like a decent chap, even if you are a bit of a wop – but it's got to be the Tudor girl. Tudors have always handled our affairs: it's traditional. Goes back a long,

long way. Almost to – well, the Tudors. Story goes, there's some connection with Bluff King Hal, don't know what. Got the hair, haven't they? They've always been solicitors, managed things for us. That's the Tudors. Sharp as a thorn, dry as a thistle. Tudors and Pyewacketts. So where is she?'

'You mean,' Jas read from the document in front of him, 'Penelope Anne Tudor, great-granddaughter of Graham Tudor? The... other executor?'

'That's the ticket. The new generation. Parents killed in a car crash or something, so it has to be her. Only one left. All the old families are running out, dying off. Bloody depressing. Soon, the whole country'll be in the hands of young upstarts like you.'

'My father,' Jas said, forgetting himself, 'is a direct descendant of the last Maharajah of Bharatpore. We too are a very old family.'

'Shame you have to do the lawyering,' said Mr Pyewackett. 'Ought to be living in a palace, riding on elephants and all that. Standards declining everywhere. About Penelope Anne –'

'There's a problem.' Jas lapsed from his aristocratic heights. 'The thing is –'

'Got the name right, didn't I? I checked pretty carefully.'

'It's not that. The thing is –'

'There you are then. Get her in here.'

'*The thing is,* she isn't a lawyer. She's still at school. She's only thirteen.'

For a moment, the dead man looked nonplussed. His eyes might have widened, but without eyelids it was difficult to tell. Instead, they seemed to pop. From close up – and the far side of the desk was rather too close – this was an alarming sight. Jas swallowed again, and wondered if this was really happening. Nothing in his years of training had prepared him to deal with a corpse, especially one that was still up and talking. He wished the teeth didn't rattle so much. It was as if Mr Pyewackett punctuated all his sentences with distant gunfire.

'She was only six when you died,' Jas continued, hanging on to some shreds of legal sanity. 'As fellow executors, this firm contacted her guardian and – er – assumed sole responsibility for... Even now, she's rather young to become involved in these matters. Five years short of her majority.'

'Piffle!' Mr Pyewackett leaned forward, jabbing at the desktop with an emphatic finger. Corpse-dust rose in a little cloud and the final joint wobbled dangerously. 'You send that girl round to see me. Doesn't matter if she's thirteen or thirty: she's a Tudor, she'll take care of things. Send her round. I can't be doing with all this nonsense. I've got my death to get on with.'

He strode out, hesitated in the corridor, and came back for his finger-joint.

Then Jas was left alone with a little drift of skin-flakes on the desk and a lingering smell of decay, slightly tinged with aftershave. Even so, it was several minutes before he got up to open the window.

Infernale

BEFORE THERE WAS a door, there would have been trees. Two trees growing close together, their branches interlacing into an arch, an arch leading nowhere. Small animals would have avoided the place and birds flown round it, but once in a while some careless or desperate creature, fleeing from a predator, might have vanished between the tree-trunks. Later, when men came, they cut down the trees and built the first door, perhaps just a couple of posts and a lintel made from crudely-shaped stones, with a rough image of one of the oldest gods set above it, as a guardian or a warning. Some said it was the gate to Hell, others, a portal to Fairyland, but few were reckless or foolhardy enough to put it to the test. Of those who did, none returned in the lifetime of kith or kin, but occasionally, a century or more later, a figure would appear with a face from long ago, white-haired, wizened, bewitched to the edge of madness, or mysteriously still young, rootless, muttering of people and places unknown.

Eventually walls came to shield the door, and the gap was closed with boards and rivets and spells, and a knob was set at the centre of the door that should never be turned. Then there were more walls and higher, corridors encircling corridors, rooms guarding rooms, and always the doors led elsewhere, and the passageways became a maze, and none knew what was inside. Sometimes the walls were torn down, or burned to the ground, but the foundations always remained, and the walls would be raised again in a different style, adapting to the changing moods of history, until rumour said they could rebuild themselves, shape-shifting to blend with the neighbourhood. For there was a neighbourhood, a city that grew until it engulfed the place, and it became a house among houses, hardly to be told apart from the others in the street.

The house had, if not an owner, at least a denizen. Legend claimed that when the first door opened *he* looked through, and saw himself, and the shadow of that bond darkened the house forever. He could not enter, because he was already there, in too many forms, in too many ages; his power and his will crept through every portal, and only the walls came in between. He did not make the house – such things are not made: they are snarls in the fabric of the universe, places where reality is twisted and fractured. But it grew to reflect his many faces, to enmesh his many webs, and those who knew of him said it must be guarded constantly, though they had no clear idea why, or against what.

It was put in the charge of a single family, an ordinary family, at least to begin with, until something infected them from the walls, a treacherous germ of magic or madness. They became eccentric, obsessive, unusually long-lived. But the house was safe in their care, sealed off from the world, and from *him*. If it had any purpose, it was forgotten. Those who were drawn to it, the curious and the adventurous and the vulnerable – the chosen few, Gifted or cursed – might find a way to enter, from the outside or within, but no one saw them come or go, and the doors seemed shut forever.

However, Time flies – it is well known for that – and at whiles even the immortals cannot keep up. An hour was yet to come when the forgotten Purpose would be remembered, and the doors would open, and all those who were lost in the mazes of the house would come crying into the world...

London, twenty-first century

PENELOPE ANNE TUDOR sat in the beige-tinted office while Jas Patel told her his story. Even though the story was carefully edited for her consumption, she found it exciting, although she had no intention of showing it. She was a pale girl with a scattering of ghost-freckles on her cheeks and forehead and straight reddish hair scraped back into a ponytail. Her mouth was small and serious, her other features tidy rather than pretty: grey eyes, neat little nose, small ears. She wore glasses for study and no makeup. In her severe school uniform – grey with maroon piping – she still looked like a child. Jas felt what little confidence he might have had evaporate at the sight of her.

He had been told she was a student who invariably got A-stars and hoped to become a lawyer in the tradition of the family. But she didn't look like someone who could deal with a walking corpse and, unsure how to broach the subject, he steered clear of it. Perhaps Mr Pyewackett would welcome her in a very bad light, or wearing a mask. Possibly she would think he was merely ill. *Very* ill. After all, children were supposed to believe what they were told, weren't they? He had tried to discuss the situation with a colleague and had been informed, in an undervoice, that the company handled some rather unusual cases, and on the whole it was best not to talk about it. Then he had contacted Mr Hayle, who had livened up at the first mention of Andrew Pyewackett.

'Good old Andy. Bit of a dry stick, mind you, bit of a sharp tongue, but a thoroughly good chap. Good old Andy. Can't believe he's still alive.'

'He isn't,' said Jas, but it failed to register with Mr Hayle, and there was no point in making an issue of it.

'Mr Pyewackett,' he told Penelope, 'may seem a little... strange... to you. In fact, he's at death's door, which can make people rather... but I hope you'll manage to be – er – polite to him.'

'I'm always polite,' Penelope said. 'My grandmother's very particular about it. I've never met anyone who was dying before. Is he very old? I looked him up in the file while I was waiting to see you and they've got his date of birth down as 1859. That must be wrong, mustn't it?'

'Typing error,' said Jas, chickening out. 'Are you quite sure you can handle this?'

'It'll be an interesting experience,' Penelope said judiciously. 'I expect it to be very beneficial for my education.'

Any thirteen-year-old who uses words like 'beneficial' is slightly scary. Jas said, in an attempt to lighten the atmosphere: 'Do they call you Penny?'

'No,' Penelope said baldly. After a minute she added: 'Some people call me Pen.'

She looked like a Pen, Jas thought, not a Penny. As in 'the pen is mightier than the sword.'

He said: 'Well – er – Pen, Mr Pyewackett is expecting you at four o'clock tomorrow. I think it's preferable he tells you everything himself. It's Number 7A, Temporal Crescent, Hampstead. Don't go to Number 7 by mistake. That's the main property, but it's – locked up. Mr Pyewackett is nervous of intruders.'

Mr Pyewackett hadn't appeared to be nervous of anything, but then, being dead would do that for you.

'I'll find it,' Pen said, with the quiet self-possession which appeared to be characteristic of her. She seemed to have no sense of humour, no natural frivolity, no *girlyness*. While it is impossible to see if someone has an imagination, Jas thought Penelope's unimaginativity was as obvious as her hair colour. He had always considered himself a serious sort of person, hard-working and conscientious to a fault, but she made him feel like a lightweight for whom legal practice was a jolly little game.

He almost thought he had been more comfortable with the corpse.

After she had gone he succumbed to guilt because he had told her so little, but consoled himself with the hope, based on no evidence whatsoever, that Mr Pyewackett would have the tact to cover his face, not to mention the rest of his anatomy, when Pen came to tea.

OUT IN THE street, Pen waited until she was a safe distance from Whitbread Tudor Hayle before she allowed herself to smile. The knot of excitement and happiness inside her was so tight she couldn't possibly unravel it all at once – she was far too grown up to skip or dance for joy, had probably been too grown up for such behaviour since she could walk. But the tension demanded some kind of release, so she smiled, and smiled, her pale face alight. She had a real job, a *legal* job, as if she was a fully-fledged lawyer, instead of a thirteen-year-old who wanted to take her GCSEs early because they were so easy, and spent her spare time reading case histories, and arguing on the Internet about famous miscarriages of justice. She had already decided to specialise in crime, breaking with family precedent, but she knew criminal cases were a long way in the future and the thrill of her first job outweighed all other considerations. It was the most magical thing that had ever happened to her, except she didn't believe in magic. Unlike her friends, she didn't read fantasy books – in fact, she read very little fiction at all since she couldn't see the point of it, though her grandmother had ensured she had a basic knowledge of the classics. But Pen preferred facts. Had Jas told her he thought she had no imagination she would have agreed with enthusiasm. School reports said she had an analytical mind, and she did her best to live up to it. Pen's best was very good. In her view, imagination just got you into trouble.

At home, Pen told her grandmother all about it, showing the eagerness she would never reveal to contemporaries. Orphaned at the age of two, she had no memory of her parents and had been brought up by her mother's mother, Eve Harkness, a veteran of flower-power and hippydom, now in her sixties and grown more conventional with time. She was on the small side, still slender, with grey-blonde hair in an elfin cut, worry-lines in her forehead, smile-lines in her cheek. Something about Pen's story made her uneasy, but then, when you are responsible for a budding teenager, practically everything makes you uneasy, so she tried to ignore it.

'You have to go and see this man who's *dying*? I thought... the firm got in touch with me about five years ago. I had the impression he was already dead. Anyway, I don't think you should be attending deathbeds, not at your age.' She sounded slightly shocked, as if Pen had said she would be visiting a brothel madam or an East End gangster.

'I'll be all right,' Pen said. 'Death isn't contagious, after all.'

'Well, I suppose it's okay,' Mrs Harkness said, doubtfully. 'I don't see what harm can come of it.'

Much later, Pen would remember her words.

THE NEXT DAY, just before four, Pen was walking along Temporal Crescent. She had expected it to be a terrace and was surprised and rather impressed to see all the houses were detached, set well back from the road with adjacent garages and bits of tree and garden behind looming walls. Each front door came with a pillared porch and was approached by at least two flights of steps, flanked by stone urns sprouting tasteful vegetation. The red eyes of burglar alarms gazed balefully from every façade and the ground floor windows were covered with painted iron grilles. Pen found Number 7 by deduction, since it preceded Number 8, but it was set even further back, the garden walls surrounded it completely, and all she could see of it was a glimpse of the roof and the second floor. There were no steps, no front door, apparently no way in at all. Every house must have a door, Pen thought, but she couldn't see one, even when she peered round the side. Number 7A was a much smaller building, perhaps originally a servants' lodge, set against the wall skirting the main property. This at least had a door, with the number on it.

Pen rang the bell.

The door was opened by a butler. Pen had never seen one, but even for a girl who read little fiction the man was instantly identifiable. Butlers are like dragons and demons and other creatures not commonly encountered everyday: you may never see them, but you know exactly what they look like.

'Miss Tudor?'

'Yes,' said Pen. It made her feel very grand to be called Miss, but she, too, could do impassive.

'Come this way, please.'

In the hall, he offered to take her coat and the small rucksack she used for school, but she declined. The rucksack contained pen and paper, in case she needed to take notes, and the coat, which was civilian issue, hid her school uniform.

They went upstairs and stopped outside a door.

'Mr Pyewackett,' the butler explained, with a diplomatic air, 'has not been accustomed to the company of young people for some years. Neither of us have. I hope you will be able to make allowances.'

Perhaps he hates children, Pen thought, trying to understand whatever nuances the butler was failing to convey. But then, why make a thirteen-year-old your executor? Of course, by the time she came to do her executing, he would be dead, so it would make little difference to him anyway.

She said: 'I'm sure I shall.'

The butler opened the door and stood aside for her to enter.

She found herself in a large dark room which, at first glance, resembled a Victorian deathbed scene. Heavy velvet curtains excluded all daylight and there was a fourposter at the far end surrounded by a quantity of dribbly candles and a low-wattage electric lamp. Her host was propped against a mound of pillows like a conventional invalid, but there all resemblance ended. Scattered across the quilt were several books at different stages of being read, a half-eaten packet of Hobnobs, a small tray with stained coffee-cup and saucer, and a couple of used hankerchieves, not paper ones but big squares of spotted silk. What looked like a vintage television set stood on a table beside the bed, and Mr Pyewackett was engaged in changing channels by stabbing at the controls with a very long, very thin bamboo pole, the other end of which had a snuffer for extinguishing the topmost candles on a chandelier.

'Look at that!' he said. 'I can switch channels without moving from my bed. Don't need to get up, don't need to ring for Quorum. Clever stuff, hey?'

Pen stared at him. She saw the lidless eyes, the withered face, the detachable teeth. His few remaining strands of hair had gone on growing after death and were splayed across the pillows like a net of cobwebs. He wore a sumptuous brocade dressing-gown and a silk cravat, and the bones protruded from his finger-ends as if from a pair of worn-out gloves.

Pen said: '–!'

'What's the matter? Never seen a dead person before?'

'N-no...'

'When I was your age, I'd seen half a dozen. Used to get taken to view the corpse every time some relative popped off. Had to kiss m' grandfather when I was eight years old – they'd baked him in embalming fluid. Disgusting. Couldn't throw up, either; wasn't done. No stamina, young people these days. Not asking you to kiss me, am I?'

Pen made an indeterminate noise.

'It's that boy Petal, isn't it? Didn't really fill you in? Should have thought you'd have realised I'd be dead, since you're supposed to be dealing with my Will. No need to bother with Wills and probate and stuff when a chap's still alive.'

'Mr Patel told me you were dying,' Pen said carefully, after a brief struggle with her vocal cords, 'not that you had actually... died.'

'Silly boy. Pussyfooting round the subject. The firm ain't what it was in your great-grandfather's day. Still, we've cleared that up now. Sit down. Quorum! get the girl some tea. Hobnob? Got to get this over in time for *The Weakest Link*. Always watch that.'

'The thing is,' Pen said, accepting a chair from the butler, who was evidently Quorum, 'I thought dead people were more... dead. I don't think I've ever heard of them staying around to watch television.'

'I'm as dead as you can get,' snapped Mr Pyewackett. 'This body won't last much longer, believe me. I'm only trying to sort things out. Television passes the time while you lawyers are meant to be finding Goodman. Sure you won't have a Hobnob?'

Pen eyed the flaking fingers clutching the packet of biscuits. 'No, thanks.'

'They go straight through me but I still get the taste.'

'Are you a zombie?' Pen asked, glad to think she had no imagination, and was therefore unable to speculate about the voyage of the Hobnob.

'No idea. Thought they were from the tropics – voodoo or something. Don't have any truck with all that. It's mostly a load of hocus-pocus, anyway. You don't want to get mixed up with magic, whatever you do.'

'I don't believe in magic,' Pen said, hanging onto that thought.

'Good girl. Good girl.' Mr Pyewackett tried to switch off the television with the bamboo pole, and inadvertently turned up the sound instead. Pen got up and pressed the appropriate button herself. 'Chip off the old block. Sharp as a thorn, dry as a thistle. That's the Tudors. Where were we?'

'Maybe you should tell me what you want me to do,' Pen suggested, taking out her notebook and felt-tip.

Okay, so he was dead. The situation was... unusual. But at least it wasn't like some stupid fantasy novel with wizards and flying carpets and talking cats and all that sort of nonsense.

'Will's pretty straightforward,' said Mr Pyewackett. 'A few conditions but no individual bequests. Everything to Goodman. Have you seen it?'

'They gave me a copy yesterday,' Pen said. 'I read it through last night.'

'There you are then. Quorum stays on here, wages all arranged. And the cat, of course.'

'What... cat?'

'That cat.'

The biggest cat Pen had ever seen heaved itself out of the shadows and thumped ponderously onto the bed. It was not only enormously fat but its long hair, brindled black, brown and orange, made it appear even larger, with the size and energy levels of a sloth. Cats shouldn't waddle but it waddled across the coverlet, helped itself to the last Hobnob, and slumped down at its master's side with its tail twitching like a monstrous caterpillar.

'His name's Felinacious,' Mr Pyewackett volunteered.

'Does he talk?' Pen asked before she could stop herself.

'Shouldn't think so. Never said anything to me. How old are you? Thirteen? Should have outgrown all that talking cat stuff. Thought you didn't believe in that sort of thing.'

'No, but...'

'Quorum'll show you the ropes. Better move in as soon I'm gone. He'll look after you.'

'I'm sorry?'

'Told young Petal, I can't wait around any more. Been dead seven years now and m' body's pretty well had it. Got to be going soon. You're the main executor: up to you to take care of things until Goodman shows up. Can't leave Number 7 without someone to keep an eye on it. Much too dangerous.'

'*Dangerous?*' Pen echoed. It had never occurred to her that her chosen profession might be dangerous, especially not this early on.

'That's what I said. Don't want people trying to get in – or out, for that matter. Your job is to stay here, watch over the place, find Goodman – or wait till he finds you. You're a Tudor: you can do it. Always trusted the Tudors.'

'My grandmother will never allow it,' Pen said, blenching slightly. 'She won't let me just go off and live on my own – even with a butler.'

Mr Pyewackett shot her a glare from his pop eyes which would have been terrifying if she hadn't gone beyond noticing such things.

'Turning yellow, are we? Showing the white feather? Bleating of grandmothers and other excuses? Not what I expect from a descendant of Bluff King Hal.'

'He wasn't bluff,' Pen said tartly. 'He was a serial killer with syphilis who created the ultimate religion of convenience – and I'm not sure about being descended from him, that's probably just family legend. What's more, I can't be both white *and* yellow. Make up your mind.'

'Aha! Sharp as a thorn –'

'I meant what I said. I have to ask my grandmother. I'm a minor, and that's the law. I know about the law.'

'Running out on your first job! What kind of a lawyer are you?'

'A legal one,' Pen said. 'What's dangerous about Number 7?'

But that was the moment when Quorum came in with the tea – good butlers always have a sense of dramatic timing – and Mr Pyewackett turned to *The Weakest Link* and declared the subject closed for the day.

Beyond the Doors
London, seventeenth century

ONLY A FEW streets away from the Grim Reaper the city changed. The patchwork walls and flaking tiles of the slums piled into the houses of the rich as if on a collision course, backyards abutting on courtyards, alleyways intersecting with avenues, ratholes and refuse-gullies threading between. Hovels rubbed shoulders with hotels; coffee houses, eating houses and bawdy houses were heaped together close to the mansions of merchants and the townhouses of the aristocracy; church towers poked skywards from huddles of crooked roofs. Here and there, unexpected gaps of green opened up, bits of leftover countryside or the gardens of the wealthy. Running Lane, Groper's Alley and Beggar's Corner were intertwined with Porkpie Street and Mincemeat Way, Queen's Square and King's Place and Viscount Terrace. High society mingled with low to watch bull-baiting and bear-baiting, cockfights, dogfights, bare-knuckle bouts – to drink and gamble and buy sex – to have their pockets picked and their purses cut – to catch crabs and scabs and the pox. Scavengers thrived. There were laws, but no one to enforce them. The thieves and the pimps and the rats and the worms lived off the underbelly of the city, though only the rats and worms grew fat.

There were many gangs. Without Mr Sheen to protect them, the boys thought they would never survive – the other gangs were run by adults, or boys big enough and strong enough to bully their way to the top of the heap. But Ghost said: 'We'll do,' and they squashed their private doubts, because Ghost was smarter than the others, because he was as pale as an angel, because his little knife came out so fast, so fast, and the blade was always bright and shiny no matter how much blood it shed. He fought off takeover attempts three times in the first week, including one by Dutch Harry, the son of a pirate who ran the toughest of the riverside gangs. He had an eye-patch, though he didn't always wear it on the same eye, and it was said he was so strong he could lift a horse, or at least a donkey, but he was clumsy and slow, and Ghost's little blade carved him up so well he was laid up for a month. It was beginning to have a reputation, that knife – nobody else had a knife which flicked out like that – and it could do a lot of damage for its size. When the fences heard about it they agreed to do business with its owner, though he was so thin and so young, because of the aura rumour gave him.

'We'll call ourselves the Lost Boys,' he told the gang. They thought it was a strange name, not tough or mean enough, but he said it came from a story, though he couldn't remember which. It was about a boy who never grew up, and sometimes he wondered if he was that boy, trapped in the city, condemned to stay thirteen forever. He wasn't trapped, he knew that – he could leave when he wished – but something inside held him there, instinct or need. Whenever he thought of going he knew, somehow, he could not.

He didn't get on with Big Belinda. She wanted him to find the young girls who arrived from the country, and bring them to her – 'So's I can give the poor things a mother's care and a chance for a better life' – but he didn't, no matter what the fee, though he knew they usually came to her in the end. They said it was more fun being a dancer than a domestic drudge, scouring pans and emptying chamberpots, but they drank too much of the geneva liquor, as strong as poison and as cheap as paint, and when their looks ran out the dancing stopped for good. Sometimes Big Belinda wanted boys too, the lucky ones she said, whom she would send to the Duke's house to sing like angels and eat to their heart's content, only no one knew what came to them, for they never returned.

Ghost had seen the Duke several times, at dogfights and bull-baiting: he was always the one backing the most vicious mastiff, or sending more challengers against the bull to be tossed and gored. He was a big man, fat but not flabby, his bloated face marked with so many vices there was barely room for them all, not just the standard seven sins but others too obscure or too cruel for even the church to have names for them. He always wore red, purpley-red or browney-red or dried-blood-red, with lacy ruffles sprouting at throat and wrist, and his chestnut wig cascading over his shoulders in rolls of fat sausage curls. His podgy hands were very white and soft, bedizened with rings – rings valuable enough to feed half the city, if anyone had been able to steal them, but no one ever made the attempt. A black slave followed him everywhere, a gigantic mute with muscles that bulged through his clothes, and it was said that the Duke himself was quick and strong despite his bulk, and could use the sword he wore with deadly skill. Maggot told how one of his boys had run away when his voice broke, babbling of how he had been whipped for his lost high notes, but nobody would take him in, because the Duke was so powerful, and two days later he was found in the creek, though whether he drowned himself or someone did it for him was never clear.

'There was marks on him most h'awful to see,' said Maggot. 'Like whipmarks, but with razor-blades sewn into the leather, so he was all over cuts and blood. They say as how the Duke does it himself. He likes to hurt people. He likes to hurt people weaker'n him.'

The boys duly shivered, except for Cherub, who sat frozen still. He was afraid Big Belinda might try to take him for the Duke, because of his choirboy looks and his singing voice.

'Your voice ain't nothing special,' said One-Ear. 'Fat Sally at the theatre sings better'n you, any day.'

But Cherub had no ear for music, and he wasn't reassured.

'I won't let her take you,' said Ghost. 'No one takes any of my gang.'

'All talk,' said Mags, who was one of the girls. 'I ain't never seen any man outface Big Bel. One o' the gents tried it, a few months back – she grabbed him by the danglies and squeezed till he squealed like a piglet. Lawks! how we laughed!'

'I'll know what to watch out for,' said Ghost. 'Thanks.'

Mags laughed again, but not unkindly. 'Ain't you the clever one?' she said. Ghost thought she was about fifteen, but the liquor was already beginning to spoil her looks. They all drank it except him, because he said it addled his brains, and he knew that to survive in the city – to look after the others – he needed to stay sharp. He had drunk alcohol in the Home when someone smuggled it in, and lain down with his head spinning, and thrown up on the quiet while his room-mates slept, but he wasn't stupid enough to touch the firewater they drank here. It was another thing that made him strange, that set him apart from the rest.

A couple of days after that he was coming home late down Running Lane when he saw the Duke's bodyguard standing by the backyard gate at Big Belinda's. He shinned up the wall, silent as the ghost they called him, and lay down on a roof to watch. And there was the Duke emerging into the yard with Big Belinda, and a boy in between them, small enough for eight though he might well have been ten, a stray from somewhere or nowhere gazing up at the Duke with big, sad eyes. The Duke touched his face with those soft white fingers, all sparkly with rubies and diamonds, and tweaked a ringlet, just hard enough to make the boy cry out, a startled cry on a high pure note that was almost musical. And Big Belinda cackled soundlessly, so all her yellow curls jiggled and danced and her bosom wobbled like twin blancmanges. She wore yellow curls some days, and some days black, but always great bunches of them, stuck with ribbons and jewels, though Mags said the jewels were paste. Ghost loathed her instinctively, the way you loathe any foul and festering thing, but not as much as he loathed the Duke. Big Belinda could be frightening – she had arms like a waggoner and her temper was legendary – but the Duke was evil, the evil hung around him like a miasma, and Ghost's skin crawled just from the nearness of him.

They haggled a little over the price – at least, Big Belinda haggled, the Duke merely paid what he had decided to pay. Then the woman bent over the child.

'You go with the nice gentleman and sing for him,' she said. 'He's a *real* gent, he is.' She wobbled again, as if at some private joke. 'You'll live in a big house, and have lots to eat. Say *thank you, Belinda.*'

''nkyou, B'linda,' the boy whispered. He might be hungry but Ghost thought he too could feel the evil, in the soft touch of the Duke's hands.

The Duke nudged him through the gate, and strode off down Running Lane with the boy and the mute at his heels, towards a closed carriage waiting in Porkpie Street. Ghost felt himself go hot all over with fury, and then cold again, cold as ice, but there was nothing he could do.

One day, he told himself, I'll get the Duke. I'll sell his rings to Wily Jake in Cripplegate and see his fat body floating in the creek with the rubbish. I swear it.

He went back to the loft on the quiet, turning and turning the thoughts in his head.

THAT NIGHT, HE had the dream again. The same dream which he had dreamed regularly ever since he got to the city. It wasn't a nightmare but it always scared him, though he didn't know why.

He was trying to get into a house with no door.

Like all dreams, it had no logic, just the need of the moment. He'd climbed over the wall into the garden – it was a very high wall, with sharpened stones on the top, but he'd stood on a bin and jumped up and cut his hands on the stones. They bled, but he didn't care. He had to get into the house. Curiosity or compulsion pulled him on, like a thread tugging at his soul. He walked all round it, but there was no door, the lower windows were barred and curtained against the light, the upper ones chintz-veiled or sealed with internal shutters. But there were creepers growing up the house, and a drainpipe, and narrow ledges, toe-holds and fingertip-holds, and he went up the wall like a lizard, hauling himself onto the ledge outside an unshuttered window on the first floor. He cut out a pane of glass, and picked at the lock with a bit of wire which he always carried for the purpose, and reached in to open the catch. Then he slid through the gap into the house.

Ghost told himself he had come to steal something, because there must be something worth stealing in a house with no door, but he wasn't in a hurry. It was quiet, and cleaner than any house he'd ever seen, with white walls and expensive rugs and a smell that was hard to describe. Not like the chemical smells of the Home, or the human smells of the city. It was more like the moon would smell on a still night, or the smell of a wind blowing from eternity – if he had ever thought in such terms. The smell of Forever. He stood for a minute or more just breathing, like someone who is taken by surprise, though there was nothing to surprise him.

He was on what must be the first floor landing, with stairs going down to the ground floor and up to the second, and corridors stretching to right and left – corridors which seemed rather too long for the size of the building he had seen from outside. But it was a large house, and he couldn't be sure. The corridors were lined with doors, and the doors were all shut, and somehow they looked as if no one had opened them for many years. In another house he would have looked inside, quick and curious, eager to find whatever there was to be found, but here he hesitated, touched a handle, drew back. He didn't fear discovery: the place was completely empty, he was certain. He could *feel* the emptiness all around him, long undisturbed, still but not tranquil, somewhere on the wrong side of peace. It unsettled him, the vacancy, and the forever-smell, and the doors that were so very shut.

He went down to the ground floor. There was a large entrance hall, with more doors – one looked like the front door, in the teeth of external evidence – and passages opening off it, but everywhere the same stillness, a hush on the edge of expectancy. He went to the nearest door, determined that this time he would see what was beyond, turned the handle, pushed it open a little way. Then stopped. He was staring into a room, with a fire crackling on the hearth, and the light flickering over old-fashioned furniture, and high shelves packed with books. A girl with her back to him was holding a spill to a table-lamp, a girl in a long dress with a waist laced small and a very full skirt. The curtains were drawn over the windows, but beyond them it was night.

He closed the door hastily, trembling. He was still standing in the hall, and it was daylight. But in the room – in the room it had been dark...

Ghost waited till he was calm again, then he went to another door. There was a long moment while he laid his hand on the knob, turning it but not pushing, holding his breath. It never occurred to him to leave the way he came, with every door unopened. The same compulsion still drew him, though he no longer felt its pull: it had become too much a part of him for that. Very cautiously, he nudged the door open a crack – just a crack...

On the other side, someone yanked it back. He was gripping the handle too tight, and it tugged him off balance. He pitched forward, into the room –

– and woke up.

He was in the loft, with the Lost Boys all around him making various whiffling snorey noises, and the safe familiar smells, and a pillow of rags for his head. Somewhere nearby there was a scream, indicating that the city went about its business as usual. He lay down, his shudders slowly subsiding, but he did not sleep again that night.

London, twenty-first century

PEN WAS BY nature a very truthful girl. As she always did her homework on schedule, invariably got top marks, and was not much given to the usual teenage indulgences of smoking, drinking, drug-taking and underage sex, it could be argued that she had rarely felt any need to lie. At least until now. But she was a lawyer, if only a fledgling one, and she understood from case studies that there was a basic difference between the *letter* of the truth and the *spirit* of the truth. When she described what had happened in Temporal Crescent, she stuck faithfully to the former, without an untrue word, while knowing that her account, with its inevitable omissions, did not subscribe to the latter. She was rather shocked to find how good at it she was, and felt both guilty and uncomfortable, but she couldn't bring herself to tell her grandmother that she had had tea with a man who'd been dead for seven years, who wanted her to come and look after a house no one lived in, in case it did something dangerous.

On the one hand, there was the possibility Mrs Harkness wouldn't believe the true story. On the other, since Pen was not the type to invent fantastic lies, she might insist on going to see Mr Pyewackett for herself, and learning the real facts – and in that event, Pen was convinced, she would never be allowed to stay in Temporal Crescent and do her job. And she wanted to. She wanted it more than anything in her life. It was maturity, responsibility, freedom. She had decided she wasn't worried about the danger element – a house surely couldn't be *dangerous*, with or without a front door. Whatever might happen there, she would handle it.

If she got the chance.

'I think I should go and see this Mr Pyewackett,' her grandmother said, as predicted.

But Pen had already worked out her response.

'He's awfully ill,' she said. 'He's going to... to be *gone* within a month. He doesn't see people at all. Only he's got this thing about my family, because the Tudors always took care of his affairs – and his ancestors' – like, from way back. He doesn't have any relatives of his own. He just wants me to stay there till the proper legatee can take over. It won't be for very long.'

'It seems a very odd request to me,' Eve Harkness said. 'Very odd. What do we know about this butler of his?'

'You're acting as if I was a kid,' Pen said. 'I know I'm still a minor, but... oh Gran, don't you see?' Now, the spirit of truth was in her voice. 'It's my chance to... to do something *legal*. It'll be an experience I can't get any other way...'

'It's just a house-sit. That won't teach you anything about the law.'

'I'd be acting as an *executor*. That's not just house-sitting. Honestly, Gran, I'm a *teenager*. If I'd lived in mediaeval times I'd probably have been married by now.'

'Yes, but you aren't. This is the twenty-first century, you're technically still a child, and you can't argue your way out of that one. I don't want to spoil what you see as a great opportunity, but...'

Pen opened her mouth, and shut it again. She knew when it was best to stay silent.

'What if I came with you? Is there anything that says you can't do your executing with an adult around?'

'I... I don't know if the house is big enough,' Pen said. She had never really expected her grandmother would permit her to go alone, much as she had wished for it. This at least was half an adventure, and half an adventure was better than none.

Besides, she wasn't – *really* – the adventurous type.

'I'll ask Quorum,' she said.

*   *   *

'How about it?' said Mr Pyewackett, the following Saturday. 'Got it all worked out yet? Ready to move in, are we?'

'My grandmother wants to come with me,' Pen said. 'She insists.'

'S'pose that's all right,' said Mr Pyewackett, rather grudgingly. 'Just don't let it stop you doing your job. She mustn't go nosing about next door, either. Can't have anyone nosing about... No more nonsense about miners and stuff, hey? You're a lawyer, aren't you? A lawyer and a Tudor. Knew my affairs would be safe in your hands. Quorum! Let's have some sherry. Can't drink to your success in tea, can we?'

When the sherry came, Pen sipped it distastefully. She wasn't keen on alcohol.

'You were going to tell me about the house,' she said. 'Number 7. Why did you say it was *dangerous*?'

'Said that, did I? Slip of the tongue. No one goes in, no one comes out. That's all that matters. See to that, and everything'll be fine.'

'If no one goes in, no one can possibly come out,' Pen said. 'That's logic.'

'Using logic on me, hey? Clever girl. You'll be one who can spot a loophole in an argument a mile off.'

'You're dodging the question,' Pen pointed out. She had honed her examination skills on invisible witnesses in the bath.

'What question?' Mr Pyewackett demanded, swivelling his unnerving glare in her direction.

But Pen had no intention of being unnerved. 'Why is the house dangerous?' she repeated obligingly.

'Ah. *That* question. Long story. Too long for now. Drink up, girl. That's my best Amontillado.'

'You're dodging again.'

'Calling me a dodger, are you? I won't have it. Speaking like that to your elders and betters – and I'm as elder and better as they get, believe me. All the same, young people – you and that boy Petal – disrespectful, insolent–'

'*Why is the house dangerous?*'

'Too young,' declared Mr Pyewackett. 'You're too young to understand. It's a matter of science. Even I don't really–'

'If I'm not too young to take care of the place,' Pen said in her best legal manner, 'then I'm not too young to know why it has to be taken care of.'

'That's the Tudors,' said Mr Pyewackett with evident appreciation. 'Sharp as a thorn, dry as a–'

'Answer the question!'

'Do I have to?' the dead man asked of no one in particular.

'I fear so, sir,' said Quorum from his stance by the sherry decanter. 'The young lady is, after all, your legal adviser.'

'Don't need any advice.'

'Nonetheless…'

'All right, all right.' Mr Pyewackett paused to take what, in a more animate figure, would have been a deep breath, but in his case he merely rattled his teeth. 'Difficult to know where to start. The house is old, you see – very old. Been a house here since heaven-knows-when. Didn't always look the same, of course: must have been Jacobean once, all limed oak and plaster, mediaeval, Roman… Go back as far as you like. There had to be a house, see. Hides the doors.'

'I couldn't see a door at all,' Pen said.

'Ah well, that's the trick. Think it doesn't have one, do you?'

'Every house must have a door,' Pen insisted.

'So where is it, hey? Any ideas?'

This is a test, she thought. If I'm clever, I can work it out. But I need to think… laterally.

'It's in here,' she said at last. 'It's in 7A. This is, like, the gatehouse. So the door must be here. Otherwise how could I watch over it?'

Mr Pyewackett grunted and Quorum, she noticed, looked at her with approval. She was careful not to appear pleased with herself, whatever she felt.

'Right,' said the corpse edgily, sending another gulp of sherry through the empty corridors of his digestive system. 'Door's in here. Quorum'll show it to you when the time comes. There's a word for people like you, girl. Can't remember it right now, but it'll come back to me. Something to do with smart... fart... tart...'

'Intelligent,' Pen supplied.

Mr Pyewackett made the noise which is always written: Harrumph!, though it doesn't actually sound much like that. His teeth closed with a snap, refused to reopen, and had to be delicately prised apart with a knife by Quorum.

'Where were we?' the dead man resumed. 'Doors. Yes. They say there was only one to begin with, but it grew. They built the walls to keep it in.'

'To keep what in? The doors?' Pen was getting confused.

'That's it. Doors to... elsewhere. Trouble is, elsewhere can be anywhere, or so they say. They've got one of those scientific names for it – a space-time prison, something like that.'

'Prism, sir,' Quorum intervened tactfully.

'Prison – prism – what's the difference? Go inside and you're lost. You could wind up anywhere, anywhen. They say the rooms shift about, so the sitting room doesn't stay the sitting room – it may turn into the bathroom overnight. And once you're in, you think you've always been in the sitting room, see? You think that's where you belong.'

'The theory of historical absorption,' Quorum elaborated, with unexpected erudition. 'If you travel into the past, history will absorb you. It is believed to be a form of defence mechanism.'

'But,' said Pen, 'but... how can history defend itself? It's not a person.'

'It has to, Miss,' Quorum said. 'Otherwise it would be changing whenever someone slipped back a century or three. History *wants* to stay the same. If it doesn't you get split universes and divergent realities and a lot of other complications.'

'Physics,' said Pen with relief. '*I see.*' It had all begun to sound a bit like fantasy, but if it was physics, she could deal with it.

And then: 'Do people often... slip back?'

'All the time,' said Quorum. 'Think about it, Miss. How many people do *you* know who are obviously living in the wrong century?'

'It's not just a matter of time travel,' Mr Pyewackett continued. 'There are magical dimensions as well, or so my father told me. Tartarus, Elysium, Elfland, Avalon. History in the sitting room and myth in the library. A load of codswallop if you ask me, but you can't take risks. In a house like that, anywhere can happen. That's why it has to be *watched*, see? All the time. But I've been the caretaker for long enough. Someone else can take over now.'

'Me,' said Pen, faintly.

'Goodman,' said Mr Pyewackett. 'Bartlemy Goodman. He's the man. Used to looking after things, so they say. Goodman – a good man. Don't believe in the power of names, but you never know. You're the stopgap; he's the next custodian. You watch the house till he comes. Find him, too. Probably just as well you'll have your grandmother. Keep you out of trouble.'

Pen didn't say anything for a while. She was still trying to take it all in, to decide what she believed. Lawyers were supposed to be naturally sceptical, to question everything, to accept nothing, to respect only the law. But you were supposed to believe your clients, whatever they told you. And her client was dead, had clearly been dead some time, and had appointed her as executor of his Will, responsible for a house which he claimed was some kind of space/time labyrinth, until the long-lost heir arrived to assume his position.

Somehow, Pen had the idea the dead couldn't lie. There would be very little point. All the things people lied *for* – keeping up appearances, material or emotional advantage, damaging an enemy or a friend – simply wouldn't matter any more. I will believe him, she decided, because he's my client. It's my job to believe him. But as soon as I can, I'm going to check the facts.

'If I'm looking after the house,' she said at last, 'how do I find this Bartlemy Goodman?'

'That's up to you,' said Mr Pyewackett cheerfully. 'Use your initiative. If you have any.'

As if it was a school project, thought Pen with secret sarcasm.

Felinacious the cat wandered in, fixed Pen with his standard baleful stare, then jumped onto the bed with much creaking of bed-springs and disarranging of covers.

'You'd better be off now,' said Mr Pyewackett. 'Time for *The X Factor.*'

Thankfully abandoning the rest of her sherry, Pen left.

Eade, twenty-first century

THE WITCH BENT over the basin, gazing into the liquid mirror. Presently, she nicked her finger with a cheese-knife, letting a single drop of blood fall onto the surface, where it spread slowly outwards in filmy scarlet rings. Fingers being prone to bleed, several more drops followed, until she applied a plaster to the cut. It hurt.

She wasn't a very good witch. She couldn't zap her enemies with lightning-flashes from her hand, nor did her eyes ever turn luminous and her hair crackle with hidden power. If witchcraft had been mathematics, she would have been at the stage of simple addition and subtraction, with a little long division thrown in when she really tried. Of course, she could add two and two to make six, a fundamental requirement for magic. Sometimes, in her case, they made eight.

She was a witch mainly because it was in her family. Her ancestors had been witches in the days when it was cool to have a hook nose and warts, and fly around on a broomstick. She couldn't do anything with a broom except sweep, and she wasn't too keen on that, her nose wasn't hooked, merely nondescript, and she didn't have any warts, only the occasional spot. At sixteen, she felt she was too young for the hook-nose-and-warts look. All she had was the gene, some magical accessories, a lot of body-piercing and an occult tattoo. But she had the instincts. She could smell trouble coming, if trouble had a smell. She didn't know what to do, but she knew a man who did, or would, if she could find him. Bartlemy Goodman, the wizard who never did magic, who had taught her the little she knew – Uncle Barty, as she called him, because he was everyone's uncle, no matter how old they were. He was an uncle sort of person. Uncle Barty, who had gone nearly a year ago, no one knew where.

Finding him, that was the hard part.

The mirror wasn't helping.

All she could see was the house – a rather grand house, with high walls cutting it off from the road, and blank windows showing nothing of what was inside. As far as she could tell, the house didn't have a door, but that might have been a defect of her spell rather than an architectural oversight. She waited for it to change into something more instructive – a vision of doom or disaster, a sickbed with phantoms gathered round its sleeping occupant, a distant figure vanishing down a winding road into eternity. But there was only the house. Probably in London, she decided, on the basis that there were a lot of houses in London. Gradually, it faded away, leaving nothing in its place.

The witch tipped the contents of the basin down the sink with a murmured outcantation to prevent anything unpleasant materialising in the drains. Then she changed the plaster on her cut – the blood had seeped through – and sat down to lay out the cards. The Tarot, with swords and pentacles, cups and wands, and the twenty-two high cards all the way from Death to the World. She shuffled awkwardly, inhibited by her injury and the fact that she wasn't naturally nimble-fingered, muttering the most effective spell she knew for such things.

'*Double-deal and deal them double*
eggs and bacon, toil and trouble,
fingers fleet as beetles' wings
fiddlefeet and twiddlestrings…
fimble famble fi-foh-fum
there we go, and here we come…'

When the pattern was complete she turned the topmost card.
It was Death.

Infernale

NO ONE BELIEVES in the Devil any more. He went out of fashion with wimples and witch-trials, made a brief comeback with the powdered wig, the bal masqué and the Marquis de Sade, popped up in the London smog somewhere between the crinoline and the bustle, and vanished for good into a world of kitsch horror films in the mid/late twentieth century. Evil went on, of course, but Evil is made by humans; we need no supernatural help for that. But there is *someone* who feeds off our evil – who feeds it and feeds off it – the Rider of Nightmares, the Eater of Souls, the God of Small Print, and if he no longer wears horns and a tail that is merely a matter of style. Modern thinking belittles him, superstition touches wood for him, children dance around his maypole – but never *widdershins*, always with the sun. He hides in folktale and fear, in legends and lies – don't speak his name, or he may hear you, don't whistle, or he may come to you. If you believe in fairies, don't clap, for there are darker things than the *sidhe* in the World Beyond Midnight. Call him a myth, call him a fantasy, for myth and fantasy do not exist.

He exists.

He exists at the top of the Dark Tower, in the circular office with the soft silent carpet, heart's-blood red, and the gleaming desktop made from the last tree of some long-lost species that grew in Eden before the Fall, and the windows that look out over all the cities in the world. A single lamp stands on the desk; the lamplight gleams on the gleaming wood, and pools on the blood-red carpet, but illuminates little else. Behind the desk a painting hangs on the wall, a painting no one ever sees; a black veil screens the canvas from view. Once in a hundred years he will make a gesture, and the veil will withdraw, and he will gaze at the picture as if reminding himself of something, though he has forgotten nothing since Time began: he is the One who never forgets. If anyone valued it, it would be the most expensive picture ever painted. The artist was the greatest of his day, perhaps of any day, but the subject – ah, the subject is *him*. It is *his* portrait. There is no visible face and little form, only the moulding of the paint, laid on thick as treacle, swelling into a shadowy density of heavy shoulders and looming presence, and in the faceless dimness the eyes, alight with their own bale. They say the artist could see through the eyes into the soul, but what would he see through the eyes of one who has no soul – the Eater of Souls – the Spirit of Emptiness and Despair? No visitor has ever looked on the painting, not even the Fellangels, his highest servants. Only he sees it, once in a hundred years, and gazes into its eyes, and knows them for his own.

'He had the Sight,' says the Devil, in the mood for conversation. 'He was human, which is to say weak, feckless, careless, and selfish. In all his life he only thought of two things: himself and his art. But his vision never failed. Talent is not given to the deserving. If I had only been able to work out the distribution system then I might have been a true creator, a giver of real gifts, instead of the great Cheat, the supreme Liar. But I never did. Sometimes I suspect there is no system. All is random.'

'But what of God?' comes the question, a whisper hushed by its own daring. 'Was there ever such a Being? A Great Designer who made the Great Pattern?'

'You ask that of *me*?' Azmordis laughs a laugh like red lightning, and the Dark Tower trembles to its very roots. 'Many have posed that question, especially in this modern age, but never – no, never – to Me! Ask it of the wind that blows without a mouth – ask it of the smile on the face of the moon – ask it of the child that was born yesterday! All you will get is the wind's breath and the moon's kiss and the child's cry. There are philosophers who will tell you that adds up to God. But I am not a philosopher.'

He calls himself the Dark Lord, all-powerful and omniscient. He would never admit there might be something he did not know.

The whisper returns, the voice of a Serafain, an infernal angel with a half-human visage and wings made of dusk and blindness.

'What did the artist give you,' he asks, 'for the privilege of painting such a picture, unique among all the pictures in the world?'

'He gave me nothing.' There may be scorn in his tone, there may be amusement. 'He had come to me for money... about three hundred and fifty years ago. He was always in debt. He offered me his soul in payment, but I refused. He put a little of his soul into every picture, you see, though he didn't know it. In the end he had none left. I took the painting instead. It is the one fragment of a human soul that I truly keep. All others wither, or slip away from me, through the Gate of Death into eternity.' He pauses, gazing at the unseen image. His hidden Self. 'When I am gone, it will be destroyed. I have commanded it. No likeness must outlast Me.'

When I am gone...

He has reigned in the Night so long...

He is old, older than the imagination of Man, and a time comes when even immortality wears out. The spirit gnaws itself, stifling in its own darkness, power galls, and the countless battles, defeats, victories all become part of a weary routine dragging him into perpetuity. Mogul emperors have been replaced by media moguls, ambitious princes by faceless businessmen, ruthless conquerors by petty politicians, eager peasants by stars of reality TV. He who once said: 'Evil be thou my Good' realises at last the endless banality to which he has doomed himself. He who once said: '*Après moi, le déluge*' vows only that when sleep takes him forever, another will sit in the empty seat, and look out over the numberless city lights, and remake Evil in his own image.

Or hers.

But the spirits are gone who might have followed him; the few who remain are weakened and jaded, left behind by the current of Progress, which flows faster than Acheron or Ifing. Lesser spirits are too lightweight and the common werekind too wayward. He must choose from among mortals, from the Gifted few, for they alone have the power and the strength he seeks. A mortal will be raised up to immortality, will wear the Horned Crown and the Cloak of Invisibility, hold the Sceptre of Fire, turn Andvari's ring. A mortal, with human imagination, human creativity, a human flair for evil, will step into the Devil's cloven footwear. And the empire of Hell will never be the same again...

'But surely,' says the Serafain, 'if humans are to take on your role, isn't it inevitable they will also take on the role of God, whether or not He exists?'

The Devil smiles a thin dark smile.

'They did that long ago.'

CHAPTER TWO
Bygone House

London, twenty-first century

PEN HAD ARRANGED to see Mr Pyewackett again on the following Wednesday, but on Tuesday she had a call on her mobile from Quorum, asking her to come around immediately. It was after school and already dark, so they were sending a taxi for her.

'I suppose your Mr Pyewackett is dying,' Mrs Harkness said.

Pen didn't answer, because she didn't want to lie. He was, after all, already dead.

Her grandmother found herself in a quandary. She had no wish to insulate Pen from reality, but there was something not quite right, in her view, about her granddaughter rushing off to attend the deathbed of a virtual stranger. Death could be peaceful, and it could be painful, and the need to protect her from ugly facts, while at the same time teaching her about them, forced her into a confused emotional dilemma.

'You can go,' she concluded eventually, 'but I'm coming with you. It's too late for you to be running off to deathbeds on your own.'

'All right,' Pen said. She knew when it was prudent to concede. 'But you have to wait downstairs.'

At 7A, Quorum seemed happy to welcome Mrs Harkness. He showed her into the sitting room, brought her tea, and offered her something to eat if she was hungry. She asked gently probing questions, and received answers which, without telling her very much, left her insensibly reassured. Mr Pyewackett was very elderly and very eccentric, his family had a long-standing connection with the Tudors, he had been extremely taken with Pen and her legal aspirations and would like to give her a chance to prove herself. And so on.

Meanwhile, the bedrooms would be prepared as soon as Mr Pyewackett had gone to his Final Reward and Quorum was looking forward to taking care of her and her granddaughter. Mrs Harkness found herself anticipating the guilty pleasure of someone else doing the housework, the cooking, the washing up...

Upstairs, the corpse said cheerily: 'Well, I'm off.'

'I thought you were going to tell me more about... about everything,' Pen said.

'No time for that. Your bloody firm's had seven years. Not my fault they've been procrastinating.'

'It isn't my firm,' Pen pointed out.

'Whitbread Tudor Hayle, ain't it? You're a Tudor. Sharp as a—'

'Never mind that. I wanted to ask you all sorts of things – about the house, and this Bartlemy Goodman, and—'

'Too late now. Here are the keys. Hang onto them: they're the only set. Don't bother trying to get them copied; there's no locksmith alive who could do it. Leaving everything in your capable hands.'

Pen stared down at the bunch of keys he had deposited in her palm. They looked unnervingly ordinary, much like any other keys she had seen. There were three of them on the ring, and only one seemed particularly ancient, a sliver of iron so crudely-shaped she couldn't imagine it turning a lock any more.

'That's the front door, that's the cellar.' Mr Pyewackett indicated the other two. 'Not sure about the third. Never found a lock it fitted. Tried a few, when I first had the place – used to go in and wander round, looking at the doors, but I never opened one. Best if you stay here. No point in inviting trouble. When Goodman turns up—'

'Supposing he doesn't?'

'You'll sort it out,' Mr Pyewackett said comfortably. 'Move in tomorrow. Don't want to leave the place empty for more than a few hours.'

'But... Quorum'll be here, won't he?'

'He's the butler. He don't count. You come around after school. He'll have supper waiting. Enjoy your digestive system while you can.' He swigged the last of the sherry, patted the cat, and lay back against the pillows.

Pen wondered if there was going to be a celestial choir, or a beam of white light coming down from the ceiling. She found it difficult to visualise Andrew Pyewackett's soul ascending to heaven under such conditions – or at all – but she felt there ought to be *something*.

The dead man said: 'Good luck, girl – though you shouldn't need it. Cheerio.'

The glow in his eyes went out as suddenly as if it had been switched off. And that was that.

Since the funeral had already taken place some seven years earlier, Quorum attended a discreet cremation the following day. That same afternoon, Pen and Mrs Harkness moved in.

THAT NIGHT THEY sat down to a supper of cheese omelette and strawberry tart, waited on by a butler, and Pen, despite the presence of her grandmother, felt a new sense of maturity, mistress of a house which, if not her own, was in her charge. (Two houses, if she was going to be precise.) She had her first job as a lawyer, if a somewhat unconventional one, and the prospect of adventure to follow – the kind of adventure in which she had never believed, that normally featured in books she never read, which meant she had only a hazy idea of what to expect, and could still hang on to her conviction that the realms of the imagination were not for her. No talking carpets, no flying cats. Time travel, it appeared, was science, and Pen had always been good at science. The elves and monsters could stay in storyland where they belonged.

Her grandmother, naturally, had been told nothing about Number 7 except that it had stood empty for many years and was 'unsuitable for occupation'. After all, that was the truth, or a small part of the truth, and Pen and Quorum, without actually discussing the matter, came to a tacit agreement that the whole truth might be rather too much for her to swallow. Although she had noticed that the house had no door at the front she simply assumed it was somewhere round the back and didn't trouble to look for it.

She worked for a small art-and-design company and rarely got home until six o'clock or later. Pen was used to having a couple of hours to herself on her return from school, normally spent on the computer with a cup of tea growing cold beside her. Now, she had Quorum to make her tea, supplemented with cake from a Hampstead patisserie, and other prospects than the Internet.

'I want to see the door,' she told him the following evening. 'The door to Number 7. Before Grandma comes home.'

'If you wish, Miss Tudor,' Quorum said, acquiescing without enthusiasm. 'But I must reiterate Mr Pyewackett's warning. Naturally, you should see the door – you need to know where it is – but it would be most unwise for you to actually enter Number 7. Also quite unnecessary.'

'Mr Pyewackett told me he went in when he was younger,' Pen said. 'He didn't open any of the doors, of course.' She carefully avoided any mention of her own intentions in that respect.

'He was the true custodian,' Quorum responded repressively. 'And although young at the time, I understand he was considerably older than you.'

'Do you think I'm just a child?' Pen said, her spine stiffening.

'Not at all, Miss Tudor. You seem, if I may say so, very mature for your age, and not at all prone to juvenile curiosity.'

'Of course I'm not,' said Pen, deciding privately that scientific curiosity was quite different from the juvenile version, should she be prone to it. 'And please... you needn't call me Miss Tudor. My name is Pen.'

'Very well, Miss Pen. If that's what you would prefer.'

He led her to the back of the house and into a utility room, with chest-freezer, washing machine, tumble-dryer, and a collection of old coats hanging on a free-standing rail, hiding the wall beyond. Quorum wheeled the rail out of the way and Pen saw the door, like a front door on the outside of a house, with steps up to the threshold, a pillared frame, a fanlight over the top and a seven on it in polished brass. It had a letterbox, though presumably that was never used, a demonic door-knocker with horns and protruding tongue, even a bell. It was painted dark green.

'This wall,' Pen said, 'does it touch the other house?' She was sure the two were completely separate.

'There is a spatial interface,' Quorum explained, switching from his Jeeves persona to scientific expert. 'Although in *this* dimension the house and the door are some way apart, they connect through another dimension, or so I have been given to understand. However, it might just be magic.'

'No magic,' Pen said positively, though she wasn't sure about spatial interfaces either. She laid a hand on the door, but it didn't give her pins-and-needles, or anything sinister; it felt exactly as a door should.

'Thank you,' she said, standing back, letting her hand slide into her pocket to touch the keys.

Quorum moved the coat-rail back into place and they left the room.

7A had four bedrooms: Quorum was on the top floor, Pen and Mrs Harkness on the first. Pen was secretly thankful she hadn't been put in Mr Pyewackett's room, since for all her pragmatic attitude she wouldn't have been entirely comfortable in a bed formerly occupied by a living corpse. (That doubtful privilege went to her grandmother.) Later that evening, scrubbing her teeth in her own private bathroom, Pen found herself anticipating the freedom of the weekend. It had been decided Mrs Harkness would go home on Saturday to clean, check the mail, attend her book club, see her friends. Quorum had already imbued her with sufficient confidence for her to consider leaving Pen in his care for the night.

On Saturday, Pen resolved, she would explore Number 7.

She lay awake for some time while the imagination she didn't have opened the dark green door and went roaming through the passageways of the forbidden house.

Beyond the Doors
London, seventeenth century

ONE-EAR CLAIMED to be the oldest of the Lost Boys. He said he was fourteen, on what basis no one knew, since he couldn't count above ten unless he took his shoes off and, like all of them, he was undernourished and undersized, but he was quick as a fox and smart as a whip, so Ghost allowed it to be true. In fact if not in name, One-Ear was his second-in-command. He had lost his left ear when he was six, or so he said, when a storekeeper set his dog on him, and the brute took it off in a single bite. Sometimes, when he had been at the gin, the storekeeper became a merchant or even a noble, and the dog got bigger, and grew several extra heads, but the gist of the story remained the same, though the scar was so clean Ghost suspected a lesser bite which had become infected, leading to amputation. One-Ear would describe being taken to a blacksmith, who cauterised the wound with a red-hot iron, which probably saved his life. The other boys looked up to him almost as much as Ghost, but he had a vicious tongue and a contemptuous manner, so only Ghost was able to love him.

Ghost loved them all, though he hid the feeling so deep inside that even he didn't know it was there.

It was One-Ear who found Tomkin.

He'd come from the country with his mother, who was looking for work, and possibly for his father, but she'd died of the flux and the cousin who took them in treated him worse than a slave. He'd run away from a beating when he met One-Ear, who brought him to the back room of the Grim Reaper for approval.

'He don't know nothing,' Filcher objected. 'He can't earn. Them as can't earn, can't eat.'

'We'll find a use for him,' One-Ear said. 'With that face, he's worth his keep. He looks as innocent as an angel in church.'

Tomkin had only been three months in the city: he hadn't yet acquired the haggard features and vagabond cunning that marked the others. Under the dirt-stains and the tear-stains he was clear-skinned and wide-eyed as an infant.

Cherub studied him appraisingly, the cynicism etched in gin on his plump little face. 'You thinking o' Big Bel?' he said. 'He looks as tender as a pullet from the king's own table. I reckon she'd get a guinea for him, easy.' He didn't say *Ghost won't like it*, but that was what they all thought.

And Ghost arrived on cue, noiseless as ever, slipping into the room like a shadow among shadows.

'A guinea for who?' he asked.

'Him,' chorused Cherub and Filcher, in unison.

'*I* found 'im,' said One-Ear, asserting his rights. 'Half o' that's mine. More'n half.'

'You know the rules,' Ghost said. 'We share the take. Bonus for whoever comes top in the day's pickings.' As he was the only one who could do the arithmetic, he could spread the bonus around without removing the incentive. 'But I don't see any guineas. I see a lost boy – like us.'

'Poor little thing,' said Mags, passing Tomkin a tankard of gin and ale mixed. He took a mouthful, turned scarlet, and choked.

'*He* ain't like us,' One-Ear said amid the laughter. 'He grew up on a farm drinking milk like a little babby. Look at 'im!'

But Ghost didn't laugh. 'He's one of us now,' he said, and his face went hard and still and scary, so the others shut up quickly, even One-Ear. 'You brought him back here. That means he's ours to look after. Big Belinda doesn't get any of my people.'

'I'll tell her that, shall I?' said Mags.

Ghost looked at her with his agate eyes. 'You tell her.'

'Nah,' she said. 'I'm no tattle-tale. But you watch out for him. If Big Bel sees 'im, she'll be round here, sure as check. She still thinks you're like old Sheen.'

'Some day,' Ghost said, 'I'll teach her different.'

Tomkin proved worth his keep after all. He wasn't much of a thief but he could warble a few popular melodies, and with his sweet sad face and the trill of his voice passers-by would be distracted from the activities of the rest of the boys. Some would give him a farthing for his pains, especially the ladies, often reaching for their purses at an inopportune moment, which rather spoiled the whole scam, but, as Ghost said, no system is ever completely foolproof. One-Ear became quite proud of his protégé, taking full credit for the new addition to their gang, and reserved the right to torment him, should any tormenting be required, permitting no one else to do so. But Cherub was jealous, seeing in Tomkin, perhaps, his own lost innocence.

It was Cherub who left him on the street when the Duke's coach came by, splashing mud over the clothes of meaner folk. That same evening Big Belinda climbed the narrow stair to the loft, squeezing her great bulk through the doorway and pointing at Tomkin with her fat finger.

'I'll give you fifteen shillings for 'im.'

'He's not for sale,' Ghost said.

'Make it twenty.'

'He's not for sale.'

'Think you're sharper than Mr Sheen, do you? And he and I doing business ten years together! Still, mebbe you're right.

You're here, and he ain't, so let's us be friendly. Twenty-five, and that's my best offer.'

'Listen,' Ghost said, and his voice went soft, and the blade came out, sudden and sharp, a-gleam in the candlelight. 'Listen carefully. This is only a small knife, and your heart might be hard to find in all that jelly – always supposing you have one – but you try this again and *I'll go looking for it*. Do you hear me?'

Big Belinda went white under the French rouge and the lead powder, white with fear and then red again with anger, but she tottered down the stairs without another word.

'Tomkin'll have to stay here for a few days,' Ghost said when she'd gone.

They cut down the stairs on his orders, since Big Belinda would never get up the ladder, and for nearly a week Tomkin was safe, until the day they returned to find the loft empty. There was blood on one of the beams where he had clung onto it in desperation, and his fingers had been smashed to make him let go. He didn't understand what use he could be to Big Belinda, but he wanted to stay with the gang.

'So they took him anyway,' Cherub said. 'We didn't get twenty-five shilling, neither.'

'Don't ever say that again,' Ghost said. He didn't bunch his fist or draw his knife: he didn't have to. He was their leader because, secretly, each of them was a little afraid of him.

Cherub never said it again.

Ghost climbed back down the ladder with One-Ear, and in Groper's Alley they found Mags. 'The Duke's men took 'im,' she said. 'He was crying something pitiful. Big Bel told 'em where to go. I wanted to warn you, but you was out.'

The knife slipped from Ghost's sleeve with a wicked little glint, even in the dark of the alley.

'Leave it,' said Mags. 'She's watchin' for you. She told us what you said. Laughed about it, she did, but she was scared underneath. She's hired a couple of bruisers to take care o' her.'

'We'll take them too,' said One-Ear.

Mags shook her head, dropping her voice to a whisper. 'She's got important friends, Big Bel. Not just the Duke – others, too. They'd send the constables arter you, mebbe even the army. You'd be strung up for sure. It ain't worth it.'

One-Ear started to speak, but Ghost silenced him. 'We can wait,' he said.

The next week in the meat market he stole a capon. The boys watched in awe as he roasted it slowly, slowly, in a big pot of herbs and wine over their small hearth. He opened up a rat, and added the blood and the guts, and water from the creek, and some of Snot's snot, and a collection of pustules he bought off a beggar who'd never thought to sell his boils before. Then he spiced it, and peppered it, and pee'd in it, all the while stirring and stirring, and the steam was still smelling of wine and herbs and chicken for all the muck that had gone into it.

'Can we try it?' asked Weasel, sniffing, and the twins nodded eagerly.

'It'll kill you,' said Ghost.

He covered the pot, which was pinched from an eatery and looked grand enough, and when it was ready he paid a little black boy from the waterfront to take it round to the gate in Running Lane, saying it was from the Duke.

'Big Bel ate the lot,' Mags confided the following morning. 'I told the girls not to touch it, like you said, but she wouldn't share. She had a bottle o' gin on the side and went to bed, and I ain't seen her since.'

'Let me know how she's feeling,' said Ghost.

But Big Belinda had lived all her life in the city, with the dirt and the diseases, and she rose at noon not a whit the worse, without even a flux to show for it. Ghost went back to the loft, and sat there sharpening his knife, silent, and thoughtful, and patient as the grave.

*   *   *

Eade, twenty-first century

IT LOOKED LIKE a gingerbread house in a fairy story. There were gabled roofs with drooping eaves, like icing running off a cake, crooked beams dark as chocolate, tiny latticed windows sunk deep into marzipan walls. The wood huddled around it, barren twigs and evergreen leaves scratching and rustling faintly in a mute wind. The 'For Sale' notice beside the front gate leaned sideways as if slightly drunk.

The boy stared at the notice with a sinking feeling inside. It had taken him so long to find the address, poring over culinary histories in second-hand bookshops, coming across that lucky mention of the family home, Thornyhill Manor, bought from the original Thorns when their last heirs died out. And now here it was, less a manor than a rambling, overgrown cottage deep in the whispering woods, a gingerbread house fit for a witch – or a cook. For Sale. Of course, it might not be empty, but it looked empty, hiding under its drooping eaves like a teenager under a hoodie, its closed door and lightless windows telling no secrets. The witch was in the Aga, the children had run away, nothing had been cooked here in a long, long time. The boy opened the gate, which creaked, like a gate that hasn't been opened in a while, and went up the path to the front door, but he knew already that he was too late. There was nobody home any more.

Gavin Lester was on a quest. Not the kind where you have to destroy a magic ring, or retrieve the Holy Grail, or even rescue a damsel in distress. At fifteen, Gavin was naturally interested in damsels, but he preferred them not to be too distressed. His quest was to find the greatest cook in the world – or at least, the man he believed might deserve that title – a cook and descendant of cooks, a man who had never hosted a TV show or penned a recipe book, an *éminence grise* of the kitchen, a repository of gourmet mysteries as ancient as the da Vinci code, and much more useful. The family name was Goodman, though sometimes it appeared translated into different languages, as Bonhomme, or Guterman. But in one form or another it featured in various tattered volumes which Gavin had unearthed among the vintage bookstores in Charing Cross Road, a name flickering through the life histories of nearly all the great chefs over the centuries: Savarin and Navarin, Carême and Béchamel, Escoffier and Ranhofer. The chefs were the heroes, fêted in their own day and immortalised all through time in the annals of *haute cuisine*, but always, somewhere in the background, was a Goodman with a finger in the pie. Gavin wanted to be a cook, not a celebrity chef or a TV star but a real cook whose sole aim in life was to make wonderful food, and he had decided that if he could only locate the Goodman of today, he could become his pupil and absorb the gastronomic wisdom of the ages.

He knew the first name would be Bartlemy because it always was – or some variation of it. Bartholomew, Barthe, Bartolème…

And now, having reached his goal, he saw the elusive Goodman slipping away from him again. He knocked, and tugged the old-fashioned bell-pull, but no one came. The trees shuffled in the wind like restless watchers, and the house appeared to hunker down between them, but the occupant had gone. Gavin got the number off the 'For Sale' board and called the estate agent, only to be told that Mr Goodman had died or departed, deeding the house to his niece, who lived locally. With the air of someone pursuing a forlorn hope to the bitter end Gavin walked into the nearby village, asked in two or three shops, traced the niece to a second-hand bookstore.

She wasn't really Bartlemy's niece, she explained, just a close friend. He had gone nearly a year ago, nobody knew where; she didn't think he was coming back.

Yes, he was a good cook.

Just a *good* cook? thought Gavin, slightly shocked, but he didn't say any more.

'Funny thing,' she said. 'You aren't the only person who's been asking. There was someone a while back, I think he was a lawyer, or he worked for some lawyers; I can't recall his name but I wrote down the firm and their number.' After a brief search, she found it. Whitbread Tudor Hayle.

'Thanks,' said Gavin.

Back home in Clapham he accessed their website. Under Wills, he came across a small advertisement requesting Bartlemy Goodman to contact them concerning a legacy from one Andrew Mortimer Pyewackett. Gavin co-opted his younger brother, the Lester computer genius, and finally brought up the Will on screen. And there was the address – another address – the end of the quest or just a further pitstop on a road going nowhere…

Number 7, Temporal Crescent.

London, twenty-first century

It was Saturday. Mrs Harkness had gone home and Quorum was out doing his weekly shop and finding out how to arrange a wireless connection for the computer – something he could have done by telephone, only Pen didn't tell him so. She wanted him out of the way for as long as possible.

When she heard him leave she went to the utility room, moved the coats, and, after some fiddling, inserted the right key in the lock. A click, and the door opened.

As 7A was against the garden wall she had been more than half expecting to find herself looking at grass and flower-beds. It's one thing to be told about a spatial interface (whatever that was), quite another to find yourself confronting one. There was no grass, no garden. She was looking at what must clearly be the entrance hall of Number 7. It was very similar to 7A, only larger. There was a parquet floor, Persian rugs, a couple of unremarkable pictures, a tall vase on a small table containing a spray of what she thought was Honesty. Pale cream walls, soft pale daylight, dimmed by the muslin curtains on the windows, a flight of stairs to an upper floor... And the doors. Lots of doors, all closed. Too many doors, Pen thought, until she realised there was a full-length mirror on one wall, doubling the number, making the hall appear bigger than it was. It's really very ordinary, she told herself. And clean. The parquet gleamed. There was no dust on the table. Someone, presumably Quorum, must come in to vacuum and flick round with a duster. Except she had the only key...

It was very quiet. She couldn't even hear the faint traffic-murmur which always lies in the background of city life. And there was a smell, or something like a smell. Long after, when she tried to describe it, she said it was the smell of something about to happen.

She went over to one of the doors, closed her fingers round the handle. She was only going to look – just to look. *History will absorb you*, Quorum had said, but she had no intention of being absorbed. She would open the door a little way, see what lay beyond, close the door again. History couldn't absorb her if she didn't pass through. She turned the handle part way... then let it slip back. No hurry. After all, for the moment at least, it was *her* house. The sensible thing would be to have a good look around first. Pen prided herself on always doing the sensible thing. She released the handle and made her way upstairs.

There was a landing, passages which must stretch the length of the house, more doors. And a draught. It was very slight but she felt it at once, the faint chill of cooler air on her cheek. To her left was a single window, closed but not shuttered; she walked over to it to check the latch. And saw the pane cut out – a single pane, sheared cleanly from the frame as if by someone who knew what they were doing. She opened the window and looked down. Quite a long way down. There was a drainpipe, a climbing plant, a couple of ledges. A monkey could do it, but surely not a human. But a monkey wouldn't know how to cut out a pane of glass.

Someone got in, Pen concluded. Someone who came to steal, at a guess: it was a big house in an upmarket residential area, and it must appear temptingly unoccupied. Someone got in, but there was no sign they ever got out...

Pen suppressed a shiver. Whoever it was could have left the way they entered, by the window – although would they have bothered to close and latch it behind them? Had someone else shut the latch? She wondered when it had happened, for how long that pane of glass had been missing. When she pressed a cautious finger against the broken edge, it didn't feel sharp, as new-broken glass should. And below the window the parquet seemed faded, as if rain or sun or both had eroded the polish and bleached the wood beneath. That could take years, she thought – perhaps decades. She must find out when Andrew Pyewackett last went inside Number 7, if Quorum knew – who did the cleaning – whether the house had a *name*, instead of just a number. A house like this *should* have a name, a title that told you something about the contents, a clue to its secrets. Bygone House, a house of doors into the past. That would be a good name.

She descended the stairs, slowly, thinking serious thoughts. In the entrance hall, she stopped. She knew she wasn't ready to explore more thoroughly – she needed some sort of safety device, to block the history absorption factor – the evidence of a clandestine intruder who had never left worried her. But she couldn't go back to 7A without doing *anything*. It was all very well being sensible but when you are psyched up for adventure, then an adventure of some sort has to happen, even if it is only a very small one. Not that Pen used the word 'adventure' anywhere in her conscious mind. It was simply that she had come there to do something, and something had to be done. She was a lawyer, and lawyers didn't run away from their duty. And there might not be that many occasions when her grandmother was out of the way.

Under the stairs was a door which, in 7A, opened on a broom cupboard. There couldn't be anything very dangerous in a broom cupboard. (It was too long since Mrs Harkness read her any children's stories, and she had forgotten about wardrobes.) She turned the handle, very gingerly, half way, all the way. Tried pulling the door towards her, but, unusually for a cupboard, it opened inward. She pushed it open a crack. Then pushed it wider...

She was looking out over a green jungly landscape that went all the way to the sky. There was a wide space of grass, like a watermeadow, stretching away until it vanished under a wall of trees – gigantic palms and monstrous shrubs with thick rubbery leaves and trees with multiple trunks and netted branches supporting great towers of foliage. Beyond, the sunrise – she was almost sure she was facing east – turned the sky to apricot gold, with a couple of curled feather-clouds hanging above it, perfectly positioned to catch the light in their filaments. A sudden ray found its way through the far-off canopy, blinking into her eye, so that for a few seconds she was dazzled and almost blinded. That was why she didn't see the creature until it charged.

She had been leaning through the gap to see better, one foot over the threshold, peering into the past – whatever past it was – and the predator, already close, must have spotted her, stalked, picked its moment to spring. Instinctively she jumped back, pulling the door shut, but it was too late. A hand or paw came round the edge, with four short claws and one long one, a curved slashing claw like a kris. It hooked itself round the door and tugged experimentally. Pen tugged back, adrenaline giving her extra strength, but the creature was far stronger. A second set of claws joined the first and the door left her control, wrenched back into the broom cupboard world. She let go, stumbled against the little table, knocked over the vase of Honesty. It shattered on the parquet, eggshell-fragments of china spraying in all directions. But Pen wasn't noticing. She was staring at the thing peering through the door.

It was as tall as a tall man, serpent-necked, lizard-skinned, striding on powerful hind legs like a huge flightless bird. Its forelimbs were short, supple as arms, tipped with the scissor-claws. Its head was half way between reptile and vulture, beak-like jaws parted in a grin full of teeth – gnawing teeth and ripping teeth and tearing-your-throat-out teeth. It looked round the hall, faintly bewildered, saw Pen. Saw *dinner*.

Bewilderment no longer mattered.

Pen knew what it was even though it had looked slightly different on film. She'd seen *Jurassic Park* on the television. She hadn't thought much of it.

'The science isn't sound,' she'd said. 'It's just an excuse for the dinosaurs. It's not believable.'

It was believable now. She bolted back into 7A, slamming the door behind her. Something hurled itself against the panels – the door shook – there was a sound of tearing wood. She pictured those curved claws sawing through the barrier, perhaps in a matter of minutes. Or less.

In 7A, the doorbell rang.

Pen raced to open it, forgetting the butler had a key. 'Quorum –'

A boy she had never seen before was standing on the steps. She took in very little about his appearance except that he was black, a year or two older than her, and wore a red-and-white striped rugger shirt. From the back of the house she could hear the unmistakable sound of a door being forced open. The horror must have showed on her face.

'What's the matter?'

'There's a velociraptor –'

'There's a *what*??'

'– in the utility room!'

The boy – reckless, curious, or merely incredulous – entered the hall from the front just as the dinosaur entered it from the back. The animal was confused by its unfamiliar surroundings, the alien smells, the strange prey with its oddly-coloured hide. It paused for an instant, head swaying from side to side, getting its bearings, checking out Pen's position and that of the newcomer. The boy returned its stare with a dropped jaw. Then the velociraptor began to advance.

As long as she lived – if she lived – Pen knew she would never forget what happened next.

The boy stepped between her and the monster. He took something out of his pocket, tried to ward off the slashing claw with one arm, reached out... There was a flash, and a buzzing noise. The dinosaur collapsed with a crash.

Felinacious emerged belatedly from the sitting room and hissed at it.

Pen said: 'Is that a stun-gun?'

'Yeah.' They were both panting, breathless with the aftermath of fear.

'How come you've got a *stun-gun*?'

'My nan got it. She's afraid of being raped.'

'Your *nan* is afraid of being raped?' Under the circumstances, it was trivial, but the remark popped out before Pen could stop herself.

'Look, ever since she lost weight she thinks she's Beyoncé, okay? She says she's got a stalker. Then she gave it to me. She says my mate Derren's in a gang.'

'Stun-guns are illegal.' It wasn't what she wanted to say, but habit took over.

'You complaining?'

'I'm sorry, I didn't mean... Thank you. Thank you for saving my life.'

'No sweat,' the boy lied. 'I just wasn't expecting random dinosaurs in Hampstead...'

'You're bleeding. Come into the kitchen. I'll patch it up.'

'Better give the beastie another blast, just in case...'

The big claw had made a cut in his arm, long but not too deep. Pen bundled it rather inexpertly in clean tea-cloths since she didn't know where to find the bandages.

'I thought you lived here?' the boy said.

'Sort of.' She saw he was trembling, perhaps from some kind of delayed shock. Then she realised she was trembling too.

'We have to put it back,' she went on. 'You must help me. I can't do it on my own.'

'I don't *must* anything.'

'Sorry,' she said again. 'I mean... please?'

'Put it back where?'

'The Jurassic, I suppose. That has to be where it came from. I don't want the butler to find it.'

The boy skimmed over an assortment of queries and plumped for: 'You've got a *butler*?' He sounded impressed.

'Yes, but he's out. We've got to move it before he gets back. If I take the head, can you get the legs? And zap it if it looks like coming round.'

'Where are we lugging it *to*?'

'The broom cupboard next door.'

The boy didn't say anything. Shock can have that effect sometimes: you don't ask the obvious questions because part of your brain's on hold. The unconscious velociraptor was heavy and awkward; they had to drag rather than lift it, its tail kept knocking into the furniture and its head lolled on the end of the serpent-neck and had to be supported against Pen's chest. The heavy jaws and jagged teeth were much too close for comfort.

In the utility room, she said: 'My name's Pen.' She would normally have introduced herself as Penelope, but when someone has just saved you from a hungry velociraptor it's time to by-pass the formalities.

'I'm Gavin.'

'Nice to meet you.' Mrs Harkness had taught her that good manners were obligatory at all times.

'Ditto,' said Gavin. 'At least... maybe. Does this sort of thing happen to you often?'

'No,' Pen said, amending it on the recollection of several conversations with a dead man. 'Not exactly.'

They bumped the dinosaur up the steps to Number 7, gave it another zap with the stun-gun, and folded back a rug so they could slide it across the hall floor.

'When I was outside,' Gavin said, 'these houses didn't look joined up. I mean, I know they aren't. I only rang your doorbell because I couldn't find the front door to Number 7.'

'*That's* the front door to Number 7,' Pen explained. 'It's a spatial interface.'

'What the frock's that?'

'What the –?'

'My mum says it. She doesn't like the f-word, so she says "frock" instead.'

'Your mum swears by a dress and your nan's afraid of being raped? Your family sound a bit – weird.'

'You've got a butler,' Gavin said accusingly, 'and a dinosaur in your front hall. *That's* weird.'

Pen backed towards the broom cupboard. Beyond, there was the vista of watermeadow and jungle, the long shadows of early morning reaching out from the trees. The sun had risen a good deal further and a variety of animals and/or birds were making a variety of screeching and whooping noises.

Gavin said: 'Is that the broom cupboard?'

'Yes.'

'There's a jungle in it.'

'Yes…'

'What is this? Frocking Narnia?'

'Please mind your language.' Pen knocked her elbow against the door-frame, said: 'Bugger,' and had reversed into the long grass before she had time to consider the risk. But the Jurassic, an era short on human beings, showed no immediate sign of taking over. Her mind stayed resolutely in the twenty-first century.

From this side the door was set in a gap in an enormous hollow tree. They hauled the velociraptor through it and dumped it on the edge of the meadow. Gavin gazed around him with an expression of awe on his face.

He said: 'Wow.' And: 'This is *wicked*.'

'Come back,' said Pen. 'Come back *now*.'

'But–'

'Your arm's bleeding through the tea-cloths. The blood-smell might attract *anything*. According to a programme I saw recently, they think tyrannosaurs were scavengers as well as hunters. Supposing a tyrannosaur rolls up? Are you sure your baby stun-gun will work on something that big?'

Reluctantly, Gavin allowed her to drag him back into the house, closing the cupboard behind them. Then they returned to 7A. The door in between shut and, rather surprisingly, locked again, though the claw-marks in the panels would remain. Pen moved the coat-rail and took Gavin upstairs to the bathroom, where a further search located enough sticking plasters to hold the cut closed (it took five), and they washed the tea-cloths out in the sink.

'Quorum mustn't know about this,' Pen said, adding: 'He's the butler.'

'You ashamed of me?'

'Not *you*, idiot. The dinosaur.'

'Okay. That figures. How come you have a butler, anyway? Are you very rich?'

'No,' Pen said. 'It's a long story. How come *you* were trying to get into Number 7?'

'I was looking for the owner.'

'There isn't one,' Pen said. 'But I'm the... the temporary custodian.' She didn't like 'caretaker'; it wasn't impressive enough.

'I was told,' Gavin said, 'the house was left to Bartlemy Goodman.'

'Oh,' said Pen, slightly nonplussed. 'Why d'you want Bartlemy Goodman?'

'*Two* long stories,' said Gavin.

For the first time, she looked at him properly. She saw classic cheekbones, velvet brown eyes, a mochaccino complexion, a sudden smile which most girls would undoubtedly consider heart-stopping. But Pen had determined some time ago that her heart would not be easily stopped. She didn't smile back.

He saw the pale face, the pale freckles, the pale red hair. He thought she was spiky and posh and probably too clever by half. And nowhere near as pretty as his ex-girlfriend, Josabeth Collins. In fact, not pretty at all, just sort of neat-looking, with the neatness of someone whose face has no obvious defects, no outstanding assets.

Nonetheless...

Anyone with a velociraptor in their broom cupboard is bound to be *interesting*.

'Let's have something to drink,' Pen suggested. 'Then we can talk.'

'Beer?' Gavin said hopefully.

'Tea,' said Pen.

Eade, twenty-first century

THE WITCH APPROACHED the gingerbread house as if she belonged there. The back-door key was where it had always been, under a stone beside the overgrown tangle of the herb garden. She murmured the spellword to release the stone, picked up the key and let herself in.

In Bartlemy's day, the door might have been left open; he had never needed the security of locks and bolts. But that day was long gone.

She went through the kitchen, remembering the aroma of past cooking, half imagining it was still there. In the drawing room she rolled back the carpet to expose the blackened scar of a hundred magic circles. She lit a fire on the hearth, not a spellfire but a real one, with logs from the log-pile and scrunched-up newspaper and the hint of a charm to get it going. The room felt slightly clammy, the way an unlived-in room will, but the fire warmed it. Then she sprinkled spellpowder round the perimeter of the circle, drew the runes of protection, spoke a word in the language of power, the language of the Stone from long ago. '*Fiumé*!'

The powder sparked into flame – not a bright ring of flame but a thin fireline, scarcely more than a glittering thread. Still, it was enough. The witch was young and very inexperienced: she had never done this on her own. But she knew what to do. She began the incantation.

Presently, a spirit appeared at the centre of the circle. It was child-sized, vaguely female, with long filmy hair and the wistful expression of someone who is always dreaming about chocolate while her mother feeds her on greens. The witch stared at it in annoyance.

'Who are you? I summoned the Child.'

'I *am* a child,' the sylph pointed out. 'I've been a child for nearly three thousand years, so I should know.'

'I summoned *the* Child,' said the witch. 'Eriost – Varli – whatever else he likes to call himself.'

'He's busy,' said the sylph. 'But I don't think he'd come for you, anyhow. I know you, even though you hide outside the boundary. You're just a village witch – the granddaughter and great-granddaughter of village witches. You shouldn't be drawing the circle. This is High Magic. It's way beyond you.'

'I've done it before,' the witch snapped. 'Give me your name.'

'If you were any good,' the spirit yawned, 'you'd know it.'

'Then *I* will give *you* a name,' said the witch, 'and beware, for it will stick to you for the *next* three thousand years – it will stick like a sticking spell – and to all who call on that name you will have to answer. I name you Airhead, also called Peabrain, spirit of –'

'My name is Finwala,' the sylph said grudgingly. 'But I can't help you. Whatever you want to know, I don't know it.'

'Airhead suits you better, Finwala,' said the witch. 'Why is the Child busy?'

'Because,' said Finwala. 'All the Old Spirits are busy. Too busy to talk to *you*, anyway.'

'Busy with *what*?' demanded the witch. It wasn't what she had meant to ask, but now she *had* asked, she wanted to know.

'Changes,' said the sylph. 'There is trouble afoot.'

'There always is,' the witch said crossly. 'Tell me something I don't know. What kind of trouble is it this time?'

'None of your business,' snapped the sylph.

'*Inserré*! I bind you in the circle – you can't leave until I give the Command – you can't leave until you answer my question. *What kind of trouble–*'

But the sylph grew pale and faint, fading to a wispy shade which seemed to tremble in an unseen wind. Her voice shrank to a far-off murmur, an echo within an echo: 'None of your business – *business, business* – trouble… *trouble*… TROUBLE…' Then, unexpectedly, she began to scream, a thin high wail that broke in the middle, like a banshee with laryngitis.

The witch let her go.

She paused for a few minutes, scowling. In the circle smoke-shapes melted and changed, elementals seeking a way in where she had left an opening, the microsprites that infest any magical process.

Eventually, she resumed the incantation. She did not intend to try the major spirits again – evidently they weren't listening, and she hadn't the power to get through – but there were others lower down the hierarchy who might respond to her call. She leafed through one of her books till she came to the section headed *Goblins, Gremlins and Grinnocks*, and placed her finger on the page with her eyes shut. When she opened them, she had a name.

'Simmoleon.' She repeated the summons, in the spelltongue and again in English for added impact. 'I summon Simmoleon.'

Within the circle, the smoke-shapes blurred – shrank inwards – condensed into solidity with disconcerting speed. A figure was standing there, a figure less than three feet high, knotty-muscled and knobble-jointed, its overlarge head resembling a lumpy and unshaven potato. It sported an ugly pout, toothbrush eyebrows, and a squint. A grinnock, thought the witch with resignation. Her knowledge of such things was rudimentary, but she had once been told a grinnock was a being somewhere between a goblin and a dwarf, solitary, sullen, and vicious: only lack of height kept them from being serial killers. Being a failed psychopath in a world too big for you would, the witch reflected, be enough to embitter anyone.

'I won't answer your questions!' the creature said.

'I haven't asked any.'

'Then don't bother, because I won't answer!' It spoke with an air of triumph out of all proportion to its size.

'Fine,' said the witch. 'I'll pen you in the circle – I'll pen you here for five hundred years – I'll taunt you with plagues and phantoms–'

'Ye wouldn't know a plague if it bit you i' the arse.'

'Oh yeah?' The witch muttered a few words under her breath. Inside the circle, tiny green flecks came buzzing out of the air and zoomed in on the grinnock, swarming round his head and stinging his horny skin. The spellring had already attracted too many elementals, and it was easy enough to work on them. He flapped his many-fingered hands, trying to beat them off, swearing in the language of his kind.

'There's a word for the likes o' you,' he said, 'and it isna *witch*!'

'Five hundred years,' she reiterated. She was short on power, but not on attitude.

It took nearly ten minutes and a range of elemental manifestations to subdue the grinnock, and by then she was concerned the perimeter might be wearing thin.

'I'm looking for someone,' the witch said.

'Puir man.'

'His name's Bartlemy Goodman.'

'Niver heard o' him.'

'He's a wizard... occasionally,' the witch elaborated. 'And a very good cook.'

Unexpectedly, a glimmer showed in the grinnock's beady little eyes. 'Can he make them buns,' he said, 'wi' sugar on the outside, and the jam i' the middle that comes out all oozy oozy when ye take a bite? I bet he canna. They call them dog-nuts, though I niver saw no dog wi'–'

'Of course he can,' the witch asserted with confidence. 'He's the best cook in the world. But I didn't know grinnocks liked doughnuts.'

'They call me Sugartop,' Simmoleon volunteered. 'Acos o' my liking for the dog-nuts, and the gen'ral sweetness o' my naitcher.'

'I should have guessed,' said the witch. 'Find Bartlemy Goodman for me, and he'll make you the doggiest dog-nuts you've ever eaten, with the sugar all crunchy on the outside, and the dough as light as an air-bubble, and the ooziest jam in the middle made from two hundred per cent fruit...'

'I dinna believe it,' said Simmoleon, but there was weakening in his voice.

Being a witch is less about magic than learning which buttons to press. 'When you bite into it the jam comes welling out and goes dripping down your chin like... like...' Perhaps because of the company she kept, the only images she could think of were to do with blood.

But her words had done the work of twenty plagues.

'Maybe I could ask around,' Simmoleon said with an air of profound reluctance. 'I could be putting an ear to the ground, and listening to the smalltalk o' the worms. What if he's dead?'

'He won't be dead,' said the witch, pushing aside the recollection of the Tarot. 'He's been alive too long. It's become a habit.'

'Ah,' said the grinnock. 'One o' *those*.'

'There's something else,' said the witch. 'I'm hearing a rumour about the Old Spirits. Some new kind of trouble...'

'What would the likes o' me be hearing about the likes o' them?'

'Rumour talks,' the witch retorted. 'And ears like yours would hear it. Think of dog-nuts. Where do you stand on chocolate cake?'

'Chocolate cake?' The grinnock's ugly face grew almost dreamy. '*Real* chocolate, wi' the icing an inch thick, all sugary buttery cocoa, and the sponge so moist and dark, dark, and that stuff i' the middle they call gooache?'

'Ganache,' said the witch. 'Yeah. Though you ice an inch thick, to that flavour must you come.' She had studied *Hamlet*. 'People have committed murder for Bartlemy Goodman's chocolate cake. As dark as the dark powers...'

'Dinna mention *him*,' Simmoleon hissed. 'If I start a-telling you things, folk will be knowing, and they'll send me into Limbo for all time...'

'You said, don't mention *him*. Which *him*?'

'Don't be naming him! If ye name him, he'll hear ye, or so they say – he'll hear ye and come to ye – though I'm thinking it'd keep him busy, the way humans throw his name around.'

'Give me *one* name,' said the witch. 'Whisper it. A name humans use.'

'Aye, well... He's been a god and he's been a demon and he's been the King o' Elfland. These days, they say he wears a suit like a man and sits at the top o' the Dark Tower pulling the strings that make the world fall down. Time was, ye'd be calling him the Divil, though now-and-now it's more like *sir*. But–'

Azmordis. The witch mouthed the name, though she did not say it.

'Sssshht!' The grinnock glanced round, furtive and scared. 'They say... *they say* – he's... *retiring*...' His potato-brown skin turned the colour of cold pasta. 'See, he's been here since the dawn o' time – he saw the first fish crawl out o' the sea and grow legs – he saw the first man and the first blow and he smelled the first blood ever shed. When the apple o' Good 'n Evil was baked in a pie, he was there to dish it out. Now, he's had enough – enough o' plots and schemes, enough o' Men and their ways, maybe even enough o' power. Aye, it'll be a dark day for mortals when he's gone.'

'How so?' said the witch, chilled and vaguely baffled.

'Ye don't follow, do ye? When the old king goes, what happens? What happens when the throne is empty? Ye've a saying among Men, better the Divil ye know…'

'Who would take over from the Devil?' the witch said slowly.

'That's the question. That's the big question. And it ain't one I'll be answering, though ye plague me all the way to eternity.'

He was becoming dim and insubstantial even as he spoke. The witch could not hold him; the *blip* of new fear broke her concentration. She was stood there, shivering, while the spellfire crumbled into ash and the dark came through the windows.

London, twenty-first century

IN THE KITCHEN at 7A, Pen looked for biscuits to go with the tea. Unfortunately, all she could find was Hobnobs. Somehow, she just didn't fancy Hobnobs any more, but Gavin accepted with enthusiasm. He looked the enthusiastic type, she decided. There was a kind of glow about him – the glow of someone who was adored by his family, popular with friends, indulged by teachers, someone who assumed life would always be nice to him because – so far – it always had been. Pen remembered her friend Matty talking once about children 'born in the sun', beloved by the Fates – people for whom the toast always falls buttered side up. Gavin definitely looked like that, Pen thought, a sunshiny person, the sort of guy who, when confronted with a velociraptor, would invariably have a stun-gun in his pocket. Someone with more than their fair share of natural luck.

Of course, she didn't believe in luck, or fate. She knew quite well these things were a matter of mathematical probabilities.

'Does your nan really look like Beyoncé?' she asked irrelevantly.

'What do *you* think?'

Felinacious rubbed his vast body against Gavin's leg, purring like a small earthquake.

'He's after the Hobnobs,' Pen explained.

'He's the fattest cat I've ever seen,' Gavin said. 'You ought to take better care of him. Shouldn't he be fed cat food – fish – something healthy?'

'It's probably too late,' said Pen. 'He's used to Hobnobs. He's not my cat, anyway. He belonged to Mr Pyewackett, who owned this house until... until recently.'

'I know,' Gavin said. 'It's in his Will. I read a copy when I was looking for Bartlemy Goodman. That's how I knew where to come. But Pyewackett died seven years ago – that's hardly recent. Goodman does own the house next door, doesn't he?'

'In a way,' Pen said. 'If you've read the Will you know who I am, anyhow. I'm the executor – Penelope Tudor.'

'But...' Gavin looked blank. 'Seven years ago you'd have been... what? Four? Five?'

'Six. Don't bother about that now. The point is, Bartlemy Goodman hasn't turned up, so I'm looking after the place.'

'Since you were *six*?'

'No. Just a few days, actually. Andrew Pyewackett... left on Tuesday.'

'But he's dead!'

'Yes,' said Pen. 'He was. But he said he couldn't move on till there was someone to watch over the house. Quorum's the butler, but he doesn't count. It had to be me.'

'You're saying,' Gavin paused, thought, started again, 'you're saying a dead man lived... *stayed* here, for seven years, *dead*, until you came along to take over?'

'Yes.'

'Like... a zombie?'

'I asked him that,' said Pen. 'He told me he didn't have any truck with voodoo.'

'You're taking the pants.'

'Pants?'

'Sorry. Mumspeak. I've got to hand it to you, you've got the best face I've ever seen for spinning a line, really deadpan, but–'

'There's a velociraptor in the broom cupboard,' Pen reminded him.

There was a long silence. The sound of munching Hobnob came at either end, with a frozen pause in the middle.

'After seven years,' Gavin said, 'a corpse would be–'

'He wasn't in great shape,' Pen said. 'But I think Quorum's managed to hoover up most of the flaky bits by now.'

More pause. More Hobnob.

'I know you're not six any more, but... aren't you rather young to be someone's executor? I thought that was a job for lawyers.'

'Sometimes,' said Pen. 'Anyway, I *am* a lawyer. At least, I'm going to be. I decided that years ago. This is my first legal job. I don't suppose you'll understand, but–'

'As a matter of fact,' Gavin said, 'I do. I've always been sure what I was going to be, too.' He looked at her with an expression on his face which she recognised though she hadn't seen it before. It was the expression she herself wore whenever she talked about her ambitions.

In that moment, they bonded, in a way they hadn't bonded over the dinosaur.

'What are you going to be?' Pen asked.

'A chef.'

'Like Jamie Oliver? On TV and everything?'

'I don't care about TV. I just want to be the *best*. It shouldn't be about churning out books and being a celeb – all I want is to make food taste brilliant. That's why I'm looking for Bartlemy Goodman.'

'*He* can't be a chef,' Pen said. 'He's meant to be... someone who takes care of things. Problems. Like the house next door.'

'He may not be a chef, exactly,' Gavin admitted. 'But he knows about cooking. He must do. He comes from this family – they go back forever – I've traced them myself. They're not famous or anything, but they're always there, behind the famous people, mentioned in passing – an acknowledgement – a footnote – a name in the margin. Always the same name, though sometimes in different languages. I don't know why they've changed nationalities, but it can't be a coincidence – it *can't* be. I've been reading up on the great chefs of the past, you see. I want to get back to their ideals, kind of sweep away all the superficial glamour that goes with cooking nowadays. Nigella pouting – Jamie Oliver being laddish – Gordon Ramsay bullying people – that isn't what it should be about. It should just be about the food. Anyway, I'm sure Bartlemy Goodman can help. He'll know things – lost secrets...'

'Are you sure this is the *right* Bartlemy Goodman?' Pen said doubtfully.

'There aren't any others,' Gavin said simply. 'So... yes, it must be. He was living in a village in the country, a place called Eade, but he left about a year ago.'

'How did you–'

'I found his address in a book. It was the Goodman family home. I went down there to see if anyone knew where he'd gone, but they didn't. He gave the house to this woman who's supposed to be his niece, only she isn't, and she's put it up for sale. I spoke to her – she was really nice – but she had no idea where he'd gone.'

'A year ago,' Pen echoed thoughtfully. 'And the people at Whitbread Hayle –' she dropped the Tudor '– couldn't find him for seven years. They obviously weren't looking very hard.'

'Then I checked out your law firm,' Gavin went on, 'and I got this address, so I came here. And now you tell me he's disappeared again.'

'He didn't disappear,' Pen said scrupulously, 'because he never actually appeared.'

'Anyway, what do you mean he *takes care of things*? What do *you* know about him?'

'Nothing,' Pen said. 'I didn't know anything about the cooking. All I do know is Mr Pyewackett didn't have any family left, so he bequeathed Number 7 to Bartlemy Goodman, because he said he was capable of looking after it. I don't even know how Mr Pyewackett got to hear of him. He would dodge questions he didn't want to answer – especially if I forgot to ask.'

Gavin said: 'What was he like, your Mr Pyewackett?'

'Like a very old corpse, with big starey eyes, sitting up in bed switching the TV on and off with a long bamboo cane because he didn't know about remotes and eating Hobnobs. That's why I don't fancy them any more. If you'd ever seen a dead person eating Hobnobs, you'd understand.'

If Gavin had harboured any lingering doubts about Pen's story, that was when they vanished. The mental picture, with Hobnobs, and her reaction to it, was eerily convincing. He said: 'About Number 7 then – what exactly is going on there?'

'It's something called a space/time prism,' Pen said. 'I don't know what that is, but all the doors open on different bits of the past, or magical dimensions, and if you go through you'll get lost, sort of absorbed into history. Like, if you're in the eighteenth century, that's where you think you belong. It stops people going around changing the course of events.'

'So knowing all that,' Gavin said, 'you went in, and opened the broom cupboard. Frocking hell.'

'What would you have done?'

He thought for a minute. 'The same, I suppose. Only...'

But at that moment they heard Quorum coming back, and further discussion had to be postponed. Pen introduced Gavin as one of her friends, demanding *sotto voce*: 'What's your surname?'

'Lester. Gavin Lester.'

Quorum cooked lunch for them, and Gavin left afterwards with a murmur of: 'I'll phone you. Don't do anything without me.'

While Pen saw no reason to pay attention to that, it was something to feel she had an ally.

PEN DIDN'T LIKE hiding things from her grandmother. There were the usual omissions in whatever she chose to repeat, mostly to do with the behaviour of her friends, or the boys who picked on her at school, calling her a swot, and other things still more impolite – but these were minor matters, too unimportant to signify. A rampant velociraptor escaping from the broom cupboard was something else. Increasingly, despite trying to cling to the letter of the truth, Pen knew she was crossing the boundary from omission into concealment. A dinosaur was too huge to be merely omitted; it had to be covered up, tucked out of sight, a guilty object thrust under a cushion on the entrance of a suspicious adult. Pen had always made a point of being Not Guilty: it was part of her creed. And now here she was, being sucked inexorably into a quagmire of deceit...

'It's client confidentiality,' she reassured herself. 'Mr Pyewackett was the client, and everything he told me was confidential.'

But he hadn't told her about the velociraptor. He *had* told her not to open the doors.

When Eve Harkness returned Pen gave a selective account of her day, explaining about Gavin and his search for Bartlemy Goodman, and how Goodman was supposed to be this amazing cook, and how she and Gavin had bonded over their separate ambitions.

'Are you going to see this boy again?' her grandmother inquired. And: 'We don't know anything about him.'

Yes we do, thought Pen. We know he's brave enough to zap a velociraptor with a stun-gun.

Aloud she said: 'He told me lots of things. Not just about the cooking. He... he's got a grandmother who thinks she looks like Beyoncé.'

'Well,' said Mrs Harkness, unexpectedly diverted, 'I've been told I look like Meryl Streep, but I can't see it myself.'

Pen was about to say *Nor can I*, and then opted for diplomacy. 'You do a bit.'

One lie leads to another, she reflected uncomfortably.

Maybe this was growing up.

CHAPTER THREE
A Tale of Two Cobblers

London, twenty-first century

MAGIC IS A force, like electricity. Nowadays, students of the subject like to discuss it in terms of thaumonuclear physics, and insist it is both a wave and particle – and, on occasion, a very big bang – none of which is particularly instructive. Our world has a low level of natural magic (except, of course, around portals and space/time prisms). Our native werecreatures are mostly tiny and virtually powerless, microsprites who are drawn to acts of sorcery and can infect susceptible minds, behaving more like airborne diseases than perilous entities. Only the Old Spirits are of any importance – beings which have been around since creation, worshipped as primitive gods, often sidelined by the march of progress, some hibernating, some withering, others gradually outwearing their taste for immortality and power, until they lapse into the everlasting slumber of Limbo. Few have survived into the present day – the Hag, the Child, the Hunter – but the Devil, Oldest of all, remains the strongest, adapting to the modern world, battening on mankind, the great User who has taken his image from our secret fears and made it real.

There was no magical strain in mortals until the time of Atlantis, when something called the Lodestone appeared, generating a magnetic field so strong that people in its vicinity were permanently affected. The Stone is now thought to have been the condensed matter of an entire galaxy, or more than one, from a universe with high levels of magic, pitchforked somehow across the barrier between the worlds. It produced a mutant gene which was passed on long after the Stone was destroyed and Atlantis fell, known as the gene for witchcraft, or the Gift – a Gift which can, if used to its full potential, totally corrupt its possessor. There is no such thing as a really good witch. Those with a minor variant of the gene can be endowed with psychological insight, the personality of a Svengali, a flair for telepathy, the Gift of the gab. Those who are truly Gifted tend to be mad, psychotic, or, in a few exceptional cases, superbly self-controlled.

The gene also attracts Luck.

Luck, as everyone knows, is one of the lesser magics, erratic, unpredictable, and quirky. The witchcraft faculty, in its weakest form, may still engender an affinity for good luck – or bad. Thus some people – like Gavin Lester – are bounced happily through life, while others are dogged by disaster, constantly shipwrecked, struck by lightning, shaken by earthquake or financial meltdown. The point about your luck tendency is that, unlike other genetic factors, it can be changed – if a person has great strength of will, or stubbornness, or the ability to go against Fate. Or – well – luck. Luck changes itself. That is its nature. You can break an apparently endless run of bad luck – but you can break a run of good luck, too.

A week after his visit to Temporal Crescent, Gavin Lester got together with his ex, Josabeth Collins. Josabeth wore a pink skirt and pink ear-rings and pink streaks in her crinkly black hair. She looked like a candidate for a girl band. Over skinny latte in Caffé Nero she talked about her career ambitions – model, actress, singer – and didn't he think she was pretty enough? Gavin said yes, of course, and thought about a pale-faced redhead who wasn't girl-band pretty, with a dinosaur in her broom cupboard. Something he called instinct told him to stick with Josabeth, to play safe, stay in the world he knew. But Gavin wanted to find Bartlemy Goodman, and learn the Secrets of Eternal Cooking, and see what else came out of Number 7. When Josabeth was in the loo, he sent a text.

Some people stretch their luck too far – until it snaps.

Beyond the Doors
London, seventeenth century

IN THE CITY, it was beginning to be spring. The weather grew warmer, and the refuse in the gutters and alleyways grew smellier, and the rats and the roaches grew fatter and more numerous. In the leftover patches of countryside that clung to the riverbanks or were preserved as private parks, leaves uncurled and shy flowers nuzzled sunward. The citizens, too, unfurled spring leaves: those who could afford it peacocked along Paul's Walk in new clothes and freshly styled wigs, those who couldn't followed them, light-fingered and quick-footed, relieving them of whatever remained in their purses when they had paid for their finery. Business flourished, both legitimate and illegitimate: traders short-changed, merchants overcharged, courtiers bribed. Lower down the social scale, beggars and brawlers, doxies and dossers made a dishonest living, or fought for scraps to survive. The Lost Boys slipped through the crowds and shinned up the buildings like monkeys in their own jungle, thriving on the earnings of their fellows.

But Ghost had other interests. When not stealing or dodging pursuit, he or another member of the gang would lurk in the vicinity of the bawdy house, watching for Big Belinda, learning her habits and her hangouts. The dressmakers she patronised, the confectioners who sold her favourite sweetmeats, the perfumiers who helped to cover – or complement – the many odours of her unwashed body. Those gentlemen whose houses she visited after the show, with a few special girls under her wing. The two hirelings were always with her. Their names were Mullen and

Cullen; one had a face scarred by disease, the other from a knife-fight, but in the dark of the alleyways it was hard to tell the difference.

That spring, Big Belinda bought a new dress of crimson satin and new hair-pieces as big as wedding bouquets, great bunches of curls said to have been shorn from the head of a child whose mother needed the money for gin. The ringlets were baby-soft and silken-smooth and pale as flax, and she wore them as a warrior wears the pelt of a slain animal, tossing them with pride.

'She knows you're watching,' Mags told Ghost. 'She knows you won't give up. They're saying in the Reaper the hirelings have a job for life.'

But one evening when the twins were on watch, she emerged from the rear gate without them. They saw her back view disappearing down Running Lane, unmistakable in a vast skirt of coquelicot stripes, her curls, yellow this time, twirling from under the sweeping brim of an overplumed hat. Ratface, who was the dominant twin, ordered his brother to follow her while he went in search of Ghost. They had already evolved a system to cover this eventuality: Pockface carried a stick of charcoal, and was to draw an arrow on the wall at every street corner, to indicate where he was going. Once Ratface had found Ghost, it was easy for them to pick up the trail.

Pockface was waiting in the backyard behind the house of Wily Jake the fence, also known as Jewish Jake, because of his hook nose and black hair. In fact, he was reputed to be Welsh, but he cultivated the Jewishness since he said it was good for business. Jews were known to be canny and cunning in financial matters, and Wily Jake did his best to maintain the standards of his adopted race. He was said to be as straight as a corkscrew, as honest as the day is short, and as kind-hearted as a crocodile, but he had his own honour – thieves' honour – and he was reliable, provided you were clear on which of his dubious qualities you wished to rely. There were, however, few reasons for Big Belinda to do business with him. She didn't handle stolen goods, only stolen bodies, and bartered lives.

'Wait till she comes out,' Ratface said, but Ghost shook his head.

'You wait,' he said, and climbed up to the first floor, entering through a window. No one expects an intruder to come from upstairs, when there are windows and doors enough on the ground floor, and Ghost always made a point of being unexpected. As he crept downstairs he heard voices talking softly in the parlour, men's voices, no sound of Big Belinda. He drew nearer, testing every board before he set his weight on it, his ears straining to discern the words.

'I won't have no part of it.' That was Wily Jake.

Then something he couldn't hear.

'I don't do vilence. I'm a businessman, I am, as honest a fence as any in the city. The coves what come looking for me, they need to know they'll be safe here. Some of my buyers are important people, see? They want dis-cretion, I give it them. I don't have no constables coming round poking their noses into my affairs. When you get vilence, you get the constables. Besides, he's a smart boy. Brings me good stuff, real quality. I don't want no harm to come to 'im. You tell Big Bel—'

'We won't hurt him, Mr Beddoes. We just want a word with him, quiet-like. A matter of dis-cretion, like you said.'

'What makes you so sure he'd 'a followed you?'

'Not him. Him you don't see. He's as soft and sneaky as your own shadow. But the other boys, they ain't that good. One of 'em come after me, and Cullen here come after 'im. Our little phantom'll be turning up soon for sure. He wants to get Big Bel on her own, don't he? He won't let slip a chance like this. He'll turn up, and we'll talk to him – quiet-like – and see he lets her alone from now on. That's all.'

'Right. That's all.' The echo was Cullen.

There was a short silence. A trap, thought Ghost. Anyone can wear a dress. He could see the hat and curls on a chair beyond the half open door. Mullen and Cullen were in the room, waiting for him. Well, let them wait. He started to retreat back upstairs.

'I don't like it,' said Wily Jake's voice from the parlour. 'They say he's pretty quick wi' that chive of his. Stuck poor old Sheen like a pig. I won't have no chives in here.'

'Don't you worry, Mr Beddoes.' Mullen again. 'I reckon I'm faster'n any brat. I'll have that chive off 'im afore he can do any harm with it.'

'I don't hold with vilence, I told you. I won't have no blood spilled here.'

'There won't be any spilling o' blood. We'll do what we have to do, nice and quiet—'

'You said you were just going to talk to him.' Wily Jake evidently wasn't convinced.

Nor was Ghost.

'That's right. Just talk.' Footsteps approached the door. 'I'm going to take a look out the back – see if the other boy's still there...'

He stepped into the hallway. Ghost didn't have time to get out of sight. There was an instant when they faced each other – Mullen was still wearing the dress – he gave a shout, pulled a knife from his bodice, threw it. Ghost dodged, vaulted the banister – the blade stuck quivering in the stair. Cullen burst out of the parlour, Wily Jake hanging ineffectually from his arm. The hall was too small for a fight, particularly one involving Big Belinda's dress and the padding necessary for Mullen to fill it. He grabbed at Ghost, who bit him. Cullen had another knife out. 'No blood!' Wily Jake was begging. 'You promised me – no blood!' His clutch hampered Cullen – the dress hampered Mullen – in the confusion only Ghost moved fast. He tried to twist himself free but the man's grip was too strong, and the switchblade flicked out, slicing through cloth and skin, blurring the stripes into a single patch of red. Mullen grunted and swore, relaxing his hold on Ghost. Wily Jake cried: 'No blood!' until Cullen hit him. And Ghost was gone through the back door and across the yard, disappearing into the labyrinth of the city.

The knife blade was small but its bite was deep. Mullen died later that night, thrown into the street by Wily Jake, who had found a moment to pick up the ancient blunderbuss he kept in a closet for special occasions.

Some people attract good luck, or bad. But Ghost attracted death. It accompanied him like a touch of darkness that followed where no shadows could be seen, seeping into his aura, slowly becoming a part of him. Every time he drew his knife, death entered a little deeper into his spirit.

There was an old woman in Farthing Alley who had the name of a witch. The church had let her be, saying she was harmless, and made a physic that could cure worms, and gallstones, and alleviate the pangs of gout, and if she did any foretelling it was after dark, to a clientele too foolish or too furtive to complain of her. The girls went to see her for charms against pregnancy and the pox, which might or might not work, but when she saw Ghost her vague stare would grow a little vaguer, and she would curse him with gipsy words, and make the sign to ward off evil, which frightened him as the Mohocks could not.

'You don't want to listen to *her*,' Mags said. 'Like as not she's been drinking her own potions, and they've addled her brain.'

But when the old woman heard what had happened to Mullen she said to Clarrie, the girl who had brought the news: 'You tell Big Belinda to let him be. You tell her. He's got a bit o' the night in him, the old night from way back, before the days o' bishop and bible. He's not one to cross, you tell her.'

'He threatened her,' Clarrie said, 'wi' that wicked little knife o' his. Big Bel don't take kindly to being threatened.'

'He's got the night in him,' the old woman repeated. 'His sort don't threaten. You'll see. Oh yes, you'll see.'

*   *   *

Infernale

THEY HAD BEEN watching the house for a long, long time. For years, centuries, perhaps millennia. Before there was a house, when there was only an empty doorway, they watched, eyes under a stone, or in the gloom of a tree-hollow. As the ages passed they became the stone, the hollow, the tree. When the old century turned they were still there, the carving on a gatepost, the pit of shadow where the sun never reached. They may be seen as the phantoms of fever, the little darknesses that remain when a nightmare has fled. They have eyes and mouths, but no speech. They are the eavesdroppers under the eaves, the listeners behind the silence, the unseen gaze that lifts the hair on your neck.

They report to no one; that is not their way. They just watch. When *he* needs to see, and hear, he will look through the holes of their eyes, and listen through the pits of their ears, and what they know, he knows. That is what they are for. They have no other being, no other awareness, but through *him*.

They move through Time like jellyfish through water, spectral transparencies that float between Then and Now, between Here and There. They are here and they are beyond the doors, in the bubbles of history where the trapped ones circulate in an endless race to nowhere. They are the spies who see everything, yet their cold curiosity has no mind, no purpose, only his.

Even now, they are watching YOU…

London, twenty-first century

MATTY FEATHERSTONE HAD held the position of Pen's best friend ever since Year Seven, when living close by meant Matty's mother shared the school run with Mrs Harkness and the two girls collaborated on homework and related issues. But they had widely divergent tastes and ideas: Matty thought all that law stuff really boring, though staying in a house with a butler must be *wicked*, and was it really, like, *her* house – until the new owner turned up – and did that mean Pen could have parties, with champagne, and no adults spoiling the fun? Pen said she wasn't too keen on parties, or champagne, and her grandmother was living there too – and anyway, she was just looking after the house, it wasn't really hers. Matty thought that sounded rather dull after all, and Pen, who had always tended to keep her own counsel, said nothing about dinosaurs, or multiple dimensions – or Gavin.

She spent some time on the computer trying to sort out what she knew (not much), and what she didn't know (a lot), opening new files and making lists in an attempt to clarify the situation. Somewhere in the chaos of whirling worlds and interlocking realities there had to be a pattern. For instance, if the remote past was in the broom cupboard, could the future be in the attic? And would there be something completely primordial in the cellar? Also, she wanted to find out who did the cleaning. Then there was the thief who had broken in and disappeared, and the third key, and the problem of entering the past without losing touch with the present… It all looked fairly hopeless, but Pen felt better for tidying up her thoughts – it made everything seem less random, somehow more manageable, even if it wasn't.

Perhaps she could write all her personal details on a piece of paper and sew it inside her clothes when venturing into the past – but her clothes might get torn or lost, and she had a sneaking suspicion that history didn't allow for cheating, and the paper would go astray, or get smudged in the wash. It couldn't be that easy or someone would have done it before…

She emerged from reflection to find Quorum standing before her announcing supper. Mrs Harkness had texted that she was working late that evening and Pen decided it was time to grasp the nettle of opportunity.

'Could we have supper together?' she asked. 'If you don't mind? Gran said she wouldn't be back till eight or nine. Besides, I'd like to talk to you.'

'I am always available for conversation, Miss Pen,' Quorum said, but he agreed to join her for supper anyway.

Over a plateful of macaroni cheese, Pen took the plunge. She would have to confide in Quorum; she needed his support. 'I've been inside Number 7,' she volunteered.

'Miss... Pen!'

'I know it's dangerous. I was very careful.' Well, she *had* been careful. Best not to discuss the incident of the broom cupboard. 'The thing is, it's my responsibility, and... and it was my decision, and there are things that have to be done, which I can't do without exploring the house. So you see...'

'Exploring! Miss Pen, this is not some children's adventure story–'

'Good, because I'm not a child.' Having jumped the first hurdle, Pen was regaining her self-possession. 'I need your help. Will you–'

'I promised your grandmother–'

'Someone's broken in there,' Pen interrupted.

'Broken in? To Number 7?'

'Yes. There's a pane of glass cut out upstairs. I don't know when it happened but the floor there looks as if the rain's been coming in for ages.'

'Oh dear.' Quorum looked anxious but resigned. 'Oh dear. I suppose I could replace it... if we go in together. You wouldn't want me to do it alone, would you? I've never been inside, you know.'

'Never mind that,' said Pen. 'The point is, somebody went in, and I don't think they came out.'

'No. Well, they wouldn't, would they? Lost in the past... It's what Mr Pyewackett was always afraid of. Nothing to be done now.'

'Yes, there is,' said Pen. 'There's always something to be done. I don't know if we could find out when they went in, or who it was, but we could look for them, and try to bring them back.'

Quorum stared at her without speaking for what felt like a full minute.

'He said you were resourceful,' he commented eventually. 'Even so, I don't think he realised quite how... Miss Pen, you aren't supposed to do this. You're supposed to just... be on guard. That's all the Pyewacketts ever did. Guard the house, keep it safe, keep people out...'

'They didn't keep people out,' Pen said brutally, 'because somebody got in. Presumably Mr Pyewackett would've noticed the broken window, if he went upstairs, so... Do you know the last time he was in Number 7?'

'Oh dear.' Quorum's brain appeared to have got stuck, like a scratched disc which keeps repeating the same phrases. 'Very resourceful... I'm afraid I... you see, I'd only been with Mr Pyewackett for thirty-one years. Not very long at all. Yes, I came here in 1975. I recall he went in some time after that. Maybe '75 or '6. He was telling me how clean it was. "I've never found anyone doing the housework," he said, "but there's not a speck of dirt. Not a speck!" I think he'd have seen – said something – if there was a window broken. I'll have to fix it, won't I? Of course, it may mend itself... eventually. I'm told the house changes every two or three centuries. Keeping up with the times. Blending in. No one notices, though. No one ever notices a thing.'

'Are you... are you an *ordinary* butler?' Pen said, suddenly conscious that all this was rather outside the range of normal butlerdom. And then, afraid she sounded rude: 'I mean – like – is your name really Quorum? That sort of thing.'

'I was christened Ronald Snibs,' he said, 'but Mr Pyewackett preferred Quorum. I don't know why. As for *ordinary*... The trouble is, when you work for someone like that, in this sort of set-up, things *rub off*. Yes, that's it. Over time, you know. Look at you. It's happening already. You were just a girl who wanted to be a lawyer, and now you're planning to go into the past and find someone who's lost. And you've only been here five minutes. *Things rub off...*'

'Am I... different?' Pen asked.

'Not exactly,' Quorum said. 'It's as if you're... more yourself. The person inside you – the person you really are – is expanding outwards. Nowadays, people are always talking about *finding themselves*, but they do it the wrong way. They look inward. You have to look *out*. That's what you've been doing, since you got here. I can see it now. You're looking *out* more. Seeing things... Oh *dear*.'

'But... isn't that a good thing?' Pen said. 'Expanding your outlook – or your inlook – or whatever...'

'It's good,' said Quorum, 'or so they say, but it can be dangerous. And what you want to do is far too dangerous for a thirteen-year-old girl. I promised your grandmother I would look after you.'

'Then help me,' Pen said. 'After all, I've got the keys to Number 7, and – I don't want to be difficult, exactly – but you can't stop me from using them... can you? So...'

'He said you were stubborn,' sighed Quorum. 'Stubborn, and resourceful... What about that boy who was here the other day? Is he involved?'

'He might be,' Pen said guardedly.

'You'll need more help than mine, Miss Pen. You'll need a strong young man to protect you. If you're going exploring, take him with you.'

'That's very sexist,' Pen said with disapprobation.

'Mr Pyewackett was a little old-fashioned at times,' said Quorum. 'It... rubs off.'

'I get that part. Let's go back to the point. First, we have to find out much more about the house. Mr Pyewackett was right: it's absolutely spotless. I want to know who the mystery cleaner is. There can't be someone shut in there who's done nothing but dust and vacuum for the past thirty years or more.'

'You never know,' said Quorum.

Somewhere in northern England, somewhere in the past

ONCE UPON A time there were two cobblers. They lived in the same town, on the same street, and they competed for the same customers, and, inevitably, they were in love with the same girl. One was older, handsome, with the steady gaze and firm handshake of a natural conman. The other was young and hungry, with a face cadaverous even in youth, and an eager light in his eyes, which frequently discouraged customers who didn't want to buy their shoes from so much blatant eagerness. The younger was the better cobbler, but the older was more popular, on account of the firmness of his handshake, even though the shoes he sold were often ill-fitting and ill-made. The older hated the younger with the weary hatred of age, but the younger hated the older with the passionate hatred of youth – a feeling intensified by the attitude of the girl, who preferred the mature charm of her older suitor to the charmless ardour of the younger.

The older was called Nicholas Cleeve and the younger was Thomas Cutforth, and their feud was the talk of the town, for in those days of few books and no television people had more time for talking if rather less to talk about. The doings of government were faint and faraway, and the only soap operas they had were on their doorstep, so they followed the saga of Cleeve versus Cutforth with an enthusiasm which embittered the younger man still further.

In the end, Nicholas Cleeve announced his engagement to the lady, and Cutforth, overcome with despair, decided there was only one thing to be done.

He sold his soul to the Devil.

The Devil is, as we know, a rather crude Christian image of the ultimate bad guy, horned, hoofed, loud-mouthed and vulgar, but behind the fairytale façade is a far darker and more subtle spirit, both deity and demon, old as Time and keeping his kingdom not in Hell but on Earth, feeding his ancient enmity for Men on their weakness and their ignorance, their subjugation and their fear. He has no use for souls, any more than a dragon has for gold; he collects them and gnaws on them, so that when death releases them there will be little left to pass beyond his reach.

Young Thom had no precise information about Hell, but he believed it was very warm, which, in the chill of his winter workshop, made it seem quite an attractive prospect. He did, however, have a wishing stone which his mother had made him swear never to touch, so of course he rubbed it, and wished, and when the Devil appeared, dressed for the part in black and looking rather suave in a demonic way, he knew he had got more than he bargained for. But his hatred was too much for him, and so he signed the usual contract, in his own blood, and in return the Devil promised he should be the most successful cobbler in the country, and triumph over his rival, and marry the girl he adored, and so on and so on.

The next morning, of course, he thought he had dreamed it. (He had been rather drunk at the time, owing to the depression following unrequited love.) Then he saw the goblin in his workshop.

It was about three feet high, with yellowy green skin, yellowy brown eyes, small stunted horns and large pointy ears. It had seven digits on each hand, though which were fingers and which thumbs Thom couldn't tell, and assorted toes in several different lengths. It was stitching at a piece of leather with incredible speed, tiny exquisite stitches rippling through its hands. Already several pairs of shoes were finished on the bench. The shoes Thom made were beautiful, but these were shoes Cinderella would never have mislaid and Imelda Marcos would have killed to wear. These shoes were *perfect*.

'What are you doing?' says Thom. '*I'm* supposed to be the cobbler. I'm the best in town.'

'I'm the best in the world,' says the goblin, unanswerably.

'But... the Devil promised–'

'He promised you'd be the most successful,' says the goblin. 'From now on, *I* make the shoes.'

It is a well-known and much-overlooked fact that the Devil cannot create anything – he cannot endow you with talent or beauty beyond your capacity – he can only cheat. Bear this in mind, if ever you seek a compact with him. The devil, quite literally, is in the small print.

With the help of the goblin, Thom became famous not only in the town but throughout the whole country. His rival grew older and wearier before his eyes. The wedding went ahead, but a year later, declining into debt, Nicholas died, reputedly choking on his own handshake, and his widow and baby daughter were left destitute. Thom married her, saying he would try to be a true father to the child, but although she was grateful to him she never loved him, and they had no children of their own. His success, being founded on the skill and genius of another, gave him no satisfaction, his marriage no affection, and it seemed to him his whole life was turned to ashes. Only his step-daughter – the child of his now-forgotten rival – made him happy, for she was the apple of his eye. His wife got sick, and died, and his beloved Isobel was all he had left.

At first he could barely endure the sight of the goblin on whom his fortune depended, but later he began to watch him at work, hoping to learn from him, and as the years passed he realised this strange magical being was the only person in whom he could confide. He tried to make shoes again, for he had been a good cobbler once, but his fingers were thick and clumsy compared with the quicksilver digits of his helper. Nonetheless, they would drink tea together, and talk, and if such a friendship was possible, they became friends.

The goblin, like all werekind, had no understanding of human morality or loyalty, and knew nothing beyond the Devil's own laws. In all his immortal existence, he had never had a friend.

Thom didn't know his name. Werefolk and spellfolk may have many names, but some will have a truename, which they keep secret, telling it only to a chosen few, since that name has great power over them, and can be used to conjure or curse. Few goblins are important enough to bear such a name, but this goblin was clever and unique amongst his kind, and he had a name to conjure with, though he told it to no one.

On her sixteenth birthday Thom was giving a party for his step-daughter, to which all the eligible young men in the area – and some from far away – would be invited. What he wanted more than anything was to make her shoes for the occasion himself. He worked on them for weeks, advised by the goblin, stitching and unstitching late into the night, determined to make them perfect, or as near perfect as possible. The goblin's shoes, as we know, *were* perfect, but even Isobel did not know of his existence, nor the deception that was her stepfather's life and livelihood. Thom sewed the shoes with minute crystals, so they sparkled like winter frost, and lined them with silk to feel soft on her feet, which, to his eyes, were the daintiest feet in the world. His soul was much eroded with the bitterness of the years, but as he made the shoes, it seemed to grow again, filling him with a new flame, and when he set the last stitch his soul went out of him, and into the shoes for his daughter to wear. So they glowed with a special glow, for even the magic of the goblin could not match the magic of a mortal soul. When they say of someone he puts his soul into his work, remember there are times when it is true.

Thom gave Isobel the shoes on the morning of her birthday, and her face lit with pleasure at the beauty of them. But privately she told her old nurse she could not wear them that night, for her new party dress was pink, with rose-coloured dancing slippers to match. The goblin, overhearing – goblins overhear everything

– stole into her room with a ladleful of the soup the cook had bubbling in the kitchen, and spilt it down the pink dress, and when Isobel saw she exclaimed in horror and surprise, for nobody knew how the accident could have happened. But it meant she would now wear her white dress, with her father's shoes. Only the goblin knew that he had put his soul into them, and if Isobel did not wear them his heart would break indeed.

That evening before the party Thom went into his workshop to thank the goblin for all his efforts, and there was the Devil sitting in Thom's own chair, very much at his ease – the Devil has plenty of ease to be at – smoking. *What* he was smoking wasn't clear, but smoke was definitely involved.

'I did not call you,' said Thom. He had given the wishing stone to the goblin to hide for him, so none other would ever find it or make use of it.

'I hear you are trying for a second chance,' said the Devil. 'Not possible, I'm afraid. No loopholes in your contract.' He snapped his fingers and the scroll appeared in his hand, unrolling by itself, and there was Thom's signature, with the blood still dripping down the page.

'You cheated,' said Thom. 'So can I.'

'I'll tell you what,' said the Devil, 'I'll offer you an extension. Only give me those shoes you've made, and a young man will come to the party tonight who will be as handsome as a god and as rich as a prince, and he will fall instantly in love with your step-daughter, marry her, and give her everything she could possibly wish for. I know how much you love her; wouldn't this be a better present than a pair of shoes?'

'Not all gods are handsome nor all princes rich,' said Thom, who had learned from his mistakes. 'And even were this youth the handsomest and richest of men, it doesn't follow that my daughter would love him. She may prefer someone plain, and poor, and kind. I will trust to her judgement, and to fate. There is nothing more you can offer me.'

The Devil smiled. It was not a pleasant sight.

'What if that young man comes to the party, and your daughter falls for him, and he marries her, and takes her far away, so you never see her again?'

'So be it,' said Thom. 'She will have my shoes.'

At that the Devil's eyes flashed red lightning, and he vanished in a puff of smoke and fury, for he knew Thom no longer belonged to him, since he had given his soul to Isobel. But behind the mask of his satanic persona is a rancorous and revengeful spirit, who never gives up, never lets go, and knows there is more than one way to cheat at cards. The goblin was still his creature, the slave he had loaned to a gentler master. Now, the Devil recalled him to his service.

'You sewed those shoes with our Thom, did you not?'

'No, lord,' said the goblin. 'He made them all himself. That was how he wanted it.'

'I see. Then take these gemstones, and sew them secretly onto each of the girl's shoes.' His hand uncurled, and in his palm lay two diamonds, as pure and bright as chips of ice. 'Once my mark is on the shoes, then you can becharm them.'

The goblin did not want to obey, but he had no choice. 'We must give the man a chance,' he demurred. 'Those are the rules. The charm must have one chance to work, one chance to fail.'

'Very well,' said the Devil, who was skilled at fixing every kind of luck. 'One chance. The charm will not work, until he dances with Isobel himself. But I defy any loving father to refrain on his daughter's birthday!' And he laughed an evil laugh, which rolled round and round the room by itself, bouncing off the walls.

The goblin knew he could not warn his friend – that was not allowed – but he put a nail in his boot, and when Thom thrust his foot into it the point drove into him, hurting him so badly he knew he would not dance that night. The nurse said there seemed to be a hex on the place, what with the spilt soup and now the hidden nail, and Thom frowned thoughtfully, because he knew that hexes are goblins' work. He thought his friend was turning against him, perhaps encouraged or coerced by the Devil, and he sighed, because he had always been told there could be no real friendship between mortal and immortal folk, and now he feared it was true.

'Yet I believed you had an honest heart,' Thom said aloud, 'whatever your nature. Now I know you are as others of your kith, mischievous and cruel.'

Hearing that the goblin might have wept, but his sort had no tears, and the heart he had grown in all the years with Thomas Cutforth swelled within him. He wrote a rhyme on a piece of paper, and unknown to Thom he slipped it in his pocket. And then Thom went limping to the party.

Isobel glittered in her white dress, and danced like a fairy in her wonderful shoes, and everyone there said they were the finest shoes Thom had ever made. There were young men there both rich and handsome, but the most charming of them all danced three dances with Isobel, and looked at her with devil's eyes, saying: 'Why do you not dance with your father on such a special day?'

'He's hurt his foot,' said Isobel. 'But indeed, I would rather dance with him than anyone else here.'

'Then tell him so,' said the charmer.

So Isobel went to her father, pleading for just one dance, if he could manage it. 'You can lean on me,' she said, 'and then it won't hurt your foot. Please try to dance with me. It's my birthday, and you are the man I love best in the world.'

Then of course Thom agreed, for he knew she would not say that much longer, and he got up, bracing himself against the pain, and followed her onto the floor. There was a whisper in his ear though nobody was nearby – *Your pocket... look in your pocket* – but he paid no attention.

They began to dance.

Immediately Isobel's shoes sparkled more brightly, and the sparkles drifted like stardust around her feet, and she seemed to be floating, spinning, dancing faster, faster... 'You go too fast,' her father cried, 'too fast for me –' But she could not slow down, her feet were no longer her own, and her shoes whirled her round and round, and the Devil's laughter rolled from floor to ceiling and back again, and there was a smell of brimstone. The charmer disappeared into his own shadow, tall and dark against the candles that lit the room, and the voice of the Devil said: 'She cannot stop! She will not stop! Your shoes will dance her till she dies! Thus the fate of all who try to cheat me of my dues!'

The guests fell back in horror, and Thom was stricken to the heart, watching his daughter's suffering, but once again the whisper came in his ear, softer than a sigh: *Look in your pocket! The rhyme – the rhyme!*

He pulled out the piece of paper – unfolded it – saw what was written there and knew it for the goblin's secret name. He read the verse aloud, softly at first, then in a stronger voice.

'*Jimminy-chu Jimminy-chu*
Unloose the charm on my daughter's shoe!'

The two diamonds flew off the shoes, and the spell was broken, and Isobel collapsed half fainting into her father's arms. And in the empty workshop Thom's ancient contract flared into flame and burned to a cinder, for the demon's hold over him was gone for good.

But the Devil's rage knew no bounds, and he shrieked like a howling wind, so all in the room covered their ears. In the shriek Thom heard the goblin's name, and knew the Devil would punish him for such a betrayal with torment beyond imagining, and at last he understood the courage and self-sacrifice of his unhuman friend. But the goblin fled fast and far, and crept through a chink in Time, and the story says that even the Devil, who sees all the kingdoms of the Earth, and all the realms of magic, could not find him. Yet he is still looking, for his memory is as long as history, and the name of every traitor is engraved in letters of fire on the darkness of his spirit...

London, twenty-first century

ON THE MONDAY, before her grandmother got back from work, Pen and Quorum went into Number 7 so he could replace the broken window pane.

'There's nothing scary in here,' Pen said. 'It's no different from any other house, really. It's just...' Quiet. Quorum glanced round often, not because he thought someone was behind him but because he knew they weren't. If Pen didn't speak for a minute or two it was easy to imagine that she had vanished, melting into the silence like a tiny ripple in a still pool.

And there were the doors, so many doors, closed but not locked – Quorum was alarmed they weren't locked – waiting, patiently, for a hand on the knob, a nudge that would open them into somewhere or nowhere. While they were on the landing Pen tried to count them, but although she counted in order, going from left to right, she kept getting a different answer. First ten, then twelve, then eleven... 'I haven't made a mistake,' she said. 'I know I haven't.'

'Maybe they move,' said Quorum. 'Maybe they change places, so quietly you don't see them. Like one of those old group photographs where the camera wheels to take in a whole line of people, and someone can run from one end of the line to the other, if they are fast enough, and get in the picture twice, even though it's a still shot. Maybe the doors don't like being counted. Remember, the act of observation –'

'– changes the behaviour of the thing observed,' said Pen. 'Yes, I know. But that's subatomic physics. These are doors.'

'Possibly the difference is just a matter of scale,' Quorum said.

He had almost finished the window and was filling in with putty.

'It'll need a daub of paint,' he added.

'*That's* an idea,' said Pen. 'I could paint numbers on the doors.'

The quiet grew a little quieter, as if the house was holding its breath.

'I don't think that would work,' said Quorum. 'The numbers would probably change, or swap around – you'd find they were all tens, or fives, or something. Like in that story about the Dancing Princesses, where the soldier put a cross on the door, only to find there were crosses on every door in the street. At least, I think it was the Dancing Princesses. You would remember better than me.'

'I'm not great on fairytales,' Pen said.

'A pity,' said Quorum. 'After all, you're in one.'

'This isn't a fairytale,' Pen retorted. 'It's real. This house… is the most real place I've ever been.'

She could sense the realness, the thickness of a door away, worlds of realness calling to her, tempting her, drawing her in…

'I'm done,' said Quorum. 'We should go now.'

He shepherded Pen down the stairs. Now she was the one looking back, though not in fear. In the hall, she said: 'I want to open one door. Just one. You're here; you can see nothing happens to me. Pull me back if I try to go through, or something.'

'Miss Pen, you mustn't–'

'I want to find out about this house. I want to… to bring back the thief who got lost… Anyway, I'm going to open a door, and that's that.'

Quorum looked frightened, but Pen was determined. She went to the door that, from its location, would have been the one to the front room, probably a sitting room. As always, it opened away from her. She peered round –

– into gloom. Instead of the fading daylight of Bygone House she was looking into a high, vaulted, stone-clad room with shadows dripping down the walls and tall arched windows admitting only the twilight of a winter evening. It was far too big a room to fit in Number 7 Temporal Crescent – in fact, less a room than a cavern – Pen glimpsed the shadowed vaults stretching away, with here and there a little puddle of light, the nearest, a few yards off, showing what looked like a lectern, with an enormous book open on it. The light came from candles on either side of the book, short candles burned down to a mere lump of wax and tall candles with only a thread of drool trickling from the flame. In the small circle of their light she could make out a figure seated at the lectern on a high stool, a figure all hunched up in voluminous dark robes, his tonsure bent over the book, his hands, in ragged gloves with the fingers cut out, clutching what seemed to be a paint brush. There was little colour in the chamber, it was a monochrome world of dimness and shade, but on the pages of the book colour bloomed, a thin tracery of colour vivid as embroidery.

When Pen had gazed into the Jurassic she had had little time for reflection. But now she thought: This is the past. The Past... and the wonder of it filled her, tightening her throat, accelerating her pulse. She must have made some slight noise, for the man at the lectern glanced round, distracted from his work, and saw her. Pen stood frozen with surprise while he clambered down off the stool and came towards her, waving his hands as if to shoo away a stray cat. He said something in a language which sounded like Latin – though she had never imagined Latin could actually be spoken.

'*Cur vos molesti me semper versatis? Nonne videre potestis me laborare conari? Ite! Ite!*'

Pen said: 'Sorry,' with an air of embarrassment and drew back, closing the door again...

Back into the present. Behind her, Quorum was clutching her sweater.

'That... didn't seem too dangerous,' she said.

'It was the Past, Miss Pen,' Quorum said, and there was a hint of a shudder in his voice. 'The Past is always dangerous.'

And then: 'What did you see?'

'I think it might have been a monastery. There was a monk, working on a book, painting pictures or doing fancy lettering, and he came over to make me go away. That was all.'

'Interaction,' said Quorum. 'Beware of interaction. That's how you get sucked in.'

'Yes,' said Pen, 'but at least we've found out what's in that room.'

'For today,' said Quorum. 'Tomorrow, who knows?'

Eade, twenty-first century

THE WITCH WAS in her bedroom, eating a doughnut. She had bought three, two for the spell and one for her, even though it meant she was getting a little sticky and was leaving sugar-prints on her great-grandmother's notebooks. Her bedroom was both a sanctum and a fane; neither parent nor vacuum cleaner ever entered there. It wasn't an ideal place for spell-casting, but it was private. And this time, she wanted the security of being in her own place.

Her mother didn't know she had the books, or the bottles with their handwritten labels and questionable contents, or the other paraphernalia of spellcasting. She wouldn't have approved, even though she didn't believe in magic; like the rest of the village, she had been afraid of great-grandmother, who had the Evil Eye, or rather, two Evil Eyes, not to mention an evil tongue. The girl had been afraid of her, too, afraid of turning into her, and for a long time after her death she hadn't touched her legacy. Now, she told herself she was a witch of a different colour; Bartlemy had taught her both technique and restraint; she could give it up any time she liked...

She drew a small circle in black lipstick round her dressing table mirror. She knew it wasn't the safest way to conjure, but she reasoned she was only calling up a small spirit, so a small circle should suffice by way of protection. Then she spoke the summons.

The mirror clouded, and presently the face of the grinnock appeared, as if trapped behind the glass.

'You're back,' he said, disagreeably.

'No, *you're* back,' said the witch. 'I conjured you.' She was determined to assert her authority right from the start.

The grinnock pushed his head out of the mirror, peering from side to side. 'You call that a circle? I ha' seen better drawed by children i' the sand, afore the waves washed it away. Ye canna believe ye can bind me wi' the grease o' your vanity box! 'Tis a mortal insult, so it is.'

'Mortal rubbish,' said the witch. 'It has touched my lips, and my lips speak the words of power, and so you are bound. Cross it if you dare.'

'Nae daring be needed,' said the grinnock, losing momentum. 'But I'm mair comfortable here. Would those be dog-nuts?'

'Doughnuts,' said the witch, assertively. She had had her doubts about the lipstick but now she was on a roll.

'Dog-nuts... dog-nits–'

'*Dough*nuts.'

'Doningfuts. Would you be off'ring them to me?'

'It depends what you've found out,' said the witch. 'Starting with Bartlemy Goodman.'

'Him. Aye. Well... he's gone.'

'Gone where?'

'Just gone. I dinna ken where.'

'You're supposed to ken,' said the witch. 'Kenning was your part of the deal. Think of sugar, all crunchy and scrunchy, and the sweet ooze of the jam, and–'

'I'm *thinking*! But old Goodman, he's gone where nary a spell can find him–'

'He's *not* dead.'

'Nay,' the grinnock replied. 'I niver said so. But he's gone where neither an oracle nor a monicle can see him, and when folks go that far, 'tis not often they come back.' By a monicle, the witch guessed, Simmoleon meant a magical spyglass. 'Ye ain't the only one a-questing and a-questioning for him. There's others would fain have the knowing of it, though they ain't asking quite so demanding-like.'

'What others?' the witch asked, demandingly. She liked the idea of being just a little dictatorial.

'Humans.' Simmoleon shrugged. 'I never heard their names. They ain't o' the witchkind. They'd be the sort what folk call sole-sitters.'

'*Sole-sitters?*' The witch was baffled.

'People what sit on things,' the grinnock suggested. 'They meddle in the Law, 'n other mortal matters. While they're sitting, I s'pose.'

'Solicitors,' the witch deduced. 'What would *solicitors* want with Bartlemy Goodman?'

'Seems they want him to live in a house,' Simmoleon said.

'Most of us do that,' the witch pointed out.

'The house of a body what died,' the grinnock explained.

'*Ah*,' said the witch.

Presently, with suitable precautions in breaching the perimeter, she gave him a doughnut. (Privately, she didn't believe in the strength of her own circle, but she had no intention of showing it.) The grinnock emerged from the mirror, and there was an interlude of sugar consumption.

'What about this business of the Devil?' the witch inquired eventually. Simmoleon hiccupped with fright, choking on a crumb, but she ignored his reaction. 'You said he's looking for a... successor?'

'Ye mustna speak of it! He's no little satter wi' goaty legs 'n a wicked grin for ye to mock! He's the Oldest of the Old – the darkest of the dark. He has the Serafain, the Nightwings – folks call them Fellangels – they fly the world for him, doing his bidding... He has kings and kingdoms i' the palm o' his hand, great folk and little, princes and peasants. Men build their cities and their towers tall as the sky, and he's there at the top. He's always there. They worship him in the heart o' the old places and at the height o' the new. They worship him wi' blood and they worship him wi' gold...'

'Globalism,' nodded the witch. 'I get the picture. He must be a hard act to follow.'

'Ye dinna want to think of it.'

'But I *am* thinking of it. I can't help it. Who could possibly succeed *him*? I suppose it would have to be another Old Spirit – the Hunter, or the Child...' Her voice faded into doubt.

'I dinna ken. Mebbe they're too set in their ways. And they were never friends o' his – spirits like that inna friendly wi' each other. There's a saying: wolves run together, but the tiger walks alone. *He* was aye one who walked alone, d'ye see?'

'So who–?'

'They say...' The grinnock hesitated, as if knowing he'd gone too far, licking his fingers with a tongue so long the tip probed his left nostril.

'There's another doughnut,' said the witch, feeling the local bakery, though not up to the Goodman standard, hadn't let her down.

The grinnock called Sugartop eyed it wistfully.

Just for a spoonful of jam he betrayed us,
Just for some sugar to sweeten his blood...

'They say...'

The witch picked up the doughnut as if to eat it herself.

'They say... he's going to take a 'prentice. A *mortal* 'prentice. One o' your kind – one o' witchkind. One o' Prospero's Children.'

'A *mortal* to succeed the Devil?' The witch was so shocked she handed over the doughnut immediately, breaking the circle without the proper incantation, but Simmoleon was too absorbed in eating to take advantage. 'But surely–'

'I shouldna ha' told ye!' The grinnock was talking with his mouth full, not a pleasant sight. A thick trickle of jam ran down his chin, bright as blood. 'If they knew... if *he* knew...' He turned pasta-pale with horror at the thought of it.

'You must find out more!'

'*Ye* find out mair!' Back in the mirror, his image was fading.

'Doningfuts!' cried the witch, as if it was a word of power. 'Remember–'

But the grinnock had gone, and she was left alone with the darkness of her thoughts.

CHAPTER FOUR
Dancers and Dragons

London, twenty-first century

BRING THE STUN-GUN, Pen texted. *Just in case*. Although she told herself she was the sole monitor of activity in Number 7, and didn't actually *need* any support, nonetheless it might be helpful to have Gavin along. Without admitting she was in any way affected by his smile, she liked him. She liked his single-minded ambition, which reminded her of her own, his focus, his sunny nature, the unmistakable aura of good fortune which clung to him so blatantly. In Bygone House, good fortune was bound to come in handy. And although her fictional reading was limited, she knew adventures went better with two.

Not that this was an adventure, of course. It was scientific research. As she explained to Gavin, she was trying to establish a pattern.

'Supposing there isn't one?'

'There's *always* a pattern,' Pen said doggedly. 'That's how everything works.'

'Clever girl, ain't you?' said Gavin. 'For your age.'

'For heaven's sake, I'm *fourteen*!' Pen lied. She knew quite well that age is the one subject on which it is always legitimate for a woman to lie.

'You look less. Maybe, if you let your hair loose–'

'I don't want it to get in the way when I'm reading!'

'You're not reading now.'

Lips thinned with resentment, Pen pulled the band off her ponytail. Her hair slithered down about her shoulders, kinked from long restraint.

'That's better,' Gavin said, on an approving note which only made her resentment worse.

'Are you ready?' she snapped, determined to remain in charge.

'If you are.'

'Come on then.'

It was Saturday, Mrs Harkness had gone home and Quorum shopping, they had a clear field. Pen unlocked the front door and they stepped through into Number 7.

She had cleared up the pieces of the broken vase when she came in with Quorum to fix the window – 'It was an accident,' she'd told him. 'I just… knocked into it' – but she saw immediately there was another in its place, filled with bare winter twigs hung with tiny stars.

'I didn't do that,' she whispered to Gavin. If you weren't struggling with an inert velociraptor, something about the atmosphere made whispering instinctive.

'What about your butler?'

'He doesn't have a key.'

Even when she peered closely, she couldn't see what the stars were made of. Each one seemed to have a minute core of pure light, encircled in its own radiance. She brushed a finger through it, and felt a faint sensation of heat.

'They're like… magic,' Gavin murmured.

'I don't believe in magic,' Pen declared resolutely.

'What, *here*? With doors opening into the past and a dinosaur in the broom cupboard?'

'It's just… weird science.'

'If you say so,' Gavin grinned. 'What should we do with the cat?'

'Oh *damn*.'

Felinacious, who could waddle very quietly for all his size, had followed them unnoticed and was now snooping round the hall.

He stopped at one door down a flight of steps and towards the back of the house, pawing the panels and miaowing.

'No, that's not the kitchen,' Pen said. 'That's just where a kitchen ought to be. Stupid animal. We should take him back, but–'

'Never mind him. He'll be okay. Cats always are. Let's open some doors first.'

'All right. The monk was in *here*... This one opposite should be a dining room or a drawing room or something – *if* the house was ordinary...' She opened it rather too quickly, anxious to go first –

Beyond the Doors
Italy, fifteenth century

THE MUSIC EXPLODED right beside her, shattering the quiet of the house. There was a whole orchestra only a little way away – fiddlers sawing until their strings twanged, the rippling fingers of a harpist, the piping treble of flute or piccolo, the bobbing keyboard of something that looked like a shrunken piano, though Pen thought it might be a clavichord or spinet. Beyond, dancers swirled in a rainbow vortex of flying silk and weaving limbs, both men and women in gaudy costumes, their faces hidden behind animal masks. And in the background there were trees hung with coloured lanterns, and a blue midnight garden twinkling with scattered lights under the honey gaze of a benevolent moon.

'A party!' said Gavin, no longer whispering but shouting in Pen's ear to make himself heard. 'Why don't we–'

'*No*. If we join in we'll never get back. Mr Pyewackett told me–'

'How did he know? I'll bet he didn't go into any of the rooms in all his life... or death. We can't possibly forget who we are in just a few minutes.'

'Someone did,' said Pen. 'I told you. Someone broke in upstairs and I *know* he never returned. We can't risk it. We–'

And then she felt something furry slide past her leg. She looked down – made a grab at empty air – Felinacious shot through her hands with a speed unnatural to him and vanished into the throng. Pen, borrowing from Gavin's mother with a dash of creative licence, said: 'Froggit! *Now* what do we do?'

A brief lull in the music facilitated communication.

'Go after him,' Gavin said brightly.

'We *can't*. Oh lord. He *is* my responsibility. I promised Mr Pyewackett I'd look after him.'

'There you are then. Although you do rather go on about your responsibilities...'

'Sorry,' said Pen, slightly taken aback.

'I thought I'd mention it,' Gavin explained, 'before it gets too boring.'

'Thank you!'

'Don't take yourself so seriously. Where were we? Yeah... the cat. I'll go after it; you wait here. That way you can remind me who I am if I decide to forget about it.'

'No, *I'll* go,' said Pen. 'It's my re–'

'Aha!'

'*It's my cat.*'

'I thought you were just the minder. Okay, get the cat, come back here. Remember that, even if you don't remember who you are. Cat, then back here. I'll wait – *this* time. But next time, I get to fetch the cat. Deal?'

Pen kept her answer to a nod which, she reasoned, was easy to misinterpret. A nod wasn't a verbal contract. Under law, she hadn't agreed to anything. Then the music started again, and she plunged forward into the Past.

She knew the cat well enough to guess he would head for food. This was a party: there were bound to be things to eat. All she had to do was find a table laden with sumptuous dishes and Felinacious would be there, picking lobster out of his teeth. Where had she put her mask? That must be it – there on the chair. The pointed snout and wide eye-slots of a weasel or stoat, its coppery fur matching her hair, its ears tufted in gold, an emerald set in its forehead. She put it on, feeling better immediately, though something was wrong with her outfit. Of course – her cousin Berenice had taken the dress out of spite, because she didn't want Penella to look pretty or enjoy herself. Berenice was like that – all curls and eyes and smile, and poison inside. So she'd borrowed these breeches from the stable boy, and found the top heaven-knows-where, because she was determined to come to the Midsummer Party, even looking like a *vagabondo*.

She was supposed to fetch the cat; she had promised Gasparo, though she couldn't really see why it mattered. But he had been so earnest about it, so concerned, and she didn't want to get him into trouble. He was her favourite of her aunt's servants – he had such a lovely smile, even though he was black, sometimes she thought him far more handsome than Ricco, whom everybody admired, or even the prince. And he'd been kind to her in her younger days, bringing her tidbits from the kitchen when she had been sent to bed supperless and in disgrace for asking Federico's tutor questions he couldn't answer. The cat belonged to her aunt: it was spoiled and overfed though not ill-natured. It would be at the supper-table, she was sure of it. Greed was its dominant emotion. She moved between the dancers, her costume attracting the occasional startled glare, treading on someone's skirt, pushed aside by someone else. Then she headed for the pavilion, running down dusky pathways, dodging courting couples. There was Ricco, with – yes, Catarinetta! – Berenice would be green with fury when she heard. And wasn't that the prince, in the little rose-grown folly, with the open blooms glowing like ghost-flowers and the shadowy leaves hiding his companion? Wasn't that the prince, murmuring: '*Tesoro... tesoro...* you are as fair as the midnight rose...' in that cool cool voice that even passion did not warm? She could see his distinctive hair gleaming in the light of the single lantern. Almost she stayed to watch, but it made her feel sly, spying on him, so she ran on.

In the pavilion was the supper-table, with whole lobsters on gilded platters, cured hams, pasties and tartlets, fresh fruits and sugared fruits and preserves. She helped herself to a frangipani tart and lifted the table-cloth, squinnying underneath to look for the cat. Sure enough, there he was, lurking in the dark with a length of fishtail protruding from his jaws, his green eyes glinting blearily in the reflected light. She dropped to her knees, calling him – '*Felinaccio! Felinaccio! Vieni – vieni qui!*' But he didn't come and she realised, reluctantly, that she would have to crawl in after him. Glancing round to check there was no one nearby to criticise her unladylike behaviour, she ducked under the hem of the linen and wriggled forward, reaching for the cat. Instead, she got the fishtail. There was a moment when she was pulling one way and the cat the other, until the fish's spine cracked under the strain and they both fell backwards. But the cat, tangled in tablecloth and still trying to finish his stolen dinner, made a slow recovery, and Penella seized a fistful of fur, hauling him out of his lair. He squealed in protest even as they emerged into the night, lashing out, hooking the cloth with a passing claw. Guests turned to stare as Penella scrambled to her feet, hanging on grimly to her captive – and the cloth with all its burden came sliding after them, sending dishes and fishes, sweetmeats and sourmeats, goblets and tartlets crashing to the ground with the slow thunder of a banqueting debacle. There was a moment's pause as the crumbs settled and the last of the platters clattered into silence. Penella did not wait for reaction to kick in. Still clutching the cat, now thankfully detached from the table-linen, she took to her heels.

It is not easy to run holding an animal of any kind, particularly a very large and heavy cat. Among the criss-crossing garden paths she looked for a place to hide, hearing the pursuit somewhere behind her. Seeing the folly now apparently empty of the prince and his *tesoro* she ducked inside – only to check when she saw that he at least was still there, standing in the lee of a pillar looking out at the moon.

'Who's under that mask?' he said, turning towards her. 'It's little Penni, isn't it? – Signorina Penella – all dressed up like a boy. What's your hurry?'

'They're after me,' she said. 'There was an accident – this stupid cat – my aunt will kill me–'

'I can't let that happen. Here–' he took her elbow, steering her away from the lantern-light to a place at the back where she could crouch out of sight. 'Now, don't make a sound. You wouldn't want to get a prince into trouble as well, would you?'

He thinks I'm still a child, she thought, smiling to herself as she squatted down in the dark. Funny how adults never notice when children grow up...

There were voices approaching, irate voices, both deep and shrill. Indignant protests – cries – demands. 'Where is he? Where's he gone? A boy with a cat – somebody's page – a servant boy. He was wearing a mask, for all the world like one of the *ospiti*! Impertinent brat – *moccioso* – where is he? We'll flay all the skin from his back... Who's there? Oh – *su Altezza. Ci perdona* – we are looking for a boy – the boy who ruined our dinner. I tell you, *sire*, he pulled the whole table over – the whole table! Everything – *everything* gone–'

'*Una catastrofia*,' said the prince, politely. His body screened Penella's hiding place. 'I have not seen any boy.' The coldness of his tone suggested that they were disturbing his moonlit solitude with matters of little importance.

The letter of the truth, thought Penella, automatically. I bet the prince is good at law.

'Of course not, *sire*. Of course...' Abashed, the intruders beat a retreat.

And then one of the prince's friends arrived – was it Lorenzo, or Vicente? 'Cesare, news from the city – for your private ear.'

The deprived banqueteers trickled away. Penella waited, wondering if it would be undiplomatic to emerge, yet certain the prince had not forgotten her. They were going to talk secrets, secrets not meant for a thirteen-year-old girl – the plots and counterplots of modern Italy. She knew the prince was ambitious and ruthless, she had heard her uncle say so, amongst his business associates, all of whom were wary of this young man with his chilly gaze and steely mind. They supported him, they feared him, behind his back they debated the wisdom of being drawn into his train. But none defied him, none challenged him. And he helped me, Penella thought. I'll never betray him. She listened while they talked, in low tones not meant for overhearing – of an ambush, an assassination, the rapid movement of troops, the even more rapid conclusion of an alliance. Then Lorenzo (or Vicente) hurried away, and the prince was left alone.

'You can come out now,' he said.

She emerged into the folly, still holding the cat, which she had muzzled with one hand in case he felt tempted to object. She had tugged off the mask now and it dangled round her neck.

'You heard all that?' he asked her.

'Of course,' she said.

His face was in shadow, but she knew he smiled. 'You seem to be a clever child.'

'I'm hardly a child. I'm thirteen. Ignazia Giancola was married younger than me.'

'Thirteen? You look less.'

Why did men always say that? It was beginning to annoy her.

'They say I'm too clever for a girl.'

'I can believe it. A clever woman is a dangerous thing. Men control the world, but women control men. Who do *you* think is at the top of the heap?'

'Is there a woman who controls you?' Penella asked, daringly, thinking of the unseen *tesoro*.

The prince laughed. 'No indeed! I play the puppeteer, and pull the strings, and men and women, armies and governments, dance to my whim. That is what it means to be a prince.'

Even princes have to obey the law, thought Penella. The law is above everyone. She was going to be a lawyer...

What was she thinking of?

'Will you tell my secrets, little one?' the prince continued. 'Will you tell your foolish cousin, in the sanctuary of your shared bedroom, whispering them into the pink hollow of her ear? Will you tell your aunt, when she threatens to punish you, thinking to deter her from her rancour? Will you tell your uncle, when you are tired of cast-off dresses, and want to purchase yourself some favours?'

'I don't wear cast-offs,' Penella said, clearing up the most important point first. 'My father left some money, so I have clothes of my own.' If Berenice doesn't hide them. 'And you know I won't tell your secrets. Otherwise you wouldn't have let me listen.'

'I could ensure your silence,' he said, one slim hand closing on her throat. 'I could kill you now. None would ever charge me with it.'

Somehow, Penella wasn't afraid. 'You won't,' she said.

He released her. Smiling. 'No, I won't. It would be a waste. I never waste anything useful.'

He thinks I'm *useful*, thought Penella, and somehow she was more flattered than if he had called her *tesoro*, or said she shone like the ghost-roses in the velvet night. He was the most powerful, the most devious, the most ruthless of princes, and he thought her *useful*. She would never forget it.

'You kept my secret,' she said. 'I will keep yours. That's the deal. *D'accordo?*'

'*D'accordo*,' said the prince. 'Very well. But you should change your clothes, and get rid of the cat, lest those who lost their dinner catch up with you.'

Penella laughed and ran off, elated by her adventure, by the moment of confidence she had shared – the confidence of a prince – even, curiously, by the memory of his lean fingers round her throat. She felt so happy, she decided – generously – that she wouldn't tell Berenice about Ricco and Catarinetta. She didn't tell secrets. Secrets were to be kept, buried in the dark, growing unseen shoots and shadowy flowers. She was so full of secrets of a sudden it made her feel mysterious and powerful. She would take the cat to Gasparo – he was waiting by the orchestra – and then… and then…

There he was, standing in the doorway of the villa, looking round for her. The expression of anxiety on his face appeared ludicrous, out of all proportion to the situation. 'Here I am,' she said. 'Don't look so worried. The greedy cat was under the banqueting table. I had to crawl in and fetch him, and his claws got caught on the cloth, pulling it off – he pulled all the food off the table – you should have seen it – it was so funny–'

But Gasparo wasn't laughing. He burst into speech, sounding both angry and frightened, only she couldn't understand what he was saying – it was just a long stream of gibberish. She drew back from him, suddenly scared – perhaps he was possessed by a devil, like that boy in the village who had fits – but he seized her arm, dragging her through the door, her and the cat, and his face was angry, so angry, and she was angry too, because he was spoiling everything, destroying the happiness of her evening. She was cursing him and struggling, and he was spouting some nonsense-language, and the cat sprang free, running into the house, and they both tumbled through the door, hearing it close behind them with a soft final snick…

'*Ragazzaccio! Mi fai male…* Gasparo – Gasparo…'

London, twenty-first century

SHE WAS IN a strange hall, in a strange house, with grey daylight and no smells. The sound of the orchestra was totally cut off and the quiet was absolute. It got into her head, numbing her thoughts, so that for a minute she stayed on her hands and knees, immobile, waiting for her brain to get back into action. Gasparo grabbed her by the shoulders, shaking her, talking and talking, though she couldn't understand a word – jumbling her thoughts like fragments in a kaleidoscope, until they fell back into a different pattern, with a different meaning. Suddenly, like tuning in a radio, his words began to make sense.

She said: 'Gavin.'

'What happened to you?' She could hear the relief, seeping gradually into his voice. 'You were gone *ages*, and then when you got back you were spouting some foreign language – Italian I think – I couldn't understand a word of it. Why wouldn't you talk English? Why wouldn't you–'

'Oh my God.' Pen spoke slowly, deliberately, cold terror oozing through her system as realisation kicked in. She pulled the mask over her head, staring at it. 'I was... being absorbed. Into the Past. It made a space for me. I had a life... a family... My God. I thought... I felt...'

'Tell me everything,' Gavin ordered. They were still sitting on the floor. 'Tell me *now*.'

'I was an orphan,' Pen said. 'I lived with my uncle and aunt and my cousins Federico and Berenice.' She pronounced it Berra-nee-chay. 'She was horrible to me. She took my dress for the party and hid it so I wouldn't be able to go. But I got these breeches from the stable-boy...'

'They're jeans,' Gavin said. '*Jeans*. Not breeches.'

'Yes. Of course. Only... I had to find the cat. It was my aunt's – fat and greedy – I knew it would be somewhere near the supper-table. I'd promised Gasparo I'd find it – I mean, I'd promised *you*. You were one of her servants. I liked you, and you were in such a state, thinking you'd get into a row if the cat was lost, so I went to get it... and then it pulled the cloth off the table, with all the food, and I had to run. The prince hid me in the folly, and told everyone to go away, and then his friend came, with news – secrets – and I listened, but he wasn't angry with me, and I said he'd kept my secret, so I'd keep his. I was so happy, sort of high, because he'd trusted me, he said I was *useful*... And then I came back to you, and you made such a fuss – such a fuss – and now... I'm here.'

She gazed at her surroundings as if seeing them for the first time. There was a smell, or a non-smell, which was elusively familiar, though she wasn't sure what it reminded her of. For all her horror, the recollection of her happiness at that fleeting connection with the prince gave her a pang sharper than regret.

Gavin slapped her face.

'You're Penelope Tudor,' he said, 'usually called Pen. You live in the twenty-first century, in Hampstead. This is the house you're looking after. Snap out of it. Come *on–*'

'I was Penella,' she said. 'The prince called me Penni.'

'Stop going on about the prince!'

Pen's pulse, quickened by the chase, the secrets, the excitement, was slowing to normal. Her breathing, too, slowed, and slowed.

Gavin said, after a pause: 'Are you back?'

'I... think so.' A whole different world had been there, a world of cloaks and daggers, schemes and stratagems, where she had lived vividly and might have died swiftly, but it was slipping away from her, leaving her with only the glimpse of a single night and an unbearable sense of loss. As reaction set in, her longing for that world sharpened fear into panic. She was trembling visibly; Gavin put his arms round her rather awkwardly, patting her hair. It was something she would have appreciated more if she hadn't been so shaken.

'I could have stayed there,' she said. 'I could have lived my entire life...' She would have died young, she knew. It was a world where people died young. Especially those who made themselves useful to the prince. 'I'm not sure who he was.'

'He?'

'The prince. Cesare. His name was Cesare. I have to... look it up, find out... I don't know what century I was in. I don't know *anything.*'

'You see?' said Gavin. 'You can't make a diagram. There's no pattern. There's nothing to hold on to.'

Pen was struggling to pull herself together. 'There's got to be,' she insisted, clutching at her belief in logic like the proverbial drowning man with the straw. 'I can Google the prince – Cesare – I know he was Italian, and the clothes looked mediaeval. Then I'll have some idea... We'd better go back now.'

Gavin drew away from her, his expression changing. 'I thought we were going to open other doors.'

'You saw what happened just now! I nearly got lost. I nearly didn't come back *ever*... We need to... to talk about things, to work out some strategy, some kind of safeguard–'

'Yeah, I know all that. But why is it you're the one having all the fun?'

'Fun!'

'Well, it was fun, wasn't it? When you got back you were all sort of lit up, going on about the prince, waving that mask around... Is that a *real* emerald?'

'I don't know.' Pen brushed away side issues. 'What does it matter?'

'It could be worth a fortune.' Gavin had taken the mask from her and was studying it hopefully. 'Anyway, it's my turn to have an adventure. I'm going to try one of the doors too.'

'Look, this is *my* house–'

'No it isn't. You're just taking care of it.'

'Well... well, it's my business what happens here, not yours. You can't –'

'I thought we were in this together?'

'I changed my mind,' Pen snapped.

'Who zapped the velociraptor?'

This was unanswerable. Pen knew she wasn't being reasonable, partly out of fear, partly from a curious resentment of the very charms that made her like Gavin.

She said: 'Okay. But–'

'I'm going to look in the broom cupboard again,' Gavin declared. 'We didn't get absorbed in the Jurassic, did we? After all, there's no way we could belong there. Dinosaurs and people didn't exist at the same time except in films. Let's see if it's still there. That way we'll have some idea how fast things change. If you're looking for a pattern, we need to know stuff like that.'

'What if the velociraptor's waiting?' Pen said doubtfully.

'I've still got the stun-gun. I charged it yesterday.'

'I suppose it might be useful to verify…' *Useful* was definitely the word of the day. *Utile*, the prince had said.

They both got up and went over to the broom cupboard, Gavin in the lead with the stun-gun at the ready. As he opened the door, Pen braced herself, feeling her heart hiccup…

Beyond the Door
Sometime in the mythical past

But the Jurassic jungle had gone. They were staring into a narrow gorge, only half a dozen yards across. Rock-faces rose almost sheer on either side; in between there was a gap of grey smoky sky. The ground was a rising slope of stones and scree, with here and there a few dry twigs thrusting upwards, or a tree-skeleton clinging to a boulder with twisted roots. A little way ahead the cliffs met, closing over the entrance to a cave. A tongue of daylight reached in until the ascending slope was swallowed in shadow, but there was nothing much to see. The tiny gorge was a dry, dead place and the cave appeared long unused.

'This doesn't look dangerous,' Gavin said, on a faint note of disappointment. Danger is always at its most attractive when it isn't happening.

'It depends what's in the cave,' said Pen.

'I'm going to have a look.'

'Why? We don't really need to know...'

'Yes we do. You're the one who wants to work out a pattern. This isn't the Jurassic any more, so let's find out when it is.'

'I had to go after the cat last time,' Pen reminded him. 'You don't have to–'

'I'm going anyway. We had a deal, remember?'

'No, we–'

Gavin stepped through into the gorge. The door was obviously in the rock-face, though why there should be a door in the rock neither of them bothered to speculate. Pen felt the cat rub against her legs and glanced down hastily, but Felinacious showed no inclination to explore further. He bent briefly to sniff the ground and drew back at once, his fur bristling, mouth open in a hiss.

Pen said: 'Gavin, look! He's scared, or angry. He smells something...'

'Stupid moggy,' said Gavin, with only a quick glance behind him. He was scrambling up the slope towards the cave. It was steeper than it looked and presently he too picked up the smell, emanating from the entrance, though his senses were far less acute than the cat's. Afterwards, he said it was like the smell you would get when someone allows a casserole to boil dry on the hob, and then doesn't open the kitchen windows for a week. It was disagreeable – particularly for an aspiring chef – but not frightening.

Not yet.

The entrance wasn't large, perhaps seven feet high and five wide. Inside, the passage seemed to broaden and the stench intensified. Gavin found himself imagining a subterranean kitchen cluttered with the residue of incompetent cooking and stacks of dirty washing up, the home perhaps of giants, or cannibals, or –

'You're not going in?' Pen called from the doorway below.

'Yes, I am. How else will we find out what's there?'

'It's dark. You haven't got a torch.'

'Another time we must come better equipped. Don't worry: I still know who I am. Whatever's here, it isn't absorbing me. Anyhow, I won't go far...'

Pen saw him move forward cautiously, one hand on the rock wall, and vanish into the dark. There was a yelp and an oath a few seconds later, and Gavin's voice came floating out: 'Stubbed my toe!' Then silence.

She thought: What if he doesn't come back?

Somehow, she knew that if the worst happened, it would be her fault.

She waited for what seemed like a very long while. This is how Gavin felt, she realised, waiting for me. We can't keep doing it like this – so *random*. If we're going to explore further we *must* be more organised – get better equipment: he's right about that – work out a system... Her responsibility (but she mustn't be boring about it). Her fault. Why did Gavin have to poke his nose in, trying to take things over? Why were boys such a pain, with their football and their toilet jokes and their idiotic obsession with machismo? Why oh why didn't he come back?

She looked at her watch, which was no help, since she hadn't looked at it when he first entered the cave.

Should she go in after him?

Felinacious had retreated into the hall, out of range of the smell, and fallen asleep.

'You're no use,' Pen said.

A shadow fell across the gorge. Pen glanced up – something was plummeting out of the sky, a winged shape, huge as a cloud, cutting off the daylight. It landed on a ledge above the cave-mouth, clutching the rock with taloned feet. At first she thought it was a pterodactyl – her mind had got stuck on dinosaurs – but then she saw it had feathers, shaggy brown feathers with a dull metallic sheen, and it was surely much bigger than a pterodactyl ought to be, at least by film and television standards. It looked rather like an eagle except that its head was crested and its curved beak over a yard long. Even as Pen watched, the beak parted and a sound emerged that was somewhere between a screech and a squawk, only far louder. Echoes carried across the unseen mountains above and bounced to and fro in the confines of the gorge. Instinctively, Pen covered her ears.

Don't come out! she cried to Gavin, inside her mind. *Whatever you do, don't come out!*

If she had read more myths and fairytales, she would have known she was looking at a roc. But she hadn't, and didn't, and all she knew was that while she stayed in the doorway it didn't pay any attention to her. With Gavin now trapped underground, that wasn't much to be thankful for.

Presently, there was the noise of movement from inside the cave. Small stones rattled and went rolling down the slope.

Something came out, but it wasn't Gavin.

Infernale

THEY SAID IT was the oldest building in the world. Of course they – whoever *they* were – were wrong, because werespirits have no capacity for original thought, and even the most powerful can only copy the ideas of Men. But when the first village was patched together out of mud and reeds, when brick was baked and stone was shaped and little walls grew upward into the first city, then *he* looked out in envy and dreamed himself a tower that would top the palaces of kings. The dwarves cut the stones, and the giants set them in place, and the foundations were bound with magic from the earliest days, when there was yet magic and to spare even in this unmagical universe. For this was *his* magic, from the chaos before the dawn of Time, and though millions of years had passed it still vibrated with the heartbeat of creation.

Everything was first then, when the sun was young and the waters were clear and clean and the air was pure from pole to pole. Men searched for their gods in the breath of the wind and the dark of the storm, and *he* named himself lord of the Earth, and supplicants came to the Dark Tower to trade for favours, leaving their souls behind. He was Azmordis, Ormuzd, Babbaloukis, Ingré Manu, Votun, Tchernobog, Agamo the Toad-God and Bale the village idol. He gave gold to the prince and blood to the warrior and land to the peasant, and the prince ate only gold and the warrior drank only blood and the peasant's land was six feet of cold earth to sleep in, and Azmordis laughed until the walls of Hell rang. He did not throw the first spear nor cast the first stone, but in his arrogance and his might he claimed Evil was of his making, and men were his creatures, and the Dark Tower stood at the centre of the world.

But time passed, and men made their own evil, and the souls he sought to feed on withered, eluding his grasp, and the Gate took them away from him. His kingdom still grew, his servants and adherents were among the mightiest on Earth, but some there were who turned from him, and kindled their own flame against the darkness of the ancient Night. There was peace and war, famine and plenty, sickness and healing, and if he was defeated or diminished one day yet he would always return more powerful than before.

In short, the usual career history for diabolical superbeings.

The Dark Tower crumbled, devoured by the passing ages, and the giants were gone who might have rebuilt it. But men worked in their stead, using not stones and spells but concrete and steel, and the tower grew taller than before, a vast black skyscraper a-glitter with sightless windows, reaching up to the clouds. In dungeons far beneath the earth prisoners were chained to their desks, pecking endlessly at their keyboards, while screens bleeped and flickered before their eyes. And on the topmost storey, so far above the world that few elevators could mount so high, Azmordis ruled from his circular office, with its blood-red carpet and gleaming desktop, the old-fashioned quill pen, the inkwell that never held ink, the paper-knife that never cut paper. If you enter that office there is only ever one file on the desk, and your name is stamped on the cover. And if you sign, whether in hope or fear, in greed or need, the price you pay will be dearer than blood. These days *he* wears a suit, or the shadow of a suit, and he looks out through the tinted glass over all the kingdoms of the world, all the cities where workers strive and struggle and fail, and their myriad lights are as numerous as the stars.

It is a terrible thing to contemplate eternity as a stockbroker.

The witch gazed into the spellfire until her eyes ached, watching the Dark Tower – though she made no attempt to peer into the circular office – listening to the smalltalk of imps and goblins. The Nightwings left by the roof, speeding out over the world on black-feathered pinions, swifter than thought.

Swifter than some people's thoughts, anyway.

'I have to find Bartlemy,' the witch said, for the hundredth time. 'He will know what to do.'

But he was gone where even the smoke-magic could not find him, somewhere outside the everyday world, through a hole in space and time to a place where imagination and reality interlock...

Beyond the Door
Sometime in the mythical past

GAVIN FELT HIS way in the dark, even slower now he was out of Pen's sight, his enthusiasm for adventure flagging. The burnt smell was so pervasive he barely noticed it. He reminded himself with satisfaction that he wasn't losing touch with the present: Pen, the house, and the events of the morning were still at the forefront of his mind. Which means, he deduced, I can't be anywhere in human history. That was a vaguely disturbing thought. At least, with history, once you'd sorted out the location and the century you might have some idea what was going on. Here, he hadn't a clue. It could be a different part of the Jurassic, or the Triassic, or some other -assic he had never heard of, or it could be a mythical place outside the range of reality, Middle-Earth or Narnia or somewhere like that. However, his mental picture of such places was a lot more scenic: caves, if any, should be hung with stalactites, glittering with quartz, lit with an eldritch glow, not like this gloomy, stinking hole.

There was a light ahead, but it wasn't eldritch. The passage had levelled out and he saw an opening some way in front filled with the dull-orange glimmer of sodium street-lamps. Gavin had read more childhood fiction than Pen, before his reading became entirely culinary, and he stopped dead. It dawned on him he was being incredibly stupid. He knew quite well what sort of creatures lived in caves, giving off a dull-orange glow. Of course, dragons didn't exist and never had, but he suspected that in Bygone House that wouldn't be a bar to stumbling over one. So much for adventure. He was going back – he was going back right now – except... He visualised himself telling Pen: 'I realised there *might* be a dragon in there, so I came away without taking a look.' It wasn't a scenario in which he shone. Burger it, he said to himself. He would go *very* quietly, and just take a peek. There would be no verbal exchanges, no riddles, none of that garbage. Just a quick peek.

He crept towards the opening, testing the ground before every step. Now, he could hear a noise like the wind whistling down a very long chimney, the sound of some large animal breathing heavily in its sleep. (Sleep was good.) He noted: 'I thought dragons snored,' and wondered why he wasn't petrified with terror. Perhaps because, after the initial shock, he knew what to expect. It was almost a cliché. Cave – reddish glow – sleeping dragon. Maybe there would be treasure, an antique hoard of gold and gems stretching away in shimmering mounds. His eyes gleamed at the prospect. Surely he could appropriate a couple of items...

He peered round the edge of the aperture into a much larger cavern.

There was no hoard. Just the dragon. It was lying on rubble and what appeared to be fragments of bone, whether human or animal he couldn't tell. Gavin guessed it was at least fifty feet long, but the tail was so looped and coiled around the floor it was impossible to be precise. Its body was just lithe enough to squeeze through the cave entrance, an ash-grey body encrusted with scales and spines, humps and bumps, only the belly glowing dimly red from the furnace inside. It lay with head slumped sideways, its eyes closed and its mouth open, displaying a jagged collection of smoke-stained teeth. A little puff of fume came from its nostrils with every exhalation. Its folded wings were bundled along its back like collapsible umbrellas, loose tucks of skin protruding between the ribbing. One foreleg was in the air, the long toes terminating in two-foot claws.

It didn't look like a cliché. It looked real – hugely, terrifyingly real – a crocodile five times bigger than it should be, winged and supple and much too hot. Dragons have several stomachs, only one of which produces flame. Special enzymes break down the fuel substances it eats to form a kind of gas called igneum, which is expelled via the oesophagus and burns when mixed with air. Dragons are of course reptiles and technically cold-blooded, but this process makes their body temperature hot enough for eggs to fry on their skin, even in sleep, and provides the glow useful for dragon-hunters operating underground. They are essentially creatures with an unnaturally high level of inbuilt heartburn. In evolutionary terms, it is hardly surprising that dragons are both magical and largely extinct.

Forgetful of his mother's training, Gavin whispered: 'Shit.' He stared – and stared – horrified, fascinated, bewitched. He could see the rhythmic swelling and shrinking of its underbelly, and the whistle of breath in its nasal passages filled the cave with hissy echoes. Somehow, he didn't think this was a dragon that did riddles. This creature wouldn't waste time on conversation. It would just eat you.

The noise from outside wrenched him abruptly from his contemplation. He drew back, stepping on something which squelched. Dragon dung. Fortunately, it was old and cold. (Fresh dragon dung will burn through clothing.) In the cavern, the dragon rolled onto its stomach and opened an eye. It was smoky red, with a slitted pupil, and it looked like the eye of no other creature in all the worlds. You felt its glance could go through both flesh and stone like a laser. It occurred to Gavin that he had no ring to make himself invisible and he was standing in the exit.

He stumbled back along the tunnel, no longer trying to be quiet. There wasn't time. Behind him, he heard the dragon's approach, far too rapid for an animal of its size and weight – the *crunch! crunch!* of claws on rubble, the scrape of tail over stone. He dived into the first recess he could find. It didn't go back far enough, and he shrank against the wall, trying to squeeze himself into a crack in the rock, knowing the dragon must see him. It shot past at speed, summoned by the screeching call outside, but there was an instant when the red gaze probed the gap – he felt it scanning him, analysing him, filing him away for future disposal, putting him on the menu for afters. His bowels loosened. He clenched every muscle against the humiliation of terror.

He knew when it issued from the cave – he heard the coughing roar as it answered its challenger. There were sounds of violent combat, crashes and thuds that made the ground shudder, shrieks of unhuman pain or rage. He had to move – he had to move *now* – it was his only chance. If he could escape under cover of the fight, get back to the door, to Pen, to the safety of Bygone

House... But the fear made him weak and stupid, penning him in that useless hole. He tried to stand, but his knees gave. The dragon's stare was supposed to be hypnotic, he remembered. It *wanted* him to wait there, till the fight was over, then it would return, scoop him out with a hooked foreclaw, carry him into the cavern and devour him at leisure...

He tottered forward into the passage, skidded and stumbled down the scree towards the entrance. The noise of combat grew – in the gap he could see dust-whorls, a threshing tail, the flare of fire. He was running now, limbs unfrozen, desperate to get out. In the cave-mouth he halted, seeing the roc for the first time, stunned by the scale of a battle between two such giants. The dragon was half turned away from him, rearing up on its hind legs, pinions spread, flame jetting from its jaws. The roc attacked from above – its brazen feathers seemed to be fireproof, and its wingbeat drove the jet back into the dragon's throat, choking it on its own breath. As it reeled Gavin sprinted from the cave. But the tail lashed sideways, hurling him against the rock with such force that for a few seconds he blacked out. He fought to stay conscious, to get back on his feet, braced himself to try again. And again the tail was there, slamming him into the tunnel. Then he understood. The dragon heard him – sensed his every move – and had no intention of letting him get away. This was a hunter who never missed a kill: the prey, once sighted, was already dead.

Push your luck too far and it may break under the strain. Gavin knew he was dinner.

The stun-gun was no good to him: it would be a mere fuel injection for a creature which ran on fire. He realised in that narrow gorge his chances of dodging the tail were nonexistent. His head was still spinning; another blow might knock him out completely. If this was Playstation he would give up, but it wasn't a game – it wasn't virtual reality – and in the gorge below, through the dust and smoke, he saw the door open in the cliff, and Pen, paler than pale, peering out, hands waving in frantic gestures. Something about the look on her face was more than he could bear.

The fight was growing increasingly vicious. Blows glanced off the rock, widening old cracks; boulders thundered down from above. Claws and jaws, talons and pinions whirled together in a vortex of destructive power. But a small corner of the dragon's mind was still on its prospective meal. Perhaps the two monsters had slain nearly all the prey in the area, the region could not sustain such predation and the conflict was vital to decide who ate what was left. Gavin was young and well-nourished, packed to the skin with soft tasty bits – liver, kidneys, sweetbreads, tripe – even those chewy knots of muscle would present no problem to a dragon. The beast would never let such a delicacy evade his hunger.

For the last time, Gavin slipped out of the cave. The tail sliced towards him – he grabbed the spiny ridge, feeling dagger-edges split his palms – vaulted clumsily over it – rolled across the ground, trying to get out of range. The dragon, infuriated, lunged with one back leg, pitching his victim almost effortlessly through the air, smashing him against the cliff. Gavin saw white pinpoints of light flickering in his vision as the impact drove breath and strength from his body. He felt a rib go but it didn't matter – he knew he couldn't run any more...

But that last tiny distraction had broken the dragon's concentration. Sensing weakness, the roc plunged – its opponent was low on fire and only a thin drift of flame crackled along the bird's crest. The huge beak thrust into the reptile's throat like a spear. Too late, the dragon tried to pull back – its body arched and spasmed – the roc shook its head, driving the mortal wound deeper and deeper. Blood fountained out, hissing and steaming as it hit the ground. The lethal tail twitched and shuddered. Pen's cry carried up the valley: 'Gavin – *now*! GAVIN–'

But Gavin was still trying to breathe.

The roc settled on its fallen enemy, turning it onto its back, exposing the thinner scaling on the belly. Gavin heard the sound – a sound to melt your guts – as talons even bigger than the dragon's ripped through hide and flesh. The fire-stomach was torn open; a little igneum must have remained, as a whoosh of flame shot upwards, then fizzled into nothing. The raptor dipped its head, lifting it again with dripping scarlet ribbons trailing from its beak. Gavin moved, groaning, struggling to inhale into squashed lungs. The bird's head tilted, watching him with a single eye. Not the red laser-stare of the dragon but the flat black glitter of generic malice. Using a boulder, Gavin pulled himself to his feet. The pain of his cracked rib twanged through his body.

'Hold on!' Pen called. 'I'm coming!'

She was running up the slope towards him – the roc's gaze swivelled to fix on her. Gavin tried to shout: *No! Stay where you are!* but his voice emerged as a croak. Then her arm went round him and somehow they were facing the bird, its neck extended, its lowered beak blood-dipped and still dangling shreds of intestine. It surveyed them first with one eye, then the other. Pen grabbed the stun-gun from Gavin's pocket.

'Didn't... feel fire,' Gavin managed.

'Those feathers seem to be metallic,' Pen said optimistically. 'Metal's a conductor. It'll feel *this*.'

But the roc evidently decided there was more meat on the dragon. It returned to its grisly meal, and the two of them staggered down the hill and through the door into the sanctuary of the house.

London, twenty-first century

BACK IN 7A, Quorum supplied hot sweet chocolate for the shock and cooked a meal which might have met Gavin's standards if he had been in a mood to register what he ate.

'You ought to see a doctor about your rib,' Pen said.

'Not much point,' Gavin said between mouthfuls. He had got his voice back when his lungs returned to normal. 'I broke one playing football once; it took ages to mend. There's nothing you can do.'

'You should have a tetanus jab for those cuts on your hand–'

'I *told* you it was dangerous,' Quorum reiterated every few minutes, agitated out of his butleresque calm. 'You young people, you don't listen–'

'We know now,' Pen said. 'Please don't go on about it. We'll be more careful next time.'

'Next time!' Quorum's tone shrilled to a squeak.

'Pen nearly got lost in the past,' Gavin said, 'and I nearly got eaten. I'm not in a hurry to open any more doors.' Over an hour later, they were both still shaking. They'd done a lot of hugging and even a little weeping when the broom cupboard was finally closed, though Gavin had attempted to rub away his tears unnoticed and Pen duly hadn't noticed them. Her colour came back with the brandy – more colour than usual – and the edge had gone from both her curiosity and her resolution.

'We did learn things,' she said. 'We learned *lots*. I'm going to put it all on the computer and see what we get.'

'Put not your trust in technology,' said Quorum. 'The house is a spatial/temporal prism – a time-twister. The hallway may be quiet but that's like the epicentre of a tornado. Beyond the doors space and time are shifting, spinning, changing. You can't pin them down.'

Pen muttered something about *patterns* which no one heard.

'You say someone is lost in there,' Quorum went on. 'I'm sure you're right. Mr Pyewackett told me hundreds have been lost, maybe thousands. There's nothing you can do. You are reckless and gallant and young, so young. Young lives are too easily thrown away. You've been lucky today – you've been lucky twice – but you can't expect to be lucky again. Go back into that house and you may never return. Then what would I say to your grandmother – to Gavin's mother?'

'Don't worry,' Gavin said. 'We're not going back.'

Pen nodded, resigned in the aftermath of horror, then said: 'Yes. I mean, no. We won't go back.'

When Gavin was leaving she asked, suddenly shy: 'Will I see you again?'

They'd only known each other a few days, but it felt like a lifetime.

(Not necessarily in a good way.)

'Of course,' he said, mildly astonished she should need to pose the question. 'I'll call you tomorrow.'

But it was she who called him, later that evening in the privacy of her room. 'I've got something,' she announced. 'I put it all on the computer, and I think I've got something.'

'Is it catching?'

Pen ignored that. 'First of all, the prince. His name was Cesare Borgia. He lived in Italy in the fifteenth century. He was a sort of military and political genius – Machiavelli wrote a book about him – though pretty unscrupulous. He died when he was only thirty-one.'

'Too late to do a rescue, then,' Gavin said pragmatically.

'That's not all,' Pen continued, a little damped. 'I've found – I think I've found – the beginning of the pattern...'

'There is no pattern. Quorum was right. Everything changes.'

'Yes, but... there could be recurring factors. Like the broom cupboard.'

'What about it?' Gavin's voice darkened at the memory.

'Monsters,' said Pen. 'Both times, it was monsters. If we opened it again–'

'No.'

'Just to look. Not go through. Just to be sure...'

'I don't *want* to be sure. Sure sounds like dead to me. Dead sure. I'm never opening that cupboard again, I'm never going into that house again, and if you're so keen on getting me killed I never want to see you again either.' He hung up, knowing he was being unfair. He was the one who'd insisted on going into the cave, out of some sort of misplaced bravado. Showing off, he thought reluctantly, kicking the thought under the table where he couldn't see it. He definitely wouldn't call Pen any more, at least for a couple of days. He would call... Josabeth Collins, in her pink skirt and her pink hair-tags, who was as pretty as a TV soap and about as predictable. With her, he would be safe.

Bored, but safe.

In 7A, Eve Harkness came back – yet again – too late to meet Gavin. When asked how they had spent the day, Pen said 'just talking.'

'You didn't go into Number 7, did you?' her grandmother said. 'Quorum tells me it's really unsafe. Something to do with the structure – rotten floorboards I suppose. If you fell through you could be badly hurt. I know you're always so sensible, but...'

'It's kept locked,' said Pen, tiptoeing round the truth. 'I couldn't get in without the key.' She didn't mention that she already had it.

She thought of adding *I wouldn't do anything silly*, but decided that was stretching a point. She still didn't want to lie if she could avoid it, though she knew that was mere nit-picking. Omission had grown to concealment, concealment to deception – she felt as if she was trying to hide a blood-splattered corpse under a hankerchief. An Italian prince, a roc and a dragon had been added to the velociraptor, and all of them seemed to be crowding her mind, weighting her tongue. At school, she was known as someone who could stay silent under taunting or peer pressure, who kept her own counsel and never spread gossip. But she had always been open with her grandmother. Until now. It was as if she had given up not just frankness but an elusive security, a firewall of protection in her life. If this was maturity, she thought, why didn't she feel strong and capable, as adults were meant to, instead of defenceless and scared?

She said goodnight to her grandmother, and went slowly to bed.

'Someone arranged those twigs next door,' she said to herself, 'and cleared up the broken vase. Someone *lives* there, whatever Mr Pyewackett said. I ought to find out who.'

She wasn't eager to explore any further – she'd been horribly frightened by the experiences of that day, and the mere idea of going there alone made her feel sick – but the urge to solve at least one little mystery hung on, an annoying niggle at the back of her thoughts.

She went into the bathroom. There was a set of false teeth in a glass beside the basin which hadn't been there before. They looked very white and shiny and faintly familiar.

'Mr Pyewackett's teeth,' she said out loud. 'What are they doing here? Surely they should have been cremated with the rest of him.'

'Nothing wrong with us,' said the teeth, in a voice alarmingly like that of Andrew Pyewackett himself. 'Why should we burn? We're good for a long trek yet. No point in wasting a decent set of teeth. Never know when *you* may need us.'

'Yuk,' said Pen.

The teeth were clacking up and down in the glass, just as they had rattled against Andrew Pyewackett's crumbling jawbone. But she felt she had gone past being surprised at anything.

'How did you get in here?'

'Had a word with Quorum. He's the butler, isn't he? Obeys orders. Told him we needed to keep an eye on you.'

'You haven't got an eye,' Pen pointed out. 'Anyway, I won't be kept an eye on in the bathroom, thank you. It's private. I go to the loo in here.'

'Hey,' said the teeth, 'we're *dentures*. We don't care about all this human modesty codswallop. Dentures don't do embarrassment.'

'I do,' said Pen.

She picked up the glass, carried it into the bedroom and placed it on the dressing table. After a moment's consideration, she fetched a hankerchief from Mr Pyewackett's old room and spread it over the top.

'Take it off!' clattered the teeth. 'Take it off!'

'Shut up,' said Pen. 'Go to sleep, or whatever it is teeth do at night. I'll take it off in the morning – *if* you behave.'

She heard the teeth grind together in frustration, and they seemed to be trying to leap out of the glass, pushing against the hankerchief, but eventually they subsided.

It's like having a parrot, Pen thought.

Presently, Felinacious came into the room, eyed the shrouded glass for a moment, then thumped onto her bed, still licking its whiskers with the satisfaction of a cat who has had a substantial fish dinner intended for others.

'No talking cats,' said Pen. 'Oh no. Just teeth.' In the glass, the dentures muttered to themselves. Pen pulled the quilt over her head and did her best to go to sleep. Worn out with terror and time lag, excitement and emotion, she succeeded almost immediately.

CHAPTER FIVE
Monster Mash

London, twenty-first century

PEN DREAMED.

The boy was outside the house, trying to get in. He had to get in, though he couldn't have said why – perhaps because the house had no door, and a house with no door was a house worth getting into. He wasn't quite a stranger to getting into other people's houses. He prowled round the garden, checking the ground floor windows, but they were all barred. Then he climbed the wall to the first storey.

'This is *him*,' Pen thought, in her dream. 'This is the thief who broke in, and was lost.'

She had thought about him, worried about him, and now her subconscious was turning worry into fantasy, showing her what might have happened. She knew she was dreaming, as you sometimes do, and she clung on to the dream, determined not to wake, eager to pursue her fancy through to the end.

She watched him cut out the pane of glass, propping it up on an external ledge. Then he reached through to find the catch, pushed the window open, and scrambled inside. She saw him clearly for the first time as he stood up, looking round the landing. Until then the dream had been following his line of vision, with only brief glimpses of the back of his head, but now she could see his face. An odd, tight, closed-in face with thin hard bones and a hard narrow mouth and eyes like dark slots. His hair was so fair it was almost white and his skin was paler than Pen's, with the dense, opaque pallor of skin that can never blush, or tan, or warm itself even a semitone. He's an albino, Pen guessed – there was one at her school, a girl a few years older, as white and delicate as porcelain – but the eyes were wrong, much too dark, brown and gleaming like polished stones. For an instant she saw him up close, and she thought: He's young. My age – not much more. Quorum was right...

In that moment his face shocked her, because it wasn't like a face in a dream. It was too vividly delineated, too intense. And for all the hardness, she sensed this was someone who hurt. This was someone who hurt all the time. But whether he hurt himself, or others, or both, she couldn't tell.

She noticed his hair was too long and he wore flared jeans which flapped about his calves.

She saw him go downstairs, and open a door (she thought it was the door through which she had seen the monk), stare into the room for a few seconds – just a few seconds – then close it again. Then he went to another door, one she was sure she hadn't tried. This time, he was more hesitant, nudging it open a very little way, craning his neck to peer through the crack. But the door was tugged wide by somebody on the far side of it, and the boy fell forward. Pen had a brief glimpse of a crowded street – a street with shops and stalls, people in old-fashioned clothes, crooked houses leaning over it, grubby patches of sky between pointed roofs. A burly-looking man had hold of the boy and was saying: 'Gotcha! I've had enough o' you varmints, sneaking into the houses of honest folk to steal what don't belong to you–' But the boy wrenched himself free, and ran off down the street, dodging through the crowd, and the man cried: 'Stop! Thief!' and some turned to stare, and others joined the chase, though no one was sure who they were chasing, and a stall was knocked over, and confusion broke out in the boy's wake like battle in the wake of a war-goddess. Then the door slammed shut, and that world was cut off, lost in the days of Long Ago, and the dream slipped away, blending with other dreams, carrying Pen on a gentle tide into oblivion...

Beyond the Doors
London, seventeenth century

GHOST WOKE FROM the dream to the accustomed gloom of the loft and a sudden snort from one of the boys, shifting in his sleep. Nearby, Weasel twitched under his blanket like a dog shaking off a fly, perhaps lost in some nightmare of Mr Sheen's wig. Snot snuggled against his brother, damp nose pressed into his side, invisible save for a clump of hair sprouting from beneath the bedding. Ratface and Pockface lay back to back, each curled in a position that mirrored the other. In slumber, all the sharpness and wariness and cunning was drained from the faces of the Lost Boys; they looked soft-cheeked and innocent as angels sleeping on a cloud, if rather dirtier. Only Ghost was always the same, asleep or awake. As a baby he had looked more like a gnome than an angel, with flaring ears on either side of a pale narrow head and puckered features. His heart was old before he was ten. Now, turned fourteen, the hardness had entered his very bones, and even sleep could not gentle it out of him. He moved amongst them like a cold, alien being – like the ghost they named him – knowing it was his differentness which made him their leader, which enabled him to protect them, if protection were possible, in the city jungle where only the strong survived.

A rat which had been hunting for scraps scurried out of his way, running over Sly's foot and disappearing into a crack in the wall. Ghost didn't like to see rats in the garret, he said they were unhealthy, but One-Ear laughed and said how could they be, they were so fat and well-fed. He would share crusts with them sometimes – there was one in particular, with a bitten ear, he seemed to have a fellow-feeling for and called it Edwin, no one knew why, though Ghost suspected it was his real name. He couldn't see if it was Edwin who ran away, the rat moved too fast, but his hard mouth grew harder at the sight of it. He knew there was a special reason not to have rats around, if only he could remember what it was.

He opened the door without a creak and slipped through into the moonlight. At that hour the city was quiet, sleeping or feigning sleep. Sudden sounds carried a long way: a cat yowled, a latch clicked. A three-quarter moon shone across the rooftops, barring the world with deep shadows and pale slabs of light. But Ghost was a night creature, in his element in the dark. The click of the latch had drawn his attention: it came from somewhere close by. A door had been opened in the furtive way you open a door when you don't want to be seen doing so. Ghost slid down the ladder and crossed the roofscape, a shadow among shadows. A few moments later he was looking down into Running Lane.

He knew which door had been opened so furtively, he knew it in his gut. He was always listening for it, somewhere just below the level of conscious thought.

The back door to Big Belinda's place.

It was perhaps two hours before dawn. The party must have wound down; what revellers there were had obviously already left. A thin slice of light issued from the door-crack, yellow against the monochrome night. A face poked out and withdrew. Then the light was cut off as two figures emerged, carrying something which looked like a long, dark bundle, sagging in the middle. Ghost knew what that bundle must be, though it was wrapped in a cloth and no details were visible. Only one thing was that size and shape, and would require such clandestine disposal. Someone else loomed briefly in the doorway, someone who could only be Big Belinda; he saw the lamplight shining through her false curls.

'Get rid of it!' She spoke very softly, but Ghost's quick ears picked up every word. 'No – not in the creek. Too close. Get the boat – take it out to the river, and make sure it's weighted. We don't want it popping up again, do we?'

Two male voices grunted acquiescence. One face was half turned, catching the light before the door closed; Ghost recognised the scarred visage of Cullen. The scars of disease, he thought, not the marks of a fight. He couldn't identify the other man with any certainty, but he guessed it must be the porter, a squat man with the build and intellectual capacity of a bulldog.

They carried their burden along the lane and through a covered way to the creek. Ghost followed, moving from roof to roof, seeing them reappear at the water's edge.

One said: 'We could just roll him in here. She wouldn't know the difference.' The porter.

'No,' said Cullen. 'She's right. Too much shit here already, and the water level's falling. The river's the place for him. We'll take him to the boat. Watch your step!'

The porter had slipped on mud or sewerage, almost falling into the creek. He swore graphically.

'Shut your mouth! D'you want half the town turning up?'

'We can't lug 'im all that way – he's a dead weight and there's no footing here for anyone carrying a load–'

'Of course he's a dead weight, blockhead. He's dead, ain't he? If you weren't so clumsy… You wait 'ere with 'im. I'll fetch the boat along and we'll row 'im the rest of the way.'

'I ain't waiting with a corpus! Not on my own I ain't.'

'You wasn't scared o' him when he was alive. What's to scare you now he's dead?' Cullen's voice – a dark grey voice with an edge like sandpaper – was scathing.

'I heard o' a dead man once, reached right out of 'is coffin to grab the cove what was burying 'im. They're terrible strong, the dead. I ain't staying 'ere to be a-strangled by a corpus.'

'Lily-livered milksop! Big Bel didn't hire you to whimper at ghost-stories! You can't bring the boat – you'd run it aground for sure. All right, all right, we'll leave 'im here and fetch it together.

There's no one about at this hour and he ain't going nowhere. Get moving.'

They deposited the bundle beside the creek and hurried off, the porter still slithering and splashing at the water's edge. Ghost dropped noiselessly down from the roof and bent over the thing on the ground. The bundle had been lashed together with string, the knots too tight to be easily loosed. He pulled out his knife to cut through them, then hesitated, unwilling to leave any sign of investigation. The knife slid out of sight again and he fumbled with the folds of cloth at one end, tugging them apart to expose what was inside. His own shadow obscured his view, but when he moved aside the moon shone clearly down on the face of the corpse. Ghost did not recognise him, seeing only that he was wigless, his hair cropped, apparently dressed in little more than his shirt. Ghost opened the cloth at chest level, looking for a stab wound or some similar cause of death. But the stains on both shirt and cloth were not blood. He unfastened the buttons; the bare torso gleamed white in the moonlight, discoloured with indistinct blotches which might have been boils. Ghost drew back, his breathing suddenly shallow. He had been less than a year in the city, but he knew what those boils might mean. Quickly he pulled the cloth back over face and chest and shinned back up to the roof.

Presently, he heard the sound of oars, sloshing through the thick water of the creek. The boat nudged into the bank and the two men got out, loading the body with some difficulty and much cursing. The additional weight grounded the dinghy too deep in the mud, and there were more oaths as they struggled to move it, and the porter lost his balance and sat down in the slime, and Ghost might have laughed to himself if he hadn't been too disturbed by what he had discovered. He guessed the man must have been a gallant from the theatre, who had come home with one of the girls, the symptoms of his sickness passing for drunkenness. By the time they knew he was dying it would have been too late to throw him out. Presumably Big Belinda imagined that getting rid of the remains in this covert manner would somehow get rid of the problem: the girls wouldn't take sick, and business would continue as usual. Stupid, thought Ghost, his upper lip thinning in something between a sneer and a snarl. The girls should be warned – Mags, Clarrie, French Sue – they should leave town *now*. But he knew already what Mags would say. *Where would we go? How would we live? Our home is here – our livelihood...*

And the boys – *his* boys – sleeping in the loft, knowing nothing of the danger that crept so close, so close... how could he protect them from *this*? What could he do? Suddenly, revenge on Big Belinda seemed a trivial matter. If the plague came, it might well prove unnecessary. How does it get here? he wondered. Does it blow on the wind? Does it flow in the water? He sensed the knowledge was there in his mind, just beyond the reach of his thought – the knowledge that might save them all – but he couldn't quite touch it, and the harder he tried the more it eluded him.

He went back to the loft and lay down in the dark, staring up at the roof beams with eyes that did not see.

Eade, twenty-first century

THE WITCH DREW the magic circle in lipstick around her mirror and chanted the invocation, but the grinnock did not come. She gazed into the basin, but there was only the blood trail uncurling on the surface of the water. At Thornyhill Manor she lit the spellfire, but all she got was a room full of smoke.

She said: 'Bugger,' and other words of conjuration, to little effect.

Eventually, after much coughing, the smoke was sucked into a kind of whirling cloud, blotting out the fire, and a hole opened at its heart. She peered into it with watering eyes but could see only blackness. And then, as her vision adapted, the blackness acquired depth and definition.

Black wings against a black sky. Not the black of night but the black of deep space arching above the atmosphere. Something that could not be clearly seen was ascending slowly, with another creature in its grip, a far smaller creature, which struggled. A soft cold voice quoted or misquoted:

'*Just for a spoonful of jam he betrayed us*
Just for some sugar to sweeten his blood...'

Suddenly, she knew the struggling thing was Simmoleon.

The wingbeats climbed higher, higher – the writhing figure was released and began to fall, screaming, down through endless layers of cloud. The black lightened to grey, grey towers of cumulus and mist-curtains which shifted and dissolved into one another. Other wings converged on the falling shape, smaller but still very large, raven's wings or vulture's wings or harpy's wings, a whole flock of them blotting it out, impeding it, until it didn't fall any more, and the screaming changed, mixing with a kind of gurgle, and then stopped altogether. The wings beat furiously. Two or three droplets escaped, streaming down through the last of the cloud, through empty air and sudden busyness, splashing red onto the ground. Feet trod on them unseeing.

She would have been horrified, but there was no time. The vision was swallowed up as if sucked into a vacuum, and then there was electric light, cosiness, a warm friendly interior. A kitchen.

She had been expecting to see a kitchen for some time – an old-fashioned kitchen with oak beams and hanging bunches of this and that and a stove or Aga, with a fat little cauldron bubbling surreptitiously on the hotplate. But this was a modern kitchen, too small for convenience and littered with knife and chopping board, bowl and saucepan, olive oil and garlic cloves, sliced onions and skinned tomatoes. The cook, too, was all wrong, too young, too handsome, too black, wearing an expression of concentration and a hooded sweatshirt with the hood down and, on the back, the lettering *Jamie Who?* A mouth-watering smell wafted out of the picture, but the witch was frowning.

In the background, a female voice complained: 'I don't see why you always have to cook. We could have got a takeaway.'

The witch stared in bewilderment as the image faded, leaving her with nothing but the smoke and a faint afterscent of frying onions. She drew back, murmuring the words to close the invocation, still frowning slightly.

'Too many cooks,' she said out loud, 'and too little broth. You can't make an omelette without putting all your eggs in one basket. I wish I knew what the hell was going on.'

Witches were supposed to know what was going on, or, if they didn't, to be able to find out. She thought of Simmoleon, falling out of the sky, and the converging wings, and the blood drops hitting the ground far below. He had been a grinnock, a lesser werecreature, ugly, amoral, unpleasant, with a sweet tooth and sour nature – a being of little account, half spirit half substance, gone now into Limbo until the world ended. She could call up another, pester and plague and bribe, but...

But she didn't.

Later that day, using less ethereal channels, she learned an address. She wasn't sure it would be much use, since if the person she wanted was there, the spells would have shown her, but it was worth investigating.

She thought about it when she went to bed, and woke in the dark hours from a nightmare of wings, her head suddenly very cold and clear.

If they knew about the grinnock, they know about me...

He knows about me.

Azmordis – Ingré Manu – the Devil – the lord of Earth – the god of Chaos and Despair – the dark Suit in the Dark Tower – *he knows about me…*

London, twenty-first century

GAVIN LASTED TWENTY-FOUR hours before calling Pen, breaking his resolution when the worry set in that if he didn't she might start exploring Number 7 on her own. It wasn't that he thought of her as a potential girlfriend: himself fifteen, he considered her far too young and in need of general prettification. Perhaps if she were to make up, grow up, jack up her skirts – but for the moment she was a mate, they had shared horrifying adventures, that was what mattered. Determined not to apologise and unsure what to say, he found himself asking her to supper.

Two nights later, with the reluctant consent of her grandmother, Pen was sitting in the Lesters' home in the less elegant part of Clapham, surrounded by his two sisters and younger brother, his mother and grandmother (his father, who did something technical for Thames Water, was at work), two cats and a hamster. To an only child orphaned at an early age, it was all a little overpowering. (The grandmother, Pen decided, did look like Beyoncé, if Beyoncé had been in her sixties and dressed by Primark.) Gavin cooked, haddock in Parma ham with some sort of ratatouille, the finer points of which clearly bypassed his family, though they all expressed appreciation except his older sister Dianna, who had a date and wanted takeaway because it was quicker. His brother Richmond apologised in an aside for the lack of chips and other sister Bobbi offered in mitigation that he made *really great* puddings, especially chocolate mousse.

'He's very good at English,' Gavin's nan confided. 'He could go to college. Cooking is all very well, but you don't get respect. College boys get respect.'

'I think cooking's a great idea,' Pen said loyally. 'Gavin could have his own restaurant, or a TV show.'

'What's TV nowadays?' Gavin's nan dismissed the notion with a wave of her hand. 'I remember when you had to be clever to be on TV; you had to be able to sing or do jokes or talk about art and things. Now, it's all this reality crap – you get just about anybody. They even had our hairdresser's daughter going off to be a model. Model – huh! Bandy Mandy! She's got no looks – no *curves* – just legs like a stick insect and nothing in her head at all. Her mum was so full of it, you couldn't get into the salon without tripping over her ego. Telly's not what it was, I told her. You've got to be loud – you've got to be *common* – to be on TV these days. Look at *Big Brother*. She didn't have any answer to that.'

Nor did Pen. Matty Featherstone was always criticising her for not watching *Big Brother*.

'What do *you* want to be?' Gavin's mum asked by way of a diversion.

'A lawyer,' Pen said.

There was a short pause. Dianna muttered: 'Boring,' not quite under her breath.

Gavin's mum said hastily: 'What sort of lawyer?'

'Crime.'

There was a collective sigh of relief, tangible if not audible. Crime was interesting. Crime was *cool*.

'Like, defending murderers and stuff?' Richmond said, impressed. 'Proving people innocent when they're wrongly accused?'

'Pen could do that,' Gavin said. 'She's pretty smart.'

'Lawyers can get good money,' said his nan, pointedly. 'Lawyers get respect.'

Fortunately for future relations between all concerned, Gavin's mum cleared the plates and they moved on to chocolate mousse.

Later, coming out of the bathroom, Pen overheard Dianna and Gavin talking in the hall.

'She looks like a kid,' Dianna was saying scornfully. 'I thought you were getting back with Josabeth–'

'Look, Pen's just a friend, okay?'

'She isn't even wearing mascara–'

'Mascara isn't a sign of maturity! Anyway, at least she doesn't spend all the time telling me how pretty she is–'

'Not much to tell!'

'– and she's really good company–'

'Yeah? She hardly opened her mouth all through supper. Too stuck up–'

'Posh off!'

Dianna slammed her way out of the house and Pen waited till Gavin went back into the living room, struggling with mortification, and anger, and an idiotic urge to burst into tears. It took more courage to go back downstairs than it would have done to open the broom cupboard again, but she put on what she hoped was a poker face and returned to the family party. She'd felt so adult of late, if not always in a good way, and now she was being condemned because she didn't wear mascara...

But Gavin smiled when she came in, and his mum offered her tea, and his nan said Dianna was a fool, always running after the boys instead of letting them run after her, which made Pen feel a very little better. After all, it didn't matter about Josabeth Collins, whoever she was, because it wasn't as if she really *fancied* Gavin: she just liked him. Sometimes.

'I'll come over at the weekend,' he told her on her way out. 'We'll talk about what to do next.'

She didn't say: *We have to go back into the house.* She didn't need to. The house was the secret which bound them together. Whatever they had told Quorum, they both knew they would go back.

'Right,' said Gavin. 'Torch. Bar of chocolate for emergency rations. Pen-knife. Stun-gun. Piece of paper reminding me who

I am. That's everything I could think of. No point in taking a mobile: there won't be any signal.'

It was Saturday, their designated day for exploration. Eve had gone home till the following day, trusting Pen to Quorum's care, and the butler himself was out shopping. The after-school slot on weekdays wasn't long enough, or so they felt. That meant weekends only, at least until the school holidays.

'I don't have a knife or a stun-gun,' Pen said. She was carrying her little rucksack, which contained a very large torch (the only one she could find), a velvet scrunchie (she was wearing her hair loose again), her personal CV, her notes on the house, two cereal bars, and a spare pair of knickers. 'Anyway, we're only going to *look*. No going through the doors any more. Right?'

'Right.'

'Right…'

'Why is there a set of false teeth on that table?'

'Don't ask.'

The teeth had taken to following Pen around in some mysterious fashion, turning up on the sideboard in the dining room during tea when her grandmother was out, or on top of the new widescreen television, or sitting – if teeth can sit – next to her laptop. Quorum denied moving them and Pen, though suspicious, believed him. The teeth hadn't spoken again: they simply grinned at her. On several occasions she had caught herself almost starting to talk to them, controlling the impulse sternly; she had no intention of becoming the sort of person who had conversations with inanimate objects, especially if the objects in question were prone to answer back. That way lay fairytales, and flying carpets, and magic. She wasn't having any of that.

They went into the utility room and through the front door into Number 7.

The quiet engulfed them like a cocoon, except that a cocoon was a safe place, and Bygone House didn't feel safe. As Quorum had said, it was like being in the still centre of something: the noises were there, on the edge of the silence, the distant murmur that was London, and the other noises, waiting beyond the doors, the unheard noises, the dragon's roar and the screech of the roc and the strumming of long-broken fiddles and the whispers of long-failed plots. Pen thought she could feel the pressure of all those countless worlds teeming and shifting around them.

She said: 'I want to find out who does the cleaning here,' but although they went up to the top floor, tiptoeing tentatively along every passage, they couldn't see anything. There was a table on each landing, one with a vase of daffodils, far too early in the year, the other with a spray of red autumn leaves from no tree Pen or Gavin could recognise. A couple of surreal landscapes hung on the walls – a desert with footprints disappearing across an endless vista of dunes, and a country lane, rutted and puddled, with more footprints, perhaps the same ones, vanishing into a wood – and in an alcove there was an ugly china dog with pointed ears and a squashed muzzle. Outside the rooms, there was nowhere for anyone to hide.

Back downstairs, Gavin said: 'If there was a flea here, we'd have seen it. There's nobody but us.'

'I suppose so. I mean, of course not. It's just…'

'D'you want to try one of the doors?' She nodded. 'Okay, so where do we start?'

After all, it was her house, at least by proxy.

'The library,' Pen said. 'That's where I saw the monk. For one thing, it wasn't dangerous. And… I'm not used to hearing Latin spoken, I only ever see it written down, but I *think* from what he said he'd been interrupted like that before. Which would mean the door sometimes opens on the same place.'

'More of your pattern idea,' Gavin said.

'If connections recur,' Pen said, 'that would be *really* significant.'

'You sound like my science teacher.'

'Good.'

Pen opened the door, more gingerly than ever, nudging it back an inch at a time…

Beyond the Doors
Amsterdam, seventeenth century

THE FIRST THING she saw was the crocodile. It was looking straight at her, its black-and-gold stare unblinking, its parted jaws a-gleam with teeth. For an instant, she stopped breathing.

Then she realised it was stuffed.

She pushed the door open further. Gavin peered past her, one arm moving to encircle her shoulders, though whether by way of protection or restraint, or simply for the reassurance of contact, neither of them could tell. They were gazing into a fair-sized room with a beamed ceiling and natural light pouring through the windows. There was a long wooden bench nearby and shelves round the walls, and every available surface was crowded with an extraordinary jumble of objects – plaster busts, steel helmets, antique glassware, globes, gourds, branches of coral, skulls both animal and human. The remaining wall space was hung with shields and antlers and assorted weaponry, and on the floor there were cauldrons stuffed into woven baskets, clam-shells and tankards and twists of driftwood. It was a collection apparently without theme or function, an Aladdin's cave of bric-a-brac from all over the world. But Pen and Gavin gave it only a brief glance. Their attention focused almost immediately on the man.

He was leaning against the bench with his back to them, one foot on an adjacent stool, a board resting on his knee with paper attached. He was very short and thickset with a fuzz of untidy hair, his clothes from some indeterminate period in history when clothes were rumpled and tucked, baggy and bulky – the sort of clothes that look uncomfortable but in this case had been worn or bullied into comfort. There was a pen behind his ear dribbling ink into his hair and he was holding a sea-shell, turning and turning it to catch the light.

Gavin whispered: 'Have you seen enough?'

'I suppose so...'

The man turned round.

He wasn't beautiful, the way the prince had been – his face, like his body, was thickset, with blunt, soft features – but there was something about his eyes, something Pen would try to recall, long after. They were eyes which didn't just look, they *saw*. Bright curious eyes, discerning and yet somehow detached – the eyes of an observer, fascinated and slightly baffled by the world he was born to see.

He smiled at them both and said something in a language they didn't understand which sounded like a cross between German and gibberish. Then he put down the sea-shell and beckoned. Pen had stepped forward before she thought about it.

Gavin said: '*Pen–!*'

'I'm all right,' she insisted.

She was only a couple of yards away from the door. The man didn't appear to be interested in who they were, or how they got there. His bright curious eyes were fixed on Pen's face. He took her by the shoulders, very gently, turning her to the light the way he had turned the shell. Then he took the pen from behind his ear, dipped it in an open ink bottle, one of several on the bench, balanced the board on his knee and began to sketch.

'For God's sake, Pen–'

'I can't talk now,' she said, without moving her lips.

The man went on sketching. His fingers were stubby and clumsy-looking, but the way he held the pen reminded Gavin suddenly of how he held a knife, when he was filleting something difficult, or slicing vegetables to a precise thickness. There was a kind of certainty in his touch. He's an artist like me, Gavin thought, not in conceit but recognition. That's why he's got all this stuff. These are things he likes to draw.

He's the greatest artist of his day, thought Pen. Perhaps of any day. And he's drawing *me...* There was a bubble of excitement and happiness swelling inside her, that special bubble she had felt only once or twice before – a happiness that had to be suppressed, a feeling too wonderful to let it escape, but she knew the glitter of it was in her face and would shine out of the picture for all time. She couldn't wait to tell her grandmother. *Mijnheer Van Rijn is drawing me...*

Gavin said something and she responded impatiently: 'I mustn't talk.'

The words came out in German and gibberish.

Gavin's expression stiffened. He reached out, taking one step into the room but still clutching the door-frame. The man said: '*Wacht*,' and went on drawing. Gavin waited. There was a quiet a little like the quiet in the house, a moment of time held in isolation – the softness of the light through the windows and Pen's stillness and the tiny scratching of pen on paper. Then the man wrote something at the bottom and passed the sheet to Pen, smiling the same smile with which he had greeted them, a half-smile at once shy and strangely self-possessed.

Pen said: '*Dankzegging*,' as if she meant it and Gavin seized her arm and yanked her abruptly back through the door – back into the twenty-first century – pulling it closed behind them. For an instant her mind blurred... Then she was herself again, or the self she ought to be, leaning on the wall and breathing deeply and trying to be normal.

London, twenty-first century

THE SKETCH WAS in her hand. A picture of a girl whose face was closed but whose eyes were open, open into the self she let no one see, the secret self that burned like a flame in a dark lantern... The signature was printed along the bottom. Rembrandt Van Rijn.

'You did it again,' Gavin said. 'I was losing you.'

'But you brought me back,' Pen said. And: 'Thanks.'

Gavin was looking at the picture. 'It's really good,' he said. 'Was that – *the* Rembrandt? The famous one? We had a talk about him at school.'

'I think so.'

'This would be worth millions,' he said, 'if anyone believed it was genuine.'

They both laughed, more from relief than anything else. Then they sat down on the stairs, unwilling to go back yet, talking things over.

'It's pretty amazing when you think about it,' Gavin said, 'meeting famous people from history and all that. I mean, *no one* else has ever done that – no one. If only we could control it better. Did you start imagining yourself a whole new life just now, like the other time?'

'I don't *imagine* it,' Pen said. 'It sort of... grows. I wasn't quite there, but I was starting to *feel* it – I lived with my grandmother, only she wasn't like my gran here, she was much older, and there was a house on the canal... No, it's gone. I can't remember any more. But each time, I grow a new self, and when I come back, something of it hangs on. It's absorbed back into the everyday me, but it's still there, like an extra layer inside my head. Do you believe in reincarnation?'

'I don't know.'

'Well, supposing you'd had lots of lives, and you could remember them all – they were all a part of who you are now...'

'Don't. My nan has a friend like that – Aisling – she's always going on about former lives, and how beautiful she was, and the adventures she had, and all the sultans and caliphs and warriors who were in love with her.'

'What does she do now?' Pen asked.

'Lives with an ageing hippy in an aromatherapy shop in Brixton.'

That disposed of reincarnation.

'D'you think it fits with your pattern theory?' Gavin said, picking up the sketch again.

'It could do,' said Pen. 'The first time through that door, there was a monk illustrating one of those mediaeval books, and now an artist's studio... There's a theme, isn't there? Art and study and so on.'

'It's a bit vague,' Gavin responded. 'Not like monsters. There's nothing vague about a monster.'

'Something you can get your teeth into,' mused Pen. 'Or vice-versa.'

Gavin tried to laugh but it didn't quite come off. The memory of his close shave with the dragon – that moment of stomach-churning, bowel-melting terror when it had looked straight into his eyes – still haunted him. In those few seconds, he hadn't liked himself. In the past, he'd never thought much about what sort of a person he was: it hadn't been necessary. Like all children of the sun, he'd accepted love and luck and general popularity as the natural order of things, without the need for gratitude or analysis. But now he'd found he could be frightened – abjectly, gut-meltingly frightened – mind and body had let him down. He'd tried to put it behind him but he couldn't: the recollection nagged at him, got between him and his chopping board, oozed into every sauce. He felt contaminated by himself.

When you have been truly afraid, there are two things you can do. You can run away from your fear, and pretend it hasn't happened. Or you can go back to it, and attempt to face it down.

The realisation of what he must do had been sneaking up on Gavin all week. He wanted to ignore it – he wanted never to go near the broom cupboard again – but he couldn't. He didn't like himself, and he didn't like not liking himself. It was that simple. If Pen had suggested a further reconnoitre, he would have accused her of wanting him dead, even though it wasn't true – he would have been angry, indignant, resistant. But she didn't. The suggestion came from him.

'So,' he said. 'So... do you... do you want to check the broom cupboard once more, just to prove your theory?'

'You're kidding,' Pen answered blankly. 'You said – *we* said – we'd never go near it again. First there was the velociraptor, then the dragon and that giant bird thing. Have you got a death wish?'

Pen had no qualms about being afraid. For one thing, she was female, and therefore unencumbered with the trappings of machismo; for another, she thought fear was part of the body's early warning system for staying alive, and as such should be treated with respect.

'If we opened that door three times,' Gavin said, 'and we got three monsters, that would be something definite. Right? I'm not saying we should go through. Just open the door, look, close it again.'

'We always say that,' Pen pointed out, 'and it never happens. Either we get dragged in, or something comes through, or– Look, a huge grizzly bear could come charging into the house, or something with tentacles could grab you and pull you into the past... We can't risk it. Not again. You nearly got killed–'

Gavin thought wretchedly that he agreed with her. He *really* didn't want to go through that door again. However...

'I'll be careful,' he said, hoping that didn't come under the heading of *Famous Last Words*.

There was no point in thinking about it any more. He went over to the door, Pen behind him. He thought turning the handle was the hardest thing he'd ever had to do...

Beyond the Doors
Somewhere in mythical Greece

THIS TIME, THERE were people. A large crowd of people, all absolutely silent. Standing. Staring. Waiting. A silent crowd is rare but despite little fidgets and shufflings from foot to foot this crowd was so quiet you could almost hear it breathing. There was something creepy about it, so many people making so little noise. Pen and Gavin were behind them, looking at the backs of countless heads, all facing the same way. Beyond the crowd was the sea, the azure blue sea of warmer climes, with sky to match. At the edge of the sea, a few yards out from the beach, a girl wearing very few clothes was chained to a rock.

'Oh sh…' said Pen, with restraint.

It was another cliché, thought Gavin. Only this time the familiarity of it didn't encourage him to relax; instead, it pressed alarm buttons. Experience teaches. The girl was olive-skinned with a mop of hair all scribble-curls and a flimsy white dress falling off one shoulder. There were heavy manacles on her wrists and a long chain joined them, running through a shank embedded in the rock. There was no label saying *Sacrifice*: the scenario was obvious without one. She turned for a minute, gazing back at the crowd, and Gavin was amazed to see there was no fear in her face; he couldn't be sure of her expression at that distance but he thought there was a trace of disdain and perhaps determination, as if, having been chosen for this fate, she was resolved to go through it with some sort of dignity.

There's nothing dignified about being eaten, Gavin said to himself. He knew.

The sea beyond the rock began to bubble ominously. Something dark was heaving itself towards the surface. Now seemed like a good time to shut the door.

'There's a monster coming for her,' Pen said, 'isn't there?'

''Fraid so.'

'We ought to do something…'

'Such as?'

'We can't just leave her there!'

'Why not?' said Gavin. 'Everyone else is!'

'But we must… we must do *something*…'

'Too right,' said Gavin, who had had enough of facing his fears. He began to close the door.

Pen lunged instinctively, taking him by surprise, and in the brief tussle that ensued the door jerked out of his grip and they both tumbled across the threshold, though Pen managed to maintain contact with the frame. Gavin swore at her – she apologised – someone in the crowd looked round and went: 'Sssh!'

When they had sorted themselves out it was too late to do anything except watch.

The sea-monster lifted its great head out of the water. It was far bigger than the dinosaur, bigger than roc or dragon: the skull alone must have been over fifteen feet long. Its enormous eyes bulged like those of a frog – accustomed to the glooms of the deep, the slotted pupils were narrowed to threads at the shock of full daylight. Its skin was fish-smooth and mottled in several shades of green; twisted fangs thrust upward from its protruding lower jaw. Strange growths crowned the head, some stiff and knobbly like horns, others more like spiny fronds or spiky fins, but whether they were part of the animal or parasitic corals and weeds it was impossible to tell. It reared up – and up – on an apparently endless length of neck, its gaze sweeping the crowd, then lowered itself towards its designated meal. The girl didn't flinch or scream; she was standing up, rigid with pride or force of will, her snaky curls streaming in the blast from the monster's breath. Gavin thought in passing that although her single garment was revealing she was so thin there wasn't much to reveal, and wondered if a creature that size would be satisfied with such a dainty. Now the head was on a level with her – the fanged muzzle drew closer – a forked tongue emerged, vividly purple, tasting her scent. The girl raised one shackled wrist, reached out... and patted it on the nose.

A gasp ran through the crowd, like the shiver of a sudden chill. Now, she was lifting both arms – the jaws parted, snapped, crunching the chains like breadsticks. Then the head dropped further, resting against the rock, and the girl stepped delicately onto the snout, barefoot on the fish-skin, walked along it, and swung herself into a sitting position behind the crown, grasping the knobbly horns. The crowd, no longer silent, was beginning to fragment. There was a clamour of exclamation and horror – small groups bunching together or fraying apart – people glancing round to see if anyone had started to run. For the first time, Gavin could see the girl full-face. She might have been beautiful, or at least good-looking, but now the change in her expression made her more terrible than the thing she bestrode. Her eyes were narrowed, her mouth widened, not smiling but in a distortion of a smile, a splendour of hatred and triumph. She might be my age, Gavin thought. Not much older. And they made her a sacrifice...

The monster stooped. The crowd splintered, dividing into separate strands of running figures which streamed along the beach. Safety lay above; but there seemed to be only two paths leading up to the bluff, and rocky outcrops enclosed the cove at either end. A wriggling shape had already been plucked from the herd. Gavin didn't look but he heard the shriek, abruptly cut off, and the indescribable sound as jaws met through flesh and bone. Pen couldn't tear her gaze from the girl: her face seemed to shudder at every bite, not with revulsion but with glee.

The creature advanced, beginning to haul its body out of the sea, water cascading from its shoulders. Webbed foreclaws mounted the sand; out in the bay, a huge fin broke the surface as the tail swirled from side to side, lashing the waves into a tumult which no swimmer could pass. A severed arm thumped onto the ground as it chewed its first victim, then, moving with astonishing speed, it picked up boulders in its mouth, hurling them to block the escape routes, penning the rest of the crowd on the beach where it could feast on them at leisure. Flight became panic as people rushed to and fro, scrabbling at the sheer rock-face, beating off both help and hindrance in the blindness of their fear. But there was one who didn't run any more. A young man, standing in the shallows, calling to the girl with anguish and passion in his voice. Her boyfriend, Pen guessed – her lover, thought Gavin – who had perhaps wept when she was chosen, and come to watch her die with a break in his heart. They couldn't understand the language but it didn't matter; his tone said more than any words. But when the girl answered her voice was cold as cold steel, with the throb in it of bitterness unsatisfied, and the monster halted only an instant, while the young man stared into its maw, not fearless but with a kind of futile defiance.

Then it took off his head.

The truncated body crumpled into the surf, staining it a dirty red. The girl howled like a Fury at the glory of her victory. The mob screeched and gibbered, already knowing none would get away. Pen felt the jolt of nausea in her stomach.

And then, at last, someone saw the door.

Why no one had seen it before the two watchers didn't know and couldn't imagine. One or two had noticed *them*, but maybe the door itself had some form of camouflage, some quirk of magic or freak science which had kept it not so much unseen as unremarked. But now somebody *saw*. A man, defeated by the cliff, tumbling onto the sand close by – lurching to his feet – blinking – pointing – calling. Other faces turned, turned towards them, arrested in mid-flight, faces ugly with desperation and terror, warped with sudden hope. There was a fraction of a second while they hesitated, unbelieving – then the whole mob came hurtling across the beach, trampling each other in their eagerness, fighting to reach the portal that was their only way of escape...

London, twenty-first century

PEN AND GAVIN didn't stop to exchange a word. As one they dived back into the house, slamming the door behind them. The gibbering mob vanished into silence. The blood-stained beach, the sea-monster, the avenging rider – all were gone. The quiet closed around them, sealing them in. The only sound was their breathing, hoarse with the aftermath of fear. They stared at one another in the dawning horror of realisation.

'Dear God,' said Pen, 'what have we done? Those people... all those people...'

After a while, Gavin said: 'Even if we'd saved them, what would they do next? This is the twenty-first century. They didn't speak our language – they wouldn't be able to cope in our world. How would they live – *here?*'

Pen shook her head numbly. 'Perhaps... they would have been absorbed. After all, we're part of history too. Only we... *killed* them.'

'No,' said Gavin hollowly. 'We didn't save them. That's all.'

'Is that any better?'

'No.'

After a further pause, he offered: 'They condemned the girl. They must have.'

'Yes, but... nobody deserves what was happening to them. Nobody deserves to be *eaten.*'

Gavin shuddered, possibly from a twinge of empathy.

He said: 'There's no point in getting the guilts. It was all a long time ago, in some half magical place. Our being there wasn't even meant.' So much for facing up to your fears. He had confronted one horror, only to saddle himself with a worse one. Another time, he would let sleeping traumas lie.

A little later Pen said: 'I wonder how she did it. The girl, I mean – taming the sea-monster.'

'Secretly feeding it monster-drops for the past few months?' Gavin suggested.

Pen smiled wanly.

'I expect she was a witch of some kind,' Gavin said. 'She looked like a witch.'

'There aren't any witches,' said Pen, but she didn't sound convinced.

Gavin said: 'Let's go home,' meaning back to 7A. 'We need more chocolate. Very hot and very chocolatey. With brandy and everything.'

'It won't change what we did,' said Pen. Her cheeks felt clammy; she realised she must have been crying.

'I know.'

They went out, leaving the Rembrandt sketch forgotten on the table. After they had gone, something stole softly down the stairs and picked it up, studying it intently for a long time.

QUORUM WAS STILL out. In the kitchen, Gavin found the chocolate, a big tin of Charbonell & Walker, and made the drinks, slightly soothed by the process of preparation. Chocolate and Armagnac had become their restorative of choice.

'We aren't doing too well, are we?' Pen said. 'It's all my fault. I was the one who wanted to go back.'

'I was just as bad,' said Gavin. 'That business with the dragon creeped me out so badly, I had to open the cupboard again, to... to prove something, I suppose. To prove I was brave, I could cope with... whatever. The trouble is, we've treated the past like reality TV. We keep forgetting it really is real.'

He passed Pen a mug of chocolate with a lavish addition of brandy.

'Here, drink this. You look all pinched and shivery.'

'Maybe I'd look better with mascara,' Pen said absently.

'*What?*'

'Sorry. It was your sister, the other night. I... I didn't mean to eavesdrop. I was coming out of the loo.'

'My sister's braindead,' Gavin said savagely. 'Don't pay any attention. The last thing you need to worry about right now is mascara.'

The shrill of the doorbell intruded abruptly. Pen put down her mug.

'Where's Quorum when you need him?' Gavin said. 'He should be around to answer the door. That's what butlers do. We're discussing heavy stuff here.'

'I'll go,' said Pen.

They both went.

There was a girl on the doorstep. A teenage girl about Pen's height with hair dyed a violent purplish auburn and cut to stick up in tufts, though much of it flopped unsuccessfully into her eyes. She had multiple ear-piercings and eyebrow-piercings, a nasal stud and the sort of lip ring known as a snake-bite. Her mascara was laid on like oil paint, an effect that might have discouraged Pen for life. She wore black – black jeans, flat black boots, short black jacket with hands thrust defensively into the pockets.

Even her rucksack was black.

She stared accusingly at Gavin and Pen. 'Who're you?'

'I live here,' Pen said, taken aback.

'Have I come to the wrong house? I'm looking for Bartlemy Goodman. I'd expected some sort of caretaker.'

'I'm the executor of Andrew Pyewackett's Will,' Pen declared, overlooking the claims of Jasveer Patel. 'We're still searching for Mr Goodman – he's the principal beneficiary. Do you know him?'

'Of course I do,' said the girl. 'I was afraid he wouldn't be here. Bugger. I really need to find him urgently.'

'Join the club,' said Gavin. 'So do we.'

'Not as urgently as me,' the girl said curtly. Her voice tended to gruff and under the makeup her face, without being precisely sullen, indicated that sullenness might be an option, if the mood took her. She glared at Pen. 'You're a bit young to be somebody's executor, aren't you? What's really going on here?'

'I *am* the executor,' Pen retorted. 'Mr Pyewackett was rather eccentric. Who are you?'

'Call me Jinx,' said the girl, carelessly. It clearly wasn't her name.

Gavin and Pen exchanged a Look.

'You can't possibly be the executor,' Jinx reiterated. 'Executors have to be lawyers, or something like that, and I know there are lawyers mixed up in all this. I can't remember the firm, but–'

'It's Whitbread Tudor Hayle,' said Pen, skating over the truth, 'and I'm Penelope Tudor.'

'She *is* a lawyer,' said Gavin, supportively. 'What are *you*, anyway? A Goth?'

'I'm a witch,' said Jinx.

Gavin and Pen swapped another Look, a longer one this time. Both of them were thinking of the Fury on the sea-monster. But this girl, whatever else she appeared, didn't seem particularly dangerous.

Pen said, without noticeable enthusiasm: 'You'd better come in.'

CHAPTER SIX
Jinx

London, twenty-first century

Jɪɴx sᴀᴛ ɪɴ the kitchen with a mug of Gavin's hot chocolate, sniffing it suspiciously.

'This has brandy in it,' she said. 'I can smell it.'

'Improves the flavour,' said Gavin.

'Uncle Barty always gives people cocoa with brandy when they've had a shock. He has a special recipe.'

'I knew it!' Gavin exclaimed, distracted from other issues. 'He's a chef, isn't he? He comes from this family of legendary cooks who worked with all the most famous chefs in the world. The name changes – sometimes it's in French, sometimes German – but it's always the same meaning. It's always Goodman. He must know all the secrets of really great cooking – the oldest recipes, the magic ingredients–'

'I don't know about *magic*,' said the witch. 'Barty's a good cook. He isn't a chef, though. He just likes making nice food.'

'Have you... have you *eaten* his cooking?' Gavin demanded, on a reverential note.

'Of course,' said Jinx. 'What else would I do with it?'

'Gavin wants to be a chef,' Pen explained. 'He thinks Mr Goodman can teach him. But Andrew Pyewackett said he was a person who looked after things – a kind of professional guardian. That's why he left him the house.'

Jinx considered this. 'That's the house without a door,' she said, evidently unfazed by the omission. 'Number 7. Why does it need a guardian?' And, after a pause: 'Could you two stop *looking* at each other like that? Anyone would think you were concealing a murder.'

'Close,' said Gavin.

'Cocoa for shock,' nodded Jinx. 'You don't have to be a witch to smell a rat. As well as the brandy.'

'What sort of witch are you?' asked Pen, stalling for time. 'Are you into – what do they call it? – Wicca?'

'Baskets,' said Jinx. (For a minute, owing to mumspeak, Gavin thought she was being offensive.) 'I don't do any of that New Age crap. I'm just an ordinary witch. The witchy kind.'

'Do you do spells?' said Gavin, on what he hoped was an ironic note.

'Sometimes,' said Jinx, guardedly. 'The spells showed me this place.' She didn't mention more mundane research into solicitors and Wills. 'I got the gene from my great-grandmother. She had a hook nose and an evil eye and put curses on people, but I'm not going to end up like that. When I'm old, I want to be more... cuddly.'

She certainly doesn't look very cuddly now, Gavin thought. The eyelashes framed her eyes like iron railings, black and spiky. If you got too close, you could be impaled on them.

'So how come you know Bartlemy Goodman?' he said. 'You called him *uncle*.'

'I grew up in the village where he lived. He isn't my uncle – he isn't anyone's uncle – but he's an uncle sort of person. He taught me... how *not* to be a witch. That's the important part. Too much magic drives you insane.' Almost as an afterthought, she added: 'He's a wizard.'

It fits, thought Pen. Damn. Mr Pyewackett must have known.

'Is *he* insane?' she asked bluntly.

'No, of course not. He doesn't use magic much – hardly at all, really. Like I said, that's the important part. He likes cooking best.' She flicked a glance at Gavin. 'He says, when you've been around fifteen hundred years, you have a lot of time to develop special interests.'

'*Fifteen–*'

'Those people you thought were his relatives – well, they were probably all him. Wizards can live a very long time if they want to.'

'Andrew Pyewackett was over a hundred and fifty,' Pen volunteered. 'But I don't think he was a wizard. It was just the house. Anyway, he was dead when I met him.'

'How dead?'

'Quite dead,' said Pen, 'but it didn't stop him talking.'

'When are you going to tell me what's going on here?' Jinx demanded.

'When are you going to tell us... everything you haven't told us already?' Gavin riposted.

'And,' said Jinx, temporarily diverted, 'why is there a set of false teeth on that worktop? I don't like the way they're looking at me...'

EXPLANATIONS TOOK A long time, and none of them were completely frank. Pen and Gavin said nothing about fear or guilt and, by unspoken consent, avoided any mention of how they had slammed the door in the face of the fleeing crowd. Jinx said: 'Oh, *portals*. I don't do portals,' in the world-weary voice of someone who knows from personal experience there are a lot of worlds to be weary of. She was sixteen, still at school (when not playing truant), and the other two instinctively resented her insider knowledge without being quite sure what it was she knew. On her part, Jinx was wary of them because they were Londoners (she had always envied people who lived in London), because Pen was much too clever and Gavin much too fit, because 7A had a butler and all the indices of class and privilege. She decided, with the ingrained superiority of her sixteen years, that they were too young to be burdened with the activities of the Oldest Spirit – the Lord of the Dark – and what he might or might not do. They had enough to worry about with Bygone House.

When Quorum returned, he was introduced to Jinx, whom he eyed rather doubtfully, and they moved their conference to the living room while he made lunch.

The teeth were waiting for them on the coffee table.

'What are *they* doing there?' Jinx said. 'Are they following us around?'

'They might be,' Pen admitted. 'They were Mr Pyewackett's teeth. I think they could be haunted. Sometimes they talk with his voice.'

'Haunted false teeth!' Gavin scoffed.

'Or they could be possessed.'

'I never heard of any demon inhabiting a set of dentures,' Jinx said. She extended her finger towards them. Suddenly, the teeth sprang, snapping viciously – Jinx pulled her finger back just in time. Gavin started violently.

'Don't *do* that!' Pen said. 'If you can't behave, I'll... I'll put you in a glass, with a hankerchief over it. Get out of that if you can.'

'We've learnt how to move around,' said the Teeth, smugly. 'You can't fence us in. We're the toughest teeth in town!'

'My God,' said Gavin. 'They *are* possessed.'

'A glass with a very heavy book on the top,' Pen muttered.

'Of course we're not possessed,' the Teeth protested. 'Ignorant boy! We're not haunted either. No one accuses you of ghostly or demonic possession, just because you want to have a conversation, do they? Talking is normal. And after three years in Andrew Pyewackett's mouth–'

'Rank,' said Pen.

'– naturally we're going to sound like him. Things rub off.'

'In this house,' Pen said severely, 'that seems to be the excuse for everything. Everything weird, anyway.'

'It could be a sort of magical infection,' Jinx suggested. 'Like chickenpox. You said Andrew Pyewackett was an animated corpse, so... maybe the teeth caught animation off him. This space/time prism... thing... puts the whole place on the edge.'

'The edge of what?' said Gavin, who suspected she didn't know what she was talking about.

'Reality,' said Jinx, who didn't, but was determined not to show it.

'Do you know why – how – you're alive?' Pen asked the Teeth.

'The witch might be right,' they said airily. 'Then again, she might not.'

'I don't believe they know any more than we do,' Gavin muttered.

'As to the *why*, we told you that. We're here in an advisory capacity, to watch over you and... give advice.'

'You didn't watch over her next door,' Gavin remarked.

'We're not stupid!'

'You haven't given me any advice,' Pen pointed out.

'Don't go next door?'

'They're useless,' said Gavin dismissively.

The Teeth made a great leap and bit him on the arm.

Beyond the Doors
London, seventeenth century

IN THE CITY, the dying started slowly, one body at a time. They carried them out late at night when no one would see, hoping to bury them quickly, quickly, so the dead would be gone with the disease they died of, but soon there was too much work for the gravediggers to keep up, and the diggers themselves were sickening, and the dead cart would creak and groan through the streets as if of its own volition, calling for its nightly cargo. To begin with, they wrapped the corpses in sheets, to hide the tell-tale boils and the last anguish on twisted features, but sheets were precious, and the corpses kept on coming. Once, a beggar stole a cloth off the cart; they found him swathed in it three days later, stiff as a plank of wood. The word *plague* crept from lip to ear like a foul whisper, for the superstitious dared not say it aloud, and the doctors who tried to treat it died with their patients, sweating and coughing in the final fever. Roses, some named it, for the red rash that flowered on their skin. *Ring-a-ring-a roses...* The pickings grew lean for both tradesmen and thieves, and when Ghost went to Wily Jake's in Cripplegate he saw the house was shut up and the windows boarded, and the woman who cooked for him peered from an upper casement, saying Wily Jake was counting pennies in hell.

'They say there's a special place for the Jewry,' she said, 'and you can bet that's where he's gone, lying his way into Purgatory to fence the gold from dead men's teeth.'

Ghost said he hoped so.

Some people fled into the country, if they had friends or family there; some locked themselves in their chambers, eating and defecating in the same confined space; some tried to go about their business, with a posy of herbs in one pocket and a prayer in the other, shrinking from contact with their fellows. The king gave orders and the clergy got in touch with God and the nobles shut themselves behind high gates and kept company with their own kind. But the plague sneaked in everywhere, slipping through keyholes and under doors, making no difference between merchant and servant, prince and peasant. In the loft the Lost Boys talked and joked a little louder each evening to drown out their fear, growing reckless as the crisis deepened, stealing from under the very noses of distracted shopkeepers, pinching food from kitchens even as the cook collapsed. Ghost told them not to go near the sick but he knew they could hardly help it; the contagion was invisible and all-pervasive, the graveyard sigh that you breathed in unawares – a man might appear healthy one moment and be dead a few hours later. Ghost's own fears grew by the day, by the hour. Every night on their return he counted his little band, and gazed hungrily into their faces, and would have hugged them if he had known how.

Then the day came when one did not return.

They found Sly in Groper's Alley, shivering and stammering from the fever. Ghost wrapped him in a blanket, and carried him into the yard beside the Grim Reaper, and stayed with him till it was over, though the boy was hallucinating and didn't seem to recognise him. He had no fear for himself, he wasn't sure why. It was as if something set him apart, rendering him impervious to the pestilence, some aspect of his strangeness, the alien quality that made him who he was. There were a few like that, the chosen few, who walked the streets without a qualm, mysteriously invulnerable – scar-faced Cullen, who was rumoured to have survived the sickness in his youth, and now drove the dead cart, growing richer with every corpse, and Big Belinda, whom nothing touched. The porter had died early on, and Clarrie, and the witch who told fortunes.

The tapster came out of the Grim Reaper, telling Ghost to take the boy away, but he would not go too close, and Ghost looked at him with stony eyes, until he backed down.

Later that night he heard the grinding wheels of the dead cart as it lumbered down Porkpie Street, and lifted the little corpse easily – it weighed almost nothing – and watched the vehicle trundle off into the dark with the hunched figure of Cullen perched up in front, like a vulture on a pile of carrion. Every so often he would ring a handbell so people knew he was coming, not a deep solemn knell but a light, tinny, clanging noise, almost like the bells on the harness of a horse in a procession. Long after, when his life in the city was all but forgotten, Ghost would wake from nightmares hearing that tuneless tinkle, and the slow ominous groan of the dead cart wheels.

Back in the loft, the other boys said little about their late companion. They were too busy trying to live, knowing the living was running out. One-Ear was feeding titbits to Edwin; the rodent looked fat and gleamy-eyed. It was a good time for rats.

'We should leave the city,' Ghost said, but they gazed at him in bewilderment. Where would they go? They knew no other place, no other life. Beyond the city was a strange country with nothing for them to steal and nowhere for them to be. Better to die here, if die they must, in the dark familiar world which was their home.

Death was fearful, but leaving the city was unthinkable.

Ghost's heart ached with a pain he barely understood, the grief of present loss, the foreknowledge of loss to come. He knew it wouldn't be long now.

Maggot was the next to go, sickening in his sleep four nights later. Ghost wanted to take him out of the loft to protect the others, but it was too late to prevent infection; they must rely on their meagre resources of youth and strength. Little Snot died almost unnoticed, and his brother Filcher vanished the following afternoon, lost in the wharfs and warehouses that bordered the river. Ghost liked to think that somehow he had escaped, though in his gut he knew it was merely a fancy. Then it was the twins' turn, Ratface going first, leaving Pockface to succumb, whimpering and abandoned, two days after. He had wanted to go with his twin, and cried piteously for Ratface to wait for him, but Ghost dared not keep the body to fester in the heat, and the corpse cart creaked inexorably on its slow rounds, parting them in death as they had never been parted in life.

'Bury them together,' Ghost told Cullen when he carried the second twin out. 'I have the money. I can pay.'

'Bury them! Ha! There's no time for burying. They'll go in the pit with the other garbage. Give me your money and I'll kiss them for you!'

Cullen made a great show of his hardiness, often embracing the bodies of the girls; Ghost shuddered to think what he might do with them when he was alone. With his disfigured face and croaking voice he was not popular among living women, but the dead could not be so particular.

'I've kissed them myself,' Ghost said, and pressed his lips to Pockface's forehead, before lifting him onto the cart.

'Your turn next,' said Cullen with more than his usual malice; he would not forget his partner's death.

Ghost shrugged and stepped back, letting the cart roll on.

A louring heat had settled over the city like a miasma, a layer of air almost too thick to breathe, warm and clammy and seething with invisible life, with evil microbeings whose presence only Ghost could sense. He could imagine them swirling around his head or the heads of his friends, crawling over lips and tongue and into nostrils and eyes. 'Bacteria,' he said, though he couldn't recall where the word came from.

'Back what?' said One-Ear.

'I ain't backt yet,' retorted Cherub. 'Not in any area.'

'We must wash,' said Ghost, groping for memories long gone astray. 'Face and hands. We must wash them off. And get rid of that rat. It's killing us all.'

'He's my friend,' responded One-Ear, stroking Edwin's throat. The rat made a sniffing, whickering noise, flicking Ghost a glance which was almost like a challenge.

Ghost rarely lost control, but stress and suffering had made him brittle. The knife flashed out, plunging into the animal's stomach, wrenched back in a gush of blood. Then he seized it by the tail and hurled it out of a window-hole, splashing Weasel's face in passing with a red spray. One-Ear started to his feet with a cry of fury which stopped at the sight of the knife.

Ghost had never used it against his own gang, never even threatened them with it. Now, he cleaned it slowly, folded it away, slowly. One-Ear stared at him in bitterness and hurt.

'He was my friend. He was one of us. You killed one of *us*. You're no different from Mr Sheen.'

Ghost was trembling, though he never trembled after a killing. 'Don't ever say that again,' he said, but his tone had lost its usual edge.

Weasel died next.

'And then there were three,' Ghost said to himself.

Ten little Indians... He was remembering a verse from long ago and far away. *A big rat swallowed one And then there were three...*

He would do anything – *anything* – to save Cherub and One-Ear. He would steal a boat and row them downriver, into the country where the air was clean – he would *make* them come, whatever they said – they were two but he was one, and strong, stronger than them both, and though they feared and hated him for it he would drag them away somewhere they could be safe, far from the leering rats and the crawling bacteria and the poisonous city stench. As in a dream he heard the bell of the dead cart and he knew it was calling for them, though they still lived and breathed and reached out to him. Then their faces blurred and the loft turned upside-down and his last thought, his very last, was that he had made a mistake, and it was him the cart was coming for – it was *him*...

Ring-a-ring-a-roses
Run through the town
Ding-a-ling the dead cart
We all fall down.

Ghost fell into a fever, and knew nothing more.

London, twenty-first century

GAVIN'S ARM WAS bandaged and the Teeth were imprisoned in a glass with an atlas on the top and the slightly dubious prospect of being let out early for good behaviour, if they were capable of it.

'Familiars,' said Jinx, knowledgeably. 'Witches often have them, a cat or a toad or something, though no one in my family ever bothered much. Of course, it isn't usual for a lawyer to have a familiar, but times change. You could start a trend.'

'I've read about familiars,' said Pen, who had googled almost everything at some stage. 'You're supposed to suckle them with a third teat. I don't have a third teat, and even if I did there is absolutely no way–'

'Let's not go there,' Gavin said hastily. 'Forget the bloody teeth. What about Bartlemy Goodman? If you came here to find him–' he was addressing Jinx '– then shouldn't you be looking? By... by magic, or whatever. *If* you know any.'

'Mr Pyewackett didn't hold with magic,' Quorum reminded them. 'He wouldn't want witchcraft going on in this house.'

'He's dead,' Jinx pointed out unnecessarily. 'Anyway, I wasn't going to do any.' She had no intention of exhibiting her inadequate skills to the two younger ones. 'What I need is to see the house next door.'

'You've seen it,' said Gavin. 'It's right there.'

'Inside.'

None of them were enthusiastic about that. Quorum said it was dangerous, Pen said it was private. Gavin simply looked mulish. Secretly, Pen didn't want anyone taking over her adventure – that is, *responsibility* – and they were all unsure about this newcomer with her body-piercings and her attitude and her offhand manner towards too many things they considered very on-hand. However, she clearly *did* know Bartlemy Goodman, and she might be of some help finding him, and she wouldn't be able to help – assuming she could – unless they gave her a chance. Or so Pen reasoned. Gavin, rather reluctantly, went along with her reasoning, and Quorum simply reiterated his warnings about danger.

'I know about danger,' said Jinx – offhandly. 'Witches do. Been there, done that.'

(Well, of course she knew about danger. It was in the dictionary, she could look it up.)

'As long as you don't touch any of the doors,' Pen said.

'If you go through,' said Gavin, 'and get lost, or eaten, or absorbed, we aren't coming to look for you.'

With as much solemnity as you can infuse into sliding a rack of coats aside and inserting a key into a lock, they went through into Number 7.

'What are those scratches?' Jinx inquired, scanning the door panels.

'That was the velociraptor,' Gavin said, and, though she didn't betray any reaction, for the first time Jinx was genuinely spooked. It is one thing to hear about a dinosaur in the broom cupboard; it's quite another to see the physical evidence. She found herself looking over her shoulder as they entered the hall, listening with witch-senses to the quiet that seemed to swallow all sound, feeling the looming not-quite-menace of the doors. This was a place so magical that no spell could enter here: it would be distorted out of shape, warped into some mutant form by the sheer pressure of overlapping space/time. Here, if you waved a wand, it might sprout a snake's head and bite you; if you kissed a prince, you might sleep for a hundred years and wake to find yourself turning into a toad. Not that Jinx had ever had anything to do with wands or princes. Her charms had always been of the most basic variety.

'Well,' said Gavin, softly – they always spoke softly there – but with scepticism, 'are you picking up any sinister vibes?'

'I don't know,' said Jinx. 'Have you dropped some?'

'That's the broom cupboard,' said Pen, hurriedly. 'And *that's* the door into the study or library or something – where I saw the monk and Rembrandt sketched me. Here's the sketch: I'd forgotten it.'

'It's quite like you,' Jinx said critically, 'in an old-fashioned sort of way. Very… sixteenth-century.'

'Seventeenth,' said Pen.

She *would* know, thought Jinx, who had picked a century at random. Smug.

She said, looking at the vase of twigs: 'So who does the cleaning and arranges the flowers and everything? Your butler?'

'No,' said Pen. 'We don't know. I've been meaning to find out. Could a magical house – a space/time prism – clean itself?'

'Of course not,' said Jinx, who hadn't a clue.

They went upstairs. By now, Jinx was becoming blasé, at least on the surface.

'More doors,' she said. 'Are they all portals, or do any of them open on ordinary rooms?'

'We haven't checked yet,' said Gavin.

Jinx touched one door-handle – she really wanted to open it, just to prove that she could, just to show she wasn't overawed – but the knob gave her pins-and-needles, and she drew her hand back sharply. She walked along the corridor, stopping in front of the alcove with the china dog, studying it with folded arms and a slight frown tugging at her pierced eyebrows. For a couple of minutes she didn't say anything at all.

'Like that, do you?' said Gavin. 'My nan would. She bought a blue cat in a junk shop in Brixton. She has a thing for china animals.' His tone suggested that while such foibles could be tolerated in a nan, they wouldn't do in someone his own age.

'I don't like it at all,' said Jinx. 'Things shouldn't try to look like what they aren't; it isn't healthy. And a china dog really mings.'

'What are you talking about?'

'Can't you see?'

Gavin and Pen stared at the object in question, but although deeply unattractive, it conveyed no hint of camouflage, no underlying mystery. It was just a china dog.

Jinx sighed, made a curious gesture with her index and little finger, and mumbled: '*Uvalé! Fia!*' with a nonchalance which hid her lack of certainty.

The china dog seemed to shrink in upon itself and turned yellow as if with a form of occult embarrassment. Its pointed ears grew a little pointier; its eyes elongated into narrow slits of umber, squinting sidelong at its audience. Paws lengthened into hands and feet, multi-fingered and multi-toed. It was more or less naked but Pen noted with relief that it wore what appeared to be a leather loincloth or boxer shorts, she couldn't tell which and didn't like to stare. (Possibly leather boxers were *de rigueur* for goblins this year.) Once its disguise had completely disseminated he – it was presumably a he – slid his gaze over the three of them, settling finally on Jinx.

'You're a witch,' he said. His speech was less archaic than that of most goblins, with no brogue or lilt but instead a trace of the Ridings in his accent.

'You're a goblin,' said Jinx.

Pen and Gavin, for the first time, were seriously impressed with their newfound ally, though Gavin wasn't showing it because he was determined to look cool and Pen wasn't showing it because this was her patch and she was too taken aback at finding it invaded.

'Are you the one who does the cleaning?' she demanded.

The goblin nodded. 'I like tidy,' he volunteered. 'I always kept workshop tidy. That's what gaffer taught me. Happen life isn't always in order, but keep job neat and house clean and your mind stays fresh. Didn't hold for him, sithee, but principle was good.'

'Who's your... gaffer?' Jinx asked.

'That was betimes,' said the goblin. 'He'll be long agone. I don't reckon much to the years or the days, here. We're on edge of too many ages to keep count.'

'How did you get in?' said Gavin. 'Through one of the doors?'

'Aye. The owd man opened it, just a crack – a crack for peeking – and I skittered through. He jumped near out of his skin, and banged door shut, and came squinnying for me round every corner, but he didn't see me again. Never a one saw me, till now.'

'Was that Andrew Pyewackett?' Pen said.

'I didn't know his name, but he was owd a long time, and he wore an owd reeky coat all sweat and mothballs, and when he was gone there was another, with a different coat that reeked the same. But they both had good shoes, the leather stitched small, though never so small or so fine as those I made for gaffer long ago.' He jerked his head at Pen's trainers. 'Your shoes now, that's quality and comfort, but they're no shoes for a lady. I could make you shoes to dance in, with leather soft as spidersilk and dewdrops for diamonds. 'Tis a gurt shame to put such dainty feet in those clumping things.' Startled and rather gratified, Pen was unable to respond.

The goblin added, with a glance at Jinx: 'Them boots are rubbish.'

'What is this?' said Gavin. 'A fashion show?'

'Never mind my boots,' Jinx interrupted, secretly annoyed. 'Why did you stay here? Are you a house goblin?'

'Nay. I have skills no house-carl could be framing. Time was, I was best in all the kingdom, happen in all the world. I doubt there's any now can make shoes like gaffer and I, not if those boots o' yourn are owt to go by. But I had to answer to a higher Master, one we don't name.' His voice dropped, and his yellow skin grew green at the memory. '*He* was my first Master, first and last, and He is one you don't betray, but I betrayed him, werefolk though I am, and now I must hide here for evermore. He waits behind every door, and beyond, in the Time Outside, but he can't see within these walls. There's too much magic for spellsight and mindsight to pierce the roke.'

'He?' said Jinx. 'Which... *He*?' And something in her tone made the others think that she already knew the answer.

'We don't name Him,' said the goblin. 'You're a witch. You should know.'

'Yes, I know,' said Jinx.

'Who are we talking about?' asked Gavin, trying to sustain a scornful attitude. 'The Devil?'

'Well,' said Jinx, 'he uses the title. Some of the time.' And he's retiring, which is confidential information, and I know it, and he knows I know, and he may be after me...

There was no point in worrying, but she did.

'The Devil,' she went on. 'Azmordis. The Lord of the Dark. He has lots of names.'

'You're saying,' Gavin persisted, 'there really is some kind of super-bad-guy out there, responsible for all the evil in the world?'

'Oh no,' said Jinx. 'People manage plenty of evil without his help; we're good at that. But I suppose he *is* a super-bad-guy, or one of them. The one at the top.'

'Then there should be a super-good-guy,' Pen said. 'Like... you know... God. You have to have balance.'

'It depends *which* God,' said Jinx. 'And what weapon He's holding.'

There was a short, depressed silence.

'This is getting silly,' Pen declared – 'You're telling me,' Gavin said – and, to the goblin: 'If you do the cleaning, why didn't you fix the broken window?'

'It was on the Outside.' The goblin almost shivered. '*He* might have looked through – might have seen me. I can't go near Outside.'

'You wouldn't like to come next door, for tea or something? You must have been awfully lonely here, all these years.'

'I can't leave this place,' the goblin reiterated. 'Not even to go Next Door. But 'tis good to see humanfolk again, especially childer, bless your bonnie face.'

Pen went slightly pink.

Jinx, aware that she was not being labelled bonnie, and her footwear was substandard, said rather sharply: 'I suppose you have a name, while we're chatting?'

'Aye. But it's not for the likes o' you. Names have power, as you well know, and I'll not be telling mine to any hagling who's passing through.'

'Rumpelstiltskin,' said Gavin.

'He was in silk trade,' said the goblin. 'I'm a cobbler.'

'Rumpelstiltskin will do,' said Jinx, 'until we learn different.'

'Can you tell us what you did,' Pen intervened, 'when you betrayed the – the – *Him*?'

'Criticised his hoofwear, probably,' muttered Gavin. Jinx was surprised into swapping a grin.

'It's a long story,' said the goblin.

'We can sit on the floor.'

THEY WENT BACK to 7A without opening any of the doors.

'That was a pretty fairytale,' said Gavin.

'He's werefolk,' said Jinx. 'What did you expect?'

'You don't mean you believe it?'

'I'm not sure. It doesn't matter. What bothers me is the part about *Him* – Azmordis. He's involved in all this: I can feel it. He's–'

'We've got time travel, magic and monsters,' said Gavin. 'We don't want the Devil as well.'

Pen was silent, thinking about something the goblin had said. *He waits behind every door...* Perhaps just a turn of phrase. Perhaps – a piece of the jigsaw, a thread in the weave, the key to the cipher.

'Whatever,' Jinx was saying. 'Look, it's time I was off. Thanks for... well, thanks.' Not that there was anything to thank them for.

'We ought to ask her back,' Gavin said in an undervoice, as she ran down the steps. 'She *is* useful. She spotted Grumbleshoestring, and she knows Goodman. We need her.'

'I suppose so.' Pen was sure her grandmother wouldn't approve of all that body-piercing. She still had to vet Gavin, and the addition of a sixteen-year-old Goth who claimed to be a witch wouldn't go down well at all.

Pen and Gavin were still hesitating when Jinx went out.

She waved carelessly, glanced right and left, and stepped into the road.

The car was parked, and there was no one in the driving seat – afterwards, Pen was certain about that. An empty car, engine off, waiting a little too far from the curb. It leaped forward without warning in a killer swerve, the engine roaring into sudden life – there were hands on the wheel, a dim shape behind the windscreen – the long white bonnet hurtled straight for Jinx. Gavin cried: 'Look out!' – clearing the steps in a single jump and racing towards her. Pen, rigid with horror, didn't move for what seemed like an age, though actually it was only a second or two. She saw Jinx check her stride, starting to turn, saw the left wing catching her a blow which flung her against another stationary car – saw Gavin make a grab for her and drag her onto the pavement. Then somehow she was there too, dropping to her knees to cradle Jinx's head on her lap, and there was blood – blood on the pavement, on Jinx's temple, on her own hands. Quorum rushed out of the house, telephone in hand, and the white car was gone, and Gavin said: 'I didn't get the number. I didn't get the bloody number,' and swore without reserve. Jinx's stiff eyelashes tried to flutter; she murmured: 'Shit' very quietly, and then went still.

For a moment Pen thought she was dead.

THE AMBULANCE WAS there in fifteen minutes, by which time Quorum had found a pulse, Pen had staunched the bleeding with towels, and Jinx had begun to recover consciousness.

'We're really racking up the injuries,' Gavin said. The rapid action had aggravated his own half-healed wounds. 'That car drove at her deliberately. We both saw it. D'you think it has something to do with... everything else?'

'It must do,' said Pen. 'But...'

At least the monsters and mirages could be shut behind the doors of Number 7. This was the real world turning against them, and there was no way to shut it out. This was Fear coming home.

They went with Jinx to the hospital and learned with relief that she wasn't seriously hurt. She had evidently struck her head on the parked car, causing possible concussion, and had suffered extensive bruising and the inevitable broken ribs where the moving vehicle had hit her. In shock from the accident and baffled by her clinical surroundings, Jinx herself was the last to realise she was going to be all right.

'If I don't make it,' she said, clutching Pen's hand, 'tell Bartlemy... about Azmordis. He has to find... the Devil's apprentice...'

'Great line,' said Gavin. 'Shame it isn't your last.'

Since her next-of-kin were in the country – Jinx said she didn't want to call them anyway, it was making too much fuss – they took her back to 7A that night, and installed her in the spare bedroom. Gavin left after supper promising to come back the next day and Pen went to look at the Teeth, which had started to chew their way through the atlas, getting stuck around South America. Once released, they jumped up and down spitting out bits of cartography and boasting of their prowess.

'We – are – the Teeth! We – are – the Teeth! We can chew up the world – at least as far as Brazil. Nothing much left after Brazil. Today, the world, tomorrow, the telephone directory! We – are – the Teeth! We–'

'You're meant to be here to help,' Pen interrupted. 'Don't you have any idea what's going on?'

'Haven't a clue! *But* we can chew!'

It had been a long day. Pen gave up and went to bed.

IN THE MORNING, Jinx was ensconced on the sofa looking fragile, with the bleared remnants of yesterday's eyeliner and mascara making her appear even more bruised than was actually the case. Pen sat on a chair beside her, realising she was stuck with the friendship whether she liked it or not and determined to make the best of it.

'Did you see who was driving that car?' she asked.

'No,' said Jinx. 'Did you?'

'When it was parked, it looked empty. Then as it shot forward there was someone there, but I couldn't make out a face or anything. I couldn't even be sure if it was a man or a woman.'

'It doesn't matter,' said Jinx. 'They were trying to kill me. That's the important bit.'

'You should tell the police.'

'The cops?' Jinx was contemptuous, evidently wishing to enhance her tough-girl image. (If she had one.) 'What good would they do?'

'They might find out whose car it was,' Pen said, struggling to hang onto reality.

Jinx didn't even bother to answer.

'You think it's... *him*?' Pen pursued, hating herself for sounding melodramatic. 'Why would he...?'

Jinx tried to shrug, and suddenly Pen saw she was shivering. A wave of feeling rushed over her, part unexpected sympathy, part remorse for her unfriendliness. She would have reached for her hand, but the other girl was huddled into her own arms, ribs twingeing at every move.

'I don't know,' she said. 'I don't know anything like enough. Or maybe I know too much. Maybe that's the problem.'

'Too much about – the Devil – Azmordis – whatever you called him?'

Jinx gave a sort of brusque half-nod.

'In stories,' said Pen, who never read any, 'when a person knows too much, they *always* get murdered before they can tell anyone. It happens so often it's a total cliché. If you tell me, now, there'll be no point in murdering you, will there? Nobody ever gets murdered for something they've already told.'

'Or we could both be killed,' Jinx said without humour. 'Bartlemy's the one I have to tell. He'll know what to do. You're... how old are you? Twelve?'

'Thirteen!'

'Whatever. You're too young to be mixed up in all this.'

'I *am* mixed up in it,' Pen said, trying not to take offence, and failing.

There was a pause – a long, brooding sort of pause. Quorum came in with tea to which Jinx added three heaped teaspoonfuls of sugar.

When he had gone Pen said: 'Bartlemy Goodman isn't here. I am. And Gavin. I mean, he isn't here right now, but he will be. He's in this too. We need to know exactly what's going on. So we can... do something about it.'

Jinx gave the kind of laugh that has no laughter in it. 'None of us can do anything about it.'

'In the hospital,' Pen persisted, fishing, 'you mentioned... the Devil's apprentice?'

More pause. More brooding.

At last Jinx said: 'All right. Since you're doing this executor thing, I suppose you should know... You said your grandmother would be back later, right?' She didn't have much use for grandmothers (or great-grandmothers), from personal experience, but another adult around was another person to look out for trouble, even if they didn't know about it. And Pen, Jinx reasoned, needed adult protection, though naturally *she* didn't.

'Yes,' said Pen, 'but I haven't told her anything about... well, anything, really.'

She was uncertain how Eve would react to their new guest, but hoped, in view of the accident, that she wouldn't object too much.

'Of course not.' Jinx tugged at her hair, a leftover gesture from when it had been longer. 'No one tells grownups the important stuff. Barty's different – your butler too. The thing is, sometimes it helps to have people there...'

'The Devil's apprentice?' Pen prompted.

'It has nothing to do with the house,' Jinx said. 'At least, I don't think so… If there's a connection, I haven't a clue what it is. This is about Azmordis. The Devil. He's retiring…'

'*Retiring*?' Pen looked blank. 'But… he's an immortal, isn't he? I thought – being the Devil was a job for life. And life is, like… forever.'

'Even immortals get old,' said Jinx, clutching her tea. 'Actually, very *very* old. The way I hear it, he's tired and jaded and just wants to sleep in Limbo until the end of Time. Whenever that is. But he has all the might of the Dark Tower, and thousands of servants and slaves, and minions and henchmen, and – and shadowy fingers in a million different pies, and centuries of plotting, and scheming, and snarling up the world, and he doesn't want to throw all that away. So he needs a successor to learn his diabolical skills and… take over. He needs an apprentice.'

This time, the nature of the pause was different. It was a pause of cold shock, of unbelief, of jumbled thoughts coming together in chaos.

Pen said at last: 'There really is a Dark Tower?'

'Yes,' said Jinx. 'Most things really are, somewhere or other. Magical dimensions and so on. Barty used to say, we have infinity and eternity. That means there's room for *everything*. Anything we can imagine, it's out there. He said, you should never underestimate the power of human imagination.' She added, a little sadly: 'He often said things like that.'

'I don't have any imagination,' Pen said. Once, she had been proud of it.

She was thinking: There's more to this girl than meets the eye. A lot more…

'So who's the apprentice going to be?'

'I don't know,' said Jinx. 'But it's a human. That's the worst part. A human with the Gift – witchkind, like me, only far more powerful. The thing is, there aren't enough of the Old Spirits left, and those there *are* all hate each other, and lesser werefolk don't have the right potential. So it has to be a human. Then they get – demonised, I suppose. Think of it: a human become immortal, with dark superpowers, ruling an evil empire as old as Time, with all the bright new ideas we humans have. Like... like atomic bombs, and germ warfare, and global warming...'

There was a long, still moment. Then Pen said: 'If you're making this up –'

Jinx made the noise generally written: 'Huh!', only it didn't sound like that. 'That's why I have to find Bartlemy,' she went on. 'He'll know what to do, if anyone does. If he doesn't–'

'What?'

'Then we're probably all going straight to Hell.'

LATER THAT DAY, Eve Harkness returned to find a teenage Goth with a questionable pseudonym and several broken ribs residing on the sofa. On interrogation, Jinx admitted she had a mother, and the mother had a phone number, and yes, she had called already, explaining she had had a slight accident, and was perfectly all right, and was staying with some people who knew Bartlemy, who was an old family friend. Anyway, she would be well enough to go home tomorrow.

Eve said: 'What about school?' and Pen said Jinx could come back, they broke up soon, and Eve found herself agreeing when she wasn't at all sure agreement was a good idea.

She didn't even know the tiresome girl's real name.

'You seem to be acquiring some very strange friends lately,' she remarked to her granddaughter when they were alone. *Lately* being since they came to Temporal Crescent.

Pen had never had many friends. Matty Featherstone, and a couple of other girls at school, and the grownups, carefully vetted, with whom she discussed law issues online. Eve had assumed it was to do with being an only child and an orphan, too clever for her age, too self-sufficient for the company of her contemporaries. She had worried about it, because she always worried – and now, suddenly, there were other teenagers in Pen's life, the boy Eve hadn't met yet, this odd-looking Goth ('Emo,' said Pen), and she was worrying all over again, because she knew nothing about them, or their parents, or why Pen had changed so abruptly. Which was irrational, and she knew it, but that didn't make it any less worrying.

She would just have to get to know Pen's new friends better – if she got the chance.

Meanwhile, why on earth was there a set of false teeth on top of the sideboard?

Beyond the Doors
London, seventeenth century

GHOST DREAMED HE was back in the Home, in bed with chickenpox. He'd had it very badly – so badly he was delirious – and he'd seen these creatures swarming above him, things with wings and pointy faces and little red eyes bright as flame, staring down at him with a kind of cold curiosity, as if they couldn't quite decide whether he was interesting or not. Even when he had begun to recover, the memory of those dark winged beings had seemed more vivid than the grey reality around him.

Now, he was trapped in a dream within a dream, and the swarm was back, clustering over him, subjecting him to the same dispassionate inspection, though what they hoped to divine he could not guess. Their faces tapered into elongated noses, with few features save for the eyes, but there must have been mouths in there somewhere since he could hear a sort of whispering, beyond the rustle of their wings, and he knew they were talking together. The odd thing was that, for all their strangeness, he wasn't afraid of them. And once again they seemed far more real than the fevered confusion of his dreams.

Beyond the swarm, the ceiling kept changing. Sometimes it was the off-white ceiling of the Home, with the discoloured patches where the damp had leaked through, and a single naked bulb dangling above him, swinging slightly whenever someone walked across the floor upstairs. Sometimes it was the underside of a roof, with criss-crossed beams and chinks here and there showing a fingerwidth of sky. Sometimes it was the curved ceiling of a caravan, and the sound of a woman whimpering close by, and the shadow of a man looming up huge and black on the wall; but that was an image from when he was very young, and he no longer knew what it meant. And then the swarm would come between, blotting out the changing ceilings, rustling and whispering, red eyes with pinpoint pupils bright as fire and cold as death.

Once or twice, Ghost thought *he* was dead, dead and buried and gazing up at the inside of a coffin, but he hoped it wasn't true, because there was something he had to do, some great anxiety hanging over him, and if he was dead it would be too late to avert disaster or change the course of his fate.

One day he woke up knowing he wasn't dead. The ceiling had beams and glimpses of sky, and the swarm had gone, and there was a normal face hanging over him, a pale face with a tired mouth and dark lank hair from which the curl had long dropped out. For a moment he thought it was Lauren from school – Lauren whose father beat her and who'd once given him a little pill that made the wallpaper climb up the walls – but then his perception shifted and the image of Lauren faded into forgetfulness, and there was Mags in her tawdry red dress with the dirty shift showing underneath, Mags with the gin on her breath and the usual sharpness in her face softened away by fatigue. Mags whose heart was kind, under the paint and the bright hard words and the bright hard jokes of her kind.

They were all just girls underneath, like his gang who were just boys – girls and boys caught up in a game where grownups made the rules, and took the winnings, and didn't stop to care when someone fell by the wayside.

Then he remembered the truth. Most of his gang were gone.

'You're going to be all right,' Mags said, touching his face. 'Ghost... can you hear me? You're going to be all right.'

'Cherub,' he said – his voice was a croaking whisper, so he hardly knew it for his own. 'Weasel. One-Ear...'

'Weasel went before: remember? Cherub's well.'

'One-Ear?'

'He got sick after you, but he... he couldn't fight it. He died this morning. He kept asking for someone called Edwin – Cherub said it was his pet rat, he said you killed it – but poor One-Ear, he didn't know what he was saying, what with the fever an' all. He was so hot, like there was a furnace in 'im, and then he died. I was afeared you'd go the same, but you fought it, three days you fought it. You always was the strong one.'

She added, touching him again with a strange new timidity: 'I'm glad you're not dead.'

'One-Ear,' Ghost repeated. He couldn't take it in. One-Ear had been his second-in-command, the boy to whom he was closest – the one who was always tough, always smart, always resilient, with the lightest fingers and the quickest feet and the sharpest tongue. Boys like One-Ear were born to dodge death and hang onto survival by the coat-tails; you could knock them down but never out; they would inevitably bounce back. One-Ear couldn't die. Not he...

'I had to kill the rat,' Ghost said. 'It was a plague rat. It brought death to us all.'

'Rats don't get plague,' said Mags. 'You was all about in the head. I daresay it was the sickness coming on. You don't want to worry about One-Ear. I reckon he's gone to a better place – he 'n Weasel 'n Clarrie 'n all of them. I don't know about church, but there's got to be a better place than here, even for the likes of us.'

'There's no better place,' said Ghost.

(The phrase meant one thing to Mags, and another to him. This was his city, and plague stalked the streets, but for Ghost there was no better place. There never would be.)

'There's just worms, and cold ground,' he said. 'That's death. There's no door to Paradise. The doors open... somewhere else, but it isn't better. Just cleaner.'

'That's the fever talking,' Mags said, 'talking nonsense, though you ain't burning now. It takes a while for your head to come right. Ghost... what's your real name? I was thinking, it ain't good to die, with no one knowing your name.'

She went on: 'Mine's Margaret Pardoe.'

'Random,' he said. 'Horwood. Random Horwood.' He answered without reflection, before the memory slipped away. If he'd reached for it, he knew it would have eluded him.

'That's a queer name,' said Mags, a fleeting smile crossing her face, like sunshine on a cloudy day. 'I never heard of that.'

'I like Ghost better,' he said. 'It fits.'

'I like Random,' she decided. 'But I won't tell it to anyone. Not if you don't want. I can keep secrets.'

'Good,' said Ghost. 'Keep mine. They are too much for me.'

That night, he heard the dead cart coming for One-Ear. Creeeak-groooan went the wheels, and clang-clatter-clang went the bell, and it seemed like the whole city went quiet with listening for it. And then there was Cullen's harsh laugh, like the cawing of a raven, and the sound of a body falling into the cart, bumping over the other bodies piled inside. Ghost slid down the ladder, and stumbled along the alleyway to the street, but he was too late, Mags and Cherub had thrown One-Ear in with the rest, and the cart was starting to roll away, creeeak-groooan, creeeak-groooan, and Cullen glanced over one shoulder to taunt him.

'I heard you made it,' he said. 'You look more dead than alive, but there! you allus did. Ghost by name and Ghost by nature –

and only a band of ghosts left for you to play the leader. Follered you all the way to the graveyard, didn't they? A line o' little ghosts, and a big Ghost leading 'em – that's a picture to warm me 'eart, haha!'

Ghost's limbs were weak and his head was dizzy but the blackness filled him with sudden strength – the strength on the other side of weakness, born of fury and the night. Somehow, he leaped onto the cart, scrambling over the corpse-pile, treading on arms and legs and faces – on One-Ear's cheek and mutilated ear-hole – the knife which had never let him down springing into his hand. Cullen was still cackling when Ghost pulled his head back and slit his throat. The cackle turned into a gurgle; blood ran down his coat and onto the road below. Ghost jumped down from the cart and watched it lumber away – creeeak-groooan, creeeak-groooan – with the dead man driving and the dead cargo heaped up behind him. When it rounded the corner he was still sitting on the box-seat, swaying gently with the motion of the vehicle, head slumped forward, reins clutched in his hand, until the cart had groaned its slow way into the dark and was lost to view.

Infernale

WHAT CAN YOU give the demon who has everything?

The gift rested on a black velvet cushion, glittering like the Koh-i-noor, sending darts of light wheeling along the dim walls. Who the giver might be did not matter: the Devil has many adherents, some of whom are the wealthiest people in the world. They send him gifts in the same way that people send presents to the Queen: the object is ostentation, not generosity.

Azmordis lifts it with one hand, turning and turning it so the darts of light skim to and fro across the room.

'A skull,' he says, in flat tones. 'A jewelled skull. How… quaint.'

Once, it was the inside of a human head. Now, every inch of bone is covered with diamonds; every gem is flawless; its value is measured in endless zeros.

'Is it worth it?' he muses. 'Calcium covered in carbon. A pretty trinket.'

'Of course I'm worth it,' snaps the skull, attempting to toss its head – a difficult feat for something with no neck. 'Just because I look like a table decoration from Accessorize–! It was not always thus, I can tell you. I stood on the worktop of the alchemist Ramon Lully when he discovered the Secret of Life–'

'What was it?' asks the Devil, mildly curious.

'I don't know. I was asleep. I only woke up when they came to murder him. I've been the prop of astrologers, actors, artists. I starred with Burbage in the first production of *Hamlet* – I was the concealed skull in that picture with a concealed skull. I stood behind Géricault while he painted *The Raft of the Medusa*. There was a basket of severed arms from the hospital under the bench and a couple of heads from the guillotine, but I had the place of honour. Gerry, I said, that hand hanging over the edge, it's all wrong. You've got to do it again. He did.'

'An interesting history,' comments Azmordis, progressing from flat to dry.

'Do you think I like this... this vulgar encrustation? I was a serious skull, I tell you. I had gravitas. I was with Poe when he wrote *The Raven*. He was groping for the *mot juste* – couldn't find it – out of his brain on laudanum. Nevermore, I said. That's the word. He scribbled it down there and then. Quoth the raven: *Nevermore*. I was an inspiration to men of genius. And now look at me!'

'Shut up,' says Azmordis, setting it down on the desk at the other end from the lamp.

'If you don't mind,' says the skull, 'I'd rather...'

'I do mind.'

A silence ensues which even the skull thinks it imprudent to break.

Presently, the Serafain who stands close by suggests: 'It's an amusing bauble.'

'It's all true,' says the skull, rather sulkily. 'I was there, I tell you. When Mother Shipton gazed into her crystal ball – when Locusta brewed her poisons – when Louis de Béchamel invented that sauce–'

'A soothsayer and a poisoner may well have owned a skull, but I find it difficult to credit that any chef would have had one,' says the Devil, more silky than sulky. 'Except among the Aztecs.'

'It wasn't the chef,' says the skull. 'It was the wizard who taught him.'

'Wizards teach the black, not the culinary arts,' says the Serafain.

'Not this one,' declares the skull.

'What was his name?' the Devil inquires, on a sudden note of interest.

'Bartholème de Bonhomme. He was not as other wizards. Not keen on becoming a megalomaniac or a supervillain. He busied himself producing small pleasures and small benefits for the good of mankind. Food, medicines, alcoholic beverages. Bit of a philanthropist, really. I expect he was hoping to stay sane. Most wizards don't. I remember Zakharion–'

'Bartholème de Bonhomme,' Azmordis repeats. 'Bartlemy Goodman. I know the man... a little. Our paths have crossed. A fat wizard who has evidently eaten too well of his own cooking.'

'Wizards are never fat,' says the Serafain, startled into contradicting his master. 'They are gaunt and cadaverous, hook-nosed and hawk-eyed. Like Cassius, they have a lean and hungry look. It goes with the terrain.'

'Nonetheless, this wizard is fat. A fat soft man with a voice as mild as milk and eyes as blue as a baby's. A wizard of little power and less importance, or so it has always seemed.' There is a pause, while that dark Mind is wrapped in a cloud of thought. The backchat of the skull has stirred ideas which might have been better left to lie. 'Until now. Now, he may be the one appointed to stand against me – the wizard chosen to contest my final purpose – even he, in all his fatness and softness. Folly! Folly and futility. Who can stand against the Lord of the Dark? Only a mortal would be so rash, and so stupid. This Goodman – this *good man* – has been named the keeper of my house, though what he keeps within he does not even know.'

'Your house?' asks the Fellangel.

'My house. The house of space and time. My house, though I can never pass the threshold, nor even see within its walls. A house of doors that has no door – a house where those who enter do not leave, and those who leave have never entered. For thousands of years men have sought to contain it: a meaningless task, since my purpose cannot be stayed, and the doorways into the vortex cannot be sealed by human hands. The house has held them long in its keeping, the chosen ones, the fortunate few. Soon, they must come to me, to fulfil their destiny – or die in the attempt. It will go ill for any who seek to stand in the way.'

'This Bartlemy Goodman,' says the seraph of Hell, 'do you think he might... stand in the way?'

'Possibly. He has the stomach for it, or at any rate, he has the stomach for something. It is a generous stomach, a stomach of noble proportion. Who knows where such a stomach may lead him?'

'The fat are neither courageous nor reckless,' the Serafain insists. 'Daring and derring-do are for the lithe and agile. Who ever heard of a fat man in a heroic last stand?'

'But he may yet block the door,' murmurs Azmordis. 'There has always been a watch on the house, but it is time for one of you to keep vigil there. When the few emerge, there should be a Nightwing on hand to greet them.'

'These few,' says the Fellangel, 'the chosen few – you mean...?'

Azmordis smiles – a smile which cannot be seen, only felt. 'The ones who seek the position of my apprentice,' he says.

'My apprentice, and my successor. The fortunate few – or not so fortunate, for those who fail. But the prize... ah, the prize is beyond mortal reckoning!'

'But they *are* mortal...'

'Indeed. Only among mortals can I find those who are still young and hungry, whose spirit is new-sharpened to a lethal edge. Men have always made my most enterprising servitors. They understand Evil as werefolk cannot, and embrace it as a cause. It is something you should appreciate. You were mortal once, long ago, before you surrendered flesh and blood and soul for immortality in my service. You knew what it was to be endowed with Youth – that magical quality which mortals alone possess, and that briefly. The house has taken only the young, the most Gifted, the most apt to evil; it has severed them from love and home – if indeed they ever knew such things – snared them in a labyrinth of magic and history. To survive they have had to scheme and cheat and kill, to cast aside kindness, weakness, debilitating affections. Only the strongest, the hardest, the most cunning and the most ruthless will have lived. They have been imprisoned in the past, frozen in their own springtide – soon to come forth, whoever they are – perhaps four, or fourteen, or forty – to compete before me for the ultimate prize. When I am gone there will be a new Lord of the Dark, born mortal, raised to immortality, and who knows? under his rule – or hers – maybe the human race will learn to regret even Me.'

The Serafain bows his head, acknowledging both Azmordis' lordship and the lordship to follow.

'Sounds like a masterplan,' says the skull. 'I was there, you know. I'm always there.'

'Shut up,' says the Devil. 'Or you won't be there next time, believe me.'

*   *   *

Eade, twenty-first century

THE ROOM WAS full of smoke. The smoke was so thick she could not see the walls, or the ceiling, or the floor; she could feel the boards under her hand, the grainy touch of old wood, but apart from that she might have been floating in a grey-yellow fog. The cloud, which should have hovered above the spellfire like a genie half way out of the bottle, had become a thick curdle of fume cramming itself into every available inch of space. The gap in its heart was a ragged cavern-mouth, as tall as a tall man, and the picture beyond grew into a reality which threatened to swallow her own. The Circular Office, the blood-coloured carpet, the veiled portrait, the Glittering Skull... And *him*, a looming shadow, a face averted, a voice ocean-deep, colder than the abyss. She was no longer a spectator observing the scene, she was part of it, a ghostly imprint on another dimension. If *he* had looked round, he would surely have seen her. Nothing would escape that unimaginable gaze.

She dared not breathe too loud, nor move, nor whisper an injunction. The smoke made her eyes water; mascara ran in black tears down her cheeks. She could only wait for it to be over, for the gap to close and the smoke to thin, breaking into separate vapours which oozed through the crack around the door and probed the blocked chimney. But even when the air cleared she still sat there, hugging her knees against her chest, shuddering uncontrollably. She was not brave enough for such visions; she had no strength to contain them. The fear knotted itself into her belly and would not go away.

She knew too much.

There was only one thing to be done. Spread it around, share her knowledge, tell someone, anyone. Pen was right – her secrets were too big to hide, too deadly to keep safe. Yet still she did not move, huddled by the fireside, dry-throated from the smoke. There was danger in Bygone House, danger on every street, danger even here, in the old empty manor – danger at the door. She heard the hinge creak in protest – a footfall too light and soft to be human – felt a warm breath on her cheek. Rigid with fright, she made a sound between a gasp and a scream.

A rough tongue rasped along her jaw – a wet nose nudged her ear. She flinched and turned... and saw the dog.

A big dog – she had forgotten how big – with long gangly legs ending in huge paws, a ragged coat, a wayward tail. His ears both lopped and cocked and his eyes were bright brown under whiskery eyebrows. He looked part lurcher, part setter, part mastiff, with a little wolf and a lot of mongrel and a trace element of Scooby Doo. He had belonged to Bartlemy for as long as Jinx could remember, which made him older than any dog should be and perhaps just a little bit magical.

She hugged him, feeling weak with relief, mumbling: 'Hoover... oh *Hoover...*'

They called him that because of his habit of mopping up crumbs, though she had a suspicion it wasn't really his name.

She had never known him leave his master.

'Where is he?' she demanded, both eager and desperate. 'Where's Uncle Barty?'

But the dog was alone.

'You would never leave him,' she said slowly, a different fear clutching at her heart. 'I *know* you wouldn't. But... he *can't* be dead. He can't be. The spells would have told me if he was dead... wouldn't they?' But the dog didn't answer, and the magic was gone, and the gingerbread house felt empty and cold.

When she had stopped shivering, she got up to leave, the dog at her heels.

CHAPTER SEVEN
The Wishing Stone

Beyond the Doors
London, seventeenth century

'YOU'RE DEAD,' SAID Mags. 'I told Big Bel. She was asking for you, hearing you'd got sick, so I said you was dead. I reckoned that was safest, what with Cullen being done in and all. You don't want her sending the constable after you, do you? Or worse.' She didn't specify what was worse.

They were sitting in the loft, she and Ghost and Cherub, sharing a stolen pie still hot from the oven (Cherub's contribution) and a mug of stout which Mags had carried up from the tavern. Frowsy sunlight leaked through the roof-holes and the half-shuttered casement, slicing across the dim interior in narrow rays glimmering with dust. In the corner Ghost's face lived up to his name, fever-white and wasted to hollows and shadows. The other two studied him doubtfully over mouthfuls of pie.

'Did you do it?' Mags asked abruptly. You weren't supposed to ask, she knew that, but she couldn't help herself. What Ghost did – or didn't do – *mattered*, more than the deeds and misdeeds of anyone else she knew.

''Course he did,' said Cherub. 'Slit his froat with that wicked little knife, didn't he? Wickedest knife I ever saw. Pops out quicker'n a tippler's pimple. I reckon that knife could've done it all on its own.'

'Ghost's not strong enough,' Mags insisted.

'Hate makes you strong,' said Ghost, from the corner.

He remembered Cullen's cackling laugh, and how he had mocked the Lost Boys, tossed in the dead cart like yesterday's rubbish.

Mags didn't say any more.

Ghost kept to the loft for the next week or so, regaining health and strength, always resilient for all his apparent fragility. Cherub stole for both of them, having no other loyalties to cling to, and Mags came when she could, for all her doubts, but no one else knew he still lived, and the business of the city – *his* city – stumbled on without him. Cherub might have had trouble with other gangs, but the epidemic had decimated them all; Dutch Harry down by the river was said to have run away to sea, and more than half the boys who had infested every alley and tenement were dead. Plague always took the poor and undernourished first. Summer hung on well past its time, dragging its feet; the jungle of backstreets and high streets, houses and hovels stewed in the last of the heat. The death-smell hung over all, so much a part of the air that even Ghost no longer noticed it.

Twice or three times Cherub reported seeing Big Belinda out on the streets, bustling along in her flounces and her curls, evidently untroubled by any need for a bodyguard. Presumably she believed what Mags had told her; at any rate, she did not seem disturbed by Cullen's death. 'It ain't as if 'e was well liked,' Cherub remarked, with airy understatement; anyone could have done it, particularly in the feckless atmosphere of the epidemic, where life was cheap, and short, and death came swiftly to the unlucky or the unwary. The one certainty, Ghost thought, was that Big Belinda herself would survive, as she always did, impervious alike to ague and plague, infection and affliction, feeding off others' misery and misfortune, fattened off the lean of the land. Nothing touched Big Belinda. Her newest ringlets were golden as guineas and the rouge on her cheeks was as red as the roses that still bloomed in the king's garden, and when she walked down the street even Death stepped around her – or so they said.

'That wicked little knife o' yourn ain't sharp enough for her,' Cherub averred. 'Her corsets are made of armour-plating and the flab on her's tougher'n raw suet. You'd need a knife sharpened by the Devil himself to cut through it.'

'I'll bear that in mind,' said Ghost.

One evening, with a change of clothes Cherub had pinched for him and his face and hair dirtied to the colour of dust, Ghost shinned down from the loft into Running Lane. The sun had sunk behind the roofline and the light was fading; Ghost disappeared into the gloaming like a shadow among shadows. Even Mags, crossing into the tavern, did not see him, nor did he call to her. He felt as if the fever had made him not only thinner but somehow less solid, a transparent being who only existed on the borders of reality, half in some other dimension of delirium or dream. The red-eyed spectres who had watched over him in his malady were gone, but occasionally he fancied he saw a wingtip flicking round a corner, or a movement on the edge of sight, too swift or too furtive to pin down. His senses seemed to be heightened: he both heard and saw more clearly, and beyond the all-pervasive death-smell his nose picked up every nuance of the city odours. Yet for all his imagined lack of substance, he himself felt intensely real, more alive than ever before; it was the world around him which appeared insubstantial, a dreamworld peopled with phantoms. Even those he knew best, Cherub and Mags, existed at one remove, as if observed through a distant lens. He wondered if this was what it was like to *be* a ghost – the spirit lives on while everything around it dies, dwindling into dimness and shades.

Death was his Gift. He did not know it with his mind but he was beginning to feel it in his heart, now most of those he had loved were gone, and rumour named *him* dead, and he was left haunting his own life like a visitant, passionless and chill.

He saw Big Belinda in Porkpie Street, turning the corner into Goldfinger Lane. It was only a glimpse but he knew her at once, more by intuition than sight, and he followed her immediately, without hesitation or thought. She was wearing her newest curls and a hat adorned with what appeared to be an entire dead cockerel; with her skirts kilted up to avoid the garbage she resembled a large plum-coloured galleon, bulging and billowing though there was little wind, sailing the streets like a flagship while lesser craft scurried out of her way. She moved quickly for all her bulk, but Ghost was quicker, flitting from shadow to shadow, keeping under cover in case she should turn around. But she never did. They went by Tight Street and Trouser Alley, by Crooked Way and Sallow Way, by Bareknuckle Court and Blazonbrass Crescent. In a place called Close Shave Alley she stopped by the door of what seemed to be a barber's and knocked twice. The door opened, and in the gap Ghost saw a dark looming figure, too dark for the evening gloom. The Duke's bodyguard. Big Belinda went inside and the door shut behind her.

Ghost waited in growing frustration. The door was closed and the single window shrouded in curtain or blind; there was no way he could eavesdrop or peer through a chink. He wondered about going round the back, but in such an alley a shop would normally have only a tiny yard, walled in, with no means of egress. When Big Belinda didn't re-emerge he approached the door and laid an ear to the panels, but he could hear no sound of movement inside, no murmur of speech. Eventually, curiosity outweighing risk, he tried the door. It was unlocked. He pushed it open, peered through the gap. Went in.

The shop was empty. The barber, if there was one, might have died or fled the city: there was no sign of occupancy. Ghost gazed round with dilating eyes, distinguishing little in the semi-darkness. The only light in the room was a thin sliver surrounding the door to what must be the basement or cellar. Once again Ghost paused to listen, but everything was quiet. He pulled the door ajar, descended the stair. At the bottom a lamp stood on an upended barrel, showing a clutter of empty boxes and bottles and a hole, partially filled in, which from the smell had been used as a midden. Ghost, long accustomed to such odours, barely wrinkled his nose. He was staring at the farther wall. There was another door, an underground door, a door that ought to go nowhere – a thick solid door of some dark wood like the door of a dungeon – a door that had no place in the basement of a poky barber's shop – incongruous, impassable, inviting.

It would not open. There was no keyhole; Ghost guessed it must be bolted on the other side. Big Belinda had gone that way: he could see her in his mind's eye, following the mute, waiting while he secured the door behind them. The mute would have been carrying a lamp or torch to light the passage: he could picture the light dwindling slowly down a long length of tunnel, and the guide's towering form stooping under the low ceiling, and the shadow of Big Belinda wavering and billowing after them. He could picture it so clearly it was almost real. He knew where the tunnel would go. Beyond Close Shave Alley was Sweet Street, and beyond that the high wall of the Duke's garden. Ghost had a vague recollection of Mr Sheen talking about the *old* Duke, the present Duke's father, who had been a friend of the king before the rebellion – the king they had executed like a criminal, though Ghost wasn't sure why. Mr Sheen had approved of the aristocracy: they were his prey. He told them how the old Duke had been imprisoned in his own house because the Tower was full, and he would have been executed too, only he escaped, no one knew how, and though the Ironclads scoured the city they couldn't find him.

'There's a secret passage, see? I knew one o' the servants, he told me about it. The Duke, 'e had it made early in the war, in case the wrong side won. 'E was a smart one, the old Duke, cunning as a thief for all his blood was blue. They say he hid in the passage ten days waiting for the soldiers to quit searching – ten days o' drinking water from the gutter and eating rats. Foul fare for a man o' his breeding, but he thrived on it. Died in France, he did, at the court o' King Louey. 'E was lean and hard and tough as a tanner's thumb, and he had more vices than a tuppenny whore, but the French cooking did for 'im in the end. *This* Duke now, he looks different, fat as a Christmas goose, but don't you be fooled, he's his father on the inside, only sharper and meaner. The old Duke, he'd kill quick as lightning, without turning a hair or breathing a prayer. But his son, he'd kill you slow, just for the fun of it.' There had been both fear and admiration in Mr Sheen's voice when he said those words, and the raven had squawked as if in affirmation. Ghost's face grew thin and hard at the memory. He thought of Tomkin, somewhere beyond that door, and the Duke behind his high wall, safe from plague and peril. There were promises to be kept, debts to be paid; that was why he had lived, surviving disease and despair, that was what he was for. At the thought, the knife came into his hand, the little blade flicking out like a serpent's tongue, but he put it away, and climbed the stair, back to the darkness of the barber's shop.

Perhaps forty minutes later the cellar door opened and Big Belinda emerged, brushing the dust from her skirts. Ghost was squatting on the top of a cupboard, trusting to the gloom to hide him, but the procuress never glanced up. She was talking, more to herself than the mute who came after her, his lamp held high.

'So he wants a new boy, does he? A sweet-faced child to sing him to sleep, to drive away his demons and open the gates of Heaven for him – and where am I to find one in *this* city? They're all dead or dying. The younger they are the faster they sicken; that's how it goes. But he wants one untouched by plague or human hand – a cherub in a city gone to hell. What's wrong with the one he's got? Lost his bloom – huh! Of course he's lost his bloom. His Haughtiness can take the bloom off in a week, whether with a belt or a riding whip. Dainty little flowers bruise easy, and then they don't look so dainty any more...'

She vanished into the alley, still talking, and the mute locked the door behind her and returned to the cellar. When he was sure he was alone Ghost slid down from the cupboard and left via the window.

Cherub, he was thinking. A cherub in a city gone to hell…

London, twenty-first century

IN TEMPORAL CRESCENT, nothing happened – for a change. Jinx had gone home; Pen's term had ended, leaving her plenty of time to develop her pattern theories; Gavin went on a date with Josabeth Collins, and found himself secretly bored. On the Sunday he came to dinner, and won Eve's approval by smiling his dazzling smile and talking a lot about cooking, though she nearly lost his when she said he was going to be another Jamie Oliver.

The following week the state schools broke up, and the next Saturday Jinx came back.

With the dog.

Felinacious took one look at him, attempted to scramble up a sheer sideboard, gouging deep claw-marks in the wood, and finally made it to the top of a chest of drawers, from which vantage point he proceeded to hiss at the enemy in the manner of a cat who has done very little hissing and can't quite get it right. Hoover lifted his lip in what, in a Rottweiler, would have been a snarl, but in his case was merely a half-hearted sneer. After this face-off, something of a comedown for both species, they decided to ignore each other.

'He's Bartlemy's dog,' Jinx explained, wincing as a rib twanged. 'I found him – or he found me – in the house where Barty used to live. I don't know where he came from. He wasn't there before. He's not an ordinary dog.'

'He looks ordinary,' Gavin said, not so much disparaging as reassured. 'He looks pure pedigree mongrel.'

Pen, who was a cat person, eyed Hoover without enthusiasm and wondered if she could order Jinx to remove him.

Probably not.

Quorum, who cleaned as well as buttled, was even less enthusiastic than Pen, conveying his feelings with pointed silences and much flourishing of brooms in Hoover's wake.

Eve said doubtfully: 'I suppose as it's Mr Goodman's dog, and this is his house...'

'He's a good guard dog,' Jinx declared. 'We need a guard dog.'

Eve thought of the burglar alarms all down the street, the grilles on the windows, the security shutters. 'All right,' she said.

Later, when she was out, Jinx told Pen and Gavin what she had seen, no longer bothering to have qualms about their youth. Qualms were a luxury she couldn't afford.

'Hoover's my familiar,' she maintained. 'On loan from Uncle Barty. You have the Teeth–' she nodded to Pen '– and I have Hoover. He looks after me. No one's tried to run me over for a week.'

'He chases cars, does he?' Gavin said, grinning. 'Bites their tyres?'

'You'd be surprised,' Jinx said darkly.

Pen surveyed her familiar – or familiars – which were sitting on a nearby shelf leering at her. She didn't know if teeth were supposed to leer, but these did. 'So,' she said, 'Azmordis has a skull studded with diamonds that's been around since the Renaissance, and we have a set of dentures. What does that tell you?'

'He's the one with the budget,' Gavin suggested.

'We could take that skull!' said the Teeth. 'We could crack that cranium! We could spit out the diamonds so they went *ping!* against the wall!'

'Only if it was a metal wall,' Gavin said.

'Shut up, or we'll bite your–'

'Is it meant to tell us anything?' Jinx demanded.

'I'm not sure.' Pen fumbled with her ideas. 'The thing is, they're sort of parallel. The Skull and the Teeth. Not-quite-identical opposites. Duality.'

'What makes them opposite?' Jinx said.

'The Teeth are on our side. We're the good guys. If there are any. At least, I... I hope we are.'

'Are we?' said Gavin. 'Not being bad guys doesn't make us heroes. As far as I can see, we're just in the way.'

'That's why we have to get involved,' said Pen. 'No one else will. I'm responsible for this house–'

'What have I told you about being responsible for everything?'

'– and we know now there are people trapped here with horrible things happening to them, turning them twisted and cruel, making them suitable candidates to be the Devil's apprentice. We have to stop it – get them out somehow–'

'Save them from themselves?' Gavin queried sceptically.

'If you're doing Devil's Advocate,' said Pen, 'I think it's in very poor taste.'

'I expect they've turned to the dark side already,' Jinx said gloomily. 'Still, she's right. We have to try. God, I hate saving the world.'

Pen and Gavin stared at her, their two very different faces wearing a single expression. There was an extremely pointed silence.

'Have you?' Gavin asked.

'Saved the world,' Pen elaborated.

'Well, not *exactly*...'

Gavin turned to Pen. 'What's your plan of action?'

'Keep opening the doors. I don't see what else we can do. I told you, I've seen that boy in dreams – the one who went through in the seventies. I don't know how... how real that is, but Quorum says dreams are significant, they can reveal things you didn't know you knew, stuff from your subconscious, suppressed memories – not just your own but other people's. If that's true, I'll recognise that boy when I see him.'

'It's a big *if*,' said Gavin.

There was a short pause.

'Look,' Jinx's voice had dropped from grumble to gruff and one hand tugged at Hoover's fur, 'I know you don't like me. I get that. I know a lot more about these things than you do, and I expect it's pissing you off. I can't help that. What's happening here is *important*, and that means we have to work together, whether we like it or not. Anyway, Pen's on the right track. When you're dealing with magic dreams can show the truth, sometimes. And if we don't open the doors we won't find out what's on the other side.'

'We?' said Gavin sharply.

Jinx scowled at him. 'I've been doing some research,' she said. 'I think there may be a way to control what's behind each door. Or at any rate, who.'

'What way?' Gavin was staying with scepticism.

'That story the goblin told us…'

'What about it?'

'He mentioned a wishing stone – sort of implied he still had it. I've been reading up on wishing stones in one of Barty's books. If Stiltz could be persuaded to lend it to us, I think it might help.'

'Stiltz?' Gavin queried.

'Rumpelstiltskin.'

'But surely that story wasn't true,' Pen said. 'Not really factually true. It was just a fairytale.'

'Take away the sparkly bits and the happy ending,' Jinx responded, 'and most fairytales are true enough. Nowadays, Cinderella comes with a divorce lawyer, and the Little Mermaid is saving up for trans-species surgery, but the basic idea always stays the same. Get pretty, get married, get rich. Whatever. Wishing stones are real, or they used to be – once upon a time, in the olden days, when reality was more flexible than it is now.

They're like... a magical pager. In theory, you can page anyone, anywhere. If the goblin has one–'

'How do they work?' said Gavin.

WISHING STONES WERE believed to have been made by the exiles from Atlantis as instruments of summoning and compulsion. How many originally existed is not known, since most of them were lost long ago. Perhaps owing to a design fault, they resembled ordinary pebbles, oval-shaped, wave-smoothed and sea-grey, unmarked save for between one and three narrow white bands circling the stone – three-banded were the most potent – so against a pebbly background only those with highly developed witchsight could distinguish them. In consequence, many were mislaid – on beaches and shingle banks, stony hillsides and cobbled streets – and never rediscovered. They were supposed to glow or change colour when activated, tingling slightly to the touch.

'The thing is,' Jinx said, launching into a speech she had rehearsed on the train to London, 'Bygone House is a space/time prism so powerful it would warp normal spells, but a wishing stone is a kind of magnet – a space/time magnet attracting a particular person, the way an everyday magnet attracts iron – so it shouldn't be distorted by the prism. I think... the house might actually *enhance* the power of the stone. It could be strong enough to work through the doors – through the time zones – focusing on the person we want to reach. A wishing stone which can summon the Devil has got to be pretty powerful to start off with.' She stopped, awaiting approbation which didn't come. 'Anyway, it must be worth a try.'

'If the goblin really has this wishing stone,' Pen said doubtfully. She didn't believe any of it. 'What do you *do* with a wishing stone to... to operate it?'

'Rub it seven times widdershins,' Jinx said promptly. 'And wish, of course. Or it might be three times. We'll have to try till we get it right.'

'What's widdershins?' asked Gavin.

'Against the sun. Anti-clockwise.'

'Anti-clockwise is only against the sun if you're facing south.'

'We'd better do it facing south then...'

'It's still only half the problem,' Pen said, secretly unconvinced by the solution. 'We have to get into the past without being absorbed, which is just as hard as finding which part of the past not to be absorbed in. There's no point in going back if you're never going to return. *And*,' she went on, becoming progressively more pessimistic, 'you say we'd have to wish for a particular person? Well, from what you overheard there should be several potential apprentices lost in Bygone House, but we don't know who they are. Except for that boy in my dream...'

'The witch-girl,' said Gavin. 'I'll bet she's one of them.'

'A witch?' queried Jinx, who hadn't heard about the girl.

'She tamed a sea monster,' Gavin said with malice aforethought, 'and set it on the villagers who tried to sacrifice her. There were body parts all over the beach. That's what I call witchcraft.'

'I call it psychosis,' said Pen.

'I call it scary,' murmured Jinx.

IT WAS RAINING on Hampstead, not the thin grey rain so typical of the English spring but a heavy persistent streaming rain worthy of a more tropical climate. Water fountained from blocked guttering and overflowed ditch and drain. Sparsely-leaved trees offered no shelter and the spray from a passing car was like the backwash of a speedboat. Felinacious had ventured out, perhaps to avoid Hoover, and now lurked in the porch, whining. Above, the cloud-roof was low and so deeply grey it turned the daylight to evening.

Over the low cloud, among the murky towers of the stormheads, there were wings too wide for rook or raven. Wings black as midnight, turning and turning on a narrowing spiral around some unseen point below. Such wings might have belonged to the condor of the Andes, or an eagle greater than any yet recorded, except that they seemed to be made of darkness, melding with the cloud-core as they veered, leaving a shadow-trail in their wake that bled slowly into the surrounding gloom. And the body – the body was not that of a bird. Streamlined, featherless, with no clear form but a face that was human or nearly so and eyes that saw not merely far but through, through swirling cloud and blurring rain, down to the house in a crescent of houses, the house with no door, to the windows with their shutters and bars, to the raindrops beating on brick and pane – saw dimly through neighbouring roof and walls, to three who sat talking close together, a dark-skinned boy and a light-skinned girl and another, also possibly a girl, with purple hair and a ring in her nose.

The wings dipped, narrowing for the dive; a darkness streaked earthward, swifter than the rain. Then there was someone on the lawn between 7 and 7A, a shadow-figure blending with the storm-grey afternoon, fading into the lee of the house. The smaller house, with lights showing, glimmering through the wet.

The people inside could be seen as vague images behind the barrier of the wall, shapes and colours that gleamed faintly with the heat of life. The observer drew nearer, eyes slitting against the rain, though no rain touched him. He appeared to be listening, his hearing more than mortal, but could catch only a rumour of what was said, voices not words. The high clear tones of one of the girls, the deeper timbre of the boy, and the third voice, lacking resonance, too low or too soft to carry. The auditor lifted his arms; wing-shadows unfurled, stretching and darkening. A single beat carried him to the roof, where he crouched beside a chimney, hearing the sound carry from the room two floors below.

'– and I don't think we should – but *you* said – we could get lost in history – it might be dangerous – bit late worrying about that – we have to find the pattern – of course it's dangerous – no pattern, just chaos – dangerous – too dangerous…'

And then the boy's voice: 'What's bothering your dog?'

The watcher had noticed the dog but had paid it no attention. He would have had to be in the room for an animal to be aware of him.

An ordinary animal…

'Hoover… What is it?'

The sound travelled upward, not exactly a growl but a preliminary rumble, conveying both suspicion and unease.

'Maybe there's a bird's nest in the chimney.' The boy again.

'No,' said the younger girl. 'We had a fire there two nights ago: remember?'

'There's someone on the roof.' The third voice, normally low-pitched, sharpening with fear. 'Don't talk!'

'What?'

'Sssh!'

'You're being paranoid. How could anyone get on the roof? We'd hear them climb up.'

'I didn't say it was anyone *human*.'

'Maybe it's Stiltz.' The younger girl sounded uncertain. 'He gets around without making any noise. Or being seen.'

'He never leaves Number 7,' the boy pointed out.

The purple-haired girl picked up a handful of ashes from the cold grate, rubbing them between her palms and muttering. There was a *whoosh!* of livid flame, livid not because it was magical but because it was half-hearted. By the time it escaped from the chimney it had fizzled to a thin jet of smoke that dispersed instantly on contact with the rain. The watcher drew back a little, eyeing it with a chilly mixture of disdain and amusement.

In the room below: 'So,' said the boy, 'that was a lance of white-hot magical energy designed to vaporise anything that got in its way?'

'I did my best.' Irritably.

'I thought it was good,' said the other girl. 'I mean, we couldn't do that.'

'We aren't supposed to. She's the witch – magic is her thing. When you ask me to cook, I don't do Pot Noodle. Anyway, there's nothing up there. False alarm. Hoover's gone quiet again...'

The dog barked once, a deep-throated bark, plainly a warning. To the spy.

The listening features flickered and changed, as if something of what he had heard disturbed or unsettled him. For a moment, the thing crouching by the chimney was no longer a night-winged phantom but a young man – a young man with a subtle, secretive face and red hair curling in the wet. Then the memory was gone. There was a whirl of shadow as he rose into the air and was swallowed up in rain.

In the room, Jinx said: 'There *was* something there. I felt it too. Anyway, Hoover's never wrong.'

For once, Gavin didn't argue.

'You watched them in your spellfire,' Pen said, 'and now they're watching us.'

It's part of the pattern, she thought. Not the kaleidoscope pattern of the space/time prism but a greater pattern, too big to see in its entirety, a pattern less glimpsed than felt – light and dark, good and evil, magic and reality, the living and the undead. A pattern of opposites woven together into a single design flowing through all the ages, intricate beyond imagining, simple beyond perception – so simple that even Pen could not quite make it out. It was like a tune on the edge of hearing, a name on the tip of her tongue...

'Where can we go,' said Gavin, 'where they *can't* watch us?'

There was only one answer.

'Next door,' said Jinx.

*   *   *

THE GOBLIN WASN'T there.

'Stiltz!' Pen called. 'Where are you?'

'Rumplestiltskin!' from Gavin. 'Crumpledforeskin!'

Pen and Jinx exchanged a look which said: *Boys*.

'Can't you summon him?' Pen asked.

'In here?' Jinx grimaced, concealing private doubts about her summoning skills. 'The space/time prism means reality is all bent and twisted. Any normal spell is liable to go pear-shaped. You could summon a goblin and get a three-toed sloth. It's simpler to look for him – there's nowhere much to hide.'

She glanced at the mirror for a minute or two and then said: 'Come out.'

They could see him under the little table, hunched up and citrus-pale with nervousness, but only in the mirror. He slid out of the reflection through the frame and re-emerged behind them.

'You want something,' he said. 'I see't in your face. But I can't help. I helped a mortal once, sithee, and now my spirit is forfeit. Werefolk shouldn't mix with humankind. No good ever comes of it.'

'Who said we wanted to do good?' snapped Jinx.

'Do you really have a wishing stone?' Pen said.

'So that's it. Aye – gaffer gave it me, long agone, but he told me to keep it safe and gi' it to no man. Wishing is vain, he said, unless you make it come true your own self, with the strength of your arm and the sweat of your brow. The good cobbler stitches his own shoon. You don't want to go a-wishing, lessen you get what you wish for. Gaffer, *he* wished for–'

'Yes, we know,' said Jinx, cutting the lecture short before it was well under way. 'You told us. But the wishing stone is our only chance of finding the people who're lost in here. There's some boy who disappeared about three decades ago, or so we think–'

'Did you see him?' Pen demanded, suddenly eager. 'He broke in through the window upstairs.'

'I saw him.' Stiltz gave what might have been a shiver. 'A skinny boy all white, even his lashes, save for his een. They were like little black holes. He was one of the doomed ones; you can allus tell. Summat in his aura. They come in like they're after fool's gold, all keen and feverish, but what they find you don't want to know. One of 'em came back once, mebbe two hundred years agone – burst through the door on the landing and sat there blubbering till he was near sick. Happen he was your age but his hair was grey from t' flaysome things he'd seen. The owd man found him, tried to get him out, but he wouldn't go through any door agin.'

'What happened to him?' Pen said.

'He died here,' said the goblin. 'Died of madness, or clemmed, or mebbe both. Wasn't nothing to be done. The owd man brought food for him, but he wouldn't eat. The doomed ones, you can't help 'em. No one can help 'em. You don't want to try.'

'Yes we do,' said Pen. 'If you would lend us the stone–'

'I dursn't,' said the goblin. 'It would be death of you. I promised gaffer–'

He didn't exactly disappear – they never saw the moment of his vanishing – but suddenly they were looking round and he was gone. Gavin swore and Pen called out, but the stillness of the house absorbed both curse and call like a fog and they didn't persist. Pen sat down on the stairs, gazing intently at nothing very much. Gavin said: 'Could we *make* him give it to us? I mean, I don't want to, but we're desperate, and the way I see it the stone isn't properly his, and there are people going mad, or suffering hideous torments... And we're only going to *borrow* it; we won't even take it out of the house.'

'Getting it from him by force would be like stealing,' said Pen. 'Also bullying. Double crime.'

'Nothing wrong with bullying,' said Jinx, deliberately nasty, 'as long as you're the bully. Besides, Stiltz is a goblin: the cobbler should never have trusted him with a genuine wishing stone, it's far too powerful, and goblins aren't trustworthy. Still... taking it by force isn't a great idea. Bad karma. In magic, everything has consequences.'

'The end justifies the means,' said Gavin.

'The means shapes the end,' said Pen.

'We don't need bad karma,' said Jinx. 'We've got enough problems.'

They thought about the boy who got out, dying on the landing because he couldn't bring himself to go through a door again. There was a moment when they all had a fleeting glimpse of what they were getting into – of a conspiracy as old as Time, of a Dark Lord in a Dark Tower, of the house shifting around them like a magician's box, so you never knew what opened where – of their own smallness and futility in the face of immeasurable odds.

'So... no force,' said Gavin. 'What *can* we try?'

'Persuasion,' said Jinx. 'I knew a grinnock who would do anything for doningfuts.'

'What's a grinnock?' said Gavin. 'And... *doningfuts?*'

'Kind of goblin,' said Jinx. 'Doughnuts. How good is your Yorkshire pudding?'

ON SUNDAY EVE took Pen, Gavin and Jinx out to lunch. They drove to a pub a little way in the country where Gavin could enjoy himself criticising the menu and Hoover could gnaw leftover bones. Jinx, who was uncomfortable around most adults, wrapped herself in an aura of sullenness and said little. Pen, who was uncomfortable with the daily deception in her life, found conversation an effort. Gavin said the mushrooms were unexpectedly good and disappeared into the kitchen to chat up the cook.

Hoover didn't waste time gnawing; he simply crunched up the bones and swallowed them.

It wasn't, Eve thought, a big success.

When Jasveer Patel arrived at 7A, around tea-time, they were all out.

He had been feeling uneasy for some while. It was a relief to know that Andrew Pyewackett was not only dead but cremated, and therefore unlikely to be hanging around his previous address, but he felt guilty leaving a thirteen-year-old girl to deal with the ensuing situation, and conscious that, as a fellow executor, there were things he should have done, though he wasn't sure what things, or how to do them. The legatee was still missing, and no one seemed to be trying to find him; Jas placed advertisements in appropriate newspapers and on the Internet but sensed in advance that it would be no use. Such methods had been essayed seven years before, without result. In a rare encounter with old Mr Hayle he broached the matter, purely on the basis of exhausting all possibilities, and was unnerved when he responded instantly: 'Goodman? Yes of course. Called me last week – no, last month. Maybe last year. Called me, anyway. Some time ago. Polite sort of chap. Asked about the Will. I gave him the address.'

'What address?' asked Jas. 'Temporal Crescent?'

'Was it? Can't say I recall. We talked about angel cakes. Nobody makes them any more. I used to like them – when I was a boy, of course.'

'Did he come to the office?' Jas said. 'Did you speak to him again?'

'No. Shame really. He said he had the original recipe.'

'But – you took his contact details – phone number – e-mail?'

'No – don't do any of that. Always leave it to the secretary. Her job.'

Jas struggled for self-control. 'Which secretary was handling calls that day?'

'None of them. Lunch hour – all out. Call came straight to me.' Mr Hayle looked faintly irritated. 'Bit annoyed about that. Shouldn't be taking my own calls, not at my time of life.'

Jas muttered under his breath in Hindi and retired to his own office to drop his head in his hands.

The senility of his superior wasn't, he reasoned, Pen's problem (after all, she was a minor with little authority in law) but in the end he decided to tell her – to see how she was getting on, if she

needed assistance or advice, if normal service had been resumed…
He'd been informed about her residence in 7A and chose a Sunday
for his call because it felt somehow more casual, off the record – he
was dropping in rather than making an official visit.

As it was, the only person there was Quorum.

'I was hoping to see Miss Tudor,' Jas explained.

'So I should suppose.' Quorum exuded austere disapproval. 'It
is, if I may say so, long overdue. For a girl of her tender age
to have to cope with her present responsibilities seems most
unsuitable. Not that she isn't doing her best – and her best is very
good – but it's time an adult took over. I trust you have some
news of Mr Goodman?'

'In a way,' said Jas, smarting inwardly. 'Apparently he called
my office, I'm not sure when, and got the details of the Will
and this address. Unfortunately, he – er – he spoke to Mr Hayle,
who's elderly and gets… confused. He didn't come here, did he?
Goodman, I mean.'

'No,' said Quorum. 'Had he done so, I would almost certainly
have admitted him. Mr Pyewackett did not believe in answering
the door.'

'Why keep a butler and buttle yourself?' said a voice in the
background which was alarmingly familiar.

'You've… you've got a parrot,' Jas hazarded, gazing past
Quorum into the hall. All he could see was a set of false teeth on
a table, grinning horribly. They looked disturbingly like the teeth
he had last seen clattering away in the mouth of the corpse.

'Not at all,' said Quorum. 'Merely an echo.'

One of the talents of the true butler – of whom there are now
very few – is the ability to lie with aplomb. Jas, though aware he
was lying, could only back down. In any case, he really wanted
to move himself from the vicinity of those teeth.

'Tell Miss Tudor I called,' he said, and fled down the steps.

Eve had just parked the car further down the street and Jinx,
insisting Hoover needed a crap, had jumped out first and was

walking along the pavement with the dog. She saw Jas departing from 7A and wondered who he was and why he was in such a hurry.

She didn't see the car until it was too late.

The same car which had gone for her – afterwards she was sure of it – long and white and gleaming. It shot forward even as Jas stepped into the road – there was a *thunk* as the bonnet hit him full on. It tossed him into the air, flipping him over with a horrible rag-doll effect of flopping limbs and loosened neck. Even before he hit the tarmac, Jinx knew he was dead.

On a neighbouring rooftop a shadow shrank towards the chimney, and something like a bird took wing into the waiting clouds.

'Do you think we should go to the funeral?' Pen said, twenty-four hours later. She looked even paler than usual and somehow pinched, as if the fear had got inside her like a chill.

Eve, horrified by the accident they had all witnessed, had finally been persuaded to go into work and leave them to nurse their trauma in peace.

'I expect he was a Hindu,' said Jinx. 'Don't they have to expose their dead on top of those special towers so they can be eaten by vultures?'

'Bloody difficult in England,' said Gavin. 'You'd have to make do with pigeons.'

'That is a custom of the Parsees,' Quorum interjected. 'Hindus cremate. The funeral will be a matter for his relatives. I cannot imagine your attendance will be required.'

'The question is,' said Jinx, '*why* was he killed? Okay, so he was coming here to tell Pen that Barty had contacted someone at his office – but he told you that anyway, before the hit-and-run, so what was the point of killing him? Unless he was going to pass on something else…'

'He Knew Too Much,' Pen said wretchedly, in capital letters.

'Are you sure it was the same car that hit you?' Gavin asked Jinx.

'Yeah. And no, I didn't see the driver, *or* the licence plate. I tried to read the numbers, but they got jumbled up. It could've been some sort of confusion spell – I ought to've been able to see them.'

'The police said it was joyriders,' Quorum remarked.

The three teenagers plainly considered this too frivolous to be worthy of comment.

'Now the guy's dead,' Jinx said to Pen after a pause, 'does that mean you're the only executor?'

'Oh no,' said Pen. 'Jasveer Patel wasn't named in Andrew Pyewackett's Will; he was just the representative appointed by the firm. They'll appoint someone else.'

'Pity,' said Jinx. 'I was thinking if they killed him, and then you, that might be their way of getting hold of the house.'

'Do you mind not killing me off so casually?'

'You know what I mean.'

There was a silence filled with frowns, and concentration on nothing very much, and gloom.

'We have to talk to Stiltz,' said Pen.

'Why?' Gavin demanded.

'Because there's no one else.'

They equipped themselves for exploration. Quorum protested, but half-heartedly; he knew it wouldn't do any good. At Jinx's insistence they took the Teeth – 'They're familiars,' she maintained. 'Backup' – though not Hoover as goblins can be afraid of dogs, and a Yorkshire pudding prepared by Gavin in a plastic lunchbox.

'There's bound to be something we haven't got,' Pen said, frowning.

'There are loads of things we haven't got,' said Gavin. 'Stun grenades, Kalashnikovs, dragon repellent. We haven't got them and we can't get them, so we'll just have to do without.'

Jinx fiddled with a ring she always wore, a coiled serpent or dragon biting its own tail. Pen thought it was a mood ring: she had noticed the glass in its eyes changed colour from time to time. At the moment it was a pale sickly green.

'I want a weapon,' Jinx said. She went into the kitchen and helped herself to a small jar of cayenne pepper.

Then they were ready.

Like an expedition heading for the Himalayas, they filed into the utility room and opened the door to Bygone House.

SMELL IS THE sense most closely associated with memory. When Pen opened the lunchbox, feeling like an evil temptress luring Stiltz towards some unspecified doom, the smell of Yorkshire pudding came out, not so much wafting as invading. A homely, folksy, friendly smell, a smell to make your mouth water, or, in the case of Stiltz, your brain. Werefolk do not need to eat, and indeed may starve a hundred years without ill effect, but they enjoy eating, and can even – as Simmoleon did – become addicted to a particular food, like a drug. The wise among them, or those who call themselves wise, say eating makes you human, and should be avoided at any price. Food, friendship, and morality are the mortal sins: any who over-indulge in them will invariably be corrupted. Stiltz had known friendship; Jinx guessed he had shared meals with his former master. And the smell, even more than the taste, should reawaken the loyalties – and the weaknesses – he had learned.

'Aye, I'll lend 'ee the stone,' he said at last. Goblins are low on resistance. 'But 'tis agin my promise, agin my instinct, agin my gut. Even if it works for you, it'll bring you no good. Once you pass a door the house will devour you, and there'll be no coming back. I shall miss your bonny face, lass–' he nodded to Pen '– and the shoon I nivver made you. But you mun go with your fate, whatever the end.'

The munching of Yorkshire pudding rather spoiled the dramatic impact of this speech.

'We *have* passed a door,' Pen pointed out. 'In fact, we've passed several. Gavin and I have, anyway. *And* we came back.' She turned to the other two. 'I think the trick is to sort of pre-programme yourself. When I chased after Felinacious I came back because I knew I had to, I had to return to Gasparo – Gavin. It was, like, this huge imperative kind of pulling me on. If somebody always stays by the door, and we fix up to meet, that ought to work even if your head gets scrambled. Anyhow, we haven't come up with anything else, and I think it's worth a try.'

'When you go,' said Jinx, 'take the Teeth. History shouldn't affect them: they're an object. They can remind you who you are – or where you're supposed to be.'

'What?' said the Teeth, slightly muffled by the pocket of Pen's jacket. 'We're not going into the past. Too dangerous. Let us out, or we'll chew our way–'

'Shut up,' said Pen, batting her pocket. 'Be quiet, or I'll... I'll take you into the past and *leave you there*. You could end up in the mouth of some old man with halitosis, or gum disease, or – they had lots of diseases, in the past. Behave yourself. I thought you were meant to be helpful.'

The Teeth subsided into a mumble of complaint which everyone decided to ignore.

'You know, you're right,' Gavin said. 'We haven't been thinking straight. Someone *has* to stay by the door – to keep it open. What if it closed while we were on the other side? The time zones change, don't they? We'd be buggered.'

There was a minute of horrified silence as the implications sank in.

Then Pen said: 'We should wedge the door somehow. Just in case. Or maybe Stiltz–'

'No,' said Jinx. 'You never rely on a goblin. Never. Not even a reliable one. One of us must wait by the door. Always.'

'I think we should have a trial run,' said Pen, 'before we go looking for the boy. Re-visit somewhere familiar. Or somewhen.'

'Like?' said Gavin.

'The Italian Renaissance wasn't too bad...'

THE WISHING STONE had three white bands, denoting maximum power. Otherwise it looked – and felt – like an ordinary pebble, fitting snugly into the palm of Pen's hand, taking warmth from her touch. Although she was the youngest they had conceded a sort of token leadership to her, partly because she was the custodian of the house – because she had assumed the role and no one could be bothered to argue – but mostly because both Gavin and Jinx preferred following Pen to following Jinx or Gavin.

'You need to face south,' Gavin reminded her, turning her in the right direction.

'Do I rub the stone three times or seven?' Pen asked.

'Well, try three first,' Jinx said, 'and if that doesn't work keep rubbing.'

'What do I say?'

'I've no idea!'

'But–'

'Make it up,' said Gavin.

Pen thought of reiterating: 'I don't believe in magic,' but decided it was rather late for that. She focused her mind on the prince – his voice, softened with moonlight and desire: *'Tesoro – tesoro–'*, the way he had called her *useful*, the feel of his hand on her throat. The image of his face came to her very vividly – the face everyone said was so beautiful, even her aunt, who wasn't the type to notice such things. And in her thought she was already Penella, child of the Renaissance, caught up in a dark web of politics and perfidy, vain ambition, broken dreams...

She opened her eyes and saw the twenty-first century, in the shape of Gavin and Jinx, only for a second or two they were

Gasparo and Teo the clown-girl, who came to town with the travelling players and was rumoured to be a witch – or a spy...

'Get on with it,' said Jinx. 'Wish!'

'I want to see Cesare,' Pen said. 'Cesare Borgia. Behind the door...'

I want to be Penella again.

She rubbed the stone with her thumb, three times widdershins. Its grey colour paled; it became translucent, like crystal, and began to glisten with an unholy pallor which spilled between her fingers. In her pocket, the Teeth champed in protest. She pushed open the door, just a crack, handed the stone to Gavin, and stepped through.

Beyond the Doors
Italy, fifteenth century

SHE WAS ON the long gallery in the Borgia palace – she'd been there once before, at a party, but there was no party now. Instead, there was a sword-fight. The time zones were overlapping in her head and she thought in a confused way that it wasn't like any sword-fight she had seen on screen, elaborate and stylish, with the swift clash of rapier on rapier and cloaks swirling and someone swinging from a chandelier. This was the kind of fight that made you realise swords were sharp pointy things which could kill you. It was ugly and untidy and vicious. There were four participants, two against two; one was already bleeding from a slash in the arm, another took a lethal thrust to the belly even as she watched. She picked up a footstool to use as a shield and dodged past, knocking into one of the combatants, who stumbled and swore and collided with a dagger. But Pen didn't wait for the final outcome. She had to find the prince. Lorenzo di Giordano had given her the message; in her *vagabondo* boy's clothes no one would pay her any attention, she knew she could get through.

They said he was ill, ill and dying, but she didn't believe it. It was a ruse to fool his enemies. The prince couldn't die – he was going to rule all Italy, and she would be there in his train, not a pawn to be married and bedded like other girls but a trusted agent, loyal and resourceful. *Utile...* She ran down a short flight of stairs, along a corridor, through a chamber where a servant was doing something with a flagon of wine. She knew there could be an assassin behind every curtain, poison in every cup. In another room two women were talking, one with her back to Pen. The other looked young and frightened: she had a puckered-rosebud mouth and red-gold hair, brighter and fairer than Pen's, crimped into a myriad of tiny waves and woven with flowers or jewels.

'He asked me to come,' she was saying. 'With him, to request is to command. I had no choice. He could die...'

'It is poison,' said her companion. 'He may suspect you. You have had cause enough to wish him dead.'

'I have done nothing – nothing...'

Pen ducked past the doorway and ran on.

Up another stair, along a passage... She guessed she'd found the right room because there was a guard on the door.

'Let me in!' she panted, breathless from running. 'I must see the prince! I have a message–'

But the guard thrust her away, drawing a poignard; she dodged the blade just in time. Behind him, the door opened, and a man in black robes emerged. For a second she thought it was Death himself – he was lean and cadaverous, hollow-cheeked and hollow-eyed as a skull – but he carried a bag, not a scythe, and she realised he must be the doctor. The guard moved aside to let him pass and she seized her opportunity, slipping behind the doctor into the room. The guard turned and shouted after her, an oath or a threat, but he was too late.

She had expected the prince to be in bed after what she had overheard, but he was on the couch, with an embroidered coverlet thrown over him and his boots tumbled on the floor.

He wore only a shirt and hose and his face was almost as white as his linen; there was a dew of sweat on cheekbone and brow and his hair straggled in damp elflocks across the cushion which supported him. But when he saw Pen he lifted his head: a faint warmth of recognition came into his eyes.

'Penni...'

'*Sire*,' said the guard, '*mi scusa* – he sneaked past when the *dottore*–'

'I know him.' For all his latent fever, Cesare spoke with his usual cool hauteur. 'Leave us.'

The guard returned to his vigil outside the door.

'Lorenzo sent me,' Pen said. 'He came to our house to ask assistance but my uncle is a traitor: he saw a messenger from the Orsini last night. I think... he gave him gold. He's holding Lorenzo, but I said I would find you. I can always slip away without being missed. Lorenzo says, now your father's dead your enemies are moving against you: the Orsini, Urbino, Malatesta... There are assassins in the palace – I saw two guards killed. Someone could come here–'

'I am done.' His hand closed over hers, gripping so tight she thought he would crush her finger-bones. 'Without my father's patronage... Too much depends on the Papacy. Whoever takes over may not be my foe, but he will never be my friend. Envy is the price of success. I know what they are saying, the backstabbers and the gossipmongers – I have risen like a star; like a star I may fall...'

'No!' she whispered. 'Not you. You're too clever for them – you always have been. Too clever and too lucky. They fear your luck...'

'Luck can change.' He smiled without humour, a smile as thin as a knife-blade. 'So why are you here for me, little one? You've denounced your uncle's treachery; if I live, I will make him pay. You must know that.'

'He hasn't asked for my loyalty, or earned it: I'm not important to him. We made a bargain, you and I, that night in the garden. You keep my secrets, I keep yours. I will never betray *you*.'

'I believe you.' His grip on her hand gentled. 'If I had the time, I would make a woman of you. But our time is running out. Still, we will try what remains of my luck.' He raised his voice, summoning the guard again. 'Fetch Don Michelotto. And see to it my sister goes back to Ferrara, with an escort. Whoever can be spared. She is in danger here.'

'But *sire*, I cannot leave you unprotected–'

'I can protect myself.' He had thrown off the coverlet and Pen saw that even in sickness he wore a long knife in his belt; the hilt was a single ruby. 'The boy will stay with me. Go!'

The guard left. Cesare dragged his boots on with an effort and pulled a black satin jacket over his shirt, though he made no attempt to fasten it. When he got to his feet his gait was uncertain; he hooked an arm round Pen for support.

'You're tall for a girl,' he said. 'Are you sure–?' He felt her breast with his other hand, as if confirming something; Pen's whole body flamed in response. In that instant she would have given herself to him without hesitation, asking for nothing – but he was walking towards the far wall, half pulling her with him, half leaning on her; the urgency of the situation excluded all else. He tweaked a boss under the mantle and a panel swung back, revealing a dark aperture and a descending stair.

'Come,' he said, not waiting for an answer. Together, they staggered down the steps.

The arm that encircled her shoulders was hard with muscle but she sensed his fragility, the aftermath of fever. She thought: 'I'm the only one left' – last of his followers, faithful to the end – and her heart seemed to swell until she felt it would burst her chest. It was a feeling beyond any she had ever known – a feeling to live for, to fight for, to die for. 'I won't live long here,' she said to herself, oblivious to the strange use of the word *here*, 'but I will *live*.'

Life is measured in passion, not in years.

They emerged into a chamber which might once have been a private chapel, though the customary religious symbols were gone. There were no windows; the walls were draped in red silk and the light came from tall candles ranged down either side of the aisle. In the space where the altar might have stood there was a pentacle drawn on the floor, surrounded with various intricate runes; above it hung a gilded Venetian mask with the horns of a goat. Cesare halted in front of it, still leaning heavily on Pen. He began to speak in a language that was not Italian nor any dialect she knew, though there were words in it she almost recognised. The outline of the pentacle and the runic sigils gleamed briefly as a streak of flame zoomed from line to line and then shot up the wall without leaving a burn. For a moment Pen thought nothing had happened – then she saw the glow behind the eye-slots of the mask. A glow which came from nowhere, irradiating the whole face, turning it from gold to pallid green, filling the empty eyes with a white dazzle. Pen had seen magicians at the fair and had heard of alchemists who could conjure gold coins that turned to sawdust once they were spent, but she had never seen anything like this. She told herself resolutely that there could be someone behind the wall lighting a flare and thrusting it through a hole – but Cesare would never be implicated in cheap tricks. He was too intelligent and too subtle.

Then the mask spoke.

She saw the gilded lips move, saw the ripple of animation travel across the moulded features. The chamber was warm but suddenly she felt very cold.

'Czesarion.' The voice was deep and grainy, as if it had been scraped over stone or splintered through wood. It was not a human voice.

'Azmordis.'

'You will call me *master*!'

'Not yet.' The strain in Cesare's tone was not due to malady; his fingers dug into Pen's arm. 'That wasn't our bargain. You promised the lordship of all Italy would be mine.'

'If you had the strength to take it. It is not my fault that your strength has failed.'

'You swore no poisoner could kill me, but my father is dead, and without his support–'

'You live. Your father was beyond my protection.'

'His life was important to me!'

'It was not in our contract.' The voice was as inexorable as fate. 'Your course is almost run. Soon, you will belong to me.'

'You said I would be immortal, invulnerable – I would outlive my enemies – my good fortune would be a byword among men–'

'So it was.' The voice sounded almost bored. 'But now the word is gone by. You will indeed outlive your enemies, though they will not know it. Your immortality is in thrall to me: you will be my vassal, my creature, until your doom runs out. *That* was our bargain. I offered you dominion, but it is slipping from your grasp.'

'Not quite.' Determination hardened him; Pen could sense the steel in his soul. What was left of his soul, anyway. 'There are those who will stand by me. I can still scheme, and bribe, sign a pact, break a bond. The common people welcomed my rule: they knew I was fair and just.'

'The common people!' The mask laughed until the gold cracked. 'When did they ever matter? The common people!'

'I am not finished yet,' Cesare insisted. 'My supporters will rally to my aid–'

'And is *this* the calibre of your support? This pale child you lean on, more girl than boy?'

'She *is* a girl,' Cesare said. 'She has kept my secrets, and betrayed her kin for me. She is a useful tool.'

Useful... That word again. It sounded less good with *strumento*.

'Kill her,' said the mask. 'She knows too much.'

Pen stared. The phrase was familiar, if only she could remember why. She wanted to laugh, though there was nothing to laugh at.

'She is faithful,' said Cesare. 'I reward fidelity.'

'Kill her,' said the mask, 'before she changes her mind.'

'I told you–'

'She brought you the bad news; she can serve no further purpose. And she has seen *me*. Do you dare trust her now? Trust is a luxury only the poor and base can afford. It is beyond the reach of the powerful.'

Pen felt Cesare hesitate, knew when he was persuaded. He drew away from her, still unsteady on his feet, reaching for the long knife. She wasn't afraid; there was no time for fear. The fantasy of her love and loyalty vanished like smoke on the wind.

'I am sorry, little one,' Cesare said. 'But the demon is right. You know... too much.'

I will not live long here, Pen thought again. And: If he had made love to me, he would still have done it. And I would have let him – I would have bared my breast for the knife...

She jumped back, needing a weapon, reaching a hand in her pocket as if she might find something there. But there was only the toy Teodora had given her, the set of teeth the puppeteer manipulated on stage, throwing his voice to make it seem they talked. She pulled them out, having nothing else. Cesare almost laughed.

'What are *those*? Would you scare me with a witch's bibelot? I am not so feeble–'

He lunged at her, adrenaline giving him strength, seizing her by the hair – the knife was poised to stab between her ribs up into the heart. But the thrust never came. The Teeth leaped from Pen's hand as if imbued with unnatural life, snapping in mid-air, plunging into Cesare's neck. The knife dropped; he gave a cry of shock and pain. Blood started to run down his throat, dyeing his shirt. The Teeth released their grip, springing back into Pen's hand, cackling maniacally. The mask began to curse in the same unknown language that Cesare had used for the summoning – the eye-slots brightened to a stinging dazzle – but Pen didn't wait to see what followed. She bolted for the stair, racing back up to the bedroom, opening the panel with a hasty shove.

'Shut up,' she told the Teeth. 'You'll bring every guard in the palace down on us.'

The Teeth ceased cackling and began to chant something incomprehensible on a low note of exultation. *We – are – the Teeth! We – are – the Teeth!*...

Pen stuffed them back in her pocket and left the room, glancing quickly round outside the door, sprinting along the passage. The Teeth seemed to be telling her something else but she couldn't understand them. It was curious how unsurprised she was that a toy should come to life and rescue her, almost as if she had expected it, though she knew that was impossible. Perhaps it was some kind of demonic possession, like the mask, except this time the demon was on her side. She'd seen such possession before, with a rabid dog, or the village idiot near her uncle's country house who had fits – only she didn't know it could happen with an object. She wondered what the priest would make of it, and decided it was best not to ask.

Now she was climbing the stair to the gallery. Teo and Gasparo were waiting for her by the door at the far end; in the excitement of her meeting with Cesare she'd forgotten. I've been ages, she thought, Gasparo will be furious...

The sword-fight was long over. The principal survivor – whichever side he was on – had fled, two were dead or dying, the one with the slash in his arm was tying a makeshift bandage with his free hand, holding one end in his mouth.

'Here,' she said. 'I'll do that.' She tied a rapid knot for him, as tight as she could – 'You should get this cleaned properly or it might get infected' – and ran on, leaving him a prey to bewilderment. She could see Gasparo's face through the half-open door: it was odd that none of the combatants seemed to have noticed. As she reached him he caught her arm, pulling her through – Teo was there, and everything was different, and as the door shut behind her she saw he was angry, so angry, just as she knew he would be...

CHAPTER EIGHT
Pirates of the Inland Sea

London, twenty-first century

'WELL,' SAID GAVIN, his tone bordering on sneer, 'how was your Borgia prince?'

Pen was recovering from the shock of transition while Gavin vented pent-up anxiety in general nastiness and Jinx reviewed their strategy.

'The wishing stone seems to have worked,' she said, 'and you *did* come back, in the end, but you were gone for ages, and–'

'Cesare made a deal with Azmordis,' Pen said. 'I saw him. I *saw* the Devil...'

'What did he look like?' Jinx demanded.

'He spoke through a mask,' Pen explained. 'It lit up with this sickly glow, and the lips moved. He told Cesare... he told him to kill me.'

'And did he?' said Gavin. 'I mean, did he try? Obviously, he didn't actually manage to–'

'He tried.' Pen went very quiet. She had wanted to see the prince again, to feel the nearness and the danger of him, to know herself his confidante, *utile*... When Azmordis gave the order, Cesare had barely hesitated. 'The Teeth saved me,' she went on at last. 'They jumped out and bit him on the neck. They were brilliant.'

'We're vampire teeth!' The dentures poked out of Pen's pocket. 'We can do time travel – we can bite the whole world!'

'Perhaps we should give them a bone,' said Gavin.

'We're not a dog. We want blood!'

'Don't be melodramatic,' Pen admonished.

'This beats living in the mouth of a corpse! We want freedom – freedom and the right to bite!'

'I knew they'd be useful,' said Jinx, slightly annoyed that no one had remembered taking the Teeth was her idea.

No one remembered it now.

'We should go back,' said Pen. 'It must be nearly lunchtime.'

'Teatime,' said Gavin. 'Or later. Your head's still upside down.'

'Whatever.'

'And we're not going back yet. I want to find that girl…'

EVENTUALLY, THE ARGUMENT ran out. Pen was too weary to persist – she thought there must be some sort of time lag involved, like jet lag only worse – and Jinx, who felt she was at the back of the queue for time travel, decided she simply wanted Gavin to get on with it. Then there was another dispute about which door to try in search of the witch-girl.

'We don't want to try the broom cupboard again,' said Pen. 'I'm monstered out.'

'What about upstairs?' Jinx suggested.

'We should stick with the magical dimensions,' Gavin said. 'Then I won't lose my memory.'

'You can't rely on that,' said Jinx. 'Where there are people, there's history. Anyhow, magic and history cross over, that's what Stiltz said.'

Gavin ignored her, possibly because he had no comeback.

'If this was a normal house, the kitchen would be *there*,' he went on, indicating the back of the hallway, where three steps led down to a door at lower ground level. 'I'm going for the one next to it – should be the utility room.'

'It might be another broom cupboard,' said Pen. 'The unobtrusive doors are always the worst.'

'I'm going to try, anyway.'

Gavin stood facing the door, rubbing the stone. He didn't know the girl's name but her face was very clear in his mind and when he said *the witch-girl* he was almost sure that would be enough. Presently, the stone began to glow and he opened the door...

He was looking into a large hall or temple, the kind with vaulting, and pillars, and gloom, the shadowy gloom of a cool place on a hot day. At the far end, beyond the pillars, he could see the sun's rays slanting in from somewhere, casting an oblique pattern across the floor. The gloom gleamed faintly with marble, and glimmered dimly with gold, as if there might be friezes along the walls, suggested rather than seen in the semi-dark. There was no one about.

Except the guard.

Gavin saw him at the last minute, just as he was stepping through the door. A man in a tunic and breastplate standing behind the sunbeams, peeing quietly into a corner. Gavin drew back at once.

Pen said: 'That's disgusting.'

Jinx nodded. 'Anyone would think it was a multi-storey car-park.'

'Quiet!' Gavin hissed. And: 'What do I do about him?'

'Your scenario,' said Jinx. 'Your problem.'

'Hit him over the head?' offered Pen.

'He's wearing a helmet!'

'Stab him in the back,' said Jinx.

'He's got body armour! I suppose I could use the stun-gun...'

'You can't go around stabbing people in the back,' Pen said, shocked, 'just because they're in the way. We're not psychopaths.'

'Speak for yourself,' muttered Jinx.

The guard finished his pee, picked up a spear which he had propped against the wall, and disappeared into the sunlight. Gavin returned the stun-gun to his rucksack on a sigh of relief.

'Take care,' said Pen as he crossed the threshold, not casually as you say it every day but in the voice of one who meant it. 'Remember to come back here.'

Gavin glanced over his shoulder by way of affirmation and headed for the unseen exit. They saw him for an instant caught in the sunlight, squinting at the sudden dazzle. Then he was gone.

Pen thought: 'What if he doesn't come back?' and felt the inevitable squeeze of panic at her heart. She knew it was pointless – it was even unfair – she had to share the risk, as well as the responsibility. But... Gavin was braver than her, rarely cautious or prudent, sometimes reckless. Where she would dodge trouble, he might walk straight into it, if only because he wasn't looking where he was going. And she didn't like this fixation with the witch-girl at all...

Jinx said: 'All this waiting is getting boring. We should've brought some sandwiches,' and switched on her iPod.

Beyond the Doors
Colchis, sometime in the mythical past

THERE WERE PEOPLE outside, a crowd of about thirty, grouped in an arc around the throne. Gavin would have stood out in his barbarian gear if anyone had been looking at him, but all their attention was fixed on the killing ground in front. It was a wide circular depression, like an arena, grass-grown and with no enclosing walls, only the guards standing at intervals leaning on their leaf-bladed spears. His fellow pirates were huddled in the middle. They looked weary, unshaven, shabby from the long voyage, dressed in rags of assorted clothing, moulting skins, oddments of dented armour. Very few had kept their helmets: Asterion, the giant Obelaos, the twins. Jaeson was bare-headed, his dark hair uncut and unkempt, torn leggings peeling from his thighs, his arms webbed with twisted sinews and jagged scars.

His pretty-boy face with its strangely wistful mouth was set into hardness and lines. Like the others, Gavin loved him despite his erratic moods, his dubious leadership skills, his bizarre obsessions. They had followed him because of the magic word *treasure*, the legendary Golden Ram of the East, and now here they were at the end of the world, in the Land Beyond the Blue, trapped by the machinations of an evil king, daring the challenge none had survived. Jaeson stood to the fore, at the head of his crew, his rust-bitten sword held loosely in his grasp. First to face danger, first to face death, as always...

Well, as sometimes. He had always been first to the feast, first to the women, if not first to the fight...

And the backup plan had failed. The underground passage had caved in, killing all Gavin's band except Penthesilé the Amazon and Jacynthe the peasant girl, who had agreed for a handful of coins to be their guide. Gavin had left them guarding the entrance to the passage in case there was any chance of escape; Jacynthe had said there was another exit, this side of the cave-in, not so close to the beach but far enough from palace and temple. Gavin hoped desperately she would not betray them.

Now, he could do nothing except watch.

He glanced at the throne: the king was leaning forward, hungry for slaughter, his profile all nose, like the beak of some voracious bird. His very name had the sound of a bird's scream: Æeetes. At his feet sat his young son in the care of a slave – a boy of five or six years old, fidgeting because he was bored.

The High Priestess stood apart, some way to his left. There were no other women present and somehow that singleness emphasised both her power and her pride. Her black hair was piled into a cone and bound with a twist of gold; more gold dangled from her ears and encircled her throat and wrists. Her small round breasts were naked, supported in gilded lily-cups, the exposed nipples painted red as blood. The silk of her dress poured over her nether limbs like clinging oil. Jaeson's gaze never left her, though whether in desire or hate Gavin could not tell. In that moment, he didn't care. The others had come for the treasure. He had come for the girl.

He had seen her long ago, on the beach with the Dromedon. The villagers had elected her for the sacrifice because of her dark skin and African eyes – the alien in their midst. What spells she had used to becharm the monster Gavin did not know, but they were strong spells, stronger than the ancient ritual which had held the creature in thrall for two decades, limiting it to devouring one in lieu of many. Gavin had peered from behind a boulder as the beast ate its fill, driven by both greed and vengeance, killing any that remained when its appetite was sated, while the girl shuddered and shuddered with the horror and the pleasure of it. He had been overlooked somehow, though she had seen him, he was sure of it. But he was of her race, the people of the far south – of the rose-coloured desert and the city of domes – the two of them astray in the unfamiliar realms north of the Inland Sea. The Dromedon had borne her far away, but he had vowed to find her, take her home, teach her gentleness again. He sensed that despite the lessons she had learned in survival and cruelty, she still had the warm heart of her desert kin…

She did not look at him, not yet. The king gave her the signal, and she struck the gong three times.

The Warriors of the Teeth filed onto the field. They were shorter than the barbarians but very thickset, armoured in overlapping metal scales like dragonskin, their cheek- and nose-guards closing over their faces so they had no visible features, no individual identity. They carried swords and javelins, and each man wore a dragon's tooth on a thong around his neck, which was supposed to make him invulnerable. They were a hundred and more; Jaeson's crew numbered twenty-five.

The Warriors threw their javelins. Those pirates who had shields raised them, but a few of the weapons got through: one man fell. Gavin couldn't see who it was. Then the fighting was hand-to-hand, and everything was confusion.

In any battle against overwhelming odds it is usual for the

weaker side to draw together into a tight knot, then their backs are protected and only so many of their opponents can confront them at any one time. But Jaeson had evidently decided to ignore this rule, relying on his men's ability not just to defend but to attack, pushing the fight towards the perimeter of the killing ground. The Warriors of the Teeth were highly trained but short on actual combat practice; Jaeson's crew had seen ambush and skirmish beyond count throughout the voyage. They were accustomed to fighting for their lives – to bad odds – to surviving if not winning. And it was quickly clear that the dragon's teeth of invulnerability should have been returned to the dragon for a refund. The linked-plate armour left men exposed at the throat and underarm, and the pirates had the advantage in height and reach. Many picked up the discarded javelins; Obelaos thrust one into an opponent straight through the armour-plating, driving the metal scales deep into his chest. Others slashed at legs and arms – Jaeson took off a man's head with a blow of such force it flew through the air and rolled to the feet of the king. The child bent to pick it up and cried when the slave pulled him away.

The chaos spread as the spectators found themselves sucked into the combat. Some of the Warriors seemed to be fighting each other: one threw off the helm which restricted his vision and Gavin saw it was a member of the crew who was supposed to have remained on board ship – his identity had been concealed by the face-guards. Jaeson must have summoned the extra men secretly, but only inside information would have allowed them to infiltrate the enemy. The Priestess, Gavin guessed, recalling how Jaeson had spoken to her, long and soft, after the banquet the previous night...

He had no sword – it had been lost in the cave-in – but he snatched one from a startled guard, kicking his legs from under him, then skirted round the back of the crowd. He was aiming for the girl. Jaeson's push into the audience had paid off: although in theory it increased the number of his opponents they were seized with panic – soldier and civilian fell over one another – only the pirates knew who to kill. But no one touched the Priestess. She stood unmoving, statue-still in the midst of the fight, frozen not with fear – Gavin was sure it wasn't fear – but perhaps with some inner intensity. Her gaze found him before he reached her, and for the first time her expression changed.

'I've seen you before,' she said. 'You were on the beach.'

'Come on!' Gavin grabbed her hand, pulling her away from the mêlée. 'We have to get out of here.'

'Why aren't you dead? They were all killed – all of them...'

'You let me live.'

'No... I let no one live...'

'*Come on!*'

A guard got in the way – Gavin wrenched his spear-butt aside and stabbed without thinking. His ribs twinged painfully from an old injury, but it barely slowed him down. The man folded to his knees, clutching a wound in his thigh. Somewhere deep inside himself Gavin was horrified – at his own reflexes, at the swift, careless action which had injured and might have taken a life – but that was ridiculous, he had been in a hundred fights, killed men he couldn't even remember. They all had. On Lemnos he had slain a woman who tried to poison his seafood stew. You had blood on your hands because that was the right place for it – otherwise the blood would be on your breast or your throat, and it would be your own.

He caught the girl's wrist again, dragging her into a run. And then they were in the temple, and the din of battle fled far away, and she stood in the shadows staring at him as if her gaze would devour his face.

'Yes,' she said. 'You were on the beach. You were one of them, one of the ones who condemned me.'

'I never condemned you,' he insisted. 'I didn't know what was happening. I was just... a traveller, passing through...'

But she barely seemed to hear him. 'They chose me, because I wasn't like them. They chained me like a goat for the sacrifice –

only I escaped, and the Dromedon brought me here, and the king made me his daughter, the High Priestess – though it was not a daughter's service he wanted. But you... you are of my people, my blood...' She laid a hand on his arm, skin to skin, touch to touch. He was far darker, but he knew they were akin. 'Jaeson wants the Golden Ram. He's greedy; I understand greed. I understand all the vices. What do *you* want?'

'I want to take you home,' he said.

At the far end of the temple the door stood ajar; he could see Penthesilé and Jacynthe waiting on the other side. Somehow, he knew that through that door was not just escape but safety, a passage where no pursuing foe could follow.

'This way...'

And then the fight broke into the temple as three Warriors burst through the entrance, crying that he was abducting the High Priestess. Jaeson was behind them, but his sword was notched and they were too many for him. Gavin swung round to defend himself, lunging, dodging, slicing. His sword clashed on metal, drew back, found flesh – there was an awkward lurch as the thrust went home. Jaeson had killed another at close range, ramming the broken blade up into his belly, seizing a spear from the dying man to confront the third. At his back, Gavin was half aware of the witch-girl's whisper, fearful now – yes, fearful – though not of the Warriors.

'Not that way... no... not *that* door! I passed that door once before – never again, no, never again...'

Footsteps, retreating. Penthesilé's shout of protest, abruptly cut off. The soft final thud as a door slammed shut...

Gavin wheeled, but it was too late. Penthesilé – Jacynthe – the door itself – had vanished. The wall of the temple was blank impassable stone.

He was trapped.

*   *   *

London, twenty-first century

'HE'S COMING BACK!' Pen tugged at Jinx's earphones, forcing her to switch to the real world. To one of the real worlds, anyway.

'He's found her,' Pen went on. 'That's the girl on the sea-monster – I'm sure it is.'

'She's wearing an awful lot of bling,' Jinx said disparagingly. 'Ancient Greek chav.'

They saw her talking earnestly to Gavin – saw him glance their way.

Pen said: 'I suppose he's persuading her to come with him.' She didn't sound particularly thrilled.

'Shit,' said Jinx. She didn't try.

Then the Warriors spilled into the temple with Jaeson in pursuit – Pen gave a gasp of horror which changed to awe as Gavin launched himself on the foremost assailant, wielding his borrowed sword with unnerving expertise. 'What's he *doing?*'

'Staying alive,' said Jinx. 'He's been absorbed – otherwise he wouldn't have a prayer.'

The witch-girl was walking towards them, staring at the doorway with terror-widened eyes. Her face was as pale as her complexion would allow, giving it a sort of greenish hue. One hand stretched out as if to ward off something.

'It's all right,' Pen said, realising belatedly that the other girl probably didn't understand her. 'We're here to help you...'

Unlike most people beyond the doors, the girl actually seemed to see *through*, into the calm alien environment of Bygone House. But whatever associations it had did nothing to reassure her. Pen and Jinx both remembered Stiltz talking about the boy who starved because he would not pass another door...

'Quick!' said Jinx, bracing her shoulder against the panels. 'We need a wedge!'

The girl made a gesture like a violent push – her lips moved on a word they couldn't hear. Pen cried out – '*No!* No don't...' – but the door swung shut with such force Jinx was thrown across the hall and the crash of its closing seemed to reverberate throughout the house. Pen thrust it open again immediately –

– and there was the temple, with pillars, but the pillars were made of jasper and the gloom was candlelit and a human sacrifice was bent backwards over the altar. Behind her, Jinx said: 'Damn,' and reached past, pulling the door closed.

They stood looking at each other while the sheer awfulness of the moment sank in.

Pen said: 'What do we do?' and hated her own helplessness, knowing she sounded little-girlish, pathetic, ineffectual. 'There's a pattern,' she reiterated, struggling to pull herself together. 'This door must be temples. If we keep opening it, maybe we'll get back to the right one.'

'How many temples were there in the... in the olden days?' Jinx demanded rhetorically. 'Anyhow, it could be any kind of religious building – church, mosque, synagogue. We don't even know if the same places recur.'

'Yes we do,' said Pen. 'The monks in the study. They'd obviously had intruders coming through the portal before.' She put her hand on the door knob.

'Wait!' Jinx interrupted. 'We're being really dumb. We've got the wishing stone, right? All we have to do is *wish* for Gavin.'

Pen relaxed, slowly, her rarest smile spreading itself across her face – the one that made her appear to light up from within. 'I'd forgotten,' she said. 'Stupid of me. Thank God – thank God. We must never, ever take the stone through any of the doors...'

'°Course not.'

The voice of Stiltz intruded from somewhere behind them. When they turned round, he was squatting on the hall table beside the vase, chewing on a dead twig.

'That'll be your third wish.'

'What d'you mean?' asked Pen. 'Does it matter?'

'You get three wishes. 'Tis the rule. That'll be third.'

'There was nothing about that in any of the books,' said Jinx.

'Nay lass, there's no excuse for 'ee. You're a witch; you know how magicks work. 'Tis allus three wishes – save when it's one, or two. But this is a three-banded wishing stone; you get three. There's one left. They don't put owt in books acos they don't need to. Everyone knows.'

'Hold on,' Jinx said, floundering. 'Isn't it three wishes *each*? Pen's had one, Gavin's had one, I haven't had any. We ought to get nine overall.'

'Nay,' said the goblin. 'You're all about in the head. Three wishes, then you mun wait a hundred years. That's how it goes, and no amount of moithering can change it.'

'Why didn't you tell us before?' said Pen.

'You didn't ask,' Stiltz retorted predictably. 'Any road, this one should've known. She's a witch... of sorts.'

Jinx ignored the jibe. 'If we use up the wish now,' she said, 'that's our lot. For the next hundred years.'

'I was going to find the boy,' said Pen. 'The boy in my dream. I *wasted* a wish on the prince. I can't believe I did that.'

I was going to have a turn, thought Jinx, but she didn't say it. 'Gavin or the boy?'

It was no contest.

'You'd better do the wishing,' said Jinx. 'I'm not sure how sincere I'd be – 'specially if he brings the chav.'

'Same door?'

'Guess so.'

Pen took the stone out of her rucksack, concentrated her thoughts on Gavin, and rubbed...

Beyond the Doors
Colchis, sometime in the mythical past

IN THE TEMPLE, they were running out of time.

'Æeetes will have sent for the army,' the girl said. With the closing of the portal she had recovered her self-possession. 'We must go now.'

'But Penthesilé – Jacynthe–' Gavin was still staring at the doorless wall.

'They can take care of themselves.' Jaeson was curt, uninterested. He must have charmed Jacynthe, made love to the Priestess, Gavin thought with familiar resignation. He does whatever it takes to get what he wants.

'The Golden Ram,' Jaeson said.

'Follow me.'

The witch-girl led them into an adjacent chamber and through a low door which opened only in response to a spellword, though she spoke so softly neither Gavin nor Jaeson heard what it was. There was a stair going down, leading to a vault beneath the temple; the only light came from torches burning in brackets along the walls, and shadows wheeled around them like dancers in an unending chain. For an instant, Gavin thought the shadows took shape, though what shape or shapes weren't clear, and moved by themselves. The girl lifted something from a recess in passing; glancing after her more closely, Gavin saw it was a set of Pan-pipes, the kind goatherds play to calm their flock. He was suddenly conscious of the strangeness of the scene: the twisting stair with the treads that seemed to shift in the wavering torchlight, and the ill-assorted trio of priestess and pirate and adventurer from the distant south. The girl's ear-rings clinked faintly as she moved and her dress whispered against her loins. Gavin was very aware of her but he suspected Jaeson's mind was otherwhere: his eyes stared past her and his faun-like features were clenched in the fixity of obsession. Then they emerged from the doorway into the vault, and all else was forgotten.

It was a treasure house. There were small chests and large chests and massive chests bound in iron, many of them open and spilling their contents across the floor: coins and beads and semi-precious stones, caskets encrusted with jewels and brimming with jewels, necklets and amulets, wine cups and loving cups, cloak-pins and brooches and daggers and crowns. The flamelight winked from heart's blood rubies, peacock emeralds, rose sapphires and star sapphires, topaz and sea-beryl and rainbow opal. And everywhere was the mellow gleam of gold – gold the corrupter, the seducer, the thief of honour. They halted and stared, oblivious to danger – danger outside and danger within – their eyes drawn irresistibly to the centre of the room, where a shallow basin of eternal oil burned steadily. Beside it on a stone plinth stood the Ram.

It was perhaps a foot high, made of solid gold – a gold so deeply, richly yellow that all other yellows would be dimmed by it. What craft had made it no man knew, but every detail was perfect, the curve of the horns, the curls of the fleece. This was the god in miniature, Ares the warlord, who showed himself to the favoured few in ram's form, and its possessor would have the power to lead an army, and conquer all who stood in his way.

Or at least, he would be very *very* rich...

As if mesmerised, Jaeson started to move towards it, but the girl held him back.

'No,' she said, and the beginning of a smile arched her mouth. 'Do you not see?'

In the flicker of the shadows and the glitter of the treasure they had somehow missed the guardian. It lay coiled among the chests and the spilled gold, its mottled skin blending with them. Its scales were amber and umber, bistre and bronze, and the interplay of light and dark along its endless body had woven it into the background like a charm of concealment. Gavin had heard of giant serpents, in the lands of his birth, but he had never seen one, never imagined that the little desert vipers could have kin so monstrous. In places, it was as thick as the girl's waist. There was the dry rasp of scale on scale, the chink of shifting coins, and its head rose, close to the Ram, forked tongue darting to taste the air. The mouth opened, showing huge fangs and the venom glands arching across its palate. Gavin raised his sword; Jaeson still had his enemy's spear.

'Leave it to me,' said the witch.

She placed the pipes to her lips and began to play.

The tune was a mere ripple of sound, soft as water; it was wavelets running over sand, dewmelt in the rising dawn. There were no words, but words shaped themselves in Gavin's head, fragments of verse half nonsense, half magic...

Hark to the piper that pipes the spell!
The chant in enchantment, the wish in the well...
List to the singer who sings of sleep –
the drift into slumber millennium deep –
no starlight in midnight, no dawnlight to creep
from hillside and shoreside to tower and keep...

The monster's head swayed and sank, the fangs folding backward as its mouth closed, the great coils settling into a creeping slumber. Gavin felt his own eyelids drooping as his mind started to drift away. There was a moment of suspended time when he lost touch with who and where he was; he thought he was an unknown boy from a magic country of warm sumptuous interiors, boxes that talked and lights that burned without a flame, a country of horseless chariots moving at fantastic speed through a city that went on forever...

'Now,' said the girl, and he woke up.

Jaeson was lifting the Ram – it seemed to be very heavy – carrying it under one arm, the spear still held in his other hand.

The Priestess had knotted the pipes into her girdle, freeing her hands to kilt her skirts, but in her haste she must have made the knot too loose, and as they fled back up the stairs the pipes slipped to the floor. Gavin bent to retrieve them, thrusting them into the deepest pocket of his breeches. The girl didn't seem to notice. They stumbled into the lighter gloom of the temple, blinking at the sunglimmer through the arched entrance. They thought it was empty save for the bodies of the fallen – the guard Gavin had taken was groaning, till Jaeson finished him off – then they saw the slave assigned to the young prince had taken refuge there, crouching in the shade beyond the sun's reach. The child brightened when he saw the Priestess and came towards her. She picked him up, while the slave cowered away from them.

'We'll take him,' she said. 'He may be useful' – as if he was a thing, another treasure stolen from the king's hoard, not a living boy.

Gavin said: 'How?' and Jaeson complained: 'He'll cry, and get in the way,' but the girl held him tight and they followed her. Out into the sun and the last throes of the fight, summoning the other pirates as they ran, heading past the battleground for the path down to the cove where they had beached their ship. Æeetes and the rest of the court had fled, no doubt unwilling to risk the wait for reinforcements, and the Warriors of the Teeth were slain or scattered. For the moment, there was no serious pursuit. Jaeson's men left their dead but the wounded were carried pig-a-back by those who had the strength for it; Obelaos, bigger and tougher even than Herakles, lifted one man easily in his arms, Asterion shared the weight of another with a fellow pirate.

At the beach, the handful left on board ship had readied everything for departure.

'What about Penthesilé?' Gavin demanded, his shoulder against the stern. Most of the crew were already at the oars.

'We can't wait,' Jaeson said as the *Argo* slid into the water. 'There'll be an entire army here any minute.' He vaulted onto the deck and Gavin swung over the side after him. He knew Penthesilé would not come.

They strained against the drag of the coastal current, and gradually the headland slipped behind them and they were out in the open sea. They saw soldiers on the beach, swarming dark figures too distant for the peril of bowshot or spear-throw. But they were few, and Jaeson frowned as he watched them. The little boy, released from his sister's clasp, was running up and down, excited and intrigued, laughing when the ship lurched and he tumbled over. Two crewmen were raising the sail as the wind picked up. The witch-girl stood beside Jaeson and Gavin, gazing towards the shore.

'The pride of the king's fleet is a trireme,' she said, 'larger than this, and swifter. We will need a strong wind and a long lead to get away.'

But the wind blew gently and their lead was still short when they saw the purple sail rounding the point, and the ram's head prow beating on their trail.

London, twenty-first century

In the ancient beige offices of Whitbread Tudor Hayle, the newest incumbent sat facing the senior partner across a crowded expanse of desk.

'So you're a Tudor,' said Mr Lazarus, who, despite his name, was still very much alive and a few years short of retirement age. 'That really is very fortunate. We like to maintain the family connection. The present generation of Hayles are in the City and the Whitbreads, I am sorry to say, have gone to America.' He spoke as if it was the modern equivalent of Sodom and Gomorrah. 'Of course, I can see the relationship. You have the colouring.'

The young man opposite him had the pallor of someone who never sees the sun and a blaze of golden-red hair worn rather too long for a lawyer, though somehow Mr Lazarus didn't like to say so.

'I'm only a distant cousin,' he said. 'This girl – Penelope, isn't it? – may not even have heard of me.' He had the faintest hint of an accent, so faint that Lazarus couldn't place it and didn't try.

'I'm sure she will be happy to know she has a family member to rely on,' the older man said comfortably. 'This business of Andrew Pyewackett's Will really has been most awkward.

There's no precedent – no precedent at all. One is used to people choosing unlikely legatees – one lady recently left a small fortune divided between a goldfish and a budgerigar, though I believe at the last count the goldfish decided to take the matter to court – but executors are supposed to be responsible adults. I daresay we should be grateful he didn't have a pet.'

'There is a dog,' said the young man. 'Or so I understand.'

'Is there? Well, well. I can see you're already well-informed. Of course, this girl has her rights, but as the firm's official representative you should be able to handle her. Yes, really a very great relief. One doesn't like to think of a minor bearing so much responsibility. There has been no sign of this Bartlemy Goodwin, no sign at all.'

'Difficult,' said the young man. 'The main house is a valuable property, isn't it? And currently unoccupied. It seems to be something of a waste. Selling is out of the question, naturally, but perhaps it could be let for a while. I might even know a suitable tenant.'

'Good, good,' said Mr Lazarus. 'I don't know why it hasn't been considered before. A waste, as you say. The girl is staying in the smaller house, at the express wish of the decedent, but there's no one in Number 7. He was against the whole idea of an occupant, I don't know why. A rather eccentric personality. But there's nothing in the Will to prevent it. I imagine it may be haunted or something – this firm does handle some rather unusual portfolios – but I trust that won't prevent you adopting a business-like approach.'

'Certainly not,' said the newcomer.

'Exactly. I can see you believe in maintaining a professional attitude. Well, I'll leave everything in your hands. Do consult if there are any problems.'

'Of course,' said the young man, who didn't look as if he ever needed to consult. Not with other lawyers, anyway.

He rose, and went back to the (beige) office formerly occupied by Jasveer Patel. There was a new laptop on the desk, a svelte, matte-black machine as slim as an after-dinner mint, with no manufacturer's logo but a complex scarlet sigil embossed on the top. The young man opened it: the keys were blank, but when he touched a switch on the side glimmering letters came and went in an assortment of different alphabets. The screensaver was a small flame dancing at the heart of a circle and instead of the touchpad there was an inset disc which lit up with the skull of a rat, fanged and with glowing red eyes. The young man pressed the left eye twice: the screen went dark, black as a black hole – there was no surface any more, only a window into emptiness. Gradually, an image appeared, an indistinct figure, more shadow than substance, sitting behind a gleaming desktop on which stood an inkless well, a quill pen, a dagger which might or might not be for cutting paper. And a skull. A skull that glistened as if it were covered in chips of ice, which of course it was.

The light from the desk lamp winked back from the skull in a thousand glancing stars, but it did not reach the seated figure. No light could illuminate *him* any more, nor ever would again.

'Master,' said the lawyer.

'Sætor.' The ice-edged, steel-cold voice sounded slightly bored.

'I'm established at the company. They've appointed me as their representative to replace Patel. All according to plan.'

'Of course. Have you anything else to report?'

'I told them I'm a Tudor. The red hair clinched it. Whether the girl will be fooled is another matter; I have the impression she's fairly intelligent.' There was a frown in his tone, more than his expression; an undercurrent of doubt.

'She's a human child.' The Shadow was contemptuous. 'What can she know? She will barely have lived before her time comes to die. Indeed, if she is not careful, it may come very soon. She does not interest me.'

'Perhaps not.' The young man was conscientiously respectful. 'But there is something about her which disturbs me, something I can't remember…'

'I see no reason for her to disturb me. You have always been adept at dealing with any trouble. Deal with it.'

'Certainly, Master.'

'The important thing is to assert control on the ground. The candidates for my apprenticeship may appear very shortly, and it is essential that *my* representative should be there to greet them and bring them to me. This weak link in the chain of guardianship is most opportune. There are those who might call it the workings of providence, and claim God is on their side. It would be ironic, would it not, if there *was* a God, and He was backing Me.'

'Good one,' said the skull. 'I like it. Nothing like a touch of religious ambiguity to get the philosophers going.'

'I was not aware that I had appointed you my personal philosopher,' said the Shadow, his coldness dropping towards permafrost. 'May I remind you that your function here is purely decorative.'

'I was being your flatterer, not your philosopher,' the skull said indignantly. 'Just leading the applause, so to speak.'

'I don't require flattery,' responded the Shadow. He lifted a finger, and the jaws locked into a sudden silence. Then his attention reverted to the lawyer. 'You have served me well, Sætor. *Usually*. Remember, I do not reward failure.'

For a second, the young man seemed to shiver, as if at a memory of utter cold.

'Of course,' the Shadow continued, silkily, 'I do not reward success, either. Success, like martyrdom, is its own reward.'

'The ancient martyrs believed they were going to Paradise,' the lawyer pointed out, less diffidently than he should have done.

'Whereas you,' said the Shadow, 'are already in Hell.'

He vanished into the void of the vacant screen, and after about half a minute the surface re-formed and the flame was back in place, dancing its little fandango at the nucleus of the circle. Presently, the young man clicked the rat and a set of desktop icons appeared which looked almost normal, until you studied them closely. He opened a window called the Infernet and began to research Bartlemy Goodman...

Beyond the Doors
Colchis, sometime in the mythical past

'How strong is your magic?' Jaeson asked the witch-girl.

The trireme was almost on them. They could see the precise carving of the ram's head prow, and the throne of Æeetes on a platform before the mast, with the small figure of the king hunched forward like some avine predator, crested with the gleaming spikes of his crown. And like an undertone to the rush and surge of their own bow-wave they could hear the drumbeat that set the pace for the oarsmen, a steady relentless throb. 'They are galley slaves,' said Jaeson. 'They have no loyalty, only the whip. Freemen row faster.'

'If they flag, they are thrown overboard with their limbs cut to draw sharks,' said the Priestess. 'They row for their lives. That is a stronger incentive than any imaginary loyalty.'

There was a long pause. Gavin listened to the regular *boom!* *boom!* and pictured the slaves chained to their oars, heaving till their muscles tore and the breath seared their lungs...

'How powerful is your magic?' Jaeson repeated.

'Magic doesn't work well on water,' said the girl. Gavin wondered if she would ask for the pipes, but her mind seemed to be elsewhere. 'It's an unstable element: it distorts the effect of any spell, no matter how potent. I thought everyone knew that. There are sea-gods I could call on, but they are as unreliable as the waves and harder to control. And there is the Dromedon, but he is far away, in the depths beyond the sun; I do not think he would hear me.'

'We're sunk,' Gavin said, and wished he had used a less appropriate verb.

'Not yet,' said the girl. 'I can summon a mist to hide us; that is simple enough, and should not go awry. It is merely a matter of drawing the water upwards, transforming it into fog – a natural process at sea. But it won't veil our escape for long unless we can slow the pursuit.'

'Nothing will do that,' Jaeson said sombrely. 'We have Æeetes' most priceless treasure – and his son. It will take more than a fog to turn him aside.'

'As you say,' the witch-girl smiled, and her eyes gleamed like black honey, 'we have his son.'

She called the child to her and lifted him up; he wrapped his arms around her neck. 'See,' she said, 'it's Papa. Wave to him!'

The boy waved blithely.

The figure of the king stiffened; his head jerked backward as if at a blow. Perhaps he had not known till then that the prince was gone; no doubt the slave, fearing retribution, had fled without reporting his defection. Æeetes leaped to his feet, shouting something at the captain who stood close by. The cry was passed on, and below decks the drumbeat quickened.

Boom ba-ba-boom ba-ba-boom ba-ba-boom...

'Give me a knife,' said the girl. The nearest rower stayed his oar to sling his dagger in her direction; it stuck in the stern beside her, vibrating from the force of the blow. Unworried, she plucked it out, holding it high in the air.

'Æeetes!' she called, and the name which was so like a gull's scream carried effortlessly across the narrowing space between the ships. 'Æeetes!'

The king shaded his eyes, staring at the girl he had called his daughter. He saw the sunglitter on the knife-blade, and the boy clinging happily to her breast.

'Tell the slaves to ship their oars,' she cried, 'or I swear, you will pick up the pieces one by one!'

The king seemed to quail visibly. In his country, they believed that the spirit would not depart unless the body was buried entire; dismembered corpses must be reassembled, or the ghost would haunt his own grave, bewailing the missing portion of his anatomy. If you quitted this life in a maimed form you could not be reborn complete in the next, or so the legend claimed. The greatest punishment that a man could suffer was to be buried minus an essential body part; men who had been castrated were thought to be reborn as women. Æeetes and his predecessors routinely castrated their enemies.

If the legend was true, Gavin thought, looking at the Priestess, perhaps that was a mistake. The female of the species...

The drumbeat halted. The three tiers of oars were raised, dripping sea. The girl still held the knife aloft, a familiar glory of triumph in her face.

Slowly, they drew away from the enemy. But the Argonauts did not cheer. Her elation was too naked, too terrible for applause. Pirates may rape and pillage – it goes with the job – but they do not kill coldly, nor shed innocent blood, not if it can be avoided. And the Priestess was a woman, young and good to look upon, shaped for gentleness and pleasure. Her stark ruthlessness appalled them.

The boy alone was untroubled, oblivious to any danger. She set him down and watched him run along the deck towards the bows, a smile curving her lips. 'I told you he would be useful,' she said.

'You wouldn't really kill him,' Jaeson said uneasily. 'There are some things no man should do – or woman – acts offensive in the sight of the gods...'

'That depends,' said the Priestess, 'which gods are watching.'

She thrust the knife through her girdle and approached the side of the ship, spreading her arms in a gesture of supplication. Gavin heard her murmuring a low-toned litany in a language he didn't understand, a language with guttural Rs and sibilant Ss and a timbre at once cool and seductive, totally unlike their rough demotic Greek. A language of poetry and passion, of grimmerie and sortilege – the language of an older world, whose ruined fanes and fallen citadels still cast a long dark shadow into the sunlight of the present day. Gavin shivered when he made out a word or two clearly, as if a cold finger had touched the nape of his neck.

'She has power, this one,' Jaeson muttered, 'but I do not like the sound of it. These are the black arts.'

'Black or not,' said Gavin, 'they may save your hide.' He leaped automatically to her defence, for all his private doubts.

All around them the mist was rising, leeched from the sluggish waves in a thin vapour which thickened as it ascended, slowly enfolding the ship in a white fuzzy blanket. They could no longer see from fore to aft and the tip of the mast vanished as the whiteness arched over them, swallowing the sun. They were encased in a cocoon of pallor which gave them the impression that although the oars dipped and rose they were not moving at all. Jaeson urged his men to pull harder, but it was difficult when there was no horizon to aim for, no sun or stars to guide them, no visible enemy to flee. Gavin took a turn at the oars, though as the official navigator (and ship's cook), he rarely did so; behind him, Asterion said in a low voice: 'I don't like this. We could be going round in circles.'

'The witch says no,' Gavin responded. The Priestess pointed ahead when Jaeson seemed in doubt.

'She may be an enchantress,' Asterion argued, 'but what does she know about sailing a ship?'

One of the things Gavin had brought from the city of the south was the mechanical device on his wrist which marked the passage of time. It divided the day into twenty-four hours, each hour into sixty minutes, each minute into sixty heartbeats. The pirates were fascinated by it, though they were not sure what it was for. In the mist, it gave time a shape and definition. Nearly an hour and a half had gone by, and Jaeson was on the oar opposite Gavin, when they heard the drumbeat again. The sound was muffled and distorted by the fog; they could not tell if it was near or far, to starboard or to port. Sometimes, it seemed to come from the sea itself, a slow implacable pounding like a gigantic pulse.

Boom... ba-ba... boom... ba... ba... boom...

'He's used the mist as a cloak, just as we did,' Jaeson said. 'He's been following our wake.'

'He doesn't know how close he is,' Asterion opined shrewdly, 'or he'd have silenced the drum.'

The witch-girl was standing in the stern; her foster-brother clung to her skirts.

She said: 'We will have to slow him down.'

Gavin and Jaeson simultaneously shelved their oars and sprang towards her.

The witch tugged the knife from her girdle, pulling the boy's head back. He gave a tiny gasp of surprise: that was all. The knife was swift and sharp. Gavin tasted the blood in his mouth, looked down and saw he was sodden with it.

He didn't make it to the ship's side before he threw up.

BOOM... BA-BA... boom... ba-ba... boom... ba-ba... boom...

JAESON STARED AT the small, limp thing which still clung to the silk of her skirt. He and Gavin had been very close when the throat opened; his ragged tunic was clammy with blood-spatter.

There was little on the girl.

'Don't mourn for him,' she said. 'He would have grown up like his father, a tyrant who tortured and killed without a qualm. They always do. He had a kitten once, but he made the slave wring its neck when it scratched him. He liked hurting things. I have spared him the burden of their pain.'

She sawed at the body with the knife; the blood ran across the deck into the bilges.

'So much blood,' Jaeson said, 'from something so small...'

'You needn't trouble about the gods,' the girl said in a tone that was almost cool, almost dry. 'Even their eyes cannot pierce the fog.'

She tossed a hand into the sea. It looked like a little flower floating on the foam, save for the red stain that veined the bubbles around it.

Then it was gone in the mist.

'We'll make that one easy for him,' she said.

The Argo was utterly silent. The pirates had stopped rowing, and gazed at her with a single face.

Presently, some way behind them, they heard the scream.

The drumbeat faltered and ceased.

Gavin had fallen to his knees in his own vomit, but he straightened up at last, his stomach emptied. 'You shouldn't have done that,' Jaeson was saying. 'You shouldn't have killed a child...'

'That's why I brought him. Don't pretend you didn't know.' She glanced at the oarsmen. 'Row! This is your chance. Take it!'

Jaeson said dully: 'Row.'

They rowed.

She threw the other hand some way to starboard, so Æeetes would have to hunt for it. The remaining body-parts followed, piece by piece. The head was last, bobbing up and down in the waves like that of a swimmer too far from the shore. Gavin and Jaeson watched till it was out of sight. Then Jaeson lowered a bucket over the side and poured water across the deck to wash away the blood. It was the sort of task he would normally have given to one of the crew.

But the blood will never really wash away, Gavin thought. His clothes were stiffening as it dried. Blood on our hands, on our heads. A child's blood. Whatever his future, we took it from him. The girl seemed to have no guilt, no remorse: the remorse and the guilt were for them. He feared her conscience had been lost long before, in the cage where she awaited her doom with the sea-monster, or some other hell-dimension he had not seen.

'He will forget,' she said to Gavin, meaning Jaeson. 'In the dark he will lie in my arms and lock the memory away in a little casket, with all the other memories you never take out, never look at, never remember again. A little casket buried deep inside, to be opened at your peril. I have a little casket too; did you know? But mine is triple-locked and loaded with chains and weighted with lead, sunken so deep no one will ever find it, not even me. One day you too will have a little casket; you'll see.'

He thought it strange, so strange, that he still didn't know her name.

But he didn't ask.

'Maybe you're right,' he said. 'When the world is wrong, people like you are always right. But I'll try to unlock it, no matter what's inside. I'll try.'

THE DOOR OPENED on a curtain of falling water, turning the sunlight all to rainbows. Pen peered round and realised they were *behind* a waterfall; through a gap beside the cascade she saw a vista of tumbled rocks, gnarly olive trees, a green secret pool where random bubbles floated at play. Arcady – though Pen didn't recognise it as such. A dragonfly zoomed above the water like a tiny iridescent helicopter. Jinx, whose knowledge of mythology was based largely on a video of *Hercules* which she had seen as a child, wondered if there would be nymphs and satyrs.

There weren't. Just the idyllic scenery, and the dragonfly.

Pen said: 'Perhaps I should go and look for Gavin.'

'Too risky,' said Jinx.

And: 'I hope he's lost the chav.'

There was an interval of birdsong and the splash-and-chatter of the fall; then they saw him. He came to the farther side of the pool and waded straight into the water without pausing to undress. He looked different – so different that for a few seconds they didn't speak or call to him: they could only stare and stare. He evidently hadn't shaved for days and the resulting stubble gave him an air of gangster toughness which should have been glamorous but wasn't. He had lost the rucksack which he had taken into the past but there was a sword lashed to his belt and his sweatshirt and jeans were blotched with rust-brown stains which looked like dried blood.

That's because they *are* dried blood, Jinx thought.

Pen, for once in her life, didn't think at all.

Gavin pulled off his sweatshirt and ducked his whole body under the water as though desperate to wash off more than the dirt. Then he began to splash towards the fall.

'Gavin!' Pen cried, her voice released at last. 'Gavin, here! Quick!'

Involuntarily, she started through the door, but Jinx held her back. 'Don't be stupid,' she said. 'He's coming this way–'

Gavin said something in a foreign language, but Pen was used to that by now and it didn't bother her. He was looking at her with stupefaction and relief, scrambling over the rocks in front of the door. She stretched out her hands to him – caught his arms – pulled him through into Number 7. Jinx yanked the door shut; there was a crunch as the latch slid home…

London, twenty-first century

THEN GAVIN WAS hugging Pen, dripping all over the carpet, shivering from the chill of the water or some other reaction.

When he could speak English again, he began to cry.

CHAPTER NINE
The Pied Piper

Beyond the Doors
London, seventeenth century

IN THE CITY, the long deadly summer was nearly over. September rain dripped from the eaves and streamed from the runnels and washed the rubbish from street to alleyway, from gutter to drain, from blockage to blockage, though no one wondered where it ended up. After the showers the city steamed like a midden. In the creek, the crust broke and piled up along the waterline or was carried in bobbing lumps towards the river. Above the Grim Reaper, in the loft, the roof leaked in several places; Ghost put buckets to catch the drips, because he said the rainwater was cleaner than anything they could get elsewhere.

'Does it matter?' Cherub asked without interest, drinking from a mug of ale Mags had brought from the tavern.

'My old ma used to say, cleanliness is next to godliness,' Mags volunteered, casting a doubtful glance at Ghost.

'There you are then,' said Cherub. 'We ain't godly, so why bother to be clean?'

'Clean water and clean food don't carry plague,' said Ghost.

'You've had it,' Cherub pointed out. 'You don't catch plague again. An I reckon if Mags and I ain't had it yet, then we ain't gonna.'

Mags grinned. Ghost noticed she still had good teeth, even and just a little discoloured, though not as good as Cherub. Cherub's teeth stayed white as ivory no matter what he ate, and shone against the dirt of his face like fresh snow on a dung heap. Ghost knew Big Belinda lusted after those teeth, as if they were a treasure she wanted to add to her hoard. Teeth like that were worth gold.

He said: 'We need to talk about the plan.'

Cherub's cheek turned pale under its patina of grime.

'I don't like it,' he said. 'I don't want to be no choirboy for the Duke.'

'It's just so I can get into the house,' said Ghost. 'You have to find the underground passage, and let me in.'

'What you going to do there?' Mags asked timidly. 'You can't do the Duke like... like they did Cullen. Nobody cared about Cullen, but a duke's a duke. They'd send the constables arter you, an' the army. They'd hunt you through every attic and cellar in the city. Being dead wouldn't save you.'

'You'd be hanged,' Cherub said with satisfaction, as if it was an achievement. 'Hanged and drawed and quartered, most like. I ain't never seen a quartering. They say there's lots of blood.'

'I won't be caught,' said Ghost. 'Whatever I do, no one's going to know I done it. No one'll be alive to know.'

The look on his face was tight and set, and Cherub shivered at the sight of it.

'What about us?' said Mags. 'We'll know...'

'You're my people,' Ghost said. 'I'll see you safe. We'll get Tomkin out, then I'll see you all safe.'

'Won't be no place safe,' said Cherub, 'if you do the Duke.'

Ghost didn't say *Trust me* because in the city no one trusted anyone. He just stared at them with those eyes that were like bits of agate, hard and dark and gleamy. You didn't argue with a stare like that.

Cherub muttered again: 'I don't like it,' but it was only a mutter. He didn't expect his leader to pay any attention.

Ghost paid no attention. 'The plan,' he said.

*   *   *

London, twenty-first century

GAVIN LAY IN his bed at home, wishing he could stop thinking. He had gone beyond exhaustion into a zone of grey weariness where his thoughts trudged round and round in circles like prisoners in an exercise yard, going nowhere. Always the same thoughts, no matter how hard he tried not to think them. Round and round in narrowing circles, spiralling inward on the same moment, the same horror, playing it over and over again the more he struggled to pull his mind away. It was growing distant now, retreating into another dimension, but somehow that only made it worse, because he knew he was getting used to it, and it would settle into his memory and become a part of it, an old familiar ugliness. His history teacher had talked recently about the Nazi concentration camps, and the few who survived the daily round of brutality and privation, and the factory line of death. Human beings can get used to anything, he had said. I don't need a little casket, Gavin thought in the wasteland of his fatigue and self-disgust. I'll get used to it…

He didn't want to sleep, for fear of what he might dream.

He had stuffed all his clothes in the washing machine as soon as he got home, a task he normally left for his mother. The rucksack was lost for good, with everything inside it, including the stun-gun. He wondered what the pirates would make of it – if they would figure out how it worked – but as it couldn't be re-charged he reasoned it wouldn't last long. He had the witch-girl's Pan-pipes in the pocket of his jeans, but he didn't know how to play them, or if the magic in their tune came from the pipes or the piper. In any case, it didn't matter. Nothing mattered now.

He thought he had been naïve, imagining he could help. No one can help anyone, he concluded gloomily. The witch-girl whose name he would probably never know had slit the boy's throat, and the blood had spurted over *him*, like a fountain, like a baptism, and now he was getting used to it. He didn't even feel sick any more.

It was obscene.

His mobile made the tinkly sound that indicated a text. It was gone one in the morning; who would text him at such an hour? He was half afraid to look at it, feeling it could only be bad news, an accusation, a condemnation...

It was from Pen.

She used predictive text, so every word was spelled out in full, and for an instant, reading it, he could almost hear her voice. 'Expect you can't sleep. Think about cooking. Think about chocolate.'

She was right, of course. She was so right it was like a warm hand closing over his. He lay back and shut his eyes, thinking about cooking the way some people count sheep. Eventually, he slipped into a dream of chocolate sponge, only someone stuck a knife into it, and the sauce spattered out all over his clothes, wet and sticky and sticking to him, so he couldn't scrub it off...

ON SUNDAY NIGHT Jinx disappeared off to the country and Pen spent the evening with her grandmother, the first evening they had had alone together for some time. Eve, who had hoped to do some adult-child bonding, found it oddly disturbing. Pen had always been serious and diligent, not given to mood-switches, still little more than a child for all her gravitas and intellectual attainments. Now, she seemed suddenly to have grown up, grown far beyond her years, until she was almost a stranger – a creature of changing moods, abstracted or distracted, who would light up for no reason and then shut herself away behind a mask of thought. Her grandmother supposed it had to do with her new responsibilities in Temporal Crescent, or perhaps her friendship with Gavin ('Not a boyfriend,' Pen had assured her), and wondered if some of it was her own imagination. Teenagers could change so quickly, transforming overnight from loving lively children into brooding adolescents who binged on alcohol and ecstasy, anime and anomie, self-obsession and self-harm. They never told you what was wrong and then blamed you for not understanding. Mrs Harkness hadn't believed Pen would go that way, but this new Pen appeared out of reach, unpredictable, capable of anything.

When she tried to put her anxieties into words, they were brushed aside as unimportant.

'There's nothing to worry about, Grandma. I'm fine. I'm always fine. I'm just getting older, like people do. It isn't a big deal.'

Which might be true, thought Mrs Harkness, but it didn't reassure her at all.

Jinx returned to Temporal Crescent on Monday morning. Eve had gone to work and Quorum was making omelettes for lunch. Pen was downstairs welcoming Hoover with more than her usual enthusiasm when the doorbell rang.

Quorum went into the hallway with the dog trotting at his heels; Hoover's ears were pricked and his hackles stirred as if at a faint cold breeze. Felinacious was curled in the chair beside Pen, overflowing the seat on two sides. Dog and cat had evidently agreed to a kind of tacit truce, where each loftily ignored the other at every possible opportunity.

Quorum returned a minute later, looking slightly discomposed. 'A young man to see you,' he said, turning his attention back to the pan. 'I told him you were at lunch, but he is most anxious to talk to you. Apparently, he comes from Whitbread Tudor Hayle – he's taken over from poor Mr Patel.'

Pen felt rather grand, being 'at lunch'. 'Perhaps he'd like to join me,' she said.

Hoover was blocking the kitchen door somehow, so the newcomer couldn't enter immediately. There was a confused moment when dog and visitor seemed to be manoeuvring for position, impeding or being impeded, then Hoover stationed himself next to Pen as if on guard and the young man came in.

'I gather you're Penelope Tudor,' he said. The hint of an accent coloured his speech, but what colour it was impossible to tell. 'My name is Seth Kayser. I believe we may be distant cousins – on my mother's side.'

Pen said nothing at all. The omelette sat in front of her, untouched.

The young man had red hair and the blanched complexion of the undead. He extended a hand towards her, a slender white hand with tapering fingers, the hand of a poet – or a poisoner.

Pen didn't take it.

Quorum asked the visitor: 'Would you care for some tea? Or coffee?'

Slowly, her brain re-engaged, wheels creaking into action. For her, it had been two days ago; for him, more than five hundred years. He doesn't recognise me, she thought. Not yet, anyway. *He doesn't remember...*

She thought blankly that this was worse than the car accident. This was the world beyond the doors reaching into Now, past invading present, evil coming home to roost...

All the way home.

She wondered how he could live so long. Hadn't Azmordis said something to him about immortality, and slavery, and doom? Perhaps he had been transformed into something more spirit than flesh, the demon servant of a demonic master. He still looked human, or nearly so, but she knew enough to realise that in the otherworld of magic and darkness, appearances can deceive. She sensed it was vital not to betray herself, not to show foreknowledge or fear. But she couldn't take his hand. Her small freckled face was closed and secretive by construction if not intent; the blandness of youth hid many things. The man who called himself Seth Kayser saw a shy, slightly awkward girl whose image bothered him for reasons he couldn't quite place, but he registered no untoward reaction, no shadow of a lie. He had had little to do with the innocent; he did not know how much such innocence can conceal.

He accepted coffee, apologised briefly for the disruption, and seated himself opposite Pen.

'I wanted to talk to you about Number 7. We need to discuss our options with a view to maximising the financial benefit...'

There was a muffled gnashing noise which Pen hoped was covered by the clatter of crockery and something thumped against her hip. The Teeth had taken to living in her pocket; she realised they were excited by the proximity of a former victim. She slapped her hand over them and produced a taut smile.

'What do you mean?' She knew she sounded stupid but it was difficult to concentrate with a set of rabid dentures champing against her palm.

'I believe the house has been vacant for some time but it's a top-of-the-range property. Even in the current market there should be no problem finding a tenant at a suitably high rent. I might possibly be able to arrange something myself—'

'No,' said Pen.

'I don't think you understand the situation. As executors, we have a duty to manage the estate in any way that will augment its value. You're a minor; you have what might be termed an honorary role. I'm sure you enjoy living here and there's no reason why you shouldn't continue to do so, but it really would be best if you left business matters up to me.'

'No,' said Pen. This was the law, and the law was one area where she was always at home. 'Actually, I understand the situation very well. I'm too young to sign cheques or anything like that but you can't let Number 7 without my permission and I won't give it so that's that.'

Belatedly aware she sounded both abrupt and rude, she added: 'I'm sorry.'

The Teeth had lapsed into stillness but Hoover put his chin on the table and glared menacingly. Quorum, conscious of undercurrents but unclear what they were, busied himself preparing coffee.

Seth Kayser looked straight into Pen's eyes. 'Why?'

The familiar worm of response wriggled inside her, but she knew it now for the worm it was. He was as cool as an iced drink on a hot day, the kind of coolness that would freeze your fingers to the glass. But he was no longer the prince, scheming to seize his kingdom, just a solicitor with a slick manner and a designer suit and all the usual jargon.

'It would be against the expressed wish of Andrew Pyewackett,' she explained. 'He expressed his wishes very strongly: Quorum will confirm that.'

'Indeed,' said the butler, setting the cafetière on the table.

'As executors,' she went on, warming to her theme, 'our first duty is to act for the deceased, in accordance with his wishes. That is what I intend to do.'

'I repeat, you are a minor. I could insist–'

'I cannot imagine your firm would want their reputation sullied with such a conflict,' Quorum interceded gently.

The lawyer's gaze narrowed. 'I would hope,' he said, still addressing himself principally to Pen, 'that this matter could be resolved without conflict of any kind. As I said, we are family, if distant. Our common colouring gives that away. I wouldn't like you to see me as an enemy.'

Cards on the table, thought Pen. He'll remember me... sooner or later.

The later the better.

'I don't know of any relationship,' she declared. 'The world is full of red-haired people who aren't my cousins.'

'I can prove it, you know,' he said lightly. 'I have the documentation. My mother's birth certificate...'

Pen shrugged. She knew he was lying, documents or no, and he probably knew that she knew, but she wanted to keep him in a state of uncertainty for a while longer. If she could.

He took a mouthful of coffee by way of courtesy and got to his feet.

'By the way,' he said, 'were you well acquainted with my predecessor? Jasveer Patel.'

'Not really,' said Pen. 'He was nice, though.'

'I was told the accident happened just outside here: is that right?'

'Yes,' Pen said shortly.

'It must have been very distressing for you,' Seth Kayser said in a voice as smooth as pouring cream.

'Yes,' said Pen.

'Accidents can happen so easily.' The threat was butterfly-light, soft as a spring breeze. 'You should be careful.'

'I think you should leave now,' Quorum said very firmly.

And then Jinx walked in – Jinx with her spiked hair standing out in all directions, her mascara-smudges, her pre-lunch expression of Neanderthal sullenness. She acknowledged the visitor with a grunt and sat down in the chair he had vacated. The tension trickled out of the moment like water from a cracked glass.

'Scrambled eggs,' she said, observing Pen's virgin plate. 'Yuk. I hate the runny bit in the middle.' She reached for the coffee.

Quorum escorted the visitor to the front door.

'I DON'T LIKE it,' Quorum said. 'Mr Pyewackett wouldn't have liked it. He didn't approve of this sort of thing.'

'He isn't here,' Pen said, 'and we are, and we're the ones in a mess. Anyhow, Jinx knows what she's doing... don't you?'

'Sort of,' said Jinx, who was selecting a bowl from a cupboard full of crockery. 'Just don't wash up that coffee cup. Don't even tip the coffee away... Don't you watch CSI?'

'What's CSI got to do with it?' asked Pen, temporarily baffled.

'DNA. Cesare – Seth Kayser – whoever he is – even if he's one of the Serafain, he's still human, or part human. I don't think humanity is something you can ever completely get rid of. His saliva should be on the cup, and in the coffee. I'm not sure if it'll be any use, but it's worth a try.'

'You're going to do some kind of scientific test?' There was relief in Quorum's voice. 'Forgive me: I thought you were about to attempt... well, magic.'

'Of course I'm going to do magic,' Jinx said. 'I'm crap at science. I'm crap at magic too, if it comes to that, but I had a brilliant teacher.'

'But...' Quorum looked daunted.

'What's DNA got to do with magic?' Pen said.

'Everything.' Having chosen a plain china bowl of suitable size, Jinx deposited it on the table with a *clunk!* that made the butler wince. 'Look, when you make an image of someone, you need some of their hair, or blood, or whatever, and then it *becomes* that person, and you can do spells on it. It's called sympathetic magic. It's very very ancient, and it's based on the idea that your blood and your hair *are* you. Modern science proves that's right – DNA. The... the formula for who you are is in every bit of your body. Right?'

'I see,' said Pen. 'It's like old herbal remedies connecting to today's medicine. Even a long time ago, people knew more than we think they did. But you aren't going to make a... a voodoo doll, are you?'

'Nope,' said Jinx. 'I'm scrying. That works in the same sort of way. If you want to see something personal – something about yourself, or people really close to you – you use your own blood. If it's someone else, someone distant, you need theirs. The books always say blood, because it's magic, and magic tends to be a bit primitive and melodramatic about things, but I'm pretty sure any physical stuff will do. My great-grandmother used hair once.'

'And you're going to use coffee?' said Quorum.

'Saliva.' Jinx poured water from the kettle into the bowl. 'This may not work – it probably won't – I'm just trying it out, okay? Please shut up now. I have to concentrate.'

She added a few drops from a couple of dark smeary bottles with handwritten labels which she had brought up from the country. She was reciting a chant, or a charm, but in a low mumble, inaudible to her listeners. Then she dripped a little of the coffee onto the surface of the water, where it fanned outwards in a brown film. There was a stagnant, vegetal odour, like a brackish pool, oddly mixed with coffee.

'Can you see anything?' Quorum said.

This time, Jinx didn't answer. She was bending forward over the bowl, scowling horribly. When she straightened up her face was greenish and she seemed short of breath.

'What is it?' demanded Pen. 'You look sick.'

'I *feel* sick. It's the smell. I must have done something wrong: it doesn't usually ming like that. Hang on; I'd better get rid of it.' Another mumble of magic words, or what Pen assumed were magic words, and Jinx tipped the murky liquid down the sink.

'Well?' Pen resumed. 'What did you see?'

'The Dark Tower... I think. A skyscraper going up and up, with thin wisps of cloud spreading round it like ripples in the air. It looked like the Dark Tower, but it was a bit blurred. There were birds circling the topmost spire, very big birds, bigger than eagles, though it was difficult to be sure 'cos there was nothing to compare them with. They might have been Nightwings. Then one of them flew away – it was flying over a city, London I suppose. I saw the river shining, and the scribble-pattern of streets, and lumpy masses of buildings, and the giant Eye–'

'The Eye of Sauron?' said Pen on a note of disbelief. She had sat through part of *Lord of the Rings* on Matty Featherstone's DVD player, mostly with her attention elsewhere.

'The London Eye,' Jinx snapped. 'I expect. A big wheel, not specially fiery. Anyhow... There was a muddled bit where the bird was swooping down very fast, then it landed on a rooftop, and folded its wings, and didn't look like a bird any more.'

'Did it look like Cesare?'

'More or less. The picture quality was rubbish. The thing is, I saw part of the street below, and I think it was here. He was on the roof – here. Or maybe Number 7. He seemed to be peering over the edge, like he was checking out the upper windows, looking for a way in.'

'He will enter there at his peril,' Quorum intoned.

'I daresay,' said Pen, 'but we have to stop him.' She was texting Gavin for the fifth time that morning. He was meant to be doing a holiday job in a restaurant near his home, cleaning the tables and stacking the dishwasher during the lunch period, but Pen thought in his present state of mind he might not be able to face it. Either he wasn't answering because he was at work, she deduced, or he wasn't answering because he didn't want to answer.

Pen hoped it was the former.

There was a long pause while Quorum washed up the bowl and Pen waited in vain for a reply and Jinx returned to frowning meditation.

Pen went to put the phone in her pocket and then remembered the Teeth had taken up residence there and were in the process of chewing their way through the lining.

'Actually,' Jinx said at last, 'I'm not certain Cesare *could* get in, even if he found a way. I was forgetting – Number 7 may be a space/time prism, but it's also a house. The ancient rules apply – at least I think so. Werefolk can't enter a house uninvited. Cesare may be part mortal, but he's also part demon now. I don't know how it works, but somehow he'd be barred from getting in.'

'Stiltz did,' Pen pointed out.

'He came through one of the inner doors,' Jinx said. 'In a way, he was already inside. No – I think Cesare hopes to *see* in, not *be* in. Remember, Azmordis said it was nearly time for the would-be apprentices to reappear. Quorum... do people often open the doors from the other side?'

'Not since I came here,' the butler said. 'Nor during Mr Pyewackett's tenure. However, he did tell me there had been instances, long before. He used to worry about it sometimes. If the doors could be opened from *beyond*, you see, anything could come through. Anything at all.'

The two girls stared at each other.

'*That*'s how most of the apprentices got there,' Pen said. 'They came in through one door and went out through another. Like that boy Stiltz talked about. All we have to do is wait.'

'And watch,' said Jinx.

She added: 'It could be a very long watch...'

Beyond the Doors
London, seventeenth century

CHERUB HAD AGREED in the end, but reluctantly.

'Big Bel won't believe it,' he said. 'She won't believe I'd go willing. I'm too smart for that.'

'Tell her your friends are all dead,' said Ghost. 'Tell her you're lonely, and hungry, and you want a soft bed and a full stomach. Tell her there's another gang moving in from the docks, ready to kill anyone who gets in their way. Let her think you're scared. Tell her you've seen the plague stalking the streets like a skeleton in a tattered shroud, pointing a bloody finger at the next person to die.'

'That's good,' Cherub said appreciatively. 'I like that. Only... if it was a skeleton, there wouldn't be any blood. The blood 'ld be all gone.'

'Whatever.'

Ghost didn't think Big Belinda would need much convincing. She wasn't one to look a gift horse in the mouth, except to check the perfection of its teeth.

Mags took Cherub through the back door into the house. Ghost waited, crouching on a ledge above Running Lane. Some time later, Big Belinda emerged, wearing a cloak though the evening was warm, with a broad hood pulled over her false curls. The smile on her face reminded Ghost of a toad which has just swallowed a particularly juicy fly. He slid off the ledge into the shadows and prepared to follow her.

But she only went as far as Porkpie Street, apparently passing a message to someone Ghost couldn't see and then, after a moment's hesitation, returning to her lair. For a few seconds, Ghost feared he was trapped. If he reached for the ledge, she would see him climb; if he ran, his retreating figure would give him away. But there was a gate on his left into a tiny yard and he slipped through, pausing at another door, hand on the knob, pulling it open a fraction in case he needed a further escape route...

He heard the tap-tap of her heels along the lane, glimpsed the shadow of her cloak outside the gate. Then she was gone. He let himself breathe again and turned, glancing through the doorway to see if he was observed...

There was a girl standing there watching him.

His first thought was that she looked very clean. Her face was as smooth and pale as an egg-shell and the straight fall of her hair had a silken gleam unlike any girl's hair that he knew. She wore odd clothes, too: very long breeches of some blue grainy material and a bulky jacket with the sleeves turned up which didn't seem to fit anywhere. There was a boy behind her whom he couldn't see clearly because his skin was so dark.

It was still daylight in the city, but the room beyond the door looked dim with the grey dimness of early evening. Like the girl, it was clean: he glimpsed pale walls and closed doors, the corner of a carpet, a segment of picture. There was something familiar about the interior, though he knew he couldn't have seen it before. A hallway with doors, many doors. Closed doors waiting to be opened...

He drew back, suddenly and horribly afraid.

The girl had been frozen in shock or surprise, but now she moved towards him. 'You're the one, aren't you?' she said. 'You're the boy who's lost.'

He didn't answer, springing back, trying to shut the door, but the dark-skinned youth wrenched it away from him.

'Don't do that!' the girl said urgently. 'You mustn't do that. Whatever happens, *you mustn't close the door.*'

Her desperation sounded ludicrous, even insane, but on some deeper level he understood. The door was a way of escape, and these people – whoever they might be – were the guardians, bizarre otherworldly beings sent to save him, or to destroy him. The clean twilit interior looked like a haven, yet something about it brought him to the edge of panic.

The boy took a rectangular object out of his pocket, slate-thin and shining like dull silver. He flipped the lid up as if it was a box, only it wasn't a box, just two flat surfaces hinged together. On the inside there were numbers and letters in clusters, which clearly had some occult significance, and a few cabbalistic signs. The boy pressed or rubbed something, and a section of the surface began to glow, though there was no discernible light source – to glow like a wishing stone, like a crystal ball, with strange colours and patterns moving through the glow like ripples on water. Then the boy spoke, as if addressing the box: 'Jinx? Get over here – quickly. Never mind supper: you can have that later. We need you. Now.'

The box spoke back.

'Okay. Coming.'

Ghost stared.

'Magic,' he said. 'Black magic.'

'No,' said the boy. 'Just technology. You'll get the hang of it.'

'Come on,' said the girl, holding out her hand. 'It's all right, really it is. We'll look after you.'

'We will?' said the boy, evidently taken aback.

'Of course we will!'

'Only... I don't think–'

'I can't come,' said Ghost. 'Not now.' Somehow, he knew that if he passed that door there would be no returning. 'I have... unfinished business. The plague took nearly all the Lost Boys, but I have to save them, the ones that are left. Cherub, and Tomkin – yes, and Mags. I promised. I promised... *myself.*'

'The Lost Boys?' said the girl, plainly confused. 'Like in *Peter Pan*?'

'That was my name for them,' Ghost explained. 'The gang. My gang.'

'Plague?' said the boy. His hands closed on the girl's shoulders, drawing her back into the shadows of the hallway.

'I've had it,' said Ghost. And: 'You couldn't get it. You're too clean.'

There was a sound of footsteps, barely audible to Ghost – noise didn't travel easily from that other place – and another girl appeared, with a dog. At least, he thought it was a girl, though she looked more like a fairground freak. There were metal rings through her ears, her eyebrows, her nose, even her lip. Her eyes were more heavily painted than any of Big Belinda's girls and her short hair was dyed a purplish bronze and stuck out like a broom in a fright.

She didn't seem anything like as clean as the other two.

The dog who accompanied her was big and shaggy and friendly-looking.

'This is him,' said the first girl. 'This is the one.'

'Has he murdered anybody yet?' asked the newcomer. Ghost recognised her voice and thought: She's the one the dark boy spoke to. The genie of the box.

Somehow, he hadn't expected a genie to look quite like that.

'Not yet,' said the boy. 'He's been too busy having the plague.'

'*Plague*?' The genie sounded apprehensive.

'It isn't that easy to catch,' said the first girl. 'Not if you're well nourished and have a strong immune system.'

'I'm not well nourished,' said the genie. 'You interrupted my supper.'

The first girl turned back to Ghost, ignoring her. 'Look,' she said, 'we're meant to help you.' ('Sez who?' said the genie.) 'If there are people you have to save, then I'm coming too. We can't lose you now.'

'Are you crazy?' This was the boy. 'You heard what he said–'

'It doesn't matter. Sometimes you have to take a little risk. Anyway, I'm going.'

The boy clenched up his anger and let it go in a sigh of resignation. 'I wish you would stop being so obstinate,' he said. 'A *little risk*! What the hell. If you're going, I'm going. Jinx can watch the door.'

'If you get the plague,' said the genie, 'and come back, and give it to me, there will be *serious trouble*.'

'Too right,' said the boy.

For all its horror, the word *plague* had an old-fashioned ring which none of those beyond the door could quite believe in.

'You can't come with me,' said Ghost, appalled. 'Not here. The city isn't a place for people like you.'

Clean people.

The girl stepped through to his side of the door. 'I'm Penelope Tudor,' she said. Not just asserting her identity but holding onto it. 'My friends call me Pen.'

'Ghost,' said Ghost. The girl offered her hand but he didn't take it. He was afraid of what might rub off on him.

'Is that what your friends call you?' asked the boy, following her. If there was a note of irony in his voice, Ghost missed it.

'I don't have friends.'

Now they were here, standing in the yard, in his world. Strangers, aliens, guardian angels.

He didn't need guardian angels.

The city air seemed to smear them with a hint of grime, a breath of dust, making them look more normal, blending them in. They were foreigners, he realised, just off a boat from somewhere far away, the spice islands or the Isles of Gold, exotic kingdoms beyond the ocean's edge. They wanted to take him with them, to a remote unimaginable country, magical as Avalon, distant as the moon, where the memories would soften and the scars would heal and he would grow up into a different person, though whether good or bad he did not know.

But first, he had things to do...

Behind them, the genie wedged something under the door to hold it open, and she and the dog sat down in the gap to wait.

IN THE LOFT, Mags said: 'Who are they?'

'They're with us,' Ghost said. 'That's all you need to know. What happened with Cherub?'

'Big Bel's sent a message to the Duke. She was that pleased when he came, she was sweating roses. You'd think she'd be worried about him having the plague, but she says like you do, if he ain't got it now, he won't never get it. There's a few what just don't. Us lucky ones.'

A rat ran across the floor of the loft. Ghost threw a boot at it – an old boot which had belonged to One-Ear – and it scurried into a corner, gnawing on a piece of pie-crust from a stolen dinner, watching them beadily.

'I hate rats,' he said.

'They're plague-carriers,' said Pen. 'That's how it got here. The rats brought it.'

'Rats don't get sick,' said Mags. 'Leastways, I never saw one what did.'

'You don't have to get sick to bring sickness,' Pen explained, with all the conviction of one who has absorbed a higher wisdom. This city might be strange to her but she was used to strange places; she thought she had been on the move all her life. 'My father's a doctor. He's travelled all over the world studying diseases. He says plague travels too, riding on the rats. It starts in some country a long way away, and the rats go on ships and take it with them.'

Mags looked unconvinced, but Ghost said: 'I knew it was rats.'

He went on: 'I daresay that's why the Duke don't get the plague. His house is locked up so tight, he even keeps the vermin out.'

And, to Mags: 'When he gives Big Bel the word, you let me know. I'll go wait in Close Shave Alley. Maybe I'll take him a brace of dead rats, just to pretty the place up.'

'You'll have to be quick, to catch them,' Gavin said.

Ghost's knife flicked out, faster than the eye could follow, cutting the air with a lethal gleam, pinning the rat to the wall. 'That quick?' he said.

When Mags had gone they waited. Pen peered through a casement, watching the raindrops puncture the mud soup in the creek below. Gavin took the Pan-pipes from his side pocket and fiddled with them, blowing experimentally, eliciting only a tuneless whistle.

'Can I try?' Ghost asked after a few minutes. 'I used to play... something. It was metal, and you blew on it, and sucked on it, and music came out. I've forgotten what it was called. A monica... something like that.'

'These are meant to be magic,' said Gavin, his mind filling with unfamiliar recollection. 'I got them in... in a souk. The man sold flying carpets too, but they didn't fly.'

A little reluctantly, he handed Ghost the pipes.

Another rat appeared from a hole in the wall, stealing the pie crust from its dead friend.

Ghost remembered Tomkin warbling his ballads for pennies, while the gang stole the sixpences and shillings that remained behind. The memory gave him a strange twisty pain inside, because most of the Lost Boys were gone, and Tomkin was singing for the Duke now, in a cold grand house full of servants and strangers. It was said the Duke did not sleep, haunted by dark deeds from his past, though no one knew what they were, nor had he ever shown even the glimmer of a conscience. But nightmares were generally supposed to torment the wicked, and only the lullabyes of the pure and innocent might cast them out.

Ghost had never sung, not even when he was happy, and the notes he had drawn from the monica had not been of a purity to ward off demons. But the pipes were different. They might even have been formed of hollow reeds, like the original pipes which the great god Pan had made in the legend. Ghost didn't know if they looked magical or not, but the thought of Tomkin made him want to play.

He put the pipes to his lips, and blew. A trill of sound emerged, uncertain but very clear, pure and sweet as the warble of a bird. He was staring at the rat as he blew, with the fixed, brooding stare he always reserved for rodents.

He paused for a minute, then tried again.

Pen and Gavin looked at Ghost. Then they looked at the rat.

It had stopped nibbling the stale pastry and was standing on its hind legs, watching Ghost. A second rat came out of the wall, then a third. And they all just stood there, watching the piper with unblinking eyes.

'Look after the girls,' Ghost said to Gavin. 'I'll be back.'

'You'll be careful, won't you?' said Mags. 'You won't go sticking the Duke with that chive?'

Ghost smiled. He didn't smile very often, if at all, and the smile was awkward, stiff from lack of use. It made a tiny crease in his cheek which hadn't been there before.

'No,' he said. 'I won't.'

The crease vanished as if it had never been.

'I'll be back.'

He disappeared down the ladder, into the dark where he belonged.

In the shop in Close Shave Alley Ghost sat in the old barber's chair, stroking the pipes. He had never learned to play, but he remembered he had been good with the monica, long ago in the Home. The other kids had listened, and asked him for their favourite tunes, until one of the grownups took it away. But back in the loft, with the pipes at his lips, all he had done was blow. The pipes had been playing *him*, taking his breath, his thought, and turning them into those few clear notes – a trill, a thrill, a warble, a babble – a fleeting cadenza of magical sound. The pipes of Pan, the goat-legged god of wildness and madness, the devil-god who came before Christ. Ghost had read about Pan, though he couldn't recall where. For tonight, he would be Pan, Pan the devil-god, blowing the pipes till the rats came dancing across the floor, their paws drumming to the rhythm of the spell...

Follow the piper who calls the tune...
by twilight and starlight and light of the moon
dance on a pinhead and spit in a spoon
a sword-dance, a fire-dance, a dance-till-you-swoon...

The door to the cellar stood ajar. Big Belinda had gone that way; soon, she must return. Ghost sat in the dark, needing neither lamp nor candle. He might not hear the bolts withdrawn but the door to the passage would heave and creak as it opened, and he would see the torchlight running ahead of them up the stair.

He waited.

In the loft, Mags and Gavin and Pen waited, listening to the rain start and stop, playing cards with a pack once the property of Mr Sheen, from which Sly had pinched all the aces...

At another door, Jinx waited, with Hoover, wishing she'd brought her iPod, forced to start thinking in order to fill up the time...

Ghost caught the noise from the cellar, saw the torch-glow leap along the wall. He blew on the pipes, softly, softly, heard the rustle of sound in the deserted shop – microscopic movements, fairy-footed, the tittupping of tiny paws... And from the stairs, heavy footsteps. The mute came in, Big Belinda following, billowing shape blending into billowing shadow. She was holding a bag which chinked with the muffled chink of coins.

Seeing the waiting figure, they halted. 'You,' said the procuress. 'I heard you was dead.' The words were sharp but there was fear at the back of them.

'Maybe,' said Ghost. He sat in the chair with one leg hooked over the arm. His face flickered in the torchlight, thin and pale as a corpse.

'You go,' he said to the mute, 'while you still can.'

The mute was staring past him at the rustle in the shadows, seeing the pairs of eyes gathering there, five pairs, ten, a dozen – small greeny eyes set close together, gleaming with a luminous gleam.

He hesitated only an instant, then ran out into Close Shave Alley.

Big Belinda loomed over the chair and its occupant. 'I ain't afraid of you,' she said. 'I ain't afraid of nobody. I've eaten bigger men than you for breakfast, tossed in the soup like chicken bones. Like chicken bones, do you hear? I run this city, not scum like you. The plague don't touch me; the king himself wouldn't raise a hand to me. See this?' She pulled a knife from the folds of her dress. It was big and ugly and the blade was saw-edged from much use. 'It's bigger than that knife o' yours, bigger and meaner. I'm going to carve you like a chicken and break your bones in my soup. I'll let the blood out of your skinny little body – if there's any in there–'

She lunged at him with the knife, but he caught her wrist in one hand and twisted it till she dropped her weapon. The pipe-music was running in his veins and he felt as strong as a god and as light as a dancer. His own knife leaped out, drawing down her arm, opening the flesh. She pulled herself backwards, clutching the wound, her mouth thinning with contempt.

'That ain't a killing cut. You can't kill me. You ain't got the goolies for it.'

'I wasn't trying to kill you,' he said. 'I only wanted the rats to smell your blood.'

And then he began to play in earnest, and the music was like birdsong and ratsong, like trilling and shrilling and squeaking, and the rats flowed across the floor towards her, clambering up her skirts, tearing through satin and brocade, through gown and petticoat and padding. She tried to shake them off, to bat them off, but her blood spattered across them and the music went on and the rats surged over her like a tidal wave over a mountain of sand. Within minutes she was borne to the ground, submerged under a heaving, squirming mass. She had begun to scream, but the scream opened a hole and the rats dived in and eventually it stopped. After a while, though the rat-pile still twitched and writhed, Ghost thought that what was underneath no longer moved. And gradually, though more and more rats came, the pile seemed to shrink, growing smaller, and smaller, until the ribs of empty corseting stuck out of the rat-tide, and bloodied ends of bone, and torn shreds of cloth, and an indigestible ball of hair whose original colour was lost.

Ghost ceased playing and stood up. The rats drew back from him; some started to trickle away. He stepped over what was left of Big Belinda and went down the stair to the cellar. He wouldn't have to wait for Cherub; the door was still open, and he blew on the pipes again, a brief whistling call, a summons, a reminder. The rats who still remained turned to watch him. Then he set off down the passage to the Duke's house.

London, twenty-first century

JINX SAT IN the doorway, thinking. Mostly, she was thinking about Bartlemy. She had tried to find him by magic, and she had tried to find him by research, and both trails had led to Bygone House and vanished there. Maybe it was time to try using her head. She knew she wasn't clever like Pen, who was clearly the sort of person who got A-stars in everything, or even like Gavin, who she suspected had more brains than he bothered to use, but she was older than both of them, in years and experience, and she was a witch of sorts, and that should give her an edge.

Bartlemy discovered this address, she reminded herself. He might have come here – he *would* have come here. He would have known the true nature of the house, even without entering; he was a wizard, after all, though he rarely used his Gift. And he would have wanted to look inside, she was sure, he would have found a way to get in, it was his house, his charge, his duty, and Bartlemy was never one to evade his duties. But he didn't go through 7A – he had no keys and Andrew Pyewackett would have had to let him in, Quorum would have seen him – not through a window, that was too clumsy and he was too fat for illicit ingress. He must have found another way, through another door... The house was full of doors. Doors that went anywhere, doors that closed – and opened. *Of course.*

Bartlemy isn't missing, she thought. He's here – he's *in the house.* There were doors into the past; there would be doors into the present. And Bartlemy, of all people, would have known how to locate such a door... from *the other side.* He got in like the witch-girl in Gavin's dream, and then, inevitably, he opened another door, crossed a threshold...

There was one person who would know.

'Stiltz!' she called, in something close to a growl. 'I'll *summon* you if you don't come! Never mind Hoover – I need to talk to you now. *Now,* do you hear?'

The goblin appeared furtively, hunched on the hall table in the lee of the vase, which was bigger than he was.

'Tell me about the wizard!' Jinx ordered. 'You knew what he was – you'd know a wizard when you saw one. He came here, didn't he? *Didn't he?* He came in through one of the doors, right?'

The goblin gave a little whimper of affirmation. His skin had turned pale as a lemon and his gaze shifted nervously between Jinx and the dog.

'You didn't think to mention it? You *knew* it was important – you must have known. Why didn't you tell us? And don't say *You didn't ask,* or I'll wring your scrawny neck, you disgusting little

Gollum!' Perhaps fortunately, Stiltz wasn't familiar with *Lord of the Rings*, and the insult meant nothing to him. 'He must have got in, looked around, and opened *another* door. Only he'd have wedged it, or put something in the gap so it couldn't close. He's not a fool, not Barty. That's what he did, isn't it? But you...' Her words came more slowly as the picture grew clearer and clearer in her mind. 'You moved it... whatever it was. You moved it, and the door closed, and he was lost...'

'Don't like doors left open,' mumbled the goblin. 'Things come through. And *he* might see us – might see in, see us hiding from him...'

'You're starting to *talk* like Gollum,' said Jinx. 'A little yellow Gollum, scared of doorses and devilses. Barty did nothing to hurt you, he never does anything mean, but I do, I'm as mean as mean gets, and if you don't tell me everything *right now* I'll shrivel you in your skin like last year's walnuts. Right now: understand?'

'He came from upstairs,' Stiltz admitted at last. 'The Fat Man.' Jinx could hear capital letters. 'He walked very quiet, for all he was so big, quiet as a wee mousie. Upstairs, that's where you're getting near the Present, sithee. He didn't look like he come out of the Past. Them as come from the Past, there's a reek about them; you can't mistake it. Maistens, they look addled, and pale as a boggart. But the Fat Man, he wasn't e'en mithered. He seed me, though I wasn't up for being noticed, but he didn't say nothing. Just give me a nod, like. Then...'

'Then?' Jinx prompted sharply.

'He opened the door. Like you said. He opened one door just to look, then another, and he went through, and didn't come back. I waited, I waited a while and a while, but he niver come again. Wasn't my blame...'

'You *closed the door*...'

'Doors mustn't be left open,' the goblin reiterated sullenly. 'Too dangerous. Anyways, I didn't shut it *deliberate*, did I? I just wanted to look... They were good ones, see? Sturdy – very sturdy – but the stitching like elf-stitch... Not cheap, not shoddy, like those.'

'What?' Jinx was bemused.

Stiltz glanced towards the object she had used for a wedge. One of her pumps, the toe-tip thrust under the door. It was all that had come to hand at the time.

'He used his shoes,' said Jinx, light dawning. 'He took off his shoes and left them in the gap. He was indoors, after all. So it must have been indoors on the other side... Have you still got them?'

'Hid them,' said the goblin.

'You'd better find them,' said Jinx. 'Or else... Which door was it? No – don't tell me. I've been stupid but I'm not being stupid any more. I can guess...'

Beyond the Doors
London, seventeenth century

THE DUKE WAS at dinner. It was a dinner such as Ghost and the Lost Boys had never seen, with pies and pasties and puddings, roasted meats and baked meats, poupetons and syllabubs – with a dozen different smells vying for air space and platter nudging on platter along an overcrowded table. Wine swilled into goblets and gurgled down throats, silver cutlery scrunched and scraped over expensive porcelain, eddying footmen scooped and served, poured and filled and re-filled. The Duke sat at the head of the table under a pyramid of caramel curls, the lace foaming over his torso like whipped cream, embroidered fruits ramping across his waistcoated stomach, so he resembled a vast sumptuous dessert, save for his eyes, which were cold and dry and watchful as a lizard's. His companions ate greedily, gorging their food and gulping their wine, their lead-whitened faces flushing under the powder, their dripping mouths crunching and chewing and chattering all at once. But the Duke ate like a chameleon, hardly moving, his hand conveying morsel to mouth before returning to curl itself round the stem of his glass, the many rings casting red glints of light across the table-linen. Above, a massive chandelier depended like a cloud full of hail, its fifty candles dropping hot wax onto the central dishes.

Presently the Duke murmured something into a footman's ear, and the servant went out, returning a few minutes later leading a boy by the hand. Cherub. Cherub washed and scrubbed and scented, his curls pomaded, his teeth polished, dressed in a wispy Grecian tunic pinned on one shoulder and shivering a little, perhaps from the cold. At a gesture from the Duke he sang, a few verses from an old ballad, the high notes clear and strong if slightly off key once or twice, but his audience was not musical. They paused between mouthfuls to praise and gush – what a treasure, an innocent, a jewel, such a rarity in today's city, where the plague had slaughtered and spoiled so many, where pretty children were few and hard to find. That milky skin – those perfect tones – he was Eros, he was Ganymede, a seraph with the voice of a skylark, a thing of beauty formed for the entertainment of the gods. The Duke was fortunate indeed to have found himself such a prize. No doubt the price had been high…?

'Very high,' said the Duke, and though they probed and prodded, he told them nothing more.

Cherub was removed until the Duke should require him again, and the footmen were sent for more sweetmeats and dainties and brandy. The other guests contended with one another in their fulsomeness, their envy, their allusions to gilded youths of classical legend. None of them realised that the boy whose beauty and high notes so enraptured them had picked their pockets not so long ago. The Duke probably knew – he always knew – but he didn't care. Cherub was his creature now.

The footmen were slow in returning so another was dispatched to hasten them, and when he too failed to reappear the Duke frowned, tugging on the bellrope. His companions – you would not call them friends – gradually fell silent, comprehending that something was not right in their world of gluttony and pleasure. The wine was sinking, the Duke was scowling, the candles guttered and smoked in the chandelier. And then the far door opened, and a boy walked in.

Not a boy like the one they had just seen, pure and perfect as Ganymede. This boy was thin and dirty and dressed in rags. His feet left prints on the floor from the mud of the streets. His face was bony and hard beyond his years, with eyes like bits of stone.

He walked forward to the end of the table, facing the Duke.

The guests gasped and swooned, fanned themselves with painted fans, sniffed at perfumed pomanders.

The Duke said: 'Quiet!' and they were quiet.

Then he fixed the boy with his lizard's stare. 'What do you want?'

'I've come for Cherub and Tomkin,' said the intruder. 'But I will give you something in return.'

'You're the boy with the knife,' said the Duke. 'The one they call Ghost. I've heard of you.'

'Good,' said Ghost. 'It's the last thing you'll ever hear.'

They saw him place the pipes to his lips and blow, emitting a cascade of notes like chirps and chirrups and squeaks transformed into a tune. A rat ran into the room and jumped on the table, dodging between the dishes, snatching a mouthful as it ran. The guests squealed. The Duke moved very swiftly for a man of his bulk, thrusting his chair back, drawing his rapier and spitting the rodent in a single stroke.

'Now,' said the Duke, tossing the dead rat aside and circling the table towards Ghost, 'it's your turn.'

Ghost took a step back. 'Rats carry plague,' he said as another scurried across the floor, and another. 'That's what I have to give you. Plague.'

The Duke sprang at him, sword extended, but a rat bit him on the ankle and he stumbled, slashing downwards, nicking his own leg. The other guests gibbered with fear.

Then Ghost played the pipes – played and played – feeling the music in his blood, in his soul, a wild rat-fandango of leaping paws and whirling whiskers and twirling tails. And somewhere inside the music were the words, a spellsong or a summons in a language that spoke to both man and beast – words that went straight to the hindbrain and became a part of the beat in his head.

Hark to the piper who pipes the call –
the call of Hunger and Greed!
Through mousehole and drainhole and hole-in-the-wall –
hurry and scurry to dance at the ball –
to leap on the tables and skip down the hall –
Come fat rats and thin rats, come large rats and small!
follow the piper and FEED!

They came from all over the city, from kitchen and midden, from cellar and cesspit, through the underground passage, through holes and tunnels and chinks in walls – great rats, small rats, lean rats, brawny rats – brown rats, black rats, grey rats, tawny rats – spilling into the room ten deep, twenty deep, scrambling over table and guests and rodent kin, till screeches and jabbers, flailing fists and threshing limbs were all overwhelmed, and diners and dinner became one huge ravening orgy. And still Ghost played, till the rats fell on each other, and the strong devoured the weak, and the fat devoured the lean, and the blood ran down the table like red gravy and the stragglers licked it clean.

But the Duke wasn't there. He came from a long line of survivors who knew when to fight and when to run away. He could stab one rat or a dozen but not a hundred, not a thousand. He was gone even as the first wave hit, slamming the door on his guests, spearing any vermin who slipped through in his wake. Outside the dining room, the servants had fled, forewarned by Ghost. The Duke heard the door rattle behind him from the weight of rats hurling themselves against it and he ran on, through the house, up stair after stair, along corridor and gallery, till he came to the tower, relic of an older building long pulled down. Solid oaken doors thudded into place as he passed, ancient bolts scraped home. At the top there was a circular chamber, with narrow windows and only one door. He barricaded himself in and sat down to wait, binding his bleeding ankle with the torn ruffles from his shirt.

In the dining room, Ghost stopped playing at last. The rats, released from the spell, tottered back to their holes with bulging stomachs and bloodied fangs. Ghost went to free Cherub and Tomkin from the room where he had locked them for safe-keeping. Cherub was sulking, embarrassed by the tunic – 'It's almost a dress!' – and Tomkin looked furtive and weepy, little like the boy they remembered.

'What happened?' Cherub demanded, looking at the dead rats, and the overturned furniture, and the red pawmarks on floor and walls.

But Ghost didn't answer.

They went through the underground passage and up the stairs to the barber's shop. Cherub stared at the debris of Big Belinda and asked no more questions. Ghost found the bag of coins, almost undamaged; gold cannot be eaten, even by rats.

Back in the loft the others greeted them with relief. Mags hugged Cherub, who grimaced, and tried to hug Tomkin, but he cried and shrank away.

'He'll be all right,' said Ghost, hoping it was true, 'in the end. Look after him. You're family now, all three of you. Take this money, go into the country, find somewhere nobody knows you, somewhere you can be free. You can do honest work – be a maid – a stableboy – jobs like that. If you stick together, you'll survive.'

'What about you?' said Mags.

'I'm going with these two. I have to.' He didn't want to, but he felt the touch of Fate, laying her fingertip on the back of his neck.

'Go quickly, before another Big Belinda comes along, or another Mr Sheen.'

'Or another Ghost?' said Cherub.

Ghost nodded. His face was so hard and tight it hurt.

'Goodbye, Random Horwood,' said Mags, and her expression screwed up as if in pain. 'I'll always remember you.'

She kissed his cheek, hastily, and he pulled back, hastily, and then he, and Pen, and Gavin climbed down the ladder, and went through Groper's Alley and Running Lane into the yard, and there was Jinx, watching the door, with her arm around Hoover. The three of them stepped through, and she removed the pump she had used as a wedge, and shut out the city and everyone in it, and Ghost stood staring round him at the twenty-first century, not knowing where or when he was.

'You need a bath,' said Pen.

'Possibly several,' added Gavin.

Jinx remembered what Stiltz had said about the people from the Past, and thought he had a point.

She said to Pen: 'What are you going to tell your gran?'

'God knows,' said Pen.

THE DUKE STAYED in the tower room a night and a day. But he was thirsty, and by the following evening he felt light-headed – lack of food, he told himself – and the rat-bite on his ankle was swollen and sore. He opened the doors very gingerly, listening at each before he slid the bolts, venturing at last into the main house. It seemed deserted: the rats had gone and the servants hadn't returned. But there were always more servants, just as there were always more rats. He felt suddenly hot, and suddenly cold; there must be a draught from somewhere, though the windows were closed.

Near the dining room he saw the paw-trails, a dead rat, a legless chair. He pushed the door open and went in.

The Duke had no nerves; he had never needed them. Prudence had kept him in the tower room, not fear. Fear was what you inflicted, not what you felt; his father had taught him that, and it was a lesson he had never unlearned.

The dining table was picked clean. So were the guests. They sat as they had sat the previous night, dressed in a few chewed rags of clothing, arm-bones, if still attached, sprawled along the table, bare skulls slumped from broken vertebrae. Fingers had not fared well, the fiddly little joints gnawed and scattered. Hunks of wig hair huddled like giant caterpillars on the floor and crawled across the stained silver. The Duke noted automatically that the table linen, as well as the china, would have to be replaced. He was proud that he noticed that. Nothing dulled the steely edge of his intelligence, or so he reassured himself. The inside of his head felt strange, thoughts swimming blearily through his brain, but that was only to be expected: he must find food and drink. Why had he come to the dining room, when he knew there would be none there? The fate of his dinner guests did not trouble him. Where there was a dukedom, where there was power, where there was money, there would always be dinner guests. He glanced round at them, his mouth curling in disdain. They died; he survived. *He survived*. That was all that mattered.

Then one of the skulls jerked upright, propping its jawbone on a fingerless wrist. It grinned at him.

Skulls always grin; it's the way they're arranged.

'Won't you join us, your Grace?' it said.

CHAPTER TEN
The Wizard's Return

London, twenty-first century

GHOST STEPPED OUT of the front door, into the street he remembered from long ago. It was the same street where he had climbed the wall to Number 7, the same houses, the marble urns and pillared porches, the feathered tops of tree and shrub behind high gates, but there were subtle differences. Like a dream which changes, so the familiar becomes alien, and known faces morph into strangers, and the place which looked the same is somewhere you have never been. There were more cars, parked nose to tail, and they looked somehow wrong, bigger, shinier, less car-shaped, gleaming eggs of glass and chrome and steel. The woman walking along the opposite pavement was dark-skinned and exotic, wearing a Muslim headscarf; there had been immigrants around in the seventies, but not in Hampstead. Some way behind her came a youth, talking into one of those new mobile telephones like Gavin had, which resembled something out of *Star Trek*. He was speaking a language which Ghost didn't recognise: he thought it might be Russian. But surely there were no Russians in London, they were the enemy, the bad guys of the Cold War, shut away behind the Iron Curtain in the icy countries of eastern Europe...

The worlds shifted in his head, memory melting into memory, different realities overlapping, mingling, dividing. For a moment his whole heart ached for *home* – for Groper's Alley and Running

Lane and the loft he had shared with the Lost Boys – but it was already slipping away, fading among the muddled images of another past, another present. He tried to think of Mags and Cherub and Tomkin, whether they had finally escaped to the country, whether he had saved them, or left them to die, but both the faces and the feelings were growing blurred, and all that remained was a formless pain which he knew would never be assuaged. And Ghost, too, was dimming, a phantom like his name, gone in the daylight of this gleaming new century. Now, there was just Random Horwood, the abandoned boy who played truant from school and planned to run away when he was old enough, to live rough, act tough, be smarter than the bullies, smarter than the law, and never lose a fight again.

Once, he remembered, he had had a mother, who had cried when they took him away, but only a little. Sometimes he had hated her, mostly he claimed to be indifferent, but occasionally he dreamed of rescuing her as he had wanted to rescue Mags and the boys, though he wasn't sure from what. But more than thirty years had passed, and she would be dead, or old (he hoped she was dead), and even if he found her she would hardly recognise him, a Peter Pan figure who had never grown up. He wondered where he was to go, what he was to do with his new life, in this new world. Would they put him in another Home, all bright and efficient, a factory processing children, and send him to school, and plug him into a computer, like Pen and her laptop, to turn him into Twenty-first Century Boy?

'You don't really exist,' Jinx had told him, evidently considering this an ideal state. 'No identification, no identity. You're an illegal immigrant from another dimension. As long as no one finds out, you'll be okay. Of course, if you're caught, you might have to claim asylum.'

'I won't let them take me to any asylum,' Random had said.

'That isn't what she meant,' said Pen. 'Don't worry. You can stay here. We'll look after you.'

They had heard the whole story now, complete with flick-knife and ratfest. It made them careful around him, as if he might too easily break apart, or implode. But looking after him, surely, was the whole point of their adventure…

They hadn't told him about the Devil yet, or that he was a candidate for the job.

Eve had been appalled by the new arrival, saying he must have run away from home, and if he didn't have a place to go she would have to call Social Services. Quorum, suppressing his own disapproval, had improvised with a skill that won admiration even from Jinx, explaining that Random was a distant relative of Andrew Pyewackett, so of course he would have to stay, at least for a short time. Eve couldn't argue with that, though clearly she wanted to. Then the butler had gone out to replenish their food supplies, saying whatever he'd done the poor boy was far too thin to be healthy.

And so Random stood looking down the street, lost not in the past but the future, numbed by his new stupidity, his ignorance, his helplessness.

Behind him, Pen said: 'Come back in.' She spoke gently, as if coaxing a stray dog.

He went in.

From the shadow under a leaf, from a crevasse in the wall, the watchers saw him go.

Infernale

It is always dark in the Dark Tower. The sun never shines beyond those black windows; if it is daylight, it will be grey daylight under louring cloud, with louring cloud beneath blanketing the lower world. As darkness deepens the cloud thins, and far off there will be drifts of tiny lights, fine as the dust of stars – the streets and flyovers, office blocks and apartment blocks of every city on the planet. It is said, there is a side road, a courtyard, an alleyway in the heart of each metropolis which will lead you to the Dark Tower, if you wish to find the way. And from the highest pinnacle the Devil looks out over his empire – *his*, he calls it, though his name is not on any deeds – as the God of the ancients once looked out, and believes, in his arrogance, that this is what he has made.

He cares nothing for industry or commerce, hedge-funds or ditch-funds, the free market or the black market: only for power. He was here from the beginning: he saw the dinosaurs come and go, and the fish crawl out of the primal sea and grow legs, and he knew the earth when it was still in the melting pot, when the fire-spirits danced their airy dances over bubbling ocean and burning land. The strength of earthquake and tsunami, of firewind and wildwind, flowed in his essence like blood. And then a band of thin-skinned apes came down from the trees, and stood up on their hind legs, and set out to rule the world. *His* world. They taught him that the powers of storm and darkness were as nothing beside the power of the imagination and the cunning of human hands. They made him in their image, and he called himself their ruler, their Dark Lord, and even now, when the world he knows has grown old and tired, he cannot let them go.

Above the circular office there is a small platform around the topmost spire, ringed with a single rail, and there he stands, he alone, though the Nightwings may come and go at his command, looping the tower in dark spirals, bringing him word of the kingdoms below. No others fly so high, or so far. He looks out over his empire, through cloud and darkness, and sees with other eyes than his own, the eyes of the watchers in the shadows. Sees a boy in a doorway, also looking out, though not in lordship and power – a boy pale and alone, afraid of what lies beneath his heart.

'Saetor!' cries the Devil. 'Saetor Czesarion!'

A shadow cuts through the cloud, swifter than sound, the boom of his wingbeat following him like an echo.

'It is time. He is here. The first of the chosen few, the honoured ones. Bring him to me!'

The Fellangel dives again, plunging earthwards like a meteor, and the cloud foams in his wake.

London, twenty-first century

RANDOM SLEPT THAT night on the sofa in the sitting room. The cushions were soft, the room was warm, and he knew he hadn't been so comfortable in a long, long while, but still he dozed uneasily, waking at intervals to see the unnatural glow of a nearby street lamp paling the window, and looking in vain for the stars through cracks in the ceiling. His dreams were haunted by the same spectres who had spied on his fever, clustering above him rustling their wings and whispering with lipless mouths. Even when he was fully awake they would take a few minutes to fade away, leftovers from the world of sleep clinging on in the darkness.

Hoover had positioned himself close by, and at times Random caught a whiff of canine halitosis as the dog sat up to check on him, or felt the rasp of a rough tongue on his arm. Despite the odour of animal breath, his nearness was reassuring. In the confusion of shifting worlds in his head, Random sensed the dog was a presence at once stable and protective, offering unspecified comfort. He let his hand fall on Hoover's neck, stroking instinctively, and somehow the act soothed him, even more than his companion, and he drifted at last into a sleep without nightmares or phantoms, waking long after daylight when Quorum brought him some tea.

In her room Pen, too, was restless, for all her weariness. On the table beside her bed the Teeth supplied rather less reassurance than Hoover. If dentures can sleep, they appeared to be sleeping, occasionally champing, or grinding together, or emitting a gurgly snore.

'You snore through your nose,' Pen muttered, 'not your teeth,' but the Teeth merely grunted, and subsided back into a gurgle.

Pen wondered if this was what it was like to sleep with a man, and whether Gavin snored, and felt herself blushing, though she never blushed, and turned her thoughts hastily elsewhere, back to the unanswered questions which had kept her awake in the first place.

What did she actually *know* about Bygone House?

The doors opened into the Past, into dimensions of myth and legend, 'worlds of the imagination,' Quorum had said once. But where *didn't* they lead? Not the future, Quorum averred, because the future hasn't happened yet, though the alternative present or near-present was always a possibility. And, as far as Pen could tell, there were no other planets or different universes. The dimensions were all more or less within this world. And somewhere in the background, like a watchful shadow, was the presence or immanence of Azmordis, the Dark Lord in the Dark Tower, an ancient spirit who had infested the space/time prism from the beginning. That's it, Pen thought, I need to go back to the beginning. I have to understand how the house actually *works*. One door to Somewhere or Nowhere, one door to Elysium or Faerie... One door. That was how it started. One door spawning others, like reflections in a multiple mirror, like an onion growing new layers...

Suddenly, she sat up, staring into the darkness.

Eureka!

The idea that had come to her was so clear, so *right*, she knew this had to be the truth about Bygone House, the pattern she had been looking for all along. She lay down again, still far from sleep, thinking her way through every twist of the maze.

IN THE MORNING, after breakfast, she explained it to the others. Eve had gone to work, but Gavin, Jinx, Random and Quorum listened while she expounded her theory with the enthusiasm of a physicist who has just discovered cold fusion.

'Because it looks like a house you expect it to behave like a house,' she said, meaning Number 7. 'But what *is* a house anyway? It's a kind of... of man-made exoskeleton. It takes our needs, our lives, and separates them into compartments, and puts walls around them. So the space/time prism looks like a house partly as camouflage, but also because that's the most appropriate shape for it. It's something that grows and functions like a living organism, like a human *mind*. It does the things minds do. It has memory and imagination.'

'You're saying the house is *alive*?' Gavin queried.

'Not exactly. It could be – I don't know – the point is, I think it acts *like* something living. Living things grow because cells divide and multiply. Well, this place started with one door, one portal, then that divided into two, and four, and so on, and the house literally grew, adding more doors, more walls, until–'

'Until when?' Gavin pursued. 'Indefinitely?'

'Until it reached its optimum size, I suppose. Like everything else. Things can only grow just so big. Otherwise the laws of science trip them up, gravity drags you down...'

'So when is a space/time prism maxed out?' Gavin wondered, still sceptical.

'How is it like a mind? Does it think?' Jinx said, from under a familiar scowl.

Since she couldn't answer the first question, Pen went for the second. 'I don't know if it thinks, but look at the way it's organised. It has doors into the past: that's memory – and magical dimensions: that's imagination. There's the study, where you get artists and monks writing books – thought and theory. Then the reception room or living room, with parties and plots and social interaction. Monsters in the broom cupboard – that might be the subconscious. Houses reflect the human mind. Number 7 looks like a house and functions like a brain. Do you see what I'm getting at?'

'It sounds most ingenious to me,' Quorum offered, politely encouraging.

'It does make sense,' Jinx said unexpectedly, frowning at her own thoughts. 'Everything shifts about in your mind, too. I mean, memories don't stay put. Different ones pop up at different times. You forget things and then you remember them. You have ideas and then they go away. The mind is a space/time prism, so... a space/time prism is a sort of mind.'

'It's an explanation,' Gavin concluded. 'I suppose time will tell whether it's the right one.'

LATER THAT MORNING they were in the sitting room explaining to Random about Azmordis, and how he was supposed to be the Devil's apprentice, or a candidate for the apprenticeship – to turn to his dark side and misuse what power he had in the service of Evil. Unfortunately, Random's youth in the seventies predated the first *Star Wars* movie, which made the explanation rather more tangled than it should have been.

They weren't calling him Ghost. Gavin had said, with a nod to Jinx, that one pretentious soubriquet in the house was more than enough.

'I have no power,' Random said. 'It must be a mistake.'

'Yes you have,' said Jinx. 'I can feel it. You made the Lost Boys follow you, right? And you use that little knife like a tooth. You flick it out like vampire fangs, like it's part of you. You kill without even trying. That's power... of a kind. You got to learn to control it.'

Random made no answer, tinkering with Gavin's mobile. He was filled with an eerie detachment, unable to believe that any of it really connected to him, neither the Gift, nor Azmordis, nor Jinx's apprehension, nor Gavin's mockery. Pen had said he might be suffering from time lag, the shock of switching dimensions after so long. He didn't feel he belonged in the present or the past: his mind planed, noting details without really taking them in. He pressed the numbers on the keypad, watching the screen light up, vaguely intrigued to find the future so... futuristic.

Pen watched him with concern. They had rescued him – or he'd rescued himself – that was something she had aimed for. It should give them a breather, a moment to pause, recoup, feel conscious of achievement, but instead she felt only an increase of disquiet, of the sense of imminent danger which had pervaded their lives for too long. She didn't actually like Random – you couldn't like someone who'd done the things he'd done – but she didn't think he was evil, not yet, not completely. They couldn't give up on him, *she* couldn't give up on him.

He'd been rescued from the house; now, he had to be rescued from himself.

Jinx left the forward drive of conversation to Pen and Gavin, muttered something about the loo, and slipped out in search of Hoover. She had a plan of her own and hoped the others would be too preoccupied to bother about her absence. As she closed the door, she heard Gavin asking about food in the world of the Past, and whether Random had managed to steal any good cooking...

IN THE HALL, Jinx fumbled in the bag Pen had left on the table, looking for the keys to Number 7.

'Hoover?'

The dog was waiting by the door to the utility room, as though he knew what she was going to do.

Together, they slipped behind the coats and into the quiet of the house next door. Jinx glanced over her shoulder once or twice, but no one seemed to have noticed her leave. In Bygone House she went down the steps to the lower ground floor, where the entrance to the kitchen should be. The dog dropped onto his haunches, looking alert.

'This could take a while,' said Jinx.

The door-knob made her fingers prickle, but she knew that was a witch-reaction and did her best to ignore it. She opened the door, very cautiously, just a couple of inches, waited about ten seconds, then closed it again. A short pause, and she repeated the process. Again. And again. And each time Hoover sniffed at the gap, then showed no further interest. Jinx was growing impatient; she didn't want to be too long, in case the others came looking for her, but this couldn't be hurried. She never opened the door enough to see anything, but occasional sounds came through – the rattle of crockery, the whistling hiss of a giant kettle, a bubbling, gurgling noise like a dragon in a soup cauldron. There were smells, too, not all of them culinary, but she clung on to the belief that what she would find through the kitchen door would be, in some shape or form, a kitchen.

Bartlemy Goodman had once told her the kitchen is the heart of a house, and if Pen was right, and the house functioned like a living organism, then surely it should have a heart. Or at least a stomach. And he would be in a kitchen, however he had managed to get there; she should have realised it long before.

The moment came when Hoover barked once, short and sharp.

'This one?' said Jinx. 'Okay… Here we go.'

She pushed the door open wide.

Beyond, she saw a square tunnel retreating into the distance until it ended in what appeared to be a blank wall. There were huge double doors on her left but no other exit and the long passageway looked like a burrow to nowhere.

She fixed a wedge under the door and Hoover lay down in the gap, adopting a pose reminiscent of the lions in Trafalgar Square.

'Stay on guard,' Jinx told him, adding, in a voice intentionally loud: 'If Smeagol-Stiltz turns up and tries to close the door, you can eat him.'

*   *   *

Beyond the Doors
Gormenghast

SHE STEPPED OVER the dog into the corridor, waiting a minute to see if anything happened. But, as far as she could tell, she was still Jinx. Perhaps this was a magical dimension. She found she was fiddling with her ring, and, glancing down, saw the snake's eyes had changed to a smoky mauve.

She had no idea what that meant.

'Here goes,' she said again. She thrust the double doors open – it took considerable effort – and went through.

It was a kitchen, as she had guessed, but a kitchen the size of a small cathedral, hung with foetid gloom and as busy as a corpse full of maggots. Ovens throbbed and belched, spits turned, fireplaces coughed out smoke, huge pots of soup or stew heaved and bubbled like volcanic pools. Flamelight from open hearth and closed stove flickered redly along the blades of saw-edged knives and glinted in the sides of those pans clean enough to glint. There were people everywhere – chefs and sous-chefs, menials and venials, scullions and rapscullions – slicing, stirring, basting, picking their noses or their teeth, preoccupied with something or nothing; but all of them completely ignored Jinx. The only person to pay her any attention was a dwarf with withered legs and impossibly long simian arms, who dropped suddenly in front of her like a lemur from a jungle canopy and cackled in her face. She produced a grimace like a kabuki mask, sticking out her tongue and hissing. The manikin flinched and swung away.

Spanning the breadth of the room was a broad wooden beam, corkscrewed with age, or heat, or damp, until it appeared more like a twisted branch than anything man-made. It was festooned with strings of onions, grizzled bunches of herbs, and strange knobbly utensils, and slung over it not far from Jinx were two limp bundles, like part-filled sacks. There was a brief, terrifying instant when she realised they were human and thought they were dead, perhaps hung there prior to cooking, then she saw they were either unconscious or asleep. On the nearest, nostril and lip rippled as a snore issued from somewhere within. Relief flooded through her; what she was seeing here was fantastic and grotesque, but not gruesome.

Not yet.

Her foot struck something and she ducked down, peering under an adjacent table to see what it was. More inert bodies, a whole row of them, vibrating with the sluggish breathing of drunken coma. The kitchen dripped grease and reeked of roasting and charring flesh, adding to the impression of some infernal region, but here the strongest smell was that of stale beer, seeping from greyish pores and exhaling from slack mouth and gurgling windpipe. Jinx stood up hastily, knocking her head on the table's edge, and backed away.

She was making her way through the room, dodging the workers and trying not to tread on any more bodies, when she found herself in a sudden oasis of calm, an area of the kitchen beyond the roar of the ovens where menials did not venture and even the smells seemed to falter, shrinking away as if in awe. On a special table all by itself stood a cake. A cake two yards long and a foot high, robed in a thick mantle of icing, the ridges of hidden layering showing along the sides like laminations in a cliff-face. But what was extraordinary about it was the decoration. Every inch of the top was covered in a vast sugar sculpture of what seemed to be a city, though Jinx decided, on looking more closely, that it was actually a building or complex of buildings. It was done with an obsessive attention to detail – towers and turrets, spires and steeples, battlements and balustrades, pillars, cupolas, gargoyles, all were exquisitely moulded, daubed with edible colorants, adorned with ivy and grasses of desiccated coconut tinted in different greens. At the centre, the six tallest chimney-stacks supported six candles in gilded holders. A man was bending over it, deft fingers daubing and tinting. A very fat man with a small concentration-frown on his large face, smooth silvery hair, pale eyelashes. He wore the white coat of a chef, spotless as virgin snow even in that place. His hat had been removed and was perched crookedly on top of a jar of dried fruits.

Jinx knew that when he looked up and saw her his eyes would be forget-me-not blue.

She waited for a little while, watching him work. Wondering how long he had been there, and whether he had stopped to eat, or sleep.

'Barty?' she said at last. 'Uncle Barty?'

He looked up.

'Good heavens!' he said. 'If it isn't Hazel. You've changed your hair. How lovely... how *lovely* to see you...'

There might have been many options for Jinx's real name – Erminwolf, or Morticia, or anything beginning with X – but not Hazel. Hazel was a country-girl name, shy and dowdy and slightly dull. She must make him swear never, ever to tell the others...

'I've been looking for you,' she said.

'You're so grown up.' He was smiling gently, taking in the body-piercing, the black-and-white makeup, the porcupine-quill eyelashes.

'That's wonderful,' she said, indicating the cake. 'It's the most amazing cake I've ever seen. What is it meant to be? I mean, *where...*?'

'It's this house,' he said simply.

'All that – is one house?'

'In Lampedusa's *The Leopard*, Don Fabrizio says it's rather vulgar to know how many rooms your house has.'

You could say that of Number 7, thought Jinx.

'It's for his lordship's birthday,' Bartlemy continued. 'He's six years old. The sixth birthday is very important – the transition from infancy to childhood. I'm hoping the Countess will be pleased with my cake.'

'Is this a real place?' Jinx asked. 'It doesn't seem real. I still know I'm *me*, for one thing. At least, I think so. Is it a magical dimension?'

'Not exactly,' he said. 'It's a place in someone's imagination. All magical dimensions come from the imagination, of course – from primitive beliefs, legends, folk-tales. But once in a while you get an individual whose imagination is so powerful he can create an entire world all by himself. His own reality. That's what this is. It isn't real as such.'

'We should go,' said Jinx. 'The cake looks finished to me.'

'I must just add a few more details...'

'If you keep adding a bit more, and a bit more, it will never be done,' said Jinx. 'Anyway, it looks perfect. More would be too much. We do have to leave. You're needed... elsewhere.'

'Is it urgent?' he said.

'It might be.' She glanced towards his feet. 'Did they give you any shoes?'

'Slippers,' he said, showing her a kind of moccasin whose pointed toe curled up like something out of the Arabian Nights.

'Good,' said Jinx. 'I'd hate you to walk across this floor barefoot.'

She took his hand, and led him carefully through the obstacle-course of the kitchen.

London, twenty-first century

IN 7A, THE doorbell rang. After Jasveer's accident and the advent of Seth Kayser the sound had become almost ominous; Quorum had just gone out, Eve wasn't due back for hours, no one was expected. The insistent *brrrrr!* intruded on them like a warning. With no butler available to answer the door Pen felt the dilemma devolved on her; she tried to see the visitor out of a window but the porch screened whoever it was from view. She mouthed: 'Should I go?' though nobody outside was likely to hear her speak.

Gavin said: 'No,' and Random said: 'Why not?' and after a few moments the bell rang again. It couldn't possibly sound more demanding but it did. Two of the things it is hardest to resist in the modern world are the doorbell and the phone. Pen tucked the Teeth into the pocket of her sweatshirt by way of protection and went to answer it.

It was Seth Kayser. She had known it would be, of course; there was a grim inevitability about his arrival, just there, just then, when Jinx and Hoover seemed to have disappeared (perhaps they had gone for a walk), and Gavin had lost the stun-gun, and all she had was a set of dentures growling in a muffled tone from her hip.

The lawyer looked different, as if exhibiting yet another incarnation of himself, somehow leaner and tougher, less human, more demon. Instead of a suit he wore a black leather jacket and faded grey jeans with the sort of rips that might have resulted from a rather stylish sword-fight. Pen was fair and Random was an albino but Seth Kayser had the bloodless pallor of a vampire. His hair shone unnaturally bright in the fleeting sunlight.

'I've come for the boy,' he said.

'You can't come in,' said Pen.

So might Gandalf have said: 'You shall not pass!' on the Bridge of Khazad-dûm. So might Marshal Pétain have declared: '*Ils ne passeront pas*' at Verdun.

It didn't do her much good.

'You can't stop me,' said the man who had been Cesare.

He thrust her aside lightly, with the casual strength of a superhero – except there are no superheroes, Pen thought. Only supervillains. She clamped a hand over the Teeth, murmuring sotto voce: 'Not yet. Not yet.' Once he saw the Teeth he could not fail to remember…

In the sitting room, Seth Kayser said to Random: 'You're the one. Come with me,' and held out his hand.

Pen and Gavin were silent. They realised that they couldn't intervene, not at this moment, though all their past efforts came to nothing. This particular choice wasn't theirs to make.

Random felt the same compulsion he had experienced when he followed them through the door. Fate leading him on. But this wasn't a ginger-haired girl and a dark-skinned boy, both too clean for comfort – this was a man with the face of a wicked angel and the poise and elegance of a steel blade. He walked into the room as if he owned it; Random sensed he would walk into any room that way. He had the aura of someone who is capable of anything, yet who can effortlessly maintain control over that potential – a wolf in sheepdog's clothing, a snake who can charm the charmer. This was someone he had wanted to be, in the Home long ago when he had fed the bully rabbit-droppings, or when he roamed the streets of a vanished city, a jackal in a world of predators far bigger and more deadly. This was Ghost, grown into a man, come back to guide him – or to haunt him.

He looked at the proffered hand but didn't take it, though his own were no longer dirty. He found he was thinking of Mags, and Cherub, and Tomkin, wondering how they had fared, and if he would forget them one day, and wishing he could see them again...

'I cannot give you everything you want,' said the guide, as if reading his mind, 'but I can teach you how to take it.' And with those words he seemed to be offering Random the world that he had lost, the friends who had gone into the dark, the hopes which had withered or failed...

'I don't think so,' Random said. *Those I loved are all dead, centuries dead; what right have I to call them back?*

Suddenly he knew that just *because* the newcomer was someone he might have been, someone he might have wanted to be, that was why he didn't trust him. He knew too much about himself, and none of it was good.

'I'll stay here,' he said, adding politely, if not quite truthfully: 'I like it here.'

'*Come with me.*'

Now, the proffered hand held a knife.

The blade was as thin as a sliver of moonlight and sharp enough to cut the wind. Random reached for his flick-knife, then remembered that it was upstairs in the room where he had slept. They had told him he wouldn't need it now. Gavin moved to help him – *how* neither of them knew – but the knife-point was at Random's stomach. He could feel the touch of it through his clothes, hardly more than a pinprick; he flattened his belly, shrinking away from it, trying not to breathe. Pen, overlooked for the minute, brought out the Teeth.

'Wait!' she whispered. If Cesare was startled his arm might jerk and the knife penetrate inadvertently...

'You and I will leave,' he told Random. 'If no one tries to prevent us, no one will get hurt. Understand?'

Random nodded. He wasn't worth anyone getting hurt, even himself. He knew that.

Seth Kayser seized him from behind. The knife shifted to his throat, a movement so swift the arm blurred. Pen wondered if now was the right time – if there was any right time. She had the element of surprise, and the Teeth. But she didn't feel heroic, only horribly scared.

She said: 'Cesare!'

He swung round, still gripping Random, his auburn brows drawn into a frown. Groping for recollection. It was so long since he had been Cesare, so long...

'Do you remember me?' If she could distract him for a few vital seconds – if the knife-hand would drop just a fraction...

'Who...? *Penni*? Penella... you were Penella...'

'Do you remember?' she repeated. The Teeth leaped from her hand.

But the man she had known had been mortal, vulnerable, weakened from the aftermath of poison. This was a demon with a demon's powers and reflexes faster than thought. He flung out his left hand, cried: '*Néfia! Estarré!*' The Teeth locked in mid-spring, thudding onto the carpet.

The knife stayed at Random's throat, cold against his skin.

'I remember.' There was a quiver in Seth Kayser's voice, but his breathing had barely quickened. 'I still have the scar. My lord told me to kill you, but I was reluctant. You were so young, so innocent, so devoted. I could have used you.' There was bewilderment in his eyes for all his arrogance. 'You are still young.'

'Work it out!' said Pen.

She thought: He doesn't understand about the house. He doesn't understand how it works...

But it didn't help them.

Seth Kayser backed into the hall, dragging his captive with him. The front door was still ajar the way he had left it when he came in. He was going to leave, taking Random, and there was nothing they could do at all...

Gavin glanced towards the rear of the house. There are few situations when you find yourself wishing for a velociraptor, but this was one of them.

What they got was Jinx. Jinx emerging from the utility room, Hoover at her side – Jinx looking somehow different, with an aura of satisfaction about her, a kind of sparkle. Jinx never sparkled.

She said: 'Hi.'

Behind her was a man they'd never seen before. A very fat man with blue eyes and an expression of mild kindliness. He wore a white coat which gave him a faintly medical air, though there was nothing else medical about him. They had no time to wonder who he was or what he was doing there. He stepped forward, his bland blue gaze scanning the room until it came to rest on Seth Kayser, Random, the knife. The mildness and kindliness of his face did not change. He looked like the sort of person who might say: 'Well, well,' or 'Dear me.'

He said: 'Dear me.'

Seth Kayser's features thinned to a predatory sharpness. 'Who are you?' he said – but he said it almost as if he knew.

'This is my house,' said the fat man.

Pen started; Gavin's mouth opened – and shut.

'*Your* house?' said the predator.

'My house,' the fat man affirmed calmly. 'You may have been invited in, but not by me. And now I am ordering you to leave.'

'I'm already leaving.'

'*Without* the boy.'

'He goes with me,' said Seth Kayser, 'or he dies. You choose. And if that dog moves a whisker nearer, I'll open his throat *now*.'

Like I did with Cullen, thought Random. Maybe that's how retribution works. Oddly, he wasn't afraid. He'd gone past being afraid of dying a long time ago...

Like the witch-girl with the child, thought Gavin, remembering the blood-spatter on his clothes...

Jinx grasped a hunk of Hoover's fur, but it wasn't necessary.

The fat man said: 'How will you explain that to your master?'

The Fellangel's face thinned and sharpened still further. He no longer looked human: his pallor had become a white mask with a flame-flicker behind the eyes.

'He told you to bring the boy back alive,' said the fat man. 'I doubt if he would thank you for his head.'

In the silence there was a wrestling of wills, challenge meeting challenge, bluff defying bluff.

Only no one was completely sure the fat man was bluffing.

'Kill him if you like,' he said. 'If you really feel rash enough to risk your master's displeasure. But living or dead, you will leave him here.'

The pause stretched out for a dozen heartbeats.

Then the Fellangel moved, swifter than sight, flowing into an arrow-streak which sped through the door and vanished into a flying shadow and the sudden boom of wings. The door swung wide and slammed shut in a blast of wind. Random pitched forward onto the parquet, startled to find he was still alive.

Pen said: 'Are you all right?'

They all looked at the fat man. He seemed as untouched by his little victory as by the confrontation which had preceded it. He still exuded mild kindliness, kindly mildness, an aura both comfortable and comforting.

He said: 'Well, well.'

They stared at him in dawning realisation.

Jinx was struggling to remember a remark Azmordis had made – something about a fat man blocking the door...

'This is Bartlemy Goodman,' she said.

AT NUMBER 7A Temporal Crescent, everything changed. Eve Harkness, returning that evening to be confronted by the new resident, was rapidly disarmed by his gentleness, his quiet capability, his manner at once beneficent and faintly implacable. She arranged to move out the following day, both relieved to be removing her granddaughter from residence with such a questionable group of friends and reassured that, under Bartlemy's aegis, a mantle of acceptability would be cast over Pen's ongoing connection with them. With Mr Goodman there she felt, insensibly, that nothing terrible could happen. Random was transformed from a delinquent stray to a poor boy in need of – and receiving – help, Gavin required only a chaperon to become perfectly suitable, and even Jinx, in the afterglow of her relationship with Uncle Barty, became just a girl in black lipstick with a few teenage hang-ups. Eve could retire from the scene and Bartlemy would take care of things. Somehow, no one could doubt his ability to take care of anything.

It took less than twenty-four hours for him to become Uncle Barty to all of them. Pen thought he was a natural uncle, the uncle everyone would have if they could choose. Since his arrival, Jinx became easier to be around, and the wary friendship between her and Pen relaxed into something more comfortable.

'I suppose it's all over now,' Pen said on the last morning, trying not to let her reluctance show. 'We rescued Random. And you found the real owner of Bygone House. There's no reason for me to come round any more.'

'You'd better,' said Jinx. 'We've just got a breathing space. You've saddled me with a serial killer, for one thing. Don't you dare walk away from that. Let's be grateful Gavin didn't bring back the psycho from Greece as well. She looked like a total shitcake.'

'Shit... cake?' Pen hazarded.

'Like a fruitcake, only with shit for fruit. If we're going to try and find the other wannabe apprentices, ten to one they'll all be like that. It's not going to make this place much fun. I'll be hitting the portals just to get away from them.'

'Portals,' said Pen with a sudden smile. 'Been there, done that.' She had never *been there, done that* before with anything. It felt good. She was nearly fourteen, she had become a real lawyer, an executor for someone who had (eventually) died, she had a Past. A past that included portals, and the adventures that lay beyond...

'Uncle Barty's going to teach me to make biscuits,' Gavin said, wandering in from the kitchen. He had been in a haze of culinary awe since supper the previous night. 'Orange biscuits, cinnamon biscuits. He says with the right biscuits you can do anything.'

'If yours are half as good as his,' Jinx said, 'you'll have your own TV show in a month.'

'I don't want my own TV show. I just want...'

(To forget. To forget how the blood spurted out, when the witch-girl sliced the boy's throat. To forget how he had felt, when the dragon looked through the crack at him – when they slammed the door against the crowd fleeing the Dromedon – to lock the bad memories in a little casket, and bury it deep, deep.

But he mustn't do that. That way lay emptiness, and coldness, and the brutalisation of the spirit.

Biscuits. Bartlemy's biscuits could do anything...)

'I just want to make good biscuits.'

'As long as we get to eat them,' Pen said.

Infernale

IN THE DARK Tower, Azmordis did not gnash his teeth. Teeth-gnashing was for small-timers. He is Shaitaan and Satanas, Bale and Baal, Ingré Manu, Utzmord, Lord of the Flies, King of the Abyss, the Shadow beyond all shadows. From the cracks in the wall, from the dark under stones, his eyes are watching, his ears listening. He knows that mortals are overflowing with good intentions, ready to pave the way to Hell. He has catalogued every human weakness, every vice, every little temptation that aspires to the name of sin. But he still does not understand their laughter, or their mercy, or the greatness of their heart. Weary ages have passed, millennia and trillennia, and he has learnt everything, and understood nothing...

'Mortals always want happy endings,' he told the Fellangel who stood by. 'Do they not know? There are no endings, only moments of transition. The door that closes must eventually open again. When I am gone, Another will take my throne. It cannot be prevented. That is the way of things.'

'The way of the Force,' nodded the Nightwing at his side.

'*What?* Ah, that is one of those human stories. They can be useful. Though I find it somewhat unrealistic that the dark side never wins. They should take a look at history. *I* win all the time.'

His servant did not contradict him. Possibly he was too polite.

'And... this time?' he murmured.

'In the end, I will win. It is... inevitable.'

But there are no endings, whispered an echo – an echo without a voice. *Only moments of transition.*

There are no endings...

In Temporal Crescent, people were eating biscuits.

About the Author

Jan Siegel has written in several different genres under several different pseudonyms, but fantasy remains her preferred form of fiction. She also works as a poet, journalist, freelance editor, and occasional teacher, her interests covering a wide range of subjects including horse riding, adventure travel and wildlife conservation.

An idealist, Siegel is continuously surprised to find fact stranger than fiction and real human beings even more bizarre than any character in a book.